The Woman in Black and Other Stories

SUSAN HILL

P

PROFILE BOOKS

This edition published in Great Britain in 2015 by
PROFILE BOOKS LTD
3 Holford Yard
Bevin Way
London WC1X 9HD
www.profilebooks.com

The Woman in Black first published in Great Britain in 1983 by
Hamish Hamilton, an imprint of Penguin Books Ltd, re-published in hardback by
Profile Books in 2011; Dolly first published by Profile Books in 2012; The Man in the
Picture first published by Profile Books in 2007; Printer's Devil Court first published
by Profile Books in 2014; The Small Hand first published by Profile Books in 2010.

1 3 5 7 9 10 8 6 4 2

Printed and bound in Great Britain by
Clays, St Ives plc

A CIP catalogue record for this book is available from the British Library.

ISBN 978 1 78125 552 0
eISBN 978 1 78283 223 2

FSC
www.fsc.org
MIX
Paper from
responsible sources
FSC® C018072

The Woman in Black and Other Stories

NOVELS
Strange Meeting
In the Springtime of the Year
I'm the King of the Castle

SHORT STORIES
*The Boy who Taught the Beekeeper to Read
and other Stories*

CRIME NOVELS
The Various Haunts of Men
The Pure in Heart
The Risk of Darkness
The Vows of Silence
The Shadows in the Street

NON-FICTION
Howards End is on the Landing

Contents

The Woman in Black

Christmas Eve

It was nine-thirty on Christmas Eve. As I crossed the long entrance hall of Monk's Piece on my way from the dining room, where we had just enjoyed the first of the happy, festive meals, towards the drawing room and the fire around which my family were now assembled, I paused and then, as I often do in the course of an evening, went to the front door, opened it and stepped outside.

I have always liked to take a breath of the evening, to smell the air, whether it is sweetly scented and balmy with the flowers of midsummer, pungent with the bonfires and leaf-mould of autumn, or crackling cold from frost and snow. I like to look about me at the sky above my head, whether there are moon and stars or utter blackness, and into the darkness ahead of me; I like to listen for the cries of nocturnal creatures and the moaning rise and fall of the wind, or the pattering of rain in the orchard trees, I enjoy the rush of air towards me up the hill from the flat pastures of the river valley.

Tonight, I smelled at once, and with a lightening heart, that there had been a change in the weather. All the previous week, we had had rain, chilling rain and a mist that lay low about the house and over the country-side. From the windows, the view stretched no farther than a yard or two down the garden. It was wretched weather, never seeming to come fully light, and raw, too. There had been no pleasure in walking, the visibility was too poor for any shooting and the dogs were permanently morose and muddy. Inside the house, the lamps were lit throughout the day and the walls of larder, outhouse and cellar oozed damp and smelled sour, the fires sputtered and smoked, burning dismally low.

My spirits have for many years now been excessively affected by the ways of the weather, and I confess that, had it not been for the air of cheerfulness and bustle that prevailed in the rest of the house, I should have been quite cast down in gloom and lethargy, unable to enjoy the flavour of life as I should like and irritated by my own susceptibility. But

Esmé is merely stung by inclement weather into a spirited defiance, and so the preparations for our Christmas holiday had this year been more than usually extensive and vigorous.

I took a step or two out from under the shadow of the house so that I could see around me in the moonlight. Monk's Piece stands at the summit of land that rises gently up for some four hundred feet from where the little River Nee traces its winding way in a north to south direction across this fertile, and sheltered, part of the country. Below us are pastures, interspersed with small clumps of mixed, broadleaf woodland. But at our backs for several square miles it is a quite different area of rough scrub and heathland, a patch of wildness in the midst of well-farmed country. We are but two miles from a good-sized village, seven from the principal market town, yet there is an air of remoteness and isolation which makes us feel ourselves to be much further from civilization.

I first saw Monk's Piece one afternoon in high summer, when out driving in the trap with Mr Bentley. Mr Bentley was formerly my employer, but I had lately risen to become a full partner in the firm of lawyers to which I had been articled as a young man (and with whom, indeed, I remained for my entire working life). He was at this time nearing the age when he had begun to feel inclined to let slip the reins of responsibility, little by little, from his own hands into mine, though he continued to travel up to our chambers in London at least once a week, until he died in his eighty-second year. But he was becoming more and more of a country-dweller. He was no man for shooting and fishing but, instead, he had immersed himself in the roles of country magistrate and churchwarden, governor of this, that and the other county and parish board, body and committee. I had been both relieved and pleased when finally he took me into full partnership with himself, after so many years, while at the same time believing the position to be no more than my due, for I had done my fair share of the donkey work and borne a good deal of the burden of responsibility for directing the fortunes of the firm with, I felt, inadequate reward – at least in terms of position.

So it came about that I was sitting beside Mr Bentley on a Sunday afternoon, enjoying the view over the high hawthorn hedgerows across the green, drowsy countryside, as he let his pony take the road back, at a gentle pace, to his somewhat ugly and over-imposing manor house. It was rare for me to sit back and do nothing. In London I lived for my work, apart from some spare time spent in the study and collecting of watercolours. I was then thirty-five and I had been a widower for the past twelve years. I had no taste at all for social life and, although in good general health, was prone to occasional nervous illnesses and conditions, as a result of the experiences I will come to relate. Truth to tell, I was growing old well before my time, a sombre, pale-complexioned man with a strained expression – a dull dog.

I remarked to Mr Bentley on the calm and sweetness of the day, and after a sideways glance in my direction he said, 'You should think of getting yourself something in this direction – why not? Pretty little cottage – down there, perhaps?' And he pointed with his whip to where a tiny hamlet was tucked snugly into a bend of the river below, white walls basking in the afternoon sunshine. 'Bring yourself out of town some of these Friday afternoons, take to walking, fill yourself up with fresh air and good eggs and cream'.

The idea had a charm, but only a distant one, seemingly unrelated to myself, and so I merely smiled and breathed in the warm scents of the grasses and the field flowers and watched the dust kicked up off the lane by the pony's hooves and thought no more about it. Until, that is, we reached a stretch of road leading past a long, perfectly proportioned stone house, set on a rise above a sweeping view down over the whole river valley and then for miles away to the violet-blue line of hills in the distance.

At that moment, I was seized by something I cannot precisely describe, an emotion, a desire – no, it was rather more, a knowledge, a simple *certainty*, which gripped me, and all so clear and striking that I cried out involuntarily for Mr Bentley to stop, and, almost before he had time to do so, climbed out of the pony trap into the lane and stood on a grassy knoll, gazing first up at the house, so handsome, so utterly right for the position it occupied, a modest house and yet sure of itself, and then looking across at the country beyond. I had no sense of having been here before, but an absolute conviction that I would come here again, that the house was already mine, bound to me invisibly.

To one side of it, a stream ran between the banks towards the meadow beyond, whence it made its meandering way down to the river.

Mr Bentley was now looking at me curiously, from the trap. 'A fine place,' he called.

I nodded, but, quite unable to impart to him any of my extreme emotions, turned my back upon him and walked a few yards up the slope from where I could see the entrance to the old, overgrown orchard that lay behind the house and petered out in long grass and tangled thicket at the far end. Beyond that, I glimpsed the perimeter of some rough-looking, open land. The feeling of conviction I have described was still upon me, and I remember that I was alarmed by it, for I had never been an imaginative or fanciful man and certainly not one given to visions of the future. Indeed, since those earlier experiences I had deliberately avoided all contemplation of any remotely non-material matters, and clung to the prosaic, the visible and tangible.

Nevertheless, I was quite unable to escape the belief – nay, I must call it more, the certain knowledge – that this house was one day to be my own home, that sooner or later, though I had no idea when, I would become the owner of it. When finally I accepted and admitted this to myself, I felt on that instant a profound sense of peace and contentment settle upon me such as I had not known for very many years, and it was with a light heart that I returned to the pony trap, where Mr Bentley was awaiting me more than a little curiously.

The overwhelming feeling I had experienced at Monk's Piece remained with me, albeit not in the forefront of my mind, when I left the country that afternoon to return to London. I had told Mr Bentley that if ever he were to hear that the house was for sale, I should be eager to know of it.

Some years later, he did so. I contacted the agents that same day and hours later, without so much as returning to see it again, I had offered for it, and my offer was accepted. A few months prior to this, I had met Esmé Ainley. Our affection for one another had been increasing steadily, but, cursed as I still was by my indecisive nature in all personal and emotional matters, I had remained silent as to my intentions for the future. I had enough sense to take the news about Monk's Piece as a good omen, however, and a week after I had formally become the owner of the house, travelled into the country with Esmé and proposed marriage to her among the trees of the old orchard. This offer, too, was accepted and very shortly afterwards we were married and moved at once to Monk's Piece. On that day, I truly believed that I had at last come out from under the long shadow cast by the events of the past and saw from his face and felt from the warmth of his handclasp that Mr Bentley believed it too, and that a burden had been lifted from his own shoulders. He had always blamed himself, at least in part, for what had happened to me – it had, after all, been he who had sent me on that first journey up to Crythin Gifford, and Eel Marsh House, and to the funeral of Mrs Drablow.

But all of that could not have been further from my conscious thought at least, as I stood taking in the night air at the door of my house, on that Christmas Eve. For some fourteen years now Monk's Piece had been the happiest of homes – Esmé's and mine, and that of her four children by her first marriage to Captain Ainley. In the early days I had come here only at weekends and holidays but London life and business began to irk me from the day I bought the place and I was glad indeed to retire permanently into the country at the earliest opportunity.

And, now, it was to this happy home that my family had once again repaired for Christmas. In a moment, I should open the front door and hear the sound of their voices from the drawing room – unless I was abruptly summoned by my wife, fussing about my catching a chill. Certainly, it was very cold and clear at last. The sky was pricked over with stars and the full moon rimmed with a halo of frost. The dampness and fogs of the past week had stolen away like thieves into the night, the paths and the stone walls of the house gleamed palely and my breath smoked on the air.

Upstairs, in the attic bedrooms, Isobel's three young sons – Esmé's grandsons – slept, with stockings tied to their bedposts. There would be no snow for them on the morrow, but Christmas Day would at least wear a bright and cheerful countenance.

There was something in the air that night, something, I suppose, remembered from my own childhood, together with an infection caught from the little boys, that excited me, old as I was. That my peace of mind was about to be disturbed, and memories awakened that I had thought forever dead, I had, naturally, no idea. That I should ever again renew my close acquaintance, if only in the course of vivid recollections and dreams, with mortal dread and terror of spirit, would have seemed at that moment impossible.

I took one last look at the frosty darkness, sighed contentedly, called to the dogs, and went in, anticipating nothing more than a pipe and a glass of good malt whisky beside the crackling fire, in the happy company of my family. As I crossed the hall and entered the drawing room, I felt an uprush of well-being, of the kind I have experienced regularly during my life at Monk's Piece, a sensation that leads on naturally to another, of heartfelt thankfulness. And indeed I did give thanks, at the sight of my family ensconced around the huge fire which Oliver was at that moment building to a perilous height and a fierce blaze with the addition of a further great branch of applewood from an old tree we had felled in the orchard the previous autumn. Oliver is the eldest of Esmé's sons, and bore then, as now, a close resemblance both to his sister Isobel (seated beside her husband, the bearded Aubrey Pearce) and to the brother next in age, Will. All three of them have good, plain, open English faces, inclined to roundness and with hair and eyebrows and lashes of a light chestnut brown – the colour of their mother's hair before it became threaded with grey.

At that time, Isobel was only twenty-four years old but already the mother of three young sons, and set fair to produce more. She had the plump, settled air of a matron and an inclination to mother and oversee her husband and brothers as well as her own children. She had been the most sensible, responsible of daughters, she was affectionate and charming, and she seemed to have found, in the calm and level-headed Aubrey Pearce, an ideal partner. Yet at times I caught Esmé looking at her wistfully, and she had more than once voiced, though gently and to me alone, a longing for Isobel to be a little less staid, a little more spirited, even frivolous.

In all honesty, I could not have wished it so. I would not have wished for anything to ruffle the surface of that calm, untroubled sea.

Oliver Ainley, at that time nineteen, and his brother Will, only fourteen months younger, were similarly serious, sober young men at heart, but for the time being they still enjoyed all the exuberance of young puppies, and indeed it seemed to me that Oliver showed rather too few signs of maturity for a young man in his first year at Cambridge and destined, if my advice prevailed with him, for a career at the Bar. Will lay on his stomach before the fire, his face aglow, chin propped upon his hands. Oliver sat nearby, and from time to time a scuffle of their long legs would break out, a kicking and shoving, accompanied by a sudden guffawing, for all the world as if they were ten years old all over again.

The youngest of the Ainleys, Edmund, sat a little apart, separating himself, as was his wont, a little distance from every other person, not out of any unfriendliness or sullen temper but because of an innate fastidiousness and reserve, a desire to be somewhat private, which had always singled him out from the rest of Esmé's family, just as he was also unlike the others in looks, being pale-skinned, and long-nosed, with hair of an extraordinary blackness, and blue eyes. Edmund was then fifteen. I knew him the least well, understood him scarcely at all, felt uneasy in his presence, and yet perhaps in a strange way loved him more deeply than any.

The drawing room at Monk's Piece is long and low, with tall windows at either end, close-curtained now, but by day letting in a great deal of light from both north and south. Tonight, festoons and swags of fresh greenery, gathered that afternoon by Esmé and Isobel, hung over the stone fireplace, and intertwined with the leaves were berries and ribbons of scarlet and gold. At the far end of the room stood the tree, candlelit and bedecked, and beneath it were piled the presents. There were flowers, too, vases of white chrysanthemums, and in the centre of the room, on a round table, a pyramid of gilded fruit and a bowl of oranges stuck all about with cloves, their spicy scent filling the air and mingling with that of the branches and the wood-smoke to be the very aroma of Christmas.

I sat down in my own armchair, drew it back a little from the full blaze of the fire, and began the protracted and soothing business of lighting a pipe. As I did so, I became aware that I had interrupted the others in the midst of a lively conversation, and that Oliver and Will at least were restless to continue.

'Well,' I said, through the first, cautious puffs at my tobacco, 'and what's all this?'

There was a further pause, and Esmé shook her head, smiling over her embroidery.

'Come ...'

Then Oliver got to his feet and began to go about the room rapidly switching off every lamp, save the lights upon the Christmas tree at the far end, so that, when he returned to his seat, we had only the immediate firelight by which to see one another, and Esmé was obliged to lay down her sewing – not without a murmur of protest.

'May as well do the job properly,' Oliver said with some satisfaction.

'Oh, you boys ...'

'Now come on, Will, your turn, isn't it?'

'No, Edmund's.'

'Ah-ha,' said the youngest of the Ainley brothers, in an odd, deep voice. 'I could an' if I would!'

'*Must* we have the lights out?' Isobel spoke as if to much smaller boys.

'Yes, Sis, we must, that's if you want to get the authentic atmosphere.'

'But, I'm not sure that I do.'

Oliver gave a low moan. 'Get on with it then, someone.'

Esmé leaned over towards me. 'They are telling ghost stories.'

'Yes,' said Will, his voice unsteady with both excitement and laughter. 'Just the thing for Christmas Eve. It's an ancient tradition!'

'The lonely country house, the guests huddled around the fireside in a darkened room, the wind howling at the casement ...' Oliver moaned again.

And then came Aubrey's stolid, good-humoured tones. 'Better get on with it then.' And so they did, Oliver, Edmund and Will vying with one another to tell the horridest, most spine-chilling tale, with much dramatic effect and mock-terrified shrieking. They outdid one another in the far extremes of inventiveness, piling agony upon agony. They told of dripping stone walls in uninhabited castles and of ivy-clad monastery ruins by moonlight, of locked inner rooms and secret dungeons, dank charnel houses and overgrown graveyards, of footsteps creaking upon staircases and fingers tapping at casements, of howlings and shriekings, groanings and scuttlings and the clanking of chains, of hooded monks and headless horsemen, swirling mists and sudden winds, insubstantial spectres and sheeted creatures, vampires and bloodhounds, bats and rats and spiders, of men found at dawn and women turned white-haired and raving lunatic, and of vanished corpses and curses upon heirs. The stories grew more and more lurid, wilder and sillier, and soon the gasps and cries merged into fits of choking laughter, as each one, even gentle Isobel, contributed more ghastly detail.

At first, I was amused, indulgent, but as I sat on, listening, in the firelight, I began to feel set apart from them all, an outsider to their circle. I was trying to suppress my mounting unease, to hold back the rising flood of memory.

This was a sport, a high-spirited and harmless game among young people, for the festive season, and an ancient tradition, too, as Will had rightly said, there was nothing to torment and trouble me, nothing of which I could possibly disapprove. I did not want to seem a killjoy, old and stodgy and unimaginative, I longed to enter into what was nothing more nor less than good fun. I fought a bitter battle within myself, my head turned away from the firelight so that none of them should chance to see my expression which I knew began to show signs of my discomfiture.

And then, to accompany a final, banshee howl from Edmund, the log that had been blazing on the hearth collapsed suddenly and, after sending up a light spatter of sparks and ash, died down so there was near-darkness. And then silence in the room. I shuddered. I wanted to get up and go round putting on every light again, see the sparkle and glitter and colour of the Christmas decorations, have the fire blazing again cheerfully, I wanted to banish the chill that had settled upon me and the sensation of fear in my breast. Yet I could not move, it had, for the moment, paralysed me, just as it had always done, it was a long-forgotten, once too-familiar sensation.

Then, Edmund said, 'Now come, stepfather, your turn,' and at once the others took up the cry, the silence was broken by their urgings, with which even Esmé joined.

'No, no.' I tried to speak jocularly. 'Nothing from me.'

'Oh, Arthur ...'

'You must know at least *one* ghost story, stepfather, everyone knows *one* ...'

Ah, yes, yes, indeed. All the time I had been listening to their ghoulish, lurid inventions, and their howling and groans, the one thought that had been in my mind, and the only thing I could have said was, 'No, no, you have none of you any idea. This is all nonsense, fantasy, it is not like this. Nothing so blood-curdling and becreepered and crude – not so ... so laughable. The truth is quite other, and altogether more terrible.'

'Come *on*, stepfather.'

'Don't be an old spoilsport.'

'Arthur?'

'Do your stuff, stepfather, surely you're not going to let us down?'

I stood up, unable to bear it any longer.

'I am sorry to disappoint you,' I said. 'But I have no story to tell!' And went quickly from the room, and from the house.

Some fifteen minutes later, I came to my senses and found myself on the scrubland beyond the orchard, my heart pounding, my breathing short. I had walked about in a frenzy of agitation, and now, realizing that I must make an effort to calm myself, I sat down on a piece of old, moss-covered stone, and began to take deliberate, steady breaths in on a count of ten and out again, until I felt the tension within myself begin to slacken and my pulse become a little steadier, my head clearer. After a short while longer, I was able to realize my surroundings once again, to note the clearness of the sky and the brightness of the stars, the air's coldness and the crispiness of the frost-stiffened grass beneath my feet.

Behind me, in the house, I knew that I must have left the family in a state of consternation and bewilderment, for they knew me normally as an even-tempered man of predictable emotions. Why they had aroused my apparent disapproval with the telling of a few silly tales and prompted such curt behaviour, the whole family would be quite at a loss to understand, and very soon I must return to them, make amends and endeavour to brush off the incident, renew some of the air of jollity. What I would not be able to do was explain. No. I would be cheerful and I would be steady again, if only for my dear wife's sake, but no more.

They had chided me with being a spoilsport, tried to encourage me to tell them the one ghost story I must surely, like any other man, have it in me to tell. And they were right. Yes, I had a story, a true story, a story of haunting and evil, fear and confusion, horror and tragedy. But it was not a story to be told for casual entertainment, around the fireside upon Christmas Eve.

I had always known in my heart that the experience would never leave me, that it was now woven into my very fibres, an inextricable part of my past, but I had hoped never to have to recollect it, consciously, and in full, ever again. Like an old wound, it gave off a faint twinge now and again, but less and less often, less and less painfully, as the years went on and my happiness, sanity and equilibrium were assured. Of late, it had been like the outermost ripple on a pool, merely the faint memory of a memory.

Now, tonight, it again filled my mind to the exclusion of all else. I knew that I should have no rest from it, that I should lie awake in a chill of sweat, going over that time, those events, those places. So it had been night after night for years.

I got up and began to walk about again. Tomorrow was Christmas Day. Could I not be free of it at least for that blessed time, was there no way of keeping the memory, and the effects it had upon me, at bay, as an analgesic or a balm will stave off the pain of a wound, at least temporarily? And then, standing among the trunks of the fruit trees, silver-grey in the moonlight, I recalled that the way to banish an old ghost that continues its hauntings is to exorcise it. Well then, mine should be exorcised. I should tell my tale, not aloud, by the fireside, not as a diversion for idle listeners – it was too solemn, and too real, for that. But I should set it down on paper, with every care and in every detail. I would write my own ghost story. Then perhaps I should finally be free of it for whatever life remained for me to enjoy.

I decided at once that it should be, at least during my lifetime, a story for my eyes only. I was the one who had been haunted and who had suffered – not the only one, no, but surely, I thought, the only one left alive, I was the one who, to judge by my agitation of this evening, was still affected by it deeply, it was from me alone that the ghost must be driven.

I glanced up at the moon, and at the bright, bright Pole star. Christmas Eve. And then I prayed, a heartfelt, simple prayer for peace of mind, and for strength and steadfastness to endure while I completed what would be the most agonizing task, and I prayed for a blessing upon my family, and for quiet rest to us all that night. For, although I was in control of my emotions now, I dreaded the hours of darkness that lay ahead.

For answer to my prayer, I received immediately the memory of some lines of poetry, lines I had once known but long forgotten. Later, I spoke them aloud to Esmé, and she identified the source for me at once.

> 'Some say that ever 'gainst that season comes
> Wherein our Saviour's birth is celebrated,
> This bird of dawning singeth all night long.
> And then, they say, no spirit dare stir abroad,
> The nights are wholesome, then no planets strike,
> No Fairy takes, nor witch hath power to charm,
> So hallowed and so gracious is that time.'

As I recited them aloud, a great peace came upon me, I was wholly myself again yet stiffened by my resolution. After this holiday when the family had all departed, and Esmé and I were alone, I would begin to write my story.

When I returned to the house, Isobel and Aubrey had gone upstairs to share the delight of creeping about with bulging stockings for their young sons, Edmund was reading, Oliver and Will were in the old playroom at the far end of the house, where there was a battered billiard table, and Esmé was tidying the drawing room, preparatory to going to bed. About that evening's incident, nothing whatsoever was said, though she wore an anxious expression, and I had to invent a bad bout of acute indigestion to account for my abrupt behaviour. I saw to the fire, damping down the flames, and knocked out my pipe on the side of the hearth, feeling quiet and serene again, and no longer agitated about what lonely terrors I might have to endure, whether asleep or awake, during the small hours of the coming night.

Tomorrow was Christmas Day, and I looked forward to it eagerly and with gladness, it would be a time of family joy and merrymaking, love and friendship, fun and laughter.

When it was over, I would have work to do.

A London Particular

It was a Monday afternoon in November and already growing dark, not because of the lateness of the hour – it was barely three o'clock – but because of the fog, the thickest of London peasoupers, which had hemmed us in on all sides since dawn – if, indeed, there had been a dawn, for the fog had scarcely allowed any daylight to penetrate the foul gloom of the atmosphere.

Fog was outdoors, hanging over the river, creeping in and out of alleyways and passages, swirling thickly between the bare trees of all the parks and gardens of the city, and indoors, too, seething through cracks and crannies like sour breath, gaining a sly entrance at every opening of a door. It was a yellow fog, a filthy, evil-smelling fog, a fog that choked and blinded, smeared and stained. Groping their way blindly across roads, men and women took their lives in their hands, stumbling along the pavements, they clutched at railings and at one another, for guidance.

Sounds were deadened, shapes blurred. It was a fog that had come three days before, and did not seem inclined to go away and it had, I suppose, the quality of all such fogs – it was menacing and sinister, disguising the familiar world and confusing the people in it, as they were confused by having their eyes covered and being turned about, in a game of Blind Man's Buff.

It was, in all, miserable weather and lowering to the spirits in the dreariest month of the year.

It would be easy to look back and to believe that all that day I had had a sense of foreboding about my journey to come, that some sixth sense, some telepathic intuition that may lie dormant and submerged in most men, had stirred and become alert within me. But I was, in those days of my youth, a sturdy, commonsensical fellow, and I felt no uneasiness or apprehension whatsoever. Any depression of my usual blithe spirits was solely on account of the fog, and of November, and that same dreariness was shared by every citizen of London.

So far as I can faithfully recall, however, I felt nothing other than

curiosity, a professional interest in what scant account o
Bentley had put before me, coupled with a mild sense of
I had never before visited that remote part of England to
now travelling – and a certain relief at the prospect of getting
the unhealthy atmosphere of fog and dankness. Moreover, I   .y
twenty-three years old, and retained a schoolboy's passion for everything
to do with railway stations and journeys on steam locomotives.

But what is perhaps remarkable is how well I can remember the minut-
est detail of that day; for all that nothing untoward had yet happened, and
my nerves were steady. If I close my eyes, I am sitting in the cab, crawling through the fog on my way to King's Cross Station, I can smell the
cold, damp leather of the upholstery and the indescribable stench of the
fog seeping in around the window, I can feel the sensation in my ears, as
though they had been stuffed with cotton.

Pools of sulphurous yellow light, as from random corners of some
circle of the Inferno, flared from the shops and the upper windows of
houses, and from the basements they rose like flares from the pit below,
and there were red-hot pools of light from the chestnut-sellers on the
street corners; here, a great, boiling cauldron of tar for the road-menders
spurted and smoked an evil red smoke, there, a lantern held high by the
lamplighter bobbed and flickered.

In the streets, there was a din, of brakes grinding and horns blowing,
and the shouts of a hundred drivers, slowed down and blinded by the fog,
and, as I peered from out the cab window into the gloom, what figures I
could make out, fumbling their way through the murk, were like ghost
figures, their mouths and lower faces muffled in scarves and veils and
handkerchiefs, but on gaining the temporary safety of some pool of light
they became red-eyed and demonic.

It took almost fifty minutes to travel the mile or so from Chambers to
the station, and as there was nothing whatsoever I could do, and I had
made allowance for such a slow start to the journey, I sat back, comforting
myself that this would certainly be the worst part of it, and turned over in
my mind the conversation I had had with Mr Bentley that morning.

I had been working steadily at some dull details of the conveyance of
property leases, forgetful, for the moment, of the fog that pressed against
the window, like a furred beast at my back, when the clerk, Tomes, came
in, to summon me to Mr Bentley's room. Tomes was a small man, thin as
a stick and with the complexion of a tallow candle, and a permanent cold,
which caused him to sniff every twenty seconds, for which reason he was

...ned to a cubby-hole in an outer lobby, where he kept ledgers and received visitors, with an air of suffering and melancholy that put them in mind of Last Wills and Testaments – whatever the business they had actually come to the lawyer about.

And it was a Last Will and Testament that Mr Bentley had before him when I walked into his large, comfortable room with its wide bay window that, on better days, commanded a fine view of the Inn of Court and gardens, and the comings and goings of half the lawyers of London. 'Sit ye down, Arthur, sit ye down.' Mr Bentley then took off his spectacles, polished them vigorously, and replaced them on his nose, before settling back in his chair, like a man content. Mr Bentley had a story to tell and Mr Bentley enjoyed being listened to.

'I don't think I ever told you about the extraordinary Mrs Drablow?'

I shook my head. It would, at any rate, be more interesting than the conveyance of leases.

'Mrs Drablow,' he repeated, and picked up the will, to wave it at me, across his partner's desk.

'Mrs Alice Drablow, of Eel Marsh House. Dead, don't you know,'

'Ah.'

'Yes. I inherited Alice Drablow, from my father. The family has had their business with this firm for ... oh ...' he waved a hand, back into the mists of the previous century and the foundation of Bentley, Haigh, Sweetman and Bentley.

'Oh yes?'

'A good age,' he flapped the paper again. 'Eighty-seven.'

'And it's her will you have there, I take it?'

'Mrs Drablow,' he raised his voice a little, ignoring my question which had broken into the pattern of his storytelling. 'Mrs Drablow was, as they say, a rum'un.'

I nodded. As I had learned in my five years with the firm, a good many of Mr Bentley's older clients were 'rum'uns'.

'Have you ever heard of the Nine Lives Causeway?'

'No, never.'

'Nor ever of Eel Marsh, in —shire?'

'No, sir.'

'Nor, I suppose, ever visited that county at all?'

'I'm afraid not.'

'Living there,' said Mr Bentley thoughtfully, 'anyone might become rum.'

'I've only a hazy idea of where it is.'

'Then, my boy, go home and pack your bags, and take the afternoon train from King's Cross, changing at Crewe and again at Homerby. From Homerby, you take the branch line to the little market town of Crythin Gifford. After that, it's a wait for the tide!'

'The *tide?*'

'You can only cross the Causeway at low tide. That takes you onto Eel Marsh and the house.'

'Mrs Drablow's?'

'When the tide comes in, you're cut off until it's low again. Remarkable place.' He got up and went to the window.

'Years since I went there, of course. My father took me. She didn't greatly care for visitors.'

'Was she a widow?'

'Since quite early in her marriage.'

'Children?'

'Children.' Mr Bentley fell silent for a few moments, and rubbed at the pane with his finger, as though to clear away the obscurity, but the fog loomed, yellow-grey, and thicker than ever, though, here and there across the Inn Yard, the lights from other chambers shone fuzzily. A church bell began to toll. Mr Bentley turned.

'According to everything we've been told about Mrs Drablow,' he said carefully, 'no, there were no children.'

'Did she have a great deal of money or land? Were her affairs at all complicated?'

'Not on the whole, Arthur, not on the whole. She owned her house, of course, and a few properties in Crythin Gifford – shops, with tenants, that sort of thing, and there's a poor sort of farm, half under water. She spent money on a few dykes here and there, but not to much purpose. And there are the usual small trusts and investments.'

'Then it all sounds perfectly straightforward.'

'It does, does it not?'

'May I ask why I'm to go there?'

'To represent this firm at our client's funeral.'

'Oh yes, of course.'

'I wondered whether to go up myself, naturally. But, to tell you the truth, I've been troubled again by my foot this past week.' Mr Bentley suffered from gout, to which he would never refer by name, though his suffering need not have given him any cause for shame, for he was an abstemious man.

'And, then, there's the chance that Lord Boltrope will need to see me. I ought to be here, do you see?'

'Ah yes, of course.'

'And then again' – a pause – 'it's high time I put a little more onto your shoulders. It's no more than you're capable of, is it?'

'I certainly hope not. I'll be very glad to go up to Mrs Drablow's funeral, naturally.'

'There's a bit more to it than that.'

'The will?'

'There's a bit of business to attend to, in connection with the estate, yes. I'll let you have the details to read on your journey. But, principally, you're going to go through Mrs Drablow's documents – her private papers ... whatever they may be. *Wherever* they may be ...' Mr Bentley grunted. 'And to bring them back to this office.'

'I see.'

'Mrs Drablow was – somewhat ... disorganized, shall I say? It may well take you a while.'

'A day or two?'

'At least a day or two, Arthur. Of course, things may have changed, I may be quite mistaken ... things may be in apple-pie order and you'll clear it all up in an afternoon. As I told you, it's very many years since I went there.'

The business was beginning to sound like something from a Victorian novel, with a reclusive old woman having hidden a lot of ancient documents somewhere in the depths of her cluttered house. I was scarcely taking Mr Bentley seriously.

'Will there be anyone to help me?'

'The bulk of the estate goes to a great-niece and -nephew – they are both in India, where they have lived for upwards of forty years. There used to be a housekeeper ... but you'll find out more when you get there.'

'But presumably she had friends ... or even neighbours?'

'Eel Marsh House is far from any neighbour.'

'And, being a rum 'un, she never made friends, I suppose?'

Mr Bentley chuckled, 'Come, Arthur, look on the bright side. Treat the whole thing as a jaunt.'

I got up.

'At least it'll take you out of this for a day or two,' and he waved his hand towards the window. I nodded. In fact, I was not by any means unattracted to the idea of the expedition, though I saw that Mr Bentley had not been able to resist making a good story better, and dramatizing the mystery of Mrs Drablow in her queer-sounding house a good way beyond the facts. I supposed that the place would merely prove cold, uncomfortable and difficult to reach, the funeral melancholy, and the papers I had to search for would be tucked under an attic bed in a dust-covered shoe-box, and contain nothing more than old receipted bills and some drafts of cantankerous letters to all and sundry – all of which was usual for such a female client. As I reached the door of his room, Mr Bentley added, 'You'll reach Crythin Gifford by late this evening, and there's a small hotel you can put up at for tonight. The funeral is tomorrow morning at eleven.'

'And, afterwards, you want me to go to the house?'

'I've made arrangements ... there's a local man dealing with it all ... he'll be in touch with you.'

'Yes, but ...'

Just then, Tomes materialized with a sniff at my shoulder.

'Your ten-thirty client, Mr Bentley.'

'Good, good, show him in.'

'Just a moment, Mr Bentley ...'

'What is the matter, Arthur? Don't dither in the doorway man, I've work to do.'

'Isn't there any more you ought to tell me, I ...'

He waved me away impatiently, and at that point Tomes returned, closely followed by Mr Bentley's ten-thirty client. I retreated.

I had to clear my desk, go back to my rooms and pack a bag, inform my landlady that I would be away for a couple of nights, and to scribble a note to my fiancée, Stella. I rather hoped that her disappointment at my sudden absence from her would be tempered by pride that Mr Bentley was entrusting me with the firm's business in such a manner – a good omen for my future prospects upon which our marriage, planned for the following year, depended.

After that, I was to catch the afternoon train to a remote corner of England, of which until a few minutes ago I had barely heard. On my way out of the building, the lugubrious Tomes knocked on the glass of his cubby-hole, and handed me a thick brown envelope marked DRABLOW. Clutching it under my arm, I plunged out, into the choking London fog.

The Journey North

As Mr Bentley had said, however far the distance and gloomy the reason for my journey, it did represent an escape from the London particular and nothing was more calculated to raise my spirits in anticipation of a treat to come than the sight of that great cavern of a railway station, glowing like the interior of a blacksmith's forge. Here, all was clangour and the cheerfulness of preparations for departure, and I purchased papers and journals at the bookstall and walked down the platform beside the smoking, puffing train, with a light step. The engine, I remember, was the Sir Bedivere.

I found a corner seat in an empty compartment, put my coat, hat and baggage on the rack and settled down in great contentment. When we pulled out of London, the fog, although still lingering about the suburbs, began to be patchier and paler, and I all but cheered. By then, a couple of other passengers had joined me in my compartment, but, after nodding briefly, were as intent on applying themselves to newspapers and other documents as myself, and so we travelled a good many uneventful miles towards the heart of England. Beyond the windows, it was quickly dark and, when the carriage blinds were pulled down, all was as cosy and enclosed as some lamplit study.

At Crewe I changed with ease and continued on my way, noting that the track began to veer towards the east, as well as heading north, and I ate a pleasant dinner. It was only when I came to change again, onto the branch line at the small station of Homerby, that I began to be less comfortable, for here the air was a great deal colder and blowing in gusts from the east with an unpleasant rain upon its breath, and the train in which I was to travel for the last hour of my journey was one of those with ancient, comfortless carriages upholstered in the stiffest of leather-cloth over unyielding horsehair, and with slatted wooden racks above. It smelled of cold, stale smuts and the windows were grimed, the floor unswept.

Until the very last second, it seemed that I was to be alone not merely in my compartment but in the entire train, but, just at the blowing of the guard's whistle, a man came through the barrier, glanced quickly along the cheerless row of empty carriages and, catching sight of me at last, and clearly preferring to have a companion, climbed in, swinging the door shut as the train began to move away. The cloud of cold, damp air that he let in with him added to the chill of the compartment, and I remarked that it was a poor night, as the stranger began to unbutton his greatcoat. He looked at me up and down inquisitively, though not in any unfriendly way, and then up at my things upon the rack, before nodding in agreement.

'It seems I have exchanged one kind of poor weather for another. I left London in the grip of an appalling fog, and up here it seems to be cold enough for snow.'

'It's not snow,' he said. 'The wind'll blow itself out and take the rain off with it by morning.'

'I'm very glad to hear it.'

'But, if you think you've escaped the fogs by coming up here, you're mistaken. We get bad frets in this part of the world.'

'Frets?'

'Aye, frets. Sea-frets, sea-mists. They roll up in a minute from the sea to land across the marshes. It's the nature of the place. One minute it's as clear as a June day, the next ...' He gestured to indicate the dramatic suddenness of his frets. 'Terrible. But if you're staying in Crythin you won't see the worst of it.'

'I stay there tonight, at the Gifford Arms. And tomorrow morning. I expect to go out to see something of the marshes later.'

And then, not particularly wishing to discuss the nature of my business with him, I picked up my newspaper again and unfolded it with a certain ostentation, and so, for some little while, we rumbled on in the nasty train, in silence – save for the huffing of the engine, and the clanking of iron wheels upon iron rails, and the occasional whistle, and the bursts of rain, like sprays of light artillery fire, upon the windows.

I began to be weary, of journeying and of the cold and of sitting still while being jarred and jolted about, and to look forward to my supper, a fire and a warm bed. But in truth, and although I was hiding behind its pages, I had read my newspaper fully, and I began to speculate about my companion. He was a big man, with a beefy face and huge, raw-looking hands, well enough spoken but with an odd accent that I took to be the local one. I put him down as a farmer, or else the proprietor of some small business. He was nearer to sixty than fifty, and his clothes were of good quality, but somewhat brashly cut, and he wore a heavy, prominent seal-ring on his left hand, and that, too, had a newness and a touch of vulgarity about it. I decided that he was a man who had made, or come into, money late and unexpectedly, and was happy for the world to know it.

Having, in my youthful and priggish way, summed up and all but dismissed him, I let my mind wander back to London and to Stella, and for the rest, was only conscious of the extreme chill and the ache in my joints, when my companion startled me, by saying, 'Mrs Drablow.' I lowered my paper, and became aware that his voice echoed so loudly through the compartment because of the fact that the train had stopped, and the only sound to be heard was the moan of the wind, and a faint hiss of steam, far ahead of us.

'Drablow,' he pointed to my brown envelope, containing the Drablow papers, which I had left lying on the seat beside me.

I nodded stiffly.

'You don't tell me you're a relative?'

'I am her solicitor.' I was rather pleased with the way it sounded.

'Ah! Bound for the funeral?'

'I am.'

'You'll be about the only one that is.' In spite of myself, I wanted to find out more about the business, and clearly my companion knew it.

'I gather she had no friends – or immediate family – that she was something of a recluse? Well, that is sometimes the way with old ladies. They turn inwards – grow eccentric. I suppose it comes from living alone.'

'I daresay that it does, Mr ... ?'

'Kipps. Arthur Kipps.'

'Samuel Daily.'

We nodded.

'And, when you live alone in such a place as that, it comes a good deal easier.'

'Come,' I said smiling, 'you're not going to start telling me strange tales of lonely houses?'

He gave me a straight look. 'No,' he said, at last, 'I am not.'

For some reason then, I shuddered, all the more because of the openness of his gaze and the directness of his manner.

'Well,' I replied in the end, 'all I can say is that it's a sad thing when someone lives for eighty-seven years and can't count upon a few friendly faces to gather together at their funeral!'

And I rubbed my hand on the window, trying to see out into the darkness. We appeared to have stopped in the middle of open country, and to be taking the full force of the wind that came howling across it. 'How far have we to go?' I tried not to sound concerned, but was feeling an unpleasant sensation of being isolated far from any human dwelling, and trapped in this cold tomb of a railway carriage, with its pitted mirror and stained, dark-wood panelling. Mr Daily took out his watch.

'Twelve miles, we're held up for the down train at Gapemouth tunnel. The hill it runs through is the last bit of high ground for miles. You've come to the flatlands, Mr Kipps.'

'I've come to the land of curious place-names, certainly. This morning, I heard of the Nine Lives Causeway, and Eel Marsh, tonight of Gapemouth tunnel.'

'It's a far-flung part of the world. We don't get many visitors.'

'I suppose because there is nothing much to see.'

'It depends what you mean by "nothing". There's the drowned churches and the swallowed-up village,' he chuckled. 'Those are particularly fine examples of "nothing to see". And we've a good wild ruin of an abbey with a handsome graveyard – you can get to it at low tide. It's all according to what takes your fancy!'

'You are almost making me anxious to get back to that London particular!'

There was a shriek from the train whistle.

'Here she comes.' And the train coming away from Crythin Gifford to Homerby emerged from Gapemouth tunnel and trundled past us, a line of empty yellow-lit carriages that disappeared into the darkness, and then immediately we were under way again.

'But you'll find everything hospitable enough at Crythin, for all it's a plain little place. We tuck ourselves in with our backs to the wind, and carry on with business. If you care to come with me, I can drop you off at the Gifford Arms – my car will be waiting for me, and it's on my way.'

He seemed keen to reassure me and to make up for his teasing exaggeration of the bleakness and strangeness of the area, and I thanked him and accepted his offer, whereupon we both settled back to our reading, for the last few miles of that tedious journey.

The Funeral of Mrs Drablow

My first impressions of the little market town – indeed, it seemed scarcely larger than an overgrown village – of Crythin Gifford were distinctly favourable. When we arrived that night, Mr Samuel Daily's car, as shining, capacious and plush a vehicle as I had travelled in in my life, took us swiftly the bare mile from the tiny station into the market square, where we drew up outside the Gifford Arms.

As I prepared to alight, he handed me his card.

'Should you need anyone ...'

I thanked him, though stressing that it was most unlikely, as I would have whatever practical help I might require to organize the late Mrs Drablow's business from the local agent, and did not intend to be in the place more than a day or two. Mr Daily gave me a straight, steady stare, and said nothing and, so as not to appear discourteous, I tucked the card carefully into my waistcoat pocket. Only then did he give the word to his driver, and move away.

'You'll find everything hospitable enough at Crythin,' he had said earlier, and so it proved. As I caught sight of the piled-up fire and the capacious armchair beside it, in the parlour of the inn, and found another fire waiting to warm me in the prettily furnished bedroom at the top of the house, my spirits rose, and I began to feel rather more like a man on holiday than one come to attend a funeral, and go through the dreary business attendant upon the death of a client. The wind had either died down or else could not be heard in the shelter of the buildings, around the market square, and the discomfort, and queer trend of the conversation of my journey, faded like a bad dream.

The landlord recommended a glass of mulled wine, which I drank sitting before the fire, listening to the murmur of voices on the other side of a heavy door leading to the public bar, and his wife made my mouth water in anticipation of the supper she proposed – home-made broth, sirloin of beef, apple and raisin tart with cream, and some Stilton cheese.

While I waited, I wrote a brief, fond note to Stella, which I would post the next morning, and while I ate heartily, I mused about the type of small house we might afford to live in after our marriage, if Mr Bentley were to continue to give me so much responsibility in the firm, so that I might feel justified in asking for an increase in salary.

All in all, and with the half-bottle of claret that had accompanied my supper, I prepared to go up to bed in a warm glow of well-being and contentment.

'You'll be here for the auction, I take it then, sir,' the landlord waited by the door, to bid me goodnight.

'Auction?'

He looked surprised. 'Ah – I thought you would have come up for that – there's a big auction of several farms that lie just south of here, and it's market day tomorrow as well.'

'Where is the auction?'

'Why here, Mr Kipps, in the public bar at eleven o'clock. We generally have such auctions as there are at the Gifford Arms, but there hasn't been one so big as this for a good many years. Then there's the lunch afterwards. We expect to serve upwards of forty lunches on market day, but it'll be a few more than that tomorrow.'

'Then I'm sorry I shall have to miss is – although I hope I shall be able to have a stroll round the market.'

'No intention to pry, sir – only I made sure you'd come for the auction.'

'That's all right – quite natural that you should. But at eleven o'clock tomorrow morning, I'm afraid that I have a sombre engagement. I'm here to attend a funeral – Mrs Drablow, of Eel Marsh House. Perhaps you knew of her?'

His face flickered with … what? Alarm, was it? Suspicion? I could not tell, but the name had stirred some strong emotion in him, all signs of which he endeavoured to suppress at once.

'I knew of her,' he said evenly.

'I am representing her firm of solicitors. I never met her. I take it she kept rather out of the way, for the most part?'

'She could hardly do otherwise, living there,' and he turned away abruptly in the direction of the public bar. 'I'll wish you goodnight, sir. We can serve breakfast at any time in the morning, to your convenience.' And he left me alone. I half moved to call him back, for I was both curious and a little irritated by his manner, and I thought of trying to get out of him exactly what he had meant by it. But I was tired and dismissed the notion, putting his remarks down to some local tales and silliness which had grown out of all proportion, as such things will do in small, out of the way communities, which have only themselves to look to for whatever melodrama and mystery they can extract out of life. For I must confess I had the Londoner's sense of superiority in those days, the half-formed belief that countrymen, and particularly those who inhabited the remoter corners of our island, were more superstitious, more gullible, more slow-witted, unsophisticated and primitive, than we cosmopolitans. Doubtless, in such a place as this, with its eerie marshes, sudden fogs, moaning winds and lonely houses, any poor old woman might be looked at askance; once upon a time, after all, she would have been branded as a witch and local legends and tales were still abroad and some extravagant folklore still half-believed in.

It was true that neither Mr Daily nor the landlord of the inn seemed anything but sturdy men of good commonsense, just as I had to admit that neither of them had done more than fall silent and look at me hard and a little oddly, when the subject of Mrs Drablow had arisen. Nonetheless, I had been left in no doubt that there was some significance in what had been left *un*said.

On the whole, that night, with my stomach full of home-cooked food, a pleasing drowsiness induced by good wine, and the sight of the low fire and inviting, turned-back covers of the deep, soft bed, I was inclined to let myself enjoy the whole business, and to be amused by it, as adding a touch of spice and local colour to my expedition, and I fell asleep most peacefully. I can recall it still, that sensation of slipping down, down into the welcoming arms of sleep, surrounded by warmth and softness, happy and secure as a small child in the nursery, and I recall waking the next morning, too, opening my eyes to see shafts of wintry sunlight playing upon the sloping white ceiling, and the delightful feeling of ease and refreshment in mind and limbs. Perhaps I recall those sensations the more vividly because of the contrast that presented with what was to come after. Had I known that my untroubled night of good sleep was to be the last such that I was to enjoy for so many terrifying, racked and weary nights to come, perhaps I should not have jumped out of bed with such alacrity, eager to be down and have breakfast, and then to go out and begin the day.

Indeed, even now in later life, though I have been as happy and at peace in my home at Monk's Piece, and with my dear wife Esmé, as any man may hope to be, and even though I thank God every night that it is all over, all long past and I will not, *cannot* come again, yet I do not believe

I have ever again slept so well as I did that night in the inn at Crythin Gifford. For I see that then I was still all in a state of innocence, but that innocence, once lost, is lost forever.

The bright sunshine that filled my room when I drew back the flowered curtains was no fleeting, early-morning visitor. By contrast with the fog of London, and the wind and rain of the previous evening's journey up here, the weather was quite altered as Mr Daily had confidently predicted that it would be.

Although it was early November and this a cold corner of England, when I stepped out of the Gifford Arms after enjoying a remarkably good breakfast, the air was fresh, crisp and clear and the sky as blue as a blackbird's egg. The little town was built, for the most part, of stone and rather austere grey slate, and set low, the houses huddled together and looking in on themselves. I wandered about, discovering the pattern of the place – a number of straight narrow streets or lanes led off at every angle from the compact market square, in which the hotel was situated and which was now filling up with pens and stalls, carts, wagons and trailers, in preparation for the market. From all sides came the cries of men to one another as they worked hammering temporary fencing, hauling up canvas awnings over stalls, wheeling barrows over the cobbles. It was as cheerful and purposeful a sight as I could have found to enjoy anywhere, and I walked about with a great appetite for it all. But, when I turned my back on the square and went up one of the lanes, at once all the sounds were deadened, so that all I heard were my own footsteps in front of the quiet houses. There was not the slightest rise or slope on the ground anywhere. Crythin Gifford was utterly flat but, coming suddenly to the end of one of the narrow streets, I found myself at once in open country, and saw field after field stretching way into the pale horizon. I saw then what Mr Daily had meant about the town tucking itself in with its back to the wind, for, indeed, all that could be seen of it from here were the backs of houses and shops, and of the main public buildings in the square.

There was a touch of warmth in the autumn sunshine, and what few trees I saw, all bent a little away from the prevailing wind, still had a few last russet and golden leaves clinging to the ends of their branches. But I imagined how drear and grey and bleak the place would be in the dank rain and mist, how beaten and battered at for days on end by those gales that came sweeping across the flat, open country, how completely cut off by blizzards. That morning, I had looked again at Crythin Gifford on the map. To north, south and west there was rural emptiness for many miles

– it was twelve to Homerby, the next place of any size, thirty to a large town, to the south, and about seven to any other village at all. To the east, there were only marshes, the estuary, and then the sea. For anything other than a day or two, it would certainly not do for me, but as I strolled back towards the market, I felt very much at home, and content, in the place, refreshed by the brightness of the day and fascinated by everything I saw.

When I reached the hotel again, I found that a note had been left for me in my absence by Mr Jerome, the agent who had dealt with such property and land business as Mrs Drablow had conducted, and who was to be my companion at the funeral. In a polite, formal hand, he suggested that he return at ten-forty, to conduct me to the church, and so, for the rest of the time until then, I sat in the front window of the parlour at the Gifford Arms, reading the daily newspapers and watching the preparations in the market place. Within the hotel, too, there was a good deal of activity which I took to be in connection with the auction sale. From the kitchen area, as doors occasionally swung open, wafted the rich smells of cooking, of roasting meat and baking bread, of pies and pastry and cakes, and from the dining room came the clatter of crockery. By ten-fifteen, the pavement outside began to be crowded with solid, prosperous-looking farmers in tweed suits, calling out greetings, shaking hands, nodding vigorously in discussion.

I was sad to be obliged to leave it all, dressed in my dark, formal suit and overcoat, with black armband and tie, and black hat in my hand, when Mr Jerome arrived – there was no mistaking him because of the similar drabness of his outfit – and we shook hands and went out onto the street. For a moment standing there looking over the colourful, busy scene before us, I felt like a spectre at some cheerful feast, and that our appearance among the men in workaday or country clothes was that of a pair of gloomy ravens. And, indeed, that was the effect we seemed to have at once upon everyone who saw us. As we passed through the square we were the focus of uneasy glances, men drew back from us slightly and fell silent and stiff, in the middle of their conversations, so that I began to be unhappy, feeling like some pariah, and glad to get away and into one of the quiet streets that led, Mr Jerome indicated, directly to the parish church.

He was a particularly small man, only five feet two or three inches tall at most, and with an extraordinary, domed head, fringed around at the very back with gingerish hair, like some sort of rough braiding around the base of a lampshade. He might have been anywhere between thirty-five and fifty-seven years of age, with a blandness and formality of manner and a somewhat shuttered expression that revealed nothing whatsoever of his own personality, his mood or his thoughts. He was courteous, business-like, and conversational but not intimate. He inquired about my journey, about the comfort of the Gifford Arms, about Mr Bentley, and about the London weather, he told me the name of the clergyman who would be officiating at the funeral, the number of properties – some half a dozen – that Mrs Drablow had owned in the town and the immediate vicinity. And yet he told me nothing at all, nothing personal, nothing revelatory, nothing very interesting.

'I take it she is to be buried in the churchyard?' I asked.

Mr Jerome glanced at me sideways, and I noted that he had very large, and slightly protuberant and pale eyes of a colour somewhere between blue and grey, that reminded me of gulls' eggs.

'That is so, yes.'

'Is there a family grave?'

He was silent for a moment, glancing at me closely again, as if trying to discover whether there were any meaning behind the apparent straight-forwardness of the question. Then he said, 'No. At least ... not here, not in this churchyard.'

'Somewhere else?'

'It is ... no longer in use,' he said, after some deliberation. 'The area is unsuitable.'

'I'm afraid I don't quite understand ...'

But, at that moment, I saw that we had reached the church, which was approached through a wrought-iron gate, between two overhanging yew trees, and situated at the end of a particularly long, very straight path. On either side, and away to the right, stood the gravestones, but to the left, there were some building which I took to be the church hall and – the one nearer to the church – the school, with a bell set high up in the wall, and from within it, the sound of children's voices.

I was obliged to suspend my inquisitiveness about the Drablow family and their burial ground, and to assume, like Mr Jerome, a profession-ally mournful expression as we walked with measured steps towards the church porch. There, for some five minutes that seemed very much longer, we waited, quite alone, until the funeral car drew up at the gate, and from the interior of the church the parson materialized beside us; and, together, the three of us watched the drab procession of the undertaker's men, bearing the coffin of Mrs Drablow, make its slow way towards us.

It was indeed a melancholy little service, with so few of us in the cold church, and I shivered as I thought once again how inexpressibly sad it was that the ending of a whole human life, from birth and childhood, through adult maturity to extreme old age, should here be marked by no blood relative or heart's friend, but only by two men connected by nothing more than business, one of whom had never so much as set eyes upon the woman during her life, besides those present in an even more bleakly professional capacity.

However, towards the end of it, and on hearing some slight rustle behind me, I half-turned, discreetly, and caught a glimpse of another mourner, a woman, who must have slipped into the church after we of the funeral party had taken our places and who stood several rows behind and quite alone, very erect and still, and not holding a prayer book. She was dressed in deepest black, in the style of full mourning that had rather gone out of fashion except, I imagined, in court circles on the most formal of occasions. Indeed, it had clearly been dug out of some old trunk or wardrobe, for its blackness was a little rusty looking. A bonnet-type hat covered her head and shaded her face, but, although I did not stare, even the swift glance I took of the woman showed me enough to recognise that she was suffering from some terrible wasting disease, for not only was she extremely pale, even more than a contrast with the blackness of her garments could account for, but the skin and, it seemed, only the thinnest layer of flesh was tautly stretched and strained across her bones, so that it gleamed with a curious, blue-white sheen, and her eyes seemed sunken back into her head. Her hands that rested on the pew before her were in a similar state, as though she had been a victim of starvation. Though not any medical expert, I had heard of certain conditions which caused such terrible wasting, such ravages of the flesh, and knew that they were generally regarded as incurable, and it seemed poignant that a woman, who was perhaps only a short time away from her own death, should drag herself to the funeral of another. Nor did she look old. The effect of the illness made her age hard to guess, but she was quite possibly no more than thirty. Before I turned back, I vowed to speak to her and see if I could be of any assistance after the funeral was over, but just as we were making ready to move away, following the parson and the coffin out of the church, I heard the slight rustle of clothing once more and realized that the unknown woman had already slipped quickly away, and gone out to the waiting, open grave, though to stand some yards back, beside another headstone, that was overgrown with moss and upon which she leaned slightly. Her appearance, even in the limpid sunshine and comparative warmth and brightness outdoors, was so pathetically wasted, so pale and gaunt with disease, that it would not have been a kindness to gaze upon her; for there was still some faint trace on her features, some lingering hint, of a not inconsiderable former beauty, which must make her feel her present condition all the more keenly, as would the victim of a smallpox, or some dreadful disfigurement of burning.

Well, I thought, there is one who cares, after all, and who knows how keenly, and surely, such warmth and kindness, such courage and unselfish purpose, can never go unrewarded and unremarked, if there is any truth at all in the words that we have just heard spoken to us in the church?

And then I looked away from the woman and back, to where the coffin was being lowered into the ground, and I bent my head and prayed with a sudden upsurge of concern, for the soul of that lonely old woman, and for a blessing upon our drab circle.

When I looked up again, I saw a blackbird on the hollybush a few feet away and heard him open his mouth to pour out a sparkling fountain of song in the November sunlight, and then it was all over, we were moving away from the graveside, I a step behind Mr Jerome, as I intended to wait for the sick-looking woman and offer my arm to escort her. But she was nowhere to be seen.

While I had been saying my prayers and the clergyman had been speaking the final words of the committal, and perhaps not wanting to disturb us, or draw any attention to herself, she must have gone away, just as unobtrusively as she had arrived.

At the church gate, we stood for a few moments, talking politely, shaking hand, and I had a chance to look around me, and to notice that, on such a clear, bright day, it was possible to see far beyond the church and the graveyard, to where the open marshes and the water of the estuary gleamed silver, and shone even brighter, at the line of the horizon, where the sky above was almost white and faintly shimmering.

Then, glancing back on the other side of the church, something else caught my eye. Lined up along the iron railings that surrounded the small asphalt yard of the school were twenty or so children, one to a gap. They presented a row of pale, solemn faces with great, round eyes, that had watched who knew how much of the mournful proceedings, and their little hands held the railings tight, and they were all of them quite silent, quite motionless. It was an oddly grave and touching sight, they looked so unlike children generally do, animated and carefree. I caught the eye of one and smiled at him gently. He did not smile back.

I saw that Mr Jerome waited for me politely in the lane, and I went quickly out after him.

'Tell me, that other woman ...' I said as I reached his side, 'I hope she can find her own way home ... she looked so dreadfully unwell. Who was she?'

He frowned.

'The young woman with the wasted face,' I urged, 'at the back of the church and then in the graveyard a few yards away from us.'

Mr Jerome stopped dead. He was staring at me.

'A young woman?'

'Yes, yes, with the skin stretched over her bones, I could scarcely bear to look at her ... she was tall, she wore a bonnet type of hat ... I suppose to try and conceal as much as she could of her face, poor thing.'

For a few seconds, in that quiet, empty lane, in the sunshine, there was such a silence as must have fallen again now inside the church, a silence so deep that I heard the pulsation of the blood in the channels of my own ears. Mr Jerome looked frozen, pale, his throat moving as if he were unable to utter.

'Is there anything the matter?' I asked him quickly. 'You look unwell.'

At last he managed to shake his head – I almost would say, that he shook himself, as though making an extreme effort to pull himself together after suffering a momentous shock, though the colour did not return to his face and the corners of his lips seemed tinged with blue.

At last he said in a low voice, 'I did not see a young woman.'

'But, surely ...' And I looked over my shoulder, back to the church-yard, and there she was again, I caught a glimpse of her black dress and the outline of her bonnet. So she had not left after all, only concealed herself behind one of the bushes or headstones, or else in the shadows of the church, waiting until we should have left, so that she could do what she was doing now, stand at the very edge of the grave in which the body of Mrs Drablow had just been laid to rest, looking down. I wondered again what connection she would have had with her, what odd story might lie behind her surreptitious visit, and what extremes of sad feeling she was now suffering, alone there. 'Look,' I said, and pointed, 'there she is again ... ought we not to ...' I stopped as Mr Jerome grabbed my wrist and held it in an agonizingly tight grip, and, looking at his face, was certain that he was about to faint, or collapse with some kind of seizure. I began looking wildly about me, in the deserted lane, wondering whatever I might do, where I could go, or call out, for help. The undertakers had left. Behind me were only a school of little children, and a mortally sick young woman under great emotional and physical strain, beside me was a man in a state of near-collapse. The only person I could conceivably reach was the clergyman, somewhere in the recesses of his church, and, if I were to go for him, I would have to leave Mr Jerome alone.

'Mr Jerome, can you take my arm ... I would be obliged if you would loosen your grip a little ... if you can just walk a few steps, back to the church ... path ... I saw a bench there, a little way inside the gate, you can rest and recover while I go for help ... a car ...'

'No!' He almost shrieked.

'But, my dear man!'

'No. I apologize ...' He began to take deep breaths and a little colour returned by degrees to his face. 'I am so sorry, it was nothing ... a passing faintness ... It will be best if you would just walk back with me towards my offices in Penn Street, off the square.'

He seemed agitated now, anxious to get away from the church and its environs.

'If you are sure ...'

'Quite sure. Come ...' and he began to walk quickly ahead of me, so quickly that I was taken by surprise and had to run a few steps to catch up with him. It took only a few minutes at that pace to arrive back in the square, where the market was in full cry and we were at once plunged into the hubbub of vehicles, the shouting of voices, of auctioneers and stallholders and buyers, and all the bleating and braying, the honking and crowing and cackling and whinnying of dozens of farm animals. At the sight and sound of it all, I noticed that Mr Jerome was looking better and, when we reached the porch of the Gifford Arms, he seemed almost lively, in a burst of relief.

'I gather you are to take me over to Eel Marsh House later,' I said after pressing him to lunch with me, and being refused.

His face closed up again. He said, 'No. I shall not go there. You can cross any time after one o'clock. Keckwick will come for you. He has always been the go-between to that place. I take it you have a key?'

I nodded.

'I shall make a start on looking out Mrs Drablow's papers and getting them in some sort of order, but I suppose I shall be obliged to go across again tomorrow, and even another day after that. Perhaps Mr Keckwick can take me early in the morning, and leave me there for the whole day? I shall have to find my way about the place.'

'You will be obliged to fit in with the tides. Keckwick will tell you.'

'On the other hand,' I said, 'if it all looks as if it may take somewhat longer than I anticipate, perhaps I might simply stay there in the house? Would anyone have any objection? It seems ridiculous to expect this man to come to and fro for me.'

'I think,' said Mr Jerome carefully, 'that you would find it more comfortable to continue staying here.'

'Well, they have certainly made me welcome and the food is first rate. Perhaps you may be right.'

'I think so.'

'So long as it causes no one any inconvenience.'

'You will find Mr Keckwick perfectly obliging.'

'Good.'

'Though not very communicative.'

I smiled. 'Oh, I'm getting very used to that.' And, after shaking hands with Mr Jerome, I went to have lunch, with four dozen or so farmers.

It was a convivial and noisy occasion, with everyone sitting at three trestle tables, which were covered in long white cloths, and shouting to one another in all directions about market matters, while half a dozen girls passed in and out bearing platters of beef and pork, tureens of soup, basins of vegetables and jugs of gravy, and mugs of ale, a dozen at a time, on wide trays. Although I did not think I knew a soul in the room, and felt somewhat out of place, especially in my funeral garb, among the tweed and corduroy, I nevertheless enjoyed myself greatly, partly, no doubt, because of the contrast between this cheerful situation and the rather unnerving events of earlier in the morning. Much of the talk might have been in a foreign language, for all I understood of the references to weights and prices, yields and breeds, but, as I ate the excellent lunch, I was happy to listen all the same, and when my neighbour to the left passed an enormous Cheshire cheese to me, indicating that I should help myself, I asked him about the auction sale which had taken place in the Inn earlier. He grimaced.

'The auction went according to expectations, sir. Do I take it you had an interest in the land yourself ?'

'No, no. It was merely that the landlord mentioned it to me yesterday evening. I gather it was quite an important sale.'

'It disposed of a very large acreage. Half the land on the Homerby side of Crythin and for several miles east as well. There had been four farms.'

'And this land about here is valuable?'

'Some is, sir. This was. In an area where much is useless because it is all marsh and salt-flat and cannot be drained to any purpose good farming land is valuable, every inch of it. There are several disappointed men here this morning.'

'Do I take it that you are one of them?'

'Me? No. I am content with what I have and if I were not it would make no odds, for I haven't the money to take on more. Besides, I would have more sense than to pit myself against such as him.'

'You mean the successful buyer?'

'I do.'

I followed his glance across to the other table. 'Ah! Mr Daily.' For there at the far end, I recognized my travelling companion of the previous night, holding up a tankard and surveying the room with a satisfied expression.

'You know him?'

'No. I met him, just briefly. Is he a large landowner here?'

'He is.'

'And disliked because of it?'

My neighbour shrugged his broad shoulders, but did not reply.

'Well,' I said, 'if he's buying up half the county, I suppose I may be doing business with him myself before the year is out. I am a solicitor looking after the affairs of the late Mrs Alice Drablow of Eel Marsh House. It is quite possible that her estate will come up for sale in due course.'

For a moment, my companion still said nothing, only buttered a thick slice of bread and laid his chunks of cheese along it carefully. I saw by the clock on the opposite wall that it was half past one, and I wanted to change my clothes before the arrival of Mr Keckwick, so that I was about to make my excuses and go, when my neighbour spoke. 'I doubt,' he said, in a measured tone, 'whether even Samuel Daily would go so far.'

'I don't think I fully understand you. I haven't seen the full extent of Mrs Drablow's land yet ... I gather there is a farm a few miles out of the town ...'

'Hoggetts!' he said in a dismissive tone. 'Fifty acres and half of it under flood for the best part of the year. Hoggetts is nothing, and it's under tenancy for his lifetime.'

'There is also Eel Marsh House and all the land surrounding it – would that be practicable for farming?'

'No, sir.'

'Well, might not Mr Daily simply want to add a little more to his empire, for the sake of being able to say that he had got it? You imply he is that type of man.'

'Maybe he is.' He wiped his mouth on his napkin. 'But let me tell you that you won't find anybody, not even Mr Sam Daily, having to do with any of it.'

'And may I ask why?'

I spoke rather sharply, for I was growing impatient of the half-hints and dark mutterings made by grown men at the mention of Mrs Drablow and her property. I had been right, this was just the sort of place where superstition and tittle-tattle were rife, and even allowed to hold sway over commonsense. Now, I expected the otherwise stalwart countryman on my left to whisper that maybe he would and, then again, maybe he would not, and how he might tell a tale, if he chose … But, instead of replying to my question at all, he turned right away from me and engaged his neighbour on the other side in a complicated discussion of crops and, infuriated by the now-familiar mystery and nonsense, I rose abruptly and left the room. Ten minutes later, changed out of my funeral suit into less formal and more comfortable clothes, I was standing on the pavement awaiting the arrival of the car, driven by a man called Keckwick.

Across the Causeway

No car appeared. Instead, there drew up outside the Gifford Arms a rather worn and shabby pony and trap. It was not at all out of place in the market square – I had noticed a number of such vehicles that morning and, assuming that this one belonged to some farmer or stockman, I took no notice, but continued to look around me, for a motor. Then I heard my name called.

The pony was a small, shaggy-looking creature, wearing blinkers, and the driver with a large cap pulled down low over his brow, and a long, hairy brown coat, looked not unlike it, and blended with the whole equipage. I was delighted at the sight, eager for the ride, and climbed up with alacrity. Keckwick had scarcely given me a glance, and now, merely assuming that I was seated, clucked at the pony and set off, picking his way out of the crowded market square and up the lane that led to the church. As we passed it, I tried to catch a glimpse of the grave of Mrs Drablow, but it was hidden from view behind some bushes. I remembered the ill-looking, solitary young woman, too, and Mr Jerome's reaction to my mention of her. But, within a few moments, I was too caught up in the present and my surroundings to speculate any further upon the funeral and its aftermath, for we had come out into open country, and Crythin Gifford lay quite behind us, small and self-contained as it was. Now, all around and above and way beyond there seemed to be sky, sky and only a thin strip of land. I saw this part of the world as those great landscape painters had seen Holland, or the country around Norwich. Today there were no clouds at all, but I could well imagine how magnificently the huge, brooding area of sky would look with grey, scudding rain and storm clouds lowering over the estuary, how it would be here in the floods of February time when the marshes turned to iron-grey and the sky seeped down into them, and in the high winds of March, when the light rippled, shadow chasing shadow across the ploughed fields.

Today, all was bright and clear, and there was a thin sun overall, though the light was pale now, the sky having lost the bright blue of the morning, to become almost silver. As we drove briskly across the absolutely flat countryside, I saw scarcely a tree, but the hedgerows were dark and twiggy and low, and the earth that had been ploughed was at first a rich mole-brown, in straight furrows. But, gradually, soil gave way to rough grass and I began to see dykes and ditches filled with water, and then we were approaching the marshes themselves. They lay silent, still and shining under the November sky, and they seemed to stretch in every direction, as far as I could see, and to merge without a break into the waters of the estuary, and the line of the horizon.

My head reeled at the sheer and startling beauty, the wide, bare openness of it. The sense of space, the vastness of the sky above and on either side made my heart race. I would have travelled a thousand miles to see this. I had never imagined such a place.

The only sounds I could hear above the trotting of the pony's hooves, the rumble of the wheels and the creak of the cart, were sudden, harsh, weird cries from birds near and far. We had travelled perhaps three miles, and passed no farm or cottage, no kind of dwelling house at all, all was emptiness. Then, the hedgerows petered out, and we seemed to be driving towards the very edge of the world. Ahead, the water gleamed like metal and I began to make out a track, rather like the line left by the wake of a boat, that ran across it. As we drew nearer, I saw that the water was lying only shallowly over the rippling sand on either side of us, and that the line was in fact a narrow track leading directly ahead, as if into the estuary itself. As we slipped on to it, I realized that this must be the Nine Lives Causeway – this and nothing more – and saw how, when the tide came in, it would quickly be quite submerged and untraceable.

At first the pony and then the trap met the sandy path, the smart noise we had been making ceased, and we went on almost in silence save for a hissing, silky sort of sound. Here and there were clumps of reeds, bleached bone-pale, and now and again the faintest of winds caused them to rattle dryly. The sun at our backs reflected in the water all around so that everything shone and glistened like the surface of a mirror, and the sky had taken on a faint pinkish tinge at the edges, and this in turn became reflected in the marsh and the water. Then, as it was so bright that it hurt my eyes to go on staring at it, I looked up ahead and saw, as if rising out of the water itself, a tall, gaunt house of grey stone with a slate roof, that now gleamed steelily in the light. It stood like some lighthouse or beacon or Martello tower, facing the whole, wide expanse of marsh and estuary, the most astonishingly situated house I had ever seen or could ever conceivably have imagined, isolated, uncompromising but also, I thought, handsome. As we neared it, I saw the land on which it stood was raised up a little, surrounding it on every side for perhaps three or four hundred yards, of plain, salt-bleached grass, and then gravel. This little island extended in a southerly direction across an area of scrub and field towards what looked like the fragmentary ruins of some old church or chapel.

There was a rough scraping, as the cart came onto the stones, and then pulled up. We had arrived at Eel Marsh House.

For a moment or two, I simply sat looking about me in amazement, hearing nothing save the faint keening of the winter wind that came across the marsh, and the sudden rawk-rawk of a hidden bird. I felt a strange sensation, an excitement mingled with alarm ... I could not altogether tell what. Certainly, I felt loneliness, for in spite of the speechless Keckwick and the shaggy brown pony I felt quite alone, outside that gaunt, empty house. But I was not afraid — of what could I be afraid in this rare and beautiful spot? The wind? The marsh birds crying? Reeds and still water?

I got down from the trap and walked around to the man.

'How long will the causeway remain passable?'

'Till five.'

So I should scarcely be able to do more than look around, get my bearings in the house, and make a start on the search for the papers, before it would be time for him to return to fetch me back again. I did not want to leave here so soon. I was fascinated by it, I wanted Keckwick to be gone, so that I could wander about freely and slowly, take it all in through every one of my senses, and by myself. 'Listen,' I said, making a sudden decision, 'it will be quite ridiculous for you to be driving to and fro twice a day. The best thing will be for me to bring my bags and some food and drink and stay a couple of nights here. That way I shall finish the business a good deal more efficiently and you will not be troubled. I'll return with you later this afternoon and then tomorrow, perhaps you could bring me back as early as is possible, according to the tides?'

I waited. I wondered if he was going to deter me, or argue, to try and put me off the enterprise, with those old dark hints. He thought for some time. But he must have recognized the firmness of my resolve at last, for he just nodded.

'Or perhaps you'd prefer to wait here for me now? Though I shall be a couple of hours. You know what suits you best.'

For answer, he simply pulled on the pony's rein, and began to turn the trap about. Minutes later, they were receding across the causeway, smaller and smaller figures in the immensity and wideness of marsh and sky, and I had turned away and walked around to the front of Eel Marsh House, my left hand touching the shaft of the key that was in my pocket.

But I did not go inside. I did not want to, yet awhile. I wanted to drink in all the silence and the mysterious, shimmering beauty, to smell the strange, salt smell that was borne faintly on the wind, to listen for the slightest murmur. I was aware of a heightening of every one of my senses, and conscious that this extraordinary place was imprinting itself on my mind and deep in my imagination, too.

I though it most likely that, if I were to stay here for any length of time, I should become quite addicted to the solitude and the quietness, and that I should turn bird-watcher, too, for there must be many rare birds, waders and divers, wild ducks and geese, especially in spring and autumn, and with the aid of books and good binoculars I should soon come to identify them by their flight and call. Indeed, as I wandered around the outside of the house, I began to speculate about living here, and to romanticize a little about how it would be for Stella and me, alone in this wild and remote spot – though the question of what I might actually do to earn our keep, and how we might occupy ourselves from day to day, I conveniently set aside.

Then, thinking thus fancifully, I walked away from the house in the direction of the field, and across it, towards the ruin. Away to the west, on my right hand, the sun was already beginning to slip down in a great, wintry, golden-red ball which shot arrows of fire and blood-red streaks across the water. To the east, sea and sky had darkened slightly to a uniform, leaden grey. The wind that came suddenly snaking off the estuary was cold.

As I neared the ruins, I could see clearly that they were indeed of some ancient chapel, perhaps monastic in origin, and all broken-down and crumbling, with some of the stones and rubble fallen, probably in recent gales, and lying about in the grass. The ground sloped a little down to the estuary shore and, as I passed under one of the old arches, I startled a bird, which rose up and away over my head with loudly beating wings and a harsh croaking cry that echoed all around the old walls and was taken up by another, some distance away. It was an ugly, satanic-looking thing, like some species of sea-vulture – if such a thing existed – and I could not suppress a shudder as its shadow passed over me, and I watched its ungainly flight away towards the sea with relief. Then I saw that the ground at my feet and the fallen stones between were a foul mess of drop-pings, and guessed that these birds must nest and roost in the walls above.

Otherwise, I rather liked this lonely spot, and thought how it would be on a warm evening at midsummer, when the breezes blew balmily from off the sea, across the tall grasses, and wild flowers of white and yellow and pink climbed and bloomed among the broken stones, the shadows lengthened gently, and June birds poured out their finest songs, with the faint lap and wash of water in the distance.

So musing, I emerged into a small burial ground. It was enclosed by the remains of a wall, and I stopped in astonishment at the sight. There were perhaps fifty old gravestones, most of them leaning over or completely fallen, covered in patches of greenish-yellow lichen and moss, scoured pale by the salt wind, and stained by years of driven rain. The mounds were grassy, and weed-covered, or else they had disappeared altogether, sunken and slipped down. No names or dates were now decipherable, and the whole place had a decayed and abandoned air.

Ahead, where the walls ended in a heap of dust and rubble, lay the grey water of the estuary. As I stood, wondering, the last light went from the sun, and the wind rose in a gust, and rustled through the grass. Above my head, that unpleasant, snake-necked bird came gliding back towards the ruins, and I saw that its beak was hooked around a fish that writhed and struggled helplessly. I watched the creature alight and, as I did so, it dis-turbed some of the stones, which toppled and fell out of sight somewhere.

Suddenly conscious of the cold and the extreme bleakness and eeri-ness of the spot and of the gathering dusk of the November afternoon, and not wanting my spirits to become so depressed that I might begin to be affected by all sorts of morbid fancies, I was about to leave, and walk briskly back to the house, where I intended to switch on a good many lights and even light a small fire if it were possible, before beginning my preliminary work on Mrs Drablow's papers. But, as I turned away, I glanced once again round the burial ground and then I saw again the woman with the wasted face, who had been at Mrs Drablow's funeral. She was at the far end of the plot, close to one of the few upright headstones, and she wore the same clothing and bonnet, but it seemed to have slipped back so that I could make out her face a little more clearly.

In the greyness of the fading light, it had the sheen and pallor not of flesh so much as of bone itself. Earlier, when I had looked at her, although admittedly it had been scarcely more than a swift glance each time, I had not noticed any particular expression on her ravaged face, but then I had, after all, been entirely taken with the look of extreme illness. Now, however, as I stared at her, stared until my eyes ached in their sockets, stared in surprise and bewilderment at her presence, now I saw that her face did wear an expression. It was one of what I can only describe – and the words seem hopelessly inadequate to express what I saw – as a desperate, yearning malevolence; it was as though she were searching for something she wanted, needed – *must have*, more than life itself, and which had been taken from her. And, towards whoever had taken it she directed the purest evil and hatred and loathing, with all the force that was available to her. Her face, in its extreme pallor, her eyes, sunken but unnaturally bright, were burning with the concentration of passionate emotion which was within her and which streamed from her. Whether or not this hatred and malevolence was directed towards me I had no means of telling – I had no reason at all to suppose that it could possibly have been, but at that moment I was far from able to base my reactions upon reason and logic. For the combination of the peculiar, isolated place and the sudden appearance of the woman and the dreadfulness of her expression began to fill me with fear. Indeed, I had never in my life been so possessed by it, never known my knees to tremble and my flesh to creep, and then to turn cold as stone, never known my heart to give a great lurch, as if it would almost leap up into my dry mouth and then begin pounding in my chest like a hammer on an anvil, never known myself gripped and held fast by such dread and horror and apprehension of evil. It was as though I had become paralysed. I could not bear to stay there, for fear, but nor had I any strength left in my body to turn and run away, and I was as certain as I had ever been of anything that, at any second, I would drop dead on that wretched patch of ground.

It was the woman who moved. She slipped behind the gravestone and, keeping close to the shadow of the wall, went through one of the broken gaps and out of sight.

The very second that she had gone, my nerve and the power of speech and movement, my very sense of life itself, came flooding back through me, my head cleared and, all at once, I was angry, yes, *angry*, with her for the emotion she had aroused in me, for causing me to experience such fear, and the anger led at once to determination, to follow her and stop her, and then to ask some questions and receive proper replies, to get to the bottom of it all.

I ran quickly and lightly over the short stretch of rough grass between the graves towards the gap in the wall, and came out almost on the edge of the estuary. At my feet, the grass gave way within a yard or two to sand, then shallow water. All around me the marshes and the flat salt dunes stretched away until they merged with the rising tide. I could see for miles. There was no sign at all of the woman in black, nor any place in which she could have concealed herself.

Who she was – or *what* – and how she had vanished, such questions I did not ask myself. I tried not to think about the matter at all but, with the very last of the energy that I could already feel draining out of me rapidly, I turned and began to run, to flee from the graveyard and the ruins and to put the woman at as great a distance behind as I possibly could. I concentrated everything upon my running, hearing only the thud of my own body on the grass, the escape of my own breath. And I did not look back.

By the time I reached the house again I was in a lather of sweat, from exertion and from the extremes of my emotions, and as I fumbled with the key my hand shook, so that I dropped it twice upon the step before managing at last to open the front door. Once inside, I slammed it shut behind me. The noise of it boomed through the house but, when the last reverberation had faded away, the place seemed to settle back into itself again and there was a great, seething silence. For a long time, I did not move from the dark, wood-panelled hall. I wanted company, and I had none, lights and warmth and a strong drink inside me, I needed reassurance. But, more than anything else, I needed an *explanation*. It is remarkable how powerful a force simple curiosity can be. I had never realized that before now. In spite of my intense fear and sense of shock, I was consumed with the desire to find out exactly who it was that I had seen, and how, I could not rest until I had settled the business, for all that, while out there, I had not dared to stay and make any investigations.

I did not believe in ghosts. Or rather, until this day, I had not done so, and whatever stories I had heard of them I had, like most rational, sensible young men, dismissed as nothing more than stories indeed. That certain people claimed to have a stronger than normal intuition of such things and that certain old places were said to be haunted, of course I was aware, but I would have been loath to admit that there could possibly be anything in it, even if presented with any evidence. And I had never had any evidence. It was remarkable, I had always thought, that ghostly apparitions and similar strange occurrences always seemed to be experienced at several removes, by someone who had known someone who had heard of it from someone they knew!

But out on the marshes just now, in the peculiar, fading light and desolation of that burial ground, I had seen a woman whose form was quite
substantial and yet in some essential respect also, I had no doubt, ghostly.
She had a ghostly pallor and a dreadful expression, she wore clothes that
were out of keeping with the styles of the present day; she had kept her
distance from me and she had not spoken. Something emanating from
her still, silent presence, in each case by a grave, had communicated itself
to me so strongly that I had felt indescribable repulsion and fear. And
she had appeared and then vanished in a way that surely no real, living,
fleshly human being could possibly manage to do. And yet ... she had not
looked in any way – as I imagined the traditional 'ghost' was supposed
to do – transparent or vaporous, she had been real, she had been there, I
had seen her quite clearly, I was certain that I could have gone up to her,
addressed her, touched her.

I did not believe in ghosts.

What other explanation was there?

From somewhere in the dark recesses of the house, a clock began to
strike, and it brought me out of my reverie. Shaking myself, I deliberately
turned my mind from the matter of the woman in the graveyards, to the
house in which I was now standing.

Off the hall ahead led a wide oak staircase and, on one side, a passage
to what I took to be the kitchen and scullery. There were various other
doors, all of them closed. I switched on the light in the hall but the bulb
was very weak, and I thought it best to go through each of the rooms in
turn and let in what daylight was left, before beginning any search for
papers.

After what I had heard from Mr Bentley and from other people once
I had arrived, about the late Mrs Drablow, I had had all sorts of wild imaginings about the state of her house. I had expected it, perhaps, to be a
shrine to the memory of a past time, or to her youth, or to the memory
of her husband of so short a time, like the house of poor Miss Havisham.
Or else to be simply cobwebbed and filthy, with old newspapers, rags and
rubbish piled in corners, all the débris of a recluse – together with some
half-starved cat or dog.

But, as I began to wander in and out of morning room and drawing
room, sitting room and dining room and study, I found nothing so dramatic or unpleasant, though it is true that there was that faintly damp,
musty, sweet-sour smell everywhere about, that will arise in any house
that has been shut up for some time, and particularly in one which,

surrounded as this was on all sides by marsh and estuary, was bound to be permanently damp.

The furniture was old-fashioned but good, solid, dark, and it had been reasonably well looked after, though many of the rooms had clearly not been much used or perhaps even entered for years. Only a small parlour, at the far end of a narrow corridor off the hall, seemed to have been much lived in – probably it had been here that Mrs Drablow had passed most of her days. In every room were glass-fronted cases full of books and, besides the books, there were heavy pictures, dull portraits and oil paintings of old houses. But my heart sank when, after sorting through the bunch of keys Mr Bentley had given me, I found those which unlocked various desks, bureaux, and writing tables, for in all of them were bundles and boxes of papers – letters, receipts, legal documents, notebooks, tied with ribbon or string, and yellow with age. It looked as if Mrs Drablow had never thrown away a single piece of paper or letter in her life, and, clearly, the task of sorting through these, even in a preliminary way, was far greater than I had anticipated. Most of it might turn out to be quite worthless and redundant, but all of it would have to be examined nevertheless, before anything that Mr Bentley would have to deal with, pertaining to the disposal of the estate, could be packed up and sent to London. It was obvious that there would be little point in my making a start now, it was too late and I was too unnerved by the business in the graveyard. Instead, I simply went about the house looking in every room and finding nothing of much interest or elegance. Indeed, it was all curiously impersonal, the furniture, the decoration, the ornaments, assembled by someone with little individuality or taste, a dull, rather gloomy and rather unwelcoming home. It was remarkable and extraordinary in only one respect – its situation. From every window – and they were tall and wide in each room – there was a view of one aspect or other of the marshes and the estuary and the immensity of the sky, all colour had been drained and blotted out of them now, the sun had set, the light was poor, there was no movement at all, no undulation of the water, and I could scarcely make out any break between land and water and sky. All was grey. I managed to let up every blind and to open one or two of the windows. The wind had dropped altogether, there was no sound save the faintest, softest suck of water as the tide crept in. How one old woman had endured day after day, night after night, of isolation in this house, let alone for so many years, I could not conceive. I should have gone mad – indeed, I intended to work every possible minute without a pause to get through the papers and be done. And yet, there was a strange fascination in looking out over the wild wide marshes, for they had an uncanny beauty, even now, in the grey twilight. There was nothing whatsoever to see for mile after mile and yet I could not take my eyes away. But for today I had had enough. Enough of solitude and no sound save the water and the moaning wind and the melancholy calls of the birds, enough of monotonous greyness, enough of this gloomy old house. And, as it would be at least another hour before Keckwick would return in the pony trap, I decided that I would stir myself and put the place behind me. A good brisk walk would shake me up and put me in good heart, and work up my appetite and if I stepped out well I would arrive back in Crythin Gifford in time to save Keckwick from turning out. Even if I did not, I should meet him on the way. The causeway was still visible, the roads back were straight and I could not possibly lose myself.

So thinking, I closed up the windows and drew the blinds again and left Eel Marsh House to itself in the declining November light.

The Sound of a Pony and Trap

Outside, all was quiet, so that all I heard was the sound of my own foot-steps as I began to walk briskly across the gravel, and even this sound was softened the moment I struck out over the grass towards the causeway path. Across the sky, a few last gulls went flying home. Once or twice, I glanced over my shoulder, half expecting to catch sight of the black figure of the woman following me. But I had almost persuaded myself now that there must have been some slope or dip in the ground upon the other side of that graveyard and beyond it, perhaps a lonely dwelling, tucked down out of sight, for the changes of light in such a place can play all manner of tricks and, after all, I had not actually gone out there to search for her hiding place, I had only glanced around and seen nothing. Well, then. For the time being I allowed myself to remain forgetful of the extreme reac-tion of Mr Jerome to my mentioning the woman that morning.

On the causeway path it was still quite dry underfoot but to my left I saw that the water had begun to seep nearer, quite silent, quite slow. I wondered how deeply the path went under water when the tide was at height. But, on a still night such as this, there was plenty of time to cross in safety, though the distance was greater, now I was traversing it on foot, than it had seemed when we trotted over in Keckwick's pony cart, and the end of the causeway path seemed to be receding into the greyness ahead. I had never been quite so alone, nor felt quite so small and insignificant in a vast landscape before, and I fell into a not unpleasant brooding, philo-sophical frame of mind, struck by the absolute indifference of water and sky to my presence.

Some minutes later, I could not tell how many, I came out of my reverie, to realize that I could no longer see very far in front of me and when I turned around I was startled to find that Eel Marsh House, too, was invisible, not because the darkness of evening had fallen, but because of a thick, damp sea-mist that had come rolling over the marshes and envel-oped everything, myself, the house behind me, the end of the causeway

path and the countryside ahead. It was a mist like a damp, clinging cob-
webby thing, fine and yet impenetrable. It smelled and tasted quite different from the yellow filthy fog of London; that was choking and thick and
still, this was salty, light and pale and moving in front of my eyes all the
time. I felt confused, teased by it, as though it were made up of millions of
live fingers that crept over me, hung on me and then shifted away again.
My hair and face and the sleeves of my coat were already damp with a veil
of moisture. Above all, it was the suddenness of it that had so unnerved
and disorientated me.

For a short time, I walked slowly on, determined to stick to my path
until I came out onto the safety of the country road. But it began to dawn
upon me that I should as likely as not become very quickly lost once I
had left the straightness of the causeway, and might wander all night in
exhaustion. The most obvious and sensible course was to turn and retrace
my steps the few hundred yards I had come and to wait at the house until
either the mist cleared, or Keckwick arrived to fetch me, or both.

That walk back was a nightmare. I was obliged to go step by slow step,
for fear of veering off onto the marsh, and then into the rising water. If
I looked up or around me, I was at once baffled by the moving, shifting
mist, and so on I stumbled, praying to reach the house, which was farther
away than I had imagined. Then, somewhere away in the swirling mist
and dark, I heard the sound that lifted my heart, the distant but unmistakable clip-clop of the pony's hooves and the rumble and creak of the
trap. So Keckwick was unperturbed by the mist, quite used to travelling
through the lanes and across the causeway in darkness, and I stopped and
waited to see a lantern – for surely he must carry one – and half wondered
whether to shout and make my presence known, in case he came suddenly
upon me and ran me down into the ditch.

Then I realized that the mist played tricks with sound as well as sight,
for not only did the noise of the trap stay further away from me for
longer than I might have expected but also it seemed to come not from
directly behind me, straight down the causeway path, but instead to be
away to my right, out on the marsh. I tried to work out the direction of
the wind but there was none. I turned around but then the sound began
to recede further away again. Baffled, I stood and waited, straining to
listen through the mist. What I heard next chilled and horrified me, even
though I could neither understand nor account for it. The noise of the
pony trap grew fainter and then stopped abruptly and away on the marsh
was a curious draining, sucking, churning sound, which went on, together

with the shrill neighing and whinnying of a horse in panic, and then I heard another cry, a shout, a terrified sobbing – it was hard to decipher – but with horror I realized that it came from a child, a young child. I stood absolutely helpless in the mist that clouded me and everything from my sight, almost weeping in an agony of fear and frustration, and I knew that I was hearing, beyond any doubt, appalling last noises of a pony and trap, carrying a child in it, as well as whatever adult – presumably Keckwick – was driving and was even now struggling desperately. It had somehow lost the causeway path and fallen into the marshes and was being dragged under by the quicksand and the pull of the incoming tide.

I began to yell until I thought my lungs would burst, and then to run forward, but then stopped, for I could see nothing and what use would that be? I could not get onto the marsh and even if I could there was no chance of my finding the pony trap or of helping its occupants, I would only, in all likelihood, risk being sucked into the marsh myself. The only thing was to get back to Eel Marsh House, to light every light and somehow try and signal with them from the windows, hoping against all reason that this would be seen, like a light-ship, by someone, somewhere, in the countryside around.

Shuddering at the dreadful thoughts racing through my mind and the pictures I could not help but see of those poor creatures being slowly choked and drowned to death in mud and water, I forgot my own fears and nervous imaginings of a few minutes earlier and concentrated on getting back to the house as quickly and safely as I could. The water was now lapping very close to the edges of the path though I could only hear it, the mist was still so thick and darkness had completely fallen, and it was with a gasp of relief that I felt the turf and then the gravel beneath my feet and fumbled my way blindly to the door of the house.

Behind me, out on the marshes, all was still and silent; save for that movement of the water, the pony and trap might never have existed.

When I got inside the house again, I managed to reach a chair in that dark hall and, sitting on it just as my legs buckled beneath me, I put my head down into my hands and gave way to an outburst of helpless sobbing as the full realization of what had just happened overcame me.

For how long I sat there, in extremes of despair and fearfulness, I do not know. But after some time I was able to pull myself together sufficiently to get up and go about the house, switching on every light that I could make work and leaving them on, though they were none of them very bright, and, in my heart, I knew that there was little chance of what was not much more than a glow from a handful of scattered lamps being seen across that misty land, even had there been any watcher or traveller on hand to glimpse them. But I had done something – all that I could do indeed – and I felt just fractionally better because of it. After that, I began searching in cupboards and sideboards and kitchen dressers until at last, at the very back of one such in the dining room, I found a bottle of brandy – thirty years old and still fully corked and sealed. I opened it, found a glass, and poured myself as large a measure as seemed sensible to be consumed by a man in a state of great shock, some hours away from his last meal.

The room had clearly not been used by Mrs Drablow for many years. The furniture had a faded bloom from the salt in the air and the candle-sticks and épergne were tarnished, the linen cloths stiffly folded and inter-leaved with yellowing tissue, the glass and china dusty.

I went back into the one room in the house that had some pretensions to comfort, for all it was chilly and musty-smelling, the little sitting-room, and there I sipped my brandy and tried as calmly as I could to work out what I should do.

But as the drink took effect I became more rather than less agitated and my brain was in an increasing turmoil. I began to be angry with Mr Bentley for sending me here, at my own foolish independence and block-headedness in ignoring all the hints and veiled warnings I had received about the place, and to long – no, to pray – for some kind of speedy deliverance and to be back in the safety and comforting busyness and clamour of London, among friends – indeed among any people at all – and with Stella.

I could not sit still in that claustrophobic and yet oddly hollow-feeling old house, but rambled about from room to room, lifting up this and that object and setting it down again hopelessly and then going upstairs, to wander into shuttered bedrooms and up again, to attics full of lumber, uncarpeted and without curtains or blinds at the tall narrow windows.

Every door was open, every room orderly, dusty, bitterly cold and damp and yet also somehow stifling. Only one door was locked, at the far end of a passage that led away from three bedrooms on the second floor. There was no keyhole, no bolt on the outside.

For some obscure reason, I became angry with that door, I kicked at it and rattled the handle hard, before giving up abruptly and returning downstairs, listening to the echo of my own footsteps as I went.

Every few moments, I went to one or other of the windows, rubbed my hand across the pane to try and see out; but, although I rubbed at a thin film of grime, enough to leave a clear space, I could not rub away the curtain of sea-mist that was so close up to the glass on the outside. As I stared into it I saw that it was still constantly shifting, like clouds, though without ever parting or dispersing.

At last I slumped down on the plush-covered sofa in the great high-ceilinged drawing room, turned my face away from the window, and gave myself up, along with the last of a second glass of the mellow, fragrant brandy, to melancholy brooding and a sort of inward-looking self-pity. I was no longer cold, no longer afraid or restless, I felt cocooned against the horrible events that had taken place out on the marshes and I allowed myself to give way, to slip down into this mindless state, which was as inchoate as the fog outside, and there to rest, wallow and find, if not peace, at least a certain relief in the suspension of all extremes of emotion.

A bell was ringing, ringing, through my ears, inside my head, its clangour sounded at once very close and oddly distant, it seemed to sway, and I to sway with it. I was trying to struggle out of some darkness which was not fixed but shifting about, as the ground seemed to be shifting beneath my feet, so that I was terrified of slipping and falling down, down, of being sucked into a horrible echoing maelstrom. The bell went on ringing. I came awake in bewilderment, to see the moon, huge as a pumpkin beyond the tall windows, in a clear black sky.

My head was thick, my mouth furred and dry, my limbs stiff. I had slept, perhaps for minutes, perhaps for some hours, I had lost my sense of time. I struggled upright and then I realized that the bell I heard was not part of the confusion of my fitful nightmare but a real bell sounding through the house. Someone was at the front door.

As I half-walked, half-fell, because of numbness in my feet and legs where I had lain cramped upon the sofa, out of the room and into the hall, I began to remember what had happened and above all – and I felt an upsurge of horror as the memory returned to me – the business of the pony and trap, from which I had heard the child screaming, out upon Eel Marsh. All the lights I had left on were still shining out and must have been seen, I thought, as I pulled open the front door, hoping against hope to see a party of searchers and helpers, strong men, people to whom I could give it all over, who would know what to do and who would, above all, take me away from this place.

But in the light of the hall as it shone out and under the full moonlight too, there stood, on the gravel drive, only one man – Keckwick.

And behind him, the pony and trap. All seemed quite real, quite normal, and completely unharmed. The air was clear and cold, the sky thick with stars. The marshes lay still and silent and gleaming silver under the moon. There was no vestige of mist or cloud, not so much as a touch of damp-ness in the atmosphere. All was so changed, so utterly changed that I might have been reborn into another world and all the rest had been some fevered dream.

'You have to wait for a fret like that to clear itself. There's no crossing over while a fret's up,' Keckwick said matter-of-factly. 'Unlucky for you, that was.'

My tongue seemed to be held fast against the roof of my mouth, my knees about to buckle beneath me.

'And, after that, there's the wait for the tide.' He looked all round him. 'Awkward place. You'll be finding that out fast enough.'

It was then that I managed to look at my watch and saw that it was almost two o'clock in the morning. The tide had just begun to recede again, revealing the Nine Lives Causeway. I had slept for almost seven hours, almost as long as I would on any normal night, but here I was with hours still to go before dawn, feeling as sick and wretched and weary as any man who has lain sleepless for hour after hour. 'I wouldn't have ex-pected you to come back at this hour,' I managed to stammer. 'It's very good of you ...'

Keckwick pushed his cap back a little in order to scratch at his forehead and I noticed that his nose and much of the lower part of his face were covered in bumps and lumps and warts and that the skin was porridgy in texture and a dark, livid red. 'I wouldn't have left you over the night,' he said at last, 'wouldn't have done that to you.'

I felt a moment of light-headedness, for we seemed to have slipped into the way of normal, practical conversation – indeed, I was glad to see him, never had I welcomed the sight of a fellow human being more in my life and to see his solid little pony that stood quietly, patiently, by.

But then the second recollection returned to me and I blurted out, 'But what happened to you, how do you manage to be here – *how did you get out?*' Then my heart lurched as I realized that of course it had not been Keckwick and his pony who had gone into the quicksand, not at all, but someone else, someone with a child, and now they were gone, dead, the marsh had taken them and the waters had closed over them and no ripple or disturbance of the faintest kind showed on that still, gleaming surface. But who, *who*, on a dark November evening in the rolling mist and the rising tide, who had been driving out, and with a child too, in that treach-erous place and why, where had they been driving to and where coming from – this was the only house for many miles, unless I had been right about the woman in black and her hidden dwelling.

Keckwick was looking straight into my face and I realized that I must appear dishevelled and wild, not at all the business-like, confident and smart young lawyer he had left at the house that afternoon. Then he indi-cated the pony trap: 'Best get in, 'he said.

'Yes – but surely ...'

He had turned away abruptly and was climbing into the driving seat. There, looking straight ahead of him, huddled into his great coat with the collar turned to cover his neck and chin, he waited. That he was fully aware of my state, knew something had happened to me and was quite unsurprised, was clear, and his manner also told me unmistakably that he did not wish to hear what it was, to ask or answer questions, to discuss the business at all. He would fetch and carry and that reliably and at any hour and he would do no more.

Silently, quickly, I went back into the house and switched off the lights and then I got into the cart and let Keckwick and his pony take me away, across the quiet, eerily beautiful marshes, under the rising moon. I fell into a sort of trance, half sleeping, half waking, rocked by the motion of the cart. My head had begun to ache miserably and my stomach to contract with spasms of nausea now and again. I did not look about me, though sometimes I glanced up into the great bowl of the night sky and at the constellations scattered there and the sight was comforting and calming to me, things in the heavens seemed still to be aright and unchanged. But nothing else was, within me or all around. I knew now that I had entered some hitherto unimagined – indeed, unbelieved-in – realm of conscious-ness, that coming to this place had already changed me and that there was no going back. For, today, I had seen things I had never dreamed of seeing and heard things too. That the woman by the graves had been ghostly I now – not believed, no – *knew*, for certainty lay deep within me, I realized that it had become fixed and immovable, perhaps during that restless, anguished sleep. But I began to suspect that the pony and trap that I had heard out on the marsh, the pony and trap with the child who had cried out so terribly and which had been sucked into the quicksands, while marsh and estuary, land and sea, had been shrouded in that sudden fog, and I lost in the midst of it – they, too, had not been real, not there, present, not substantial, but ghostly also. What I had heard, I had heard, as clearly as I now heard the roll of the cart and the drumming of the pony's hooves, and what I had seen – the woman with the pale wasted face, by the grave of Mrs Drablow and again in the old burial ground – I had seen. I would have sworn to that on oath, on any testament. Yet they had been, in some sense I did not understand, unreal, ghostly, things that were dead.

Having accepted so much, I at once felt calmer and so we left the marsh and the estuary behind us and clopped along the lane in the middle of that quiet night. I supposed that the landlord of the Gifford Arms could be knocked up and persuaded to let me in, and then I intended to go up to that comfortable bed and sleep again, to try and shut out all these things from my head and my heart and not think of them more. Tomorrow, in daylight, I would recover myself and then plan what I was going to do. At this moment I knew that more than anything else I did not want to have to go back to Eel Marsh House and must try to find some way of extricating myself from any more dealings with the affairs of Mrs Drablow. Whether I would make some excuse to Mr Bentley or endeavour to tell him the truth and hope not to be ridiculed I did not try and decide.

It was only as I was getting myself ready for bed – the landlord having proved most sympathetic and accommodating – that I began to think again about the extraordinary generosity of Keckwick, in coming out for me the moment the mist and tides enabled him to do so. He would surely have been expected to shrug his shoulders, retire and plan to collect me first thing in the morning. But he must have waited up and perhaps even kept his pony harnessed, in his concern that I should not have to spend a night alone in that house. I was profoundly grateful to him and I made a note that he should receive a generous reward for his pains.

It was after three o'clock when I climbed into bed, and it would not be light for another five hours. The landlord had said I was to sleep on as long as I chose, no one would disturb me and a breakfast would be provided at any time. He, too, in his different way, had seemed as anxious for my welfare as Keckwick, though about them both there was the same extreme reserve, a barrier put up against all inquiry which I had the sense not to try and break down. Who could tell what they themselves had seen or heard, how much more they knew about the past and all manner of events, not to mention rumours and hearsay and superstition about those events, I could not guess. The little I had experienced was more than enough and I was reluctant to begin delving into any explanations.

So I thought that night, as I laid my head on the soft pillow and fell eventually into a restless, shadowy sleep, across which figures came and went, troubling me, so that once or twice I half-woke myself, as I cried out or spoke a few incoherent words, I sweated, I turned and turned about, trying to free myself from the nightmares, to escape from my own semi-conscious sense of dread and foreboding, and all the time, piercing through the surface of my dreams, came the terrified whinnying of the pony and the crying and calling of that child over and over, while I stood, helpless in the mist, my feet held fast, my body pulled back, and while behind me, though I could not see, only sense her dark presence, hovered the woman.

Mr Jerome is Afraid

When I awoke, it was again to see the pleasant bedroom filled with bright winter sunshine. But it was with a great sense of weariness and bitterness, too, that I contrasted my present state with that of the previous morning, when I had slept so well and woken so refreshed and sprung out of bed eager to begin the day. And was it only yesterday? I felt as if I had journeyed so far, in spirit if not in time experienced so much and been so churned about within my formerly placid and settled self that it might have been years since then. Now, I felt heavy and sick in my head, stale and tired and jangled too, my nerves and my imagination were all on edge.

But, after a while, I forced myself to rise, as I could hardly feel worse than I did lying in the bed that now felt as lumpish and uncomfortable as a heap of potato sacks. Once I had drawn back the curtains on a sharp blue sky and taken a good hot bath, followed by a rinse of my head and neck under the cold tap, I began to feel less frowsty and depressed, more composed and able to think in an orderly way about the day ahead. Over breakfast, for which I had a better appetite than I had expected, I put to myself the various alternatives. Last night I had been adamant and would have brooked no possible opposition – I was having nothing more to do with Eel Marsh and the Drablow business but would telegraph to Mr Bentley, leave matters in the hands of Mr Jerome and take the first available train to London.

In short, I was going to run away. Yes, that was how I saw it in the bright light of day. I attached no particular blame to my decision. I had been as badly frightened as a man could be. I did not think that I would be the first to run from physical risks and dangers, although I had no reason to suppose myself markedly braver than the next person. But these other matters were altogether more terrifying, because they were intangible and inexplicable, incapable of proof and yet so deeply affecting. I began to realize that what had frightened me most – and, as I investigated my own thoughts and feelings that morning, what continued to frighten me – was not what I had seen – there had been nothing intrinsically repellent or horrifying about the woman with the wasted face. It was true that the ghastly sounds I had heard through the fog had greatly upset me but far worse was what emanated from and surrounded these things and arose to unsteady me, an atmosphere, a force – I do not exactly know what to call it – of evil and uncleanness, of terror and suffering, of malevolence and bitter anger. I felt quite at a loss to cope with any of these things.

'You'll find Crythin a quieter place today,' the landlord said, as he came to clear away my plate and replenish my pot of coffee. 'Market day brings everyone from miles about. There'll be little enough happening this morning.'

He stood for a moment, looking at me closely and I again felt it necessary to apologize for having had him get up and come down to let me in, the previous night. He shook his head 'Oh, I had rather that than have you spend an ... an uncomfortable night anywhere else.'

'As it happened, my night was a bit disturbed in any case. I seemed to have an overdose of bad dreams and be generally restless.'

He said nothing.

'I think what I need this morning is some exercise in the fresh air. Perhaps I'll walk into the countryside a mile or so, look at the farms belonging to some of the men who were all here doing their market business yesterday.'

What I meant was that I planned to turn my back upon the marshes and walk steadfastly in the opposite direction.

'Well, you'll find it nice and easy walking, we're flat as a bed-sheet for many miles about. Of course, you could go a good deal further, if you want to be on horseback.'

'Alas, I have never ridden in my life and I confess I don't feel in the mood to start today.'

'Or else,' he said suddenly with a smile, 'I can lend you a good stout bicycle.'

A bicycle! He saw my expression change. As a boy I had bicycled regularly and far, and indeed Stella and I still sometimes took the train out towards one of the locks and cycled for miles along the Thames towpath with a picnic in our baskets.

'You'll find it around the back, in the yard there. Just help yourself, sir, if the fancy takes you.' And he left the dining room.

The idea of bicycling for an hour or so, to blow away the clinging cobwebs and staleness of the night, to refresh and restore me, was extremely cheering, and I knew that my mood was uprising. Moreover, I was not going to run away.

Instead, I decided to go and talk to Mr Jerome. I had formed some notion of asking for help in sorting out Mrs Drablow's papers – perhaps he had an office boy he could spare, for I was now sure that, in daylight and with company, I was strong enough again to face Eel Marsh House. I would return to the town well before dark and work as methodically and efficiently as possible. Nor would I take any walk in the direction of the burial ground.

It was remarkable how physical well-being had improved my spirits and, as I stepped outside into the market square, I felt once again my normal, equable, cheerful self, while every so often a spurt of glee arose inside me at the anticipation of my bicycle ride.

I found the office of Horatio Jerome, Land and Estate Agent – two poky, low-ceilinged rooms, over a corn merchant's store, in the narrow lane leading off the square – and expected also to find an assistant or clerk, to whom to give my name. But there was no one. The place was silent, the outer waiting room dingy and empty. So after hovering about for a few moments I went to the only other closed door and knocked. There was a further pause and then the scraping of a chair and some quick footsteps. Mr Jerome opened the door.

It was clear at once that he was by no means pleased to see me. His face took on the closed-up, deadened look of the previous day and he hesitated before eventually inviting me into his office and cast odd half-glances at me, before looking quickly away again, to a point over my shoulder. I paused, waiting, I suppose, for him to inquire how I had fared at Eel Marsh House. But he said nothing at all and so I began to put my proposal to him.

'You see I had had no idea – I don't know whether you had – of the volume of papers belonging to Mrs Drablow. Tons of the stuff and most of it I've no doubt so much waste, but it will have to be gone through item by item, nevertheless. It seems clear that, unless I am to take up residence in Crythin Gifford for the foreseeable future, I shall have to have some help.'

Mr Jerome's expression was one of panic. He shifted his chair back, further away from me, as he sat behind his rickety desk, so that I thought that, if he could have gone through the wall into the street, he would like to have done so.

'I'm afraid *I* can't offer you help, Mr Kipps. Oh, no.'

'I wasn't thinking that you would do anything personally,' I said in a soothing tone. 'But perhaps you have a young assistant.'

'There is no one. I am quite on my own. I cannot give you any help at all.'

'Well, then, help me to find someone – surely the town will yield me a young man with a modicum of intelligence, and keen to earn a few pounds, whom I may take on for the job?'

I noticed that his hands, which rested on the sides of his chair, were working, rubbing, fidgeting, gripping and ungripping in agitation.

'I'm sorry – this is a small place – young people leave – there are no openings.'

'But I am offering an opening – albeit temporary.'

'You will find no one suitable.' He was almost shouting at me.

Then I said, very calmly and quietly, 'Mr Jerome, what you mean is not that there is no one available, that no young person – or older person for that matter – could be found in the town or the neighbourhood able and free to do the work if a thorough search were to be made. There would not I am sure be many applicants but certainly we should be able to find one or two possible candidates for the job. But you are backing away from speaking out the truth of the matter, which is that I should not find a soul willing to spend any time out at Eel Marsh House, for fear of the stories about that place proving true – for fear of encountering what I have already encountered.'

There was absolute silence. Mr Jerome's hands continued to scrabble about like the paws of some struggling creature. His pale domed forehead was beaded with perspiration. Eventually he got up, almost knocking over his chair as he did so, and went over to the narrow window to look out through the dirty pane onto the houses opposite and down into the quiet lane below. Then, with his back to me, he said at last, 'Keckwick came back for you.'

'Yes. I was more grateful than I can say.'

'There's nothing Keckwick doesn't know about Eel Marsh House.'

'Do I take it he fetched and carried sometimes for Mrs Drablow?'

He nodded. 'She saw no one else. Not ...' his voice trailed away.

'Not another living soul,' I put in evenly.

When he spoke again he sounded husky and tired. 'There are stories,' he said, 'tales. There's all that nonsense.'

'I can believe it. Such a place would breed marsh monsters and creatures of the deep and Jack o'Lanterns by the cart-load.'

'You can discount most of it.'

'Of course. But not all.'

'You saw that woman in the churchyard.'

'I saw her again. I went for a walk all around the ground Eel Marsh House stands on, after Keckwick had left me yesterday afternoon. She was in that old burial ground. What are the ruins – some church or chapel?'

'There was once a monastery on that island – long before the house was ever built. Some small community that cut itself off from the rest of the world. There are records of it in the county histories. It was abandoned, left to decay – oh, centuries ago.'

'And the burial ground?'

'There was ... some later use. A few graves.'

'The Drablows?'

He turned suddenly to face me. There was a sickly greyish pallor over his skin now and I realized how seriously he was affected by our conversation and that he would probably prefer not to continue. I had to make my arrangements but I decided, at that moment, to abandon the attempt to work with Mr Jerome and to telephone instead, directly to Mr Bentley in London. For that purpose, I would return to the hotel.

'Well,' I said, 'I'm not going to be put out by a ghost or several ghosts, Mr Jerome. It was unpleasant and I confess that I shall be glad when I have found a companion to share my work out at the house. But it will have to be done. And I doubt if the woman in black can have any animosity towards *me*. I wonder who she was? *Is?*' I laughed though it came out sounding quite false into the room. 'I hardly know how to refer to her!'

I was trying to make light of something that we both knew was gravely serious, trying to dismiss as insignificant, and perhaps even non-existent, something that affected us both as deeply as any other experience we had undergone in our lives, for it took us to the very edge of the horizon where life and death meet together. 'I must face it out, Mr Jerome. Such things one must face.' And even as I spoke I felt a new determination arise within me.

'So I said.' Mr Jerome was looking at me pityingly. 'So I said ... once.'

But his fear was only serving to strengthen my resolve. He had been weakened and broken, by what? A woman? A few noises? Or was there more that I should discover for myself ? I knew that, if I asked him, he would refuse to answer and, in any case, I was uncertain whether I wanted to be filled up with all these frightening and weird tales of the nervous Mr

Jerome's past experiences at Eel Marsh House. I decided that, if I were to get to the truth of the business, I should have to rely upon the evidence of my own senses and nothing more. Perhaps, after all, I should do better *not* to have an assistant.

I took my leave of Mr Jerome, remarking as I went that in all probability I should see nothing more of the woman or of any other peculiar visitors to the late Mrs Drablow's house.

'I pray that you do not,' Mr Jerome said, and he held onto my hand with a sudden fierce grip as he shook it. 'I pray that you do not.'

'Don't worry about it,' I called, deliberately making myself sound carefree and cheerful, and I ran lightly down the staircase, leaving Mr Jerome to his agitation.

I returned to the Gifford Arms and, instead of telephoning, wrote a letter to Mr Bentley. In it I described the house and its hoard of papers and explained that I should have to stay longer than anticipated and that I expected to hear if Mr Bentley required me to return at once to London, and make some other arrangements. I also made a light remark about the bad reputation Eel Marsh House enjoyed locally and said that for this reason – but also for others rather more mundane – it might be difficult for me to get any help, though I was anxious to try. The whole business, nevertheless, should be completed within the week and I would arrange for the dispatch of as many papers as seemed to be important to London.

Then, putting the letter on the table in the lobby, to be collected at noon, I went out and found the landlord's bicycle, a good, old-fashioned sit-up-and-beg with a large basket on the front almost like that sported by the butcher-boys in London. I mounted it and pedalled out of the square and away, up one of the side streets towards the open country. It was the perfect day for bicycling, cold enough to make the wind burn against my cheeks as I went, bright and clear enough for me to be able to see a long way in all directions across that flat, open landscape.

I intended to cycle to the next village, where I hoped to find another country inn and enjoy some bread and cheese and beer for lunch but, as I reached the last of the houses, I could not resist the urge that was so extraordinarily strong within me to stop and look, not westwards, where I might see farms and fields and the distant roofs of a village, but east. And there they lay, those glittering, beckoning, silver marshes with the sky pale at the horizon where it reached down to the water of the estuary. A thin breeze blew off them with salt on its breath. Even from as far away as this I could hear the mysterious silence, and once again the haunting, strange beauty of it all aroused a response deep within me. I could not run away from that place, I would have to go back to it, not now, but soon, I had fallen under some sort of spell of the kind that certain places exude and it drew me, my imaginings, my longings, my curiosity, my whole spirit, towards itself.

For a long time, I looked and looked and recognized what was happening to me. My emotions had now become so volatile and so extreme, my nervous responses so near the surface, so rapid and keen, that I was living in another dimension, my heart seemed to beat faster, my step to be quicker, everything I saw was brighter, its outlines more sharply, precisely defined. And all this since yesterday. I had wondered whether I looked different in some essential way so that, when I eventually returned home, my friends and family would notice the change. I felt older and like a man who was being put to trial half fearful, half wondering, excited, completely in thrall.

But now, managing to suspend this acute emotional state and in order to help myself retain my normal equilibrium, I would take some exercise, and so I turned the bicycle and remounted and pedalled steadily down the country road, putting my back firmly to the marshes.

Spider

I returned some four hours and thirty-odd miles later in a positive glow of well-being. I had ridden out determinedly across the countryside, seeing the very last traces of golden autumn merging into the beginnings of winter, feeling the rush of pure cold air on my face, banishing every nervous fear and morbid fancy by energetic physical activity. I had found my village inn and eaten my bread and cheese and even, afterwards, made myself free of a farmer's barn to sleep for an hour.

Coming back into Crythin Gifford I felt like a new man, proud, satisfied, and most of all eager and ready to face and to tackle the worst that Mrs Drablow's house and those sinister surrounding marshes might have in store for me. In short, I was defiant, defiant and cheerful, and so I spun around a corner into the square and almost smack into a large motor car which was negotiating the narrow turn in the oncoming direction. As I swerved, braked and scrambled somehow off my machine, I saw that the car belonged to my railway travelling companion, the man who had been buying up farms at yesterday's auction, Mr Samuel Daily. Now, he was bidding his driver slow down and leaning out of the window to ask me how I did.

'I've just had a good spin out into the countryside and I shall do justice to my dinner tonight,' I said cheerfully.

Mr Daily raised his eyebrows. 'And your business?'

'Mrs Drablow's Estate? Oh, I shall soon have all that in order, though I confess there will be rather more to do than I had anticipated.'

'You have been out to the house?'

'Certainly.'

'Ah.'

For a few seconds we looked at each other, neither one apparently willing to press the subject a little further. Then, preparing to remount my bicycle once I was out of his way, I said breezily, 'To tell the truth, I'm enjoying myself. I am finding the whole thing rather a challenge.'

Mr Daily continued to regard me steadily until I was forced to shift about and glance away, feeling like nothing so much as a schoolboy caught out in blustering his way through a fabricated tale.

'Mr Kipps,' he said, 'you are whistling in the dark. Let me give you that dinner you say you've such an appetite for. Seven o'clock. Your landlord will direct you to my house.' Then he motioned to the driver, sat back and did not give me another glance.

Once back at the hotel, I began to make serious arrangements for the next day or so for, although there had been a grain of truth in Mr Daily's accusation, I was nonetheless in a firmly determined frame of mind and more than ready to go ahead with the business at Eel Marsh House. Accordingly, I asked for a hamper of provisions to be got ready and, in addition, went out myself into the town and bought some additional supplies – packets of tea and coffee and sugar, a couple of loaves of bread, a tin of biscuits, fresh pipe tobacco, matches and so forth. I also purchased a large torch lantern and a pair of Wellington boots. Far at the back of my mind, I retained a vivid recollection of my walk on the marshes in the fog and rising tide. If that were ever to happen again – though I prayed fervently it would not – I determined to be as well prepared, at least for any physical eventuality, as I could be.

When I told the landlord of my plan – that I intended to spend tonight at his inn and then the next two over at Eel Marsh House – he said nothing at all but I knew full well that he was recalling at the same moment as I was myself how I had arrived, banging violently on his door in the early hours of that morning, the shock from my experiences etched upon my face. When I asked if I could again borrow the bicycle he merely nodded. I told him that I wanted to retain my room and that, depending on how speedily I got through the work on Mrs Drablow's papers, I should be taking my final leave towards the end of the week.

I have often wondered since what the man actually thought of me and the enterprise I was blithely undertaking, for it was clear that he knew as much as anyone not only of the stories and rumours attaching to Eel Marsh House but of the truth too. I suspect that he would have preferred me to be gone altogether but was making it his business neither to voice an opinion nor to give warning or advice. And my manner that day must have indicated clearly that I would brook no opposition, heed no warning, even from within myself. I was by now almost pigheadedly bent upon following my course.

That much Mr Samuel Daily ascertained within a few moments of my arriving at his house that evening and he watched me and let me babble, saying nothing himself for the best part of our meal.

I had found my way there without difficulty and been duly impressed upon my arrival. He lived in an imposing, rather austere country park, which reminded me of something that a character in the novels of Jane Austen might have inhabited, with a long, tree-lined carriage drive up to a porticoed front, stone lions and urns mounted upon pillars on either side of a short flight of steps, a balustraded walk, overlooking rather dull, formal lawns with close-clipped hedges. The whole effect was grand and rather chilling and somehow quite out of keeping with Mr Daily himself. He had clearly bought the place because he had made enough money to do so and because it was the biggest house for miles around but, having bought it, he did not seem very much at ease within it and I wondered how many rooms stood empty and unused for much of the time, for apart from a few household staff only he and his wife lived here, though they had one son, he told me, married and with a child of his own.

Mrs Daily was a quiet, shy-seeming, powdery-looking little woman, even more ill at ease in her surroundings than he. She said little, smiled nervously, crocheted something elaborate with very fine cotton.

Nonetheless, they both made me warmly welcome, the meal was an excellent one, of roast pheasant and a huge treacle tart, and I began to feel comfortably at home.

Before and during supper and over coffee, which Mrs Daily poured out for us in the drawing room, I listened to the story of Samuel Daily's life and rising fortunes. He was not so much boastful, as exuberantly gleeful, at his own enterprise and good luck. He listed the acres and properties he owned, the number of men in his employ or who were his tenants, told me of his plans for the future which were, so far as I could ascertain, simply to become the biggest landlord in the county. He talked about his son and his young grandson too, for both of whom he was building up this empire. He might be envied and resented, I thought, particularly by those who competed with him for the purchase of land and property. But he could surely not be disliked, he was so simple, so direct, so unashamed of his ambitions. He seemed astute and yet unsubtle, a keen bargainer, but thoroughly honest. As the evening went on I found myself taking to him more and more warmly and confiding in him too, telling him of my own albeit small-seeming ambitions, if Mr Bentley would give me a chance, and about Stella and our prospects for the future.

It was not until the timid Mrs Daily had retired and we were in the study, a decanter of good port and another of whisky on the small table between us, that my reason for being in the area was so much as referred to.

Mr Daily poured me a generous glass of port wine and as he handed it over said, 'You're a fool if you go on with it.'

I took a sip or two calmly and without replying, though something in the bluntness and abruptness of his speaking had given rise to a spurt of fear deep within me, which I suppressed at once.

'If you mean you think I should give up the job I've been sent here to do and turn tail and run ...'

'Listen to me, Arthur.' He had begun to use my Christian name in an avuncular way, while not offering me the use of his. 'I'm not going to fill you up with a lot of women's tales ... you'd find those out fast enough if you ask about the place. Maybe you already have.'

'No,' I said, 'only hints – and Mr Jerome turning a little pale.'

'But you went out there to the place.'

'I went there and I had an experience I shouldn't care to go through again, though I confess I can't explain it.'

And then I told him the full story, of the woman with the wasted face at the funeral and in the old burial ground, and of my walk across the marsh in the fog and the terrible sounds I had heard there. He sat impassively, a glass at his hand, and listened without interrupting me until I had reached the end.

'It seems to me, Mr Daily,' I said, 'that I have seen whatever ghost haunts Eel Marsh and that burial ground. A woman in black with a wasted face. Because I have no doubt at all that she was whatever people call a ghost, that she was not a real, living, breathing human being. Well, she did me no harm. She neither spoke nor came near me. I did not like her look and I liked the ... the power that seemed to emanate from her towards me even less, but I have convinced myself that it is a power that cannot do more than make me feel afraid. If I go there and see her again, I am prepared.'

'And the pony and trap?'

I could not answer because, yes, that had been worse, far worse, more terrifying because it had been only heard not seen and because the cry of that child would never, I was sure, leave me for the rest of my life.

'I shook my head. 'I won't run away.'

I felt strong, sitting there at Samuel Daily's fireside, resolute, brave and stout-hearted, and I also – and he saw it – felt proud of being so. Thus, I thought, would a man go into battle, thus armed would he fight with giants.

'You shouldn't go there.'

'I'm afraid I'm going.'

'You shouldn't go there alone.'

'I could find no one to go with me.'

'No,' he said, 'and you would not.'

'Good God, man, Mrs Drablow lived alone there for what was it? – sixty odd years – to a ripe old age. She must have come to terms with all the ghosts about the place.'

'Aye.' He stood up. 'Maybe that's just what she did do. Come – Bunce will take you home.'

'No – I'd prefer to walk. I'm getting a taste for fresh air.'

As it happened, I had come on the bicycle but, confronted with the grandeur of the Daily home, had hidden it in a ditch beyond the outer gates, feeling that it did not look quite right to bicycle up that carriage drive.

As I thanked him for the evening's hospitality and was getting into my coat, he seemed to be mulling something over, and at the last moment he said suddenly, 'You are still set on it?'

'I am.'

'Then take a dog.'

I laughed. 'I haven't got a dog.'

'I have.' And he strode in front of me, out of the house, down the steps and into the darkness at the side of the house where presumably the outbuildings were situated. I waited, amused, and rather touched by his concern for me, speculating idly about what use a dog would be against any spectral presence, but not reluctant to take up Mr Daily's offer. I liked dogs well enough and it would be a fellow creature, warm-blooded and breathing in that cold, empty old house.

After a few moments there came the pat and scrabble of feet, followed by Mr Daily's measured tread.

'Take her,' he said, 'bring her back when you are done.'

'Will she come with me?'

'She'll do what I tell her.'

I looked down. At my feet stood a sturdy little terrier with a rough brindle coat and bright eyes. She wagged her tail briefly, acknowledging me, but otherwise was still, close to Daily's heels.

'What's her name?'

'Spider.'

The dog's tail flicked again.

'All right,' I said, 'I'll be glad of her company, I confess. Thank you.' I turned and began to walk off down the broad drive. After a few yards I turned and called. 'Spider. Here. Come, girl, Spider.' The dog did not stir and I felt foolish. Then Samuel Daily chuckled, snapped his fingers and spoke a word. At once, Spider bounded after me and stuck obediently to my heels.

I retrieved the bicycle, when I was sure that I could no longer be seen from the house, and the dog ran cheerfully after me down the quiet, moonlit lane, towards the town. My spirits rose. In a strange way, I was looking forward to the morrow.

In the Nursery

The fine clear weather still held, there was sunshine and blue sky again, when I drew my curtains. I had slept lightly and restlessly, troubled by snatches of peculiar, disconnected dreams. Perhaps I had eaten and drunk too well and richly with Mr Daily. But my mood was unchanged, I was determined and optimistic, as I dressed and breakfasted, and then began to make preparations for my stay at Eel Marsh House. The little dog Spider had, somewhat to my surprise, slept motionlessly at the foot of my bed. I had taken to her, though I knew little of the way of dogs. She was spirited, lively and alert and yet completely biddable, the expression in her bright eyes, fringed a little by shaggy hair that formed itself somewhat comically into the shape of beetling eyebrows, seemed to me highly intelligent. I thought I was going to be very glad of her.

Just after nine o'clock the landlord summoned me to the telephone. It was Mr Bentley, crisp and curt – for he greatly disliked using the instrument. He had received my letter and agreed that I should stay until I had at least made some sort of sense of the Drablow papers and managed to sort out what looked as if it needed to be dealt with, from all the out-of-date rubbish. I was to parcel up and dispatch anything I thought important, leave the remainder in the house for the attention of the legatees at some future date and then return to London.

'It's an odd sort of place,' I said.

'She was an odd sort of woman.' And Mr Bentley clapped the receiver down hard, blistering my ear.

By nine-thirty I had the bicycle basket and panniers packed and ready, and I set off, Spider bounding behind me. I could not leave it any later or the tide would have risen across the causeway and it occurred to me, as I bowled over the wide open marshes, that I was burning my boats, at least in a small way – if I had left anything important behind, I could not return to fetch it for some hours.

The sun was high in the sky, the water glittering, everywhere was light,

light and space and brightness, the very air seemed somehow purified and more exhilarating. Sea birds soared and swooped, silver-grey and white, and ahead, at the end of the long straight path, Eel Marsh House beckoned to me.

For half an hour or so after my arrival, I worked busily at establishing myself there, domestically. I found crockery and cutlery in the somewhat gloomy kitchen at the back of the house, washed, dried and laid it out for my later use and made over a corner of the larder to my provisions. Then, after searching through drawers and cupboards upstairs, I found clean linen and blankets and set them to air before a fire I had built in the drawing room. I made other fires too, in the little parlour and in the dining room, and even succeeded, after some trial and error, in getting the great black range alight, so that by evening I hoped to have hot water for a bath.

Then I let up the blinds and opened some windows and established myself at a large desk in one of the bays of the morning room that had, I thought, the finest view of the sky, the marshes, the estuary. Beside me, I set two chests of papers. Then, with a pot of tea at my right hand and the dog Spider at my feet, I commenced work. It was pretty tedious going but I persevered patiently enough, untying and cursorily examining bundle after bundle of worthless old papers, before tossing them into an empty box I had set beside me for the purpose. There were ancient household accounts and tradesmen's bills and receipts of thirty and forty years or more before; there were bankers' statements and doctors' prescriptions and estimates from carpenters, glaziers and decorators; there were many letters from persons unknown – and Christmas and anniversary cards, though nothing dating from recent years. There were accounts from department stores in London and scraps of shopping lists and measurements.

Only the letters themselves I reserved for later perusal. Everything else was waste. From time to time, to alleviate the boredom, I looked out of the wide windows at the marshes, unshadowed still and quietly beautiful in the winter sunlight. I made myself a lunch of ham and bread and beer and then a little after two o'clock, I called to Spider and went outside. I felt very calm and cheerful, a little cramped after my morning spent at the desk, a little bored, but in no way nervous. Indeed, all the horrors and apparitions of my first visit to the house and the marshes had quite evaporated, along with the mists that had for that short time engulfed me. The air was crisp and fresh and I walked all around the perimeter of the land upon which Eel Marsh House stood, occasionally tossing a stick for the dog to chase happily after and retrieve, breathing in the clean air deeply, entirely relaxed. I even ventured as far as the ruin of the burial ground and Spider dashed in and out, searching for real or imaginary rabbits, digging occasionally in a frantic burst with her front paws and then bounding excitedly away. We saw no one. No shadow fell across the grass.

For a while, I wandered among the old gravestones, trying to decipher some of the names but without any success, until I reached the corner where, that last time, the woman in black had been standing. There, on the headstone against which – I was fairly certain I remembered aright – she had been leaning, I thought I could make out the name of Drablow: the letters were encrusted with a salt deposit blown, I suppose, off the estuary over years of bad winter weather.

In L ... g Mem ...
... net Drablow
... 190...
... nd of He ...
... iel ... low
Bor ...

I remembered that Mr Jerome had hinted at some Drablow family graves, no longer used, in a place other than the churchyard and supposed that this was the resting place of ancestors from years back. But it was quite certain that there was nothing and no one except old bones here now and I felt quite unafraid and tranquil as I stood there, contemplating the scene and the place which had previously struck me as eerie, sinister, evil, but which now, I saw, was merely somewhat melancholy because it was so tumbledown and unfrequented. It was the sort of spot where, a hundred years or more earlier, romantically minded poets would have lingered and been inspired to compose some cloyingly sad verse.

I returned to the house with the dog, for already the air was turning much colder, the sky losing its light as the sun declined.

Indoors, I made myself some more tea and built up the fires and, before settling down again to those dull, dull papers, browsed at random among the bookshelves in the drawing room and chose myself some reading matter for later that evening, a novel by Sir Walter Scott and a volume of John Clare's poetry. These I took upstairs and placed on the locker of the small bedroom I had chosen to appropriate, mainly because it was at the front of the house but not so large and cold as the others and therefore, I thought, it would probably be cosier. From the window I could see the section of marsh away from the estuary and, if I craned my neck, the line of Nine Lives Causeway.

As I worked on into the evening and it grew dark, so I lit every lamp I could find, drew curtains and fetched in more coal and wood for the fires from a bunker in an outhouse I had located outside the scullery door.

The pile of waste paper grew in the box, by contrast with the few packets I thought ought to be examined more closely, and I fetched other boxes and drawersful from about the house. At this rate I should be through by the end of another day and a half at the most. I had a glass of sherry and a rather limited but not unpleasant supper which I shared with Spider and then, being tired of work, took a final turn outside before locking up.

All was quiet, there was not the slightest breeze. I could scarcely hear even the creeping of the water. Every bird had long since hidden for the night. The marshes were black and silent, stretching away from me for miles.

I have recounted the events – or rather, the non-events – of that day at Eel Marsh House in as much detail as I remember, in order to remind myself that I was in a calm and quite unexcitable state of mind. And that the odd events which had so frightened and unnerved me were all but forgotten. If I thought of them at all, it was mentally, as it were, to shrug my shoulders. Nothing else had happened, no harm had befallen me. The tenor of the day and the evening had been even, uninteresting, ordinary. Spider was an excellent companion and I was glad of the sound of her gentle breathing, her occasional scratching or clattering about, in that big, empty old house. But my main sensation was one of tedium and a certain lethargy, combined with a desire to finish the job and be back in London with my dear Stella. I remembered that I meant to tell her that we should get a small dog, as like Spider as possible, once we had a house of our own. Indeed, I decided to ask Mr Samuel Daily that if there were ever a chance of Spider having a litter of puppies he should reserve one for me.

I had worked assiduously and with concentration and taken some fresh air and exercise. For half an hour or so after retiring to bed I read *The Heart of Midlothian*, the dog settled on a rug at the foot of my bed. I think I must have fallen asleep only a few moments after putting the lamp out and slept quite deeply too, for when I awoke – or was awakened – very suddenly, I felt somewhat stunned, uncertain, for a second or two, where

I was and why. I saw that it was quite dark but once my eyes were fully focused I saw the moonlight coming in through the window, for I had left the rather heavy, thick-looking curtains undrawn and the window slightly ajar. The moon fell upon the embroidered counterpane and on the dark wood of wardrobe and chest and mirror with a cold but rather beautiful light, and I thought that I would get out of bed and look at the marshes and the estuary from the window.

At first, all seemed very quiet, very still, and I wondered why I had awoken. Then, with a missed heart-beat, I realized that Spider was up and standing at the door. Every hair of her body was on end, her ears were pricked, her tail erect, the whole of her tense, as if ready to spring. And she was emitting a soft, low growl from deep in her throat. I sat up para-lysed, frozen, in the bed, conscious only of the dog and of the prickling of my own skin and of what suddenly seemed a different kind of silence, ominous and dreadful. And then, from somewhere within the depths of the house – but somewhere not very far from the room in which I was – I heard a noise. It was a faint noise, and, strain my ears as I might, I could not make out exactly what it was. It was a sound like a regular yet inter-mittent bump or rumble. Nothing else happened. There were no foot-steps, no creaking floorboards, the air was absolutely still, the wind did not moan through the casement. Only the muffled noise went on and the dog continued to stand, bristling at the door, now putting her nose to the gap at the bottom and snuffling along, now taking a pace backwards, head cocked and, like me, listening. And, every so often, she growled again.

In the end, I suppose because nothing else happened and because I did have the dog to take with me, I managed to get out of bed, though I was shaken and my heart beat uncomfortably fast within me. But it took some time for me to find sufficient reserves of courage to enable me to open the bedroom door and stand out in the dark corridor. The moment I did so, Spider shot ahead and I heard her padding about, sniffing intently at every closed door, still growling and grumbling down in her throat.

After a while, I heard the odd sound again. It seemed to be coming from along the passage to my left, at the far end. But it was still quite impossible to identify. Very cautiously, listening, hardly breathing, I ven-tured a few steps in that direction. Spider went ahead of me. The passage led only to three other bedrooms on either side and, one by one, regaining my nerve as I went, I opened them and looked inside each one. Nothing, only heavy old furniture and empty unmade beds and, in the rooms at the back of the house, moonlight. Down below me on the ground floor of the house, silence, a seething, blanketing, almost tangible silence, and a musty darkness, thick as felt.

And then I reached the door at the very end of the passage. Spider was there before me and her body, as she sniffed beneath it, went rigid, her growling grew louder. I put my hand on her collar, stroked the rough, short hair, as much for my own reassurance as for hers. I could feel the tension in her limbs and body and it answered to my own.

This was the door without a keyhole, which I had been unable to open on my first visit to Eel Marsh House. I had no idea what was beyond it. Except the sound. It was coming from within that room, not very loud but just to hand, on the other side of that single wooden partition. It was a sound of something bumping gently on the floor, in a rhythmic sort of way, a familiar sort of sound and yet one I still could not exactly place, a sound that seemed to belong to my past, to waken old, half-forgotten memories and associations deep within me, a sound that, in any other place, would not have made me afraid but would, I thought, have been curiously comforting, friendly.

But, at my feet, the dog Spider began to whine, a thin, pitiful, frightened moan, and to back away from the door a little and press against my legs. My throat felt constricted and dry and I had begun to shiver. There was something in that room and I could not get to it, nor would I dare to, if I were able. I told myself it was a rat or a trapped bird, fallen down the chimney into the hearth and unable to get out again. But the sound was not that of some small, panic-stricken creature. Bump bump. Pause. Bump bump. Pause. Bump bump. Bump bump. Bump bump.

I think that I might have stood there, in bewilderment and terror, all night, or else taken to my heels, with the dog, and run out of the house altogether, had I not heard another, faint sound. It came from behind me, not directly behind but from the front of the house. I turned away from the locked door and went back, shakily, groping along the wall to my bedroom, guided by the slant of moonlight that reached out into the darkness of the corridor. The dog was half a pace ahead of me.

There was nothing in the room at all, the bed was as I had left it, there had been no disturbances; then I realized that the sounds had been coming not from within the room but outside it, beyond the window. I pulled it up as far as the sash would allow and looked out. There lay the marshes, silver-grey and empty, there was the water of the estuary, flat as a mirror with the full moon lying upturned upon it. Nothing. No one. Except, like a wash from far, far away, so that I half wondered if I were remembering and reliving the memory, a cry, a child's cry. But no. The slightest of breezes stirred the surface of the water, wrinkling it, and passing dryly through the reed beds and away. Nothing more.

I felt something warm against my ankle and, looking down, saw that it was Spider, very close to me and gently licking my skin. When I stroked her, I realized that she was calm again, her body relaxed, her ears down. I listened. There was no sound in the house at all. After a while, I went back along the passage to the closed door. Spider came quite happily and stood obediently there, perhaps waiting for the door to be opened. I put my head close to the wood. Nothing. Absolute silence. I put my hand on the door-handle, hesitated as I felt my heart again begin to race, but drew in several deep breaths and tried the door. It would not open, though the rattling of it echoed in the room beyond, as if there were no carpet on the floor. I tried it once more and pushed against it slightly with my shoulder. It did not give.

In the end I went back to bed. I read two further chapters of the Scott novel, though without fully taking in their meaning, and then switched out my lamp. Spider had settled again on the rug. It was a little after two o'clock.

It was a long time before I slept.

The first thing I noticed on the following morning was a change in the weather. As soon as I awoke, a little before seven, I felt that the air had a dampness in it and that it was rather colder and, when I looked out of the window, I could hardly see the division between land and water, water and sky, all was a uniform grey, with thick cloud lying low over the marsh and a drizzle. It was not a day calculated to raise the spirits and I felt un-refreshed and nervous after the previous night. But Spider trotted down the stairs eagerly and cheerfully enough and I soon built up the fires again and stoked the boiler, had a bath and breakfast and began to feel more like my everyday self. I even went back upstairs and along the corridor to the door of the locked room, but there was no strange sound from within, no sound at all.

At nine o'clock I went out, taking the bicycle and pedalling hard, to work up a good head of speed across the causeway and through the country lanes back to Crythin, with Spider bounding behind me and taking off every so often, to burrow briefly in a ditch or start after some creature that flitted away across the fields.

I had the landlord's wife refill my hamper with plenty of food and bought more from the grocer's. With both of them and with Mr Jerome, whom I met in a side street, I spoke briefly and jestingly and I said nothing whatsoever about the business at Eel Marsh House. Daylight, even such a dreary damp affair as it was, had once again renewed my nerve and resolve and banished the vapours of the night. Moreover, there was a fond letter from Stella, full of gratifying exclamations of regret at my absence and pride in my new responsibility, and it was with this warming my inside pocket that I cycled back towards the marshes and the house, whistling as I went.

Although it was not yet lunch-time I was obliged to put on most of the lamps in the house, for the day lowered, and the light was too poor to work by, even directly in front of the window. Looking out, I saw that the cloud and drizzle had thickened, so that I could scarcely see beyond the grass that ran down to the edges of the water and, as the afternoon began to draw in, they had merged together to form a fog. Then my nerve began to falter a little and I decided I might pack up and return to the comfort of the town. I went to the front door and stepped out. At once the dampness clung to my face and to my clothes like a fine web. There was a stronger wind now, whipping off the estuary and going through to my bones, with its raw coldness. Spider ran off a yard or two and then stopped and looked back at me, uncertain, not anxious to walk far in such dreary weather. I could not see the ruin or the walls of the old burial ground, away across the field, the low-lying cloud and mist had blotted them out. Neither could I see the causeway path, not only because of that but because the tide had now covered it over completely. It would be late at night before it was clear again. I could not after all retreat to Crythin Gifford.

I whistled the dog who came at once and gladly, and returned to Mrs Drablow's papers. So far I had found only one interesting-looking, slim packet of documents and letters, and I decided that I would give myself the possible diversion of reading them that evening after supper. Until then I cleared several more piles of rubbish and was cheered by the sight of the several now-empty boxes and drawers, depressed by those that still remained full and unsifted.

The first packet of letters, bundled together and tied with narrow purple ribbon, were all written in the same hand, between a February of about sixty years before and the summer of the following year. They were sent first from the manor house of a village I remembered from the map as being some twenty miles away from Crythin Gifford, and later from a lodge in the Scottish countryside beyond Edinburgh. All were addressed to 'My dear' or 'Dearest Alice' and signed for the most part 'J' but occasionally 'Jennet'. They were short letters, written in a direct, rather naïve manner, and the story they told was a touching one and not particularly unfamiliar. The writer, a young woman and apparently a relative of Mrs Drablow, was unmarried and with child. At first, she was still living at home, with her parents; later, she was sent away. Scarcely any mention was made of the child's father, except for a couple of references to P. 'P will not come back here.' And: 'I think P was sent abroad.' In Scotland, a son was born to her and she wrote of him at once with a desperate, clinging affection. For a few months the letters ceased, but when they began again it was at first in passionate outrage and protest, later, in quiet, resigned bitterness. Pressure was being exerted upon her to give up the child for adoption; she refused, saying over and over again that they would 'never be parted'.

'He is mine. Why should I not have what is mine? He shall not go to strangers. I shall kill us both before I let him go.'

Then the tone changed.

'What else can I do? I am quite helpless. If you and M are to have him I shall mind it less.' And again, 'I suppose it must be.'

But at the end of the last letter of all was written in a very small, cramped hand: 'Love him, take care of him as your own. But he is mine, he can *never* be yours. Oh, forgive me. I think my heart will break. J.'

In the same packet, there was a simple document drawn up by a lawyer, declaring that Nathaniel Pierston, infant son of Jennet Humfrye was become by adoption the child of Morgan Thomas Drablow of Eel Marsh House, Crythin Gifford, and of his wife Alice. Attached to this were three other papers. The first was a reference from a Lady M – in Hyde Park Gate – for a nursemaid called Rose Judd.

I had read and set this aside, and was about to open the next, a single folded sheet, when I looked up suddenly, startled into the present by a noise.

Spider was at the door, growling the same, low growl of the previous night. I looked round at her and saw that her hackles were up. For a moment I sat, too terrified to move. Then I recalled my decision to seek out the ghosts of Eel Marsh House and confront them, for I was sure – or I had been sure, in the hours of daylight – that the harder I ran away from those things, the closer they would come after me and dog my heels, and the greater would be their power to disturb me. And so, I laid down the papers, got to my feet and went quietly to open the door of the small parlour in which I had been sitting.

At once, Spider shot out of the room as though after a hare and made for the staircase, still growling. I heard her scurry along the passage above and then stop. She had gone to the locked door and even from below I could hear it again, the odd, faint, rhythmic noise – bump bump, pause, bump bump, pause, bump bump …

Determined to break in if I possibly could, and to identify the noise and whatever was making it, I went into the kitchen and scullery, in search of a strong hammer or chisel or other forcing tool. But, not finding anything there and remembering that there was a wood axe in the outhouse where the fuel was stored, I opened the back door and, taking my torch with me, stepped outside.

There was still a mist and a drizzling dampness in the air, though nothing like the dense, swirling fog of the night when I had crossed the causeway path. But it was pitch dark: there was neither moonlight nor any stars visible and I stumbled about on my way to the shed in spite of the beam from my torch.

It was when I had located the axe and was making my way back to the house that I heard the noise and, when I heard it, so close that I thought it was only a few yards from the house, turned back, instead of going on, walked quickly around to the front door, expecting to greet a visitor.

As I came onto the gravel, I shone my torch out into the darkness in the direction of the causeway path. It was from there that the clip-clop of the pony's hooves and the rumbling and creaking of the trap were coming. But I could see nothing. And then, with an awful cry of realization, I knew. There was no visitor – or at least no real, human visitor – no Keckwick. The noise was beginning to come from a different direction now, as the pony and trap left the causeway and struck off across the open marsh.

I stood, hideously afraid, straining into the murky, misty distance with my ears, to try and detect any difference between this sound and that of a real vehicle. But there was none. If I could have run out of there, seen my way, I must surely have been able to reach it, climb up onto it, challenge its driver. As it was, I could do nothing, but stand, stand as still and stiff as a post, rigid with fear and yet inwardly in a turmoil of nervous apprehension and imaginings and responses.

Then I realized that the dog had come down and was beside me on the gravel, her body absolutely still, ears pricked, facing the marsh and the source. The pony trap was going further away now, the noise of its wheels was becoming muffled and then there was the sound of splashing water and churning mud, the noise of the pony plunging about in terror. It was happening, the whole thing was caught up in the quicksands and sinking, sinking, there was a terrible moment when the waters began to close around it and to gurgle, and then, above it all, and above the whinnying and struggling of the pony, the child's cry, that rose and rose to a scream of terror and was then slowly choked and drowned; and, finally, silence.

Then nothing, save the lap and eddy of the water far away. My whole body was trembling, my mouth dry, the palms of my hands sore where I had dug my nails into them as I had stood, helplessly, hearing that dreadful sequence of sounds repeated again, as it would be repeated in my head a thousand times forever after.

That the pony and trap and the crying child were not real I had no shadow of a doubt, that their final drive across the marshes and their disappearance into the treacherous quicksands had not just taken place a hundred yards away from me in the darkness, of this I was now certain. But I was equally certain that once, who knew how long ago, but one actual day, this dreadful thing had indeed taken place, here on Eel Marsh. A pony and trap with whoever was its driver, together with a child passenger, had been swallowed up and drowned within a few moments. At the very thought of it, let alone at this awful ghostly repetition of the whole event, I was more distressed than I could bear. I stood shivering, cold from the mist and the night wind and from the sweat that was rapidly cooling on my body.

And then, hair bristling, with eyes a-start, the dog Spider took a couple of steps backwards, half lifted her front paws off the ground and began to howl, a loud, prolonged, agonized and heart-stopping howl.

In the end, I had to lift her up and carry her inside the house – she would not move in answer to any call. Her body was stiff in my arms and she was clearly in a state of distress, and, when I set her down on the floor of the hall, she clung close to my heels

In a curious way, it was her fearfulness that persuaded me that I must retain control of myself, rather as a mother will feel obliged to put a brave face on things in order to calm her frightened child. Spider was only a dog but nevertheless I felt obliged to soothe and reassure her, and, in doing so, was able to calm myself and gather some inner strength. But, after a few moments of allowing herself to be stroked and petted under my hand, the dog broke away and, alert again and growling, made for the stairs. I followed her quickly, switching on every light I could find as I went. As

I expected, she had made for the passage, with the locked door at the end of it, and already I could hear the noise, that maddeningly familiar bump that tantalized me because I still could not identify it.

I was breathing fast as I ran to the corner and my heart seemed to be leaping about madly within me. But, if I had been afraid at what had happened in this house so far, when I reached the end of the short corridor and saw what I did see now, my fear reached a new height, until for a minute I thought I would die of it, *was* dying, for I could not conceive of a man's being able to endure such shocks and starts and remain alive, let alone in his right senses.

The door of the room from which the noise came, the door which had been securely locked, so that I had not been able to break it down, the door to which there could not be a key – that door was now standing open. Wide open.

Beyond it lay a room, in complete darkness, save for the first yard or two immediately at the entrance, where the dim light from the bulb on the landing outside fell onto some shining, brown floor-covering. Within, I could hear both the noise – louder now because the door was open – and the sound of the dog, pattering anxiously about and sniffing and snuffling as she went.

I do not know how long I stood there in fear and trembling and in dreadful bewilderment. I lost all sense of time and ordinary reality. Through my head went a tumbling confusion of half-thoughts and emotions, visions of spectres and of real fleshy intruders, ideas of murder and violence, and all manner of odd, distorted fears. And, all the time, the door stood wide open and the rocking continued. Rocking. Yes. I came to, because I had realized at last what the noise within the room was – or, at least, what it reminded me of closely. It was the sound of the wooden runners of my nurse's rocking chair, when she had sat beside me every night while I went to sleep, as a small child, rocking, rocking. Sometimes, when I was ill and feverish or had wakened from the throes of some nightmare, she or my mother had come to me and lifted me out of my bed and sat with me in that same chair, holding me and rocking until I was soothed and sleepy again. The sound that I had been hearing was the sound that I remembered from far back, from a time before I could clearly remember anything else. It was the sound that meant comfort and safety, peace and reassurance, the regular, rhythmical sound at the end of the day, that lulled me asleep and into my dreams, the sound that meant that one of the two people in the world to whom I was closest and whom

I most loved was nearby. And so, as I stood there in the dark passageway, listening, the sound began to exert the same effect upon me now until I felt hypnotized by it into a state of drowsiness and rest, my fears and the tensions in my body they had aroused began to slip away, I was breathing slowly and more deeply and felt a warmth creeping into my limbs. I felt that nothing could come near to harm or afright me, but I had a protector and guardian close at hand. And, indeed, perhaps I had, perhaps all I had ever learned and believed in the nursery about unseen heavenly spirits surrounding, upholding and preserving us was indeed true; or perhaps it was only that my memories aroused by the rocking sound were so positive and so powerfully strong that they overcame and quite drove out all that was sinister and alarming, evil and disturbed.

Whichever might be the case, I knew that I now had courage enough to go into that room and face whatever might be there and so, before the conviction faltered, and my fears could return, I walked in, as determinedly and boldly and firmly as I could. As I did so I put my hand up to the light switch on the wall but when I pressed it no illumination came and, shining my torch onto the ceiling, I saw that the socket was bare of any light bulb. But the beam from my own lamp was quite strong and bright, it gave me ample light for my purpose and now, as I went into the room, Spider gave a low whine from one corner, but did not come over to me. Very slowly and cautiously I looked around the room.

It was almost the room I had just been remembering, the room to which the sound I had identified belonged. It was a child's nursery. There was the bed in one corner, the same sort of low narrow wooden bed that I myself had once slept in, and beside it and facing the open fireplace at an angle stood the rocking chair and that too was the same or very similar, a low-seated, tall, ladder-backed chair made of dark wood – elm, perhaps, and with wide, worn, curved runners. As I watched, stared until I could stare no harder, it rocked gently and with gradually decreasing speed, in the way any such chair will continue to rock for a time after someone has just got out of it.

But no one had been there. The room had been empty. Anyone who had just left it must have come out into the corridor and confronted me, I would have had to move aside to let them pass.

I shone a torch rapidly all around the wall. There was the chimney breast and fireplace, there was the window, closed and bolted and with two wooden bars across it, such as all nurseries have to guard the children from falling out; there was no other door.

Gradually the chair rocked less and less, until the movements were so slight I could scarcely see or hear them. Then they stopped and there was absolute silence.

The nursery was fully furnished and equipped and in such good order that the occupant of it might only have gone away for a night or two or even simply taken a walk, there was none of the damp, bare, unlived-in feeling of all the other rooms of Eel Marsh House. Carefully and cautiously, almost holding my breath, I explored it. I looked at the bed, made up and all complete with sheets and pillows, blankets and counterpane. Beside it was a small table and on the table a tiny wooden horse and a night-light with the candle half burnt away, still in place and with water in the holder. In the chest of drawers and wardrobe there were clothes, underclothes, day clothes, formal clothes, play clothes, clothes for a small boy of six or seven years old, beautiful, well-made clothes, in the style of those which my own parents wore as children in those formal photographs we still have about the house, the styles of sixty years or more ago.

And then there were the child's toys, so many toys and all of them most neatly and meticulously ordered and cared for. There were rows of lead soldiers, arranged in regiments, and a farm, set out with painted barns and fences, haycocks and little wooden stooks of corn and on a big board. There was a model ship complete with masts and sails of linen, yellowed a little by age, and a whip with a leather thong, lying beside a polished spinning top. There were games of ludo and halma, draughts and chess, there were jigsaw puzzles of country scenes and circuses and the 'Boyhood of Raleigh', and in a small wooden chest there was a monkey made of leather and a cat and four kittens knitted from wool, a furry bear and a bald doll with a china head and a sailor suit. The child had had pens and brushes, too, and bottles of coloured inks and a book of nursery rhymes and another of Greek stories and a Bible and a prayer book, a set of dice and two packs of playing cards, a miniature trumpet and a painted musical box from Switzerland and a Black Sambo made of tin with jointed arms and legs.

I picked things up, stroked them, even smelled them. They must have been here for half a century, yet they might have been played with this afternoon and tidied away tonight. I was not afraid now. I was puzzled. I felt strange, unlike myself, I moved as if in a dream. But for the moment at least there was nothing here to frighten or harm me, there was only emptiness, an open door, a neatly made bed and a curious air of sadness, of something lost, missing, so that I myself felt a desolation, a grief in my own heart. How can I explain? I cannot. But I remember it, as I felt it.

The dog was sitting quietly now on the rag rug beside the child's bed and in the end, because I had examined everything and could not explain any of it and did not want to be in that sad atmosphere any longer, I went out, after taking a last slow look around, closing the door behind me.

It was not late but I had no more energy left to go on reading Mrs Drablow's papers, I felt drained, exhausted, all the emotions that had poured into me and out again leaving me like something thrown up on a calm beach at the end of a storm.

I made myself a drink of hot water and brandy and did my round of the house, banking up the fires and locking the doors before going to bed, to read Sir Walter Scott.

Just before doing so, I went down the passage-way that led to the nursery. The door was still closed as I had left it. I listened, but there was no sound at all from within. I did not disturb the silence or the emptiness again but went quietly back to my own room at the front of the house.

Whistle and I'll Come to You

During the night the wind rose. As I had lain reading I had become aware of the stronger gusts that blew every so often against the casements. But when I awoke abruptly in the early hours it had increased greatly in force. The house felt like a ship at sea, battered by the gale that came roaring across the open marsh. Windows were rattling everywhere and there was the sound of moaning down all the chimneys of the house and whistling through every nook and cranny.

At first I was alarmed. Then, as I lay still, gathering my wits, I reflected on how long Eel Marsh House had stood here, steady as a lighthouse, quite alone and exposed, bearing the brunt of winter after winter of gales and driving rain and sleet and spray. It was unlikely to blow away tonight. And then, those memories of childhood began to be stirred again and I dwelt nostalgically upon all those nights when I had lain in the warm and snug safety of my bed in the nursery at the top of our family house in Sussex, hearing the wind rage round like a lion, howling at the doors and beating upon the windows but powerless to reach me. I lay back and slipped into that pleasant, trance-like state somewhere between sleeping and waking, recalling the past and all its emotions and impressions vividly, until I felt I was a small boy again.

Then from somewhere, out of that howling darkness, a cry came to my ears, catapulting me back into the present and banishing all tranquillity.

I listened hard. Nothing. The tumult of the wind, like a banshee, and the banging and rattling of the window in its old, ill-fitting frame. Then yes, again, a cry, that familiar cry of desperation and anguish, a cry for help from a child somewhere out on the marsh.

There was no child. I knew that. How could there be? Yet how could I lie here and ignore even the crying of some long-dead ghost?

'Rest in peace,' I thought, but this poor one did not, could not..

After a few moments I got up. I would go down into the kitchen and make myself a drink, stir up the fire a little and sit beside it trying, trying to shut out that calling voice for which I could do nothing, and no one had been able to do anything for ... how many years?

As I went out onto the landing, Spider the dog following me at once, two things happened together. I had the impression of someone who had just that very second before gone past me on their way from the top of the stairs to one of the other rooms, and, as a tremendous blast of wind hit the house so that it all but seemed to rock at the impact, the lights went out. I had not bothered to pick up my torch from the bedside table and now I stood in the pitch blackness, unsure for a moment of my bearings.

And the person who had gone by, and who was now in this house with me? I had seen no one, felt nothing. There had been no movement, no brush of a sleeve against mine, no disturbance of the air, I had not even heard a footstep. I had simply the absolutely certain sense of someone just having passed close to me and gone away down the corridor. Down the short narrow corridor that led to the nursery whose door had been so firmly locked and then, inexplicably, opened.

For a moment I actually began to conjecture that there was indeed someone – another human being – living here in this house, a person who hid themselves away in that mysterious nursery and came out at night to fetch food and drink and to take the air. Perhaps it was the woman in black. Had Mrs Drablow harboured some reclusive old sister or retainer, had she left behind her a mad friend that no one had known about? My brain span all manner of wild, incoherent fantasies as I tried desperately to provide a rational explanation for the presence I had been so aware of. But then they ceased. There was no living occupant of Eel Marsh House other than myself and Samuel Daily's dog. Whatever was about, whoever I had seen, and heard rocking, and who had passed me by just now, whoever had opened the locked door was not 'real'. No. But what *was* 'real'? At that moment I began to doubt my own reality.

The first thing I must have was a light and I groped my way back across to my bed, reached over it and got my hand to the torch at last, took a step back, stumbled over the dog who was at my heels and dropped the torch. It went spinning away across the floor and fell somewhere by the window with a crash and the faint sound of breaking glass. I cursed but managed, by crawling about on my hands and knees, to find it again and to press the switch. No light came on. The torch had broken.

For a moment I was as near to weeping tears of despair and fear, frustration and tension, as I had ever been since my childhood. But instead of crying I drummed my fists upon the floorboards, in a burst of violent rage, until they throbbed.

It was Spider who brought me to my senses by scratching a little at my arm and then my licking the hand I stretched out to her. We sat on the floor together and I hugged her warm body to me, glad of her, thoroughly ashamed of myself, calmer and relieved, while the wind boomed and roared without, and again and again I heard that child's terrible cry borne on the gusts towards me.

I would not sleep again, of that I was sure, but nor did I dare to go down the stairs in that utter darkness, surrounded by the noise of the storm, unnerved by the awareness I had had of the presence of that other one. My torch was broken. I must have a candle, some light, however faint and frail, to keep me company. There was a candle near at hand. I had seen it earlier, on the table beside the small bed in the nursery.

For a very long time, I could not summon up sufficient courage to grope my way along that short passage to the room which I realized was somehow both the focus and the source of all the strange happenings in the house. I was lost to everything but my own fears, incapable of decisive, coherent thought, let alone movement. But gradually I discovered for myself the truth of the axiom that a man cannot remain indefinitely in a state of active terror. Either the emotion will increase until, at the prompting of more and more dreadful events and apprehensions, he is so overcome by it that he runs away or goes mad; or he will become by slow degrees less agitated and more in possession of himself.

The wind continued to howl across the marshes and batter at the house but that was, after all, a natural sound and one that I could recognize and tolerate, for it could not hurt me in any way. And the darkness did not brighten and would not for some hours but there is no more in the simple state of darkness itself to make a man afraid than in the sound of a storm wind. Nothing else happened at all. All sense of another one's presence had faded away, the faint cries of the child ceased at last and from the nursery at the end of the passage came not the faintest sound of the rocking chair or of any other movement. I had prayed, as I had crouched on the floorboards with the dog clutched to me, prayed that whatever had disturbed me and was within the house should be banished or at least that I should gain possession of myself enough to confront and overcome it.

Now, as I got to my feet unsteadily, aching and stiff in every limb, so great had been the tension of my body, I did at last feel able to make some move, though I was profoundly relieved that, so far as I could tell, there was, for the moment at least, nothing worse to face up to than my blind journey down the corridor to the nursery, in search of the candle.

That journey I made, very slowly and in mounting trepidation but successfully, for I found my way to the bedside and took up the candle in its holder and, grasping it tightly, began to fumble with my hand along the walls and the furniture, back towards the door.

I have said that there were no other strange and dreadful happenings that night, nothing else to make me afraid except the sound of the wind and the completeness of the dark, and in a sense that is true, for the nursery was quite empty and the rocking chair still and silent, all, so far as I could tell, was as it had been before. I did not know then to what I could possibly attribute the feelings that swept over me from the moment I entered the room. I felt not fear, not horror, but an overwhelming grief and sadness, a sense of loss and bereavement, a distress mingled with utter despair. My parents were both alive, I had one brother, a good many friends and my fiancée, Stella. I was still a young man, Apart from the inevitable loss of elderly aunts and uncles and grandparents I had never experienced the death of anyone close to me, never truly mourned and suffered the extremes of grief. Never yet. But the feelings that must accompany the death of someone as close to my heart and bound up with my own being as it was possible to be, I knew then, in the nursery of Eel Marsh House. They all but broke me, yet I was confused and puzzled, not knowing any reason at all why I should be in the grip of such desperate anguish and misery. It was as though I had, for the time that I was in the room, become another person, or at least experienced the emotions that belong to another.

It was as alarming and strange an occurrence as any of those more outward, visible and audible that had taken place over these past few days.

When I left the room and closed the door behind me and stood in the corridor again, the feelings dropped away from me like a garment that had been put over my shoulders for a short time and then removed again. I was back within my own person, my own emotions, I was myself again.

I returned unsteadily to my bedroom, found the matches that I kept in my coat pocket along with my pipe and tobacco and lit the candle at last. As I gripped the hoop of the tin holder in my fingers my hand trembled so that the yellow flame flickered and swerved about, reflecting here and there crazily upon walls and door, floor and ceiling, mirror and counterpane. But it was a comfort and a relief nonetheless and in the end it burned brightly and well, as I became less agitated.

I saw the face of my watch. It was barely three o'clock and I hoped that the candle would burn until dawn, which on a stormy day at this fag end of the year would come late.

I sat up in bed, wrapped in my coat, and read Sir Walter Scott as best I could by the meagre flame. Whether it went out before the first thin grey light sneaked into the room I do not know, for in the end and without meaning to do so I fell asleep. When I awoke it was into a watery, washed-out dawn, I was uncomfortable and stale, the candle had burned to the last drop of wax and guttered out, leaving only a black stain at its base, and my book was fallen onto the floor.

Once again it was a noise that had awakened me. Spider was scratching and whining at the door and I realized that it was some hours before the poor creature had been let out. I got up and dressed briskly, went downstairs and opened the front door. The sky was swollen and streaked with rain clouds, everything looked drab and without colour and the estuary was running high. But the wind had died down, the air was lighter and very cold.

At first the dog trotted across the gravel towards the scrubby grass, anxious to relieve herself, while I stood yawning, trying to get some life and warmth into my body by beating my arms and stamping my feet. I decided that I would put on a coat and boots and go for a brisk walk across the field, to clear my head, and was turning to go back into the house when, from far out on the marshes, I heard, unmistakably clean and clear, the sound of someone whistling, as one whistles to summon a dog.

Spider stopped dead in her tracks for a split second and then, before I could restrain her, before I had fully gathered my wits, she set off, as though after a hare, running low and fast away from the house, away from the safety of the grass and out across the wet marshes. For a few moments I stood amazed and bewildered and could not move, only stare, as Spider's small form receded into that great open expanse. I could see no one out there, but the whistle had been real, not a trick of the wind. Yet I would have sworn it had not come from any human lips. Then, even as I looked, I saw the dog falter and slow down and finally stop and I realized in horror that she was floundering in mud, fighting to maintain her balance from the pull beneath her feet. I ran as I have never run before, heedless of my own safety, desperate to go to the aid of the brave, bright little creature who had given me such consolation and cheer in that desolate spot.

At first the path was firm, though muddy, beneath my feet and I could make good speed. The wind coming across the estuary was bitingly cold on my face and I felt my eyes begin to smart and water, so that I had to wipe them in order to see my way clearly. Spider was yelping loudly now, afraid but still visible, and I called to her, trying to reassure her. Then I, too, began to feel the stickiness and the unsteadiness of the ground as it became boggier. Once I plunged my leg down and it stuck fast in a watery hole until I managed to exert all my strength and get free. All around me the water was swollen and murky, the tide of the estuary was now high, running across the marshes themselves, and I was obliged to wade rather than walk. But at last, out of breath and straining with every movement, I got almost within reach of the dog. She could scarcely hold up now, her legs and half her body had disappeared beneath the whirling, sucking bog and her pointed head was held up in the air as she struggled and yelped all the while. I tried two or three times to stride across to her but each time I had to pull free abruptly for fear of going under myself. I wished that I had got a stick to throw across to her, as some sort of grappling hook with which to grab hold of her collar. I felt a second of pure despair, alone in the middle of the wide marsh, under the fast-moving, stormy sky, with only water all around me and that dreadful house the only solid thing for miles around.

But aware that, if I gave into panic, I should most certainly be lost, I thought furiously and then, very cautiously, lay down full length on the marsh mud, keeping my lower body pressed as hard as I could onto a small island of solid ground and, reaching and stretching my trunk and my arms forward, inch by inch, gasping for breath until, just as the last of her body sank, I lunged out and grabbed the dog about the neck and hauled and strained and tugged with all the force I could, a strength I would never have dreamed I could have summoned up, born of terror and desperation; and after an agonizing time, when we both fought for our lives against the treacherous quicksand that tried to pull us both down into itself and I felt my grip on the slippery wet fur and wet flesh of the dog almost give, at last I knew that I would hold and win. I strained as hard as ever I could to drag my body backwards onto firmer ground. As I did so, the dog's body suddenly gave and the tug of war was over as I fell back, holding her tight, the two of us soaked with water and mud, my chest burning and my lungs almost bursting, my arms feeling as if they had been dragged from their sockets, as indeed they almost had.

We rested, panting, exhausted, and I wondered if I would ever be able to get up, I felt suddenly so faint and weak and lost in the middle of the marsh. The poor dog was making choking noises now and rubbing her head against me over and over, no doubt both terrified and also in great pain, for I had nearly asphyxiated her as I had clutched so hard around her neck. But she was alive and so was I and, gradually, a little warmth from each of our bodies and the pause revived us and cradling Spider like a child in my arms, I began to stumble back across the marshes towards the house. As I did so and within a few yards of it, I glanced up. At one of the upper windows, the only window with bars across it, the window of the nursery, I caught a glimpse of someone standing. A woman. That woman. She was looking directly towards me.

Spider was whimpering in my arms and making occasional little retching coughs. We were both trembling violently. How I reached the grass in front of the house I shall never know but, as I did so, I heard a sound. It was coming from the far end of the causeway path which was just beginning to be visible as the tide began to recede. It was the sound of a pony trap.

A Packet of Letters

There was a bright light and I was staring into it – or, rather, I felt that *it* was boring into *me*, boring through my eyes right into my brain and I struggled to turn my head away and my head seemed to be very light, scarcely set on my shoulders at all, but spinning, floating like blown thistledown!

Then abruptly the light was removed and when I opened my eyes the normal world and ordinary things in it came into focus again. I found myself lying, propped up on the couch in the morning room, with the large, red, concerned face of Mr Samuel Daily looming over me. In his hand he held a pocket torch, with which, I realized, he must have been peering into my eyes, in a crude attempt to arouse me.

I sat up, but at once the walls began to shift and buckle forward and I was obliged to lie back again weakly. And then, in a rush, everything came back to me with great force, the chase after the dog across the wet marshes and the struggle to free her, the sight of the woman in black at the nursery window and then those sounds which had caused my fears to mount to such a height that I had lost control of myself and my senses and fallen unconscious.

'But the trap – the pony and trap …'

'At the front door.'

I stared.

'Oh, I still like to make use of it now and again. It's a pleasant way to travel when there's nothing to hurry over and it's a sight safer than a motor car across that causeway.'

'Ah.' I felt a surge of relief as I realized the plain facts of the matter, that the noise I had heard had been that of a real pony and cart.

'What did you think?' He was looking at me keenly.

'A pony and cart –'

'Yes?'

'I'd – heard others. Another.'

'Keckwick, perhaps,' he said evenly.

'No, no'. I sat up, more cautiously and the room stayed firm.

'You take care now.'

'I'm better – I'm all right. It was …' I wiped my brow. 'I should like a drink.'

'At your elbow.'

I turned and saw a jug of water and a glass and I drank thirstily, beginning to feel more and more refreshed and my nerves to be steadier as I did so.

Realizing it, Mr Daily moved away from my side to a chair opposite and sat himself down.

'I had you on my mind,' he said at last. 'I wasn't happy. It began to unsettle me.'

'Isn't it quite early in the morning – I've become confused …'

'Early enough. I kept waking. As I said, I had you on my mind.'

'How strange.'

'Was it? Not as it seems to me. Not strange at all.'

'No.'

'A good job I came when I did.'

'Yes, indeed, I'm very grateful. You must have – what? Carried me in here, I remember nothing about it.'

'I've dragged heavier than you with one arm around my neck – there's not much flesh on your bones.'

'I'm extremely glad to see you, Mr Daily.'

'You've good reason.'

'I have.'

'People have drowned on that marsh before now.'

'Yes. Yes, I know that now. I felt that I was being pulled under and the dog with me.' I stared up. 'Spider…'

'She is here. She'll do.'

I looked to where he nodded, to the dog down on the rug between us. At the sound of her name, she bumped her tail, but otherwise she lay, the mud drying on her coat in clots and streaks, and pasted thickly to her leg, looking as limp and exhausted as I myself felt.

'Now, when you've come to a bit more, you'd better get whatever you need and we'll be off.'

'Off ?'

'Aye. I came to see how you were faring in this godforsaken place. I have seen. You had better come back home with me and recover yourself.'

I did not answer for a few moments but lay back and went over in my mind the sequence of events of the previous night and of this morning – and, indeed, further back than that, from my first visit here. I knew that there had been hauntings by the woman in black and perhaps by some other occupant of this house. I knew that the sounds I had heard out on the marsh were ghostly sounds. But although these had been terrifying, and inexplicable, I thought that if I had to I could go over them again, if only because I had been growing more and more determined to find out what restless soul it was who wanted to cause these disturbances and why, *why*. If I could uncover the truth, perhaps I might in some way put an end to it all forever.

But what I couldn't endure more was the atmosphere surrounding the events: the sense of oppressive hatred and malevolence, of someone's evil and also of terrible grief and distress. These, which seemed to invade my own soul and take charge of me, these were what I could no longer bear. I told Mr Daily that I would be glad and grateful to go back with him and to rest at his house if only for a short while. But I was worried, not wanting to leave the mystery unexplained and knowing, too, that at the same time someone would have to finish, at some point, the necessary work of sorting out and packing up Mrs Drablow's papers.

This I mentioned now.

'And what have you found here, Mr Kipps? A map to buried treasure?'

'No. A great quantity of rubbish, old waste paper, and precious little of interest, let alone of value. Frankly, I doubt whether there will be anything. But the job will have to be done at some time or other. We are obliged to it.'

I got up and began to walk about the room, trying my limbs and finding them more or less steady.

'For now, I don't mind confessing that I shall be pretty glad to let up and leave the lot of it behind. There were just one or two papers I should like to go over again for my own curiosity. There is a packet of old letters with a few documents attached. I was reading them late last night. I shall bring those with me.

Then, while Mr Daily began to go round the downstairs rooms, drawing the blinds, checking that all the fires were extinguished, I went first to the room in which I had been working to gather together the bundle of letters and then upstairs for my few belongings. I was no longer at all afraid because I was leaving Eel Marsh House at least for the time being and because of the large and reassuring presence of Mr Samuel

Daily. Whether I would ever return here I did not know but certainly if I did so it would not be alone. I felt altogether calm, therefore, as I reached the top of the staircase and turned towards the small bedroom I had been using, the events of the previous night seeming far in the past and with no more power to harm me than a particularly bad nightmare.

I packed up my bag quickly, closed the window and drew down the blind. On the floor lay the remnants of the shattered torch and I swept them together into a corner with the edge of my foot. All was quiet now, the wind had been dropping since dawn, though, if I closed my eyes, I could hear again its moaning and crying and all the banging and rattling it had given rise to in the old house. But, although that had contributed to my nervousness, I could perfectly well sort out those incidental events – the storm, the bumps and creaks, the darkness, from the ghostly happenings and the atmosphere surrounding them. The weather might change, the wind drop, the sun shine, Eel Marsh House might stand quiet and still. It would be no less dreadful. Whoever haunted it and whatever terrible emotions still possessed them would continue to disturb and distress anyone who came near here, that I knew.

I finished picking up my belongings and left the room. As I reached the landing I could not prevent myself from glancing quickly and half-fearfully along the passage that led to the nursery.

The door was ajar. I stood, feeling the anxiety that lay only just below the surface begin to rise up within me, making my heart beat fast. Below, I heard Mr Daily's footsteps and the pitter-patter of the dog as it followed him about. And, reassured by their presence, I summoned up my courage and made my way cautiously towards that half-open door. When I reached it I hesitated. She had been there. I had seen her. Whoever she was, this was the focus of her search or her attention or her grief – I could not tell which. This was the very heart of the haunting.

There was no sound now. The rocking chair was still. Very slowly I pushed open the door wider and wider, inch by inch, and took a few steps forward until I could see all the way into the room.

It was in a state of disarray as might have been caused by a gang of robbers, bent on mad, senseless destruction. Whereas the bed had been made up neatly, now the clothes were pulled off anyhow and bundled up or trailing onto the floor. The wardrobe door and the drawers of the small chest were pulled open and all the clothes they contained half dragged out, and left hanging like entrails from a wounded body. The lead soldiers had been knocked down like a set of ninepins and the wooden animals from the ark strewn about the shelf, books lay open, their jackets torn, puzzles and games were all jumbled up in a heap together in the centre of the floor. Soft toys were split and unclothed, the tin Sambo was smashed as by a hammer blow. The bedside table and the small cupboard were overturned. And the rocking chair had been pushed into the centre, to preside, tall-backed and erect, like a great brooding bird, over the wreck.

I crossed the room to the window, for perhaps the vandals had gained an entry here. It was tight-bolted and rusted over and the wooden bars were fast and firm. No one had entered here.

As I climbed unsteadily up into Mr Daily's pony trap which waited in the drive, I stumbled and he was obliged to grip my arm and support me until I could regain my strength and I saw that he peered intensely into my face and recognized by its pallor that I had suffered a new shock. But he said nothing about it, only wrapped a heavy rug about my legs, set Spider on my knees for the greater warmth and comfort of us both and then clicked at the pony to turn about.

We left the gravel and went across the rough grass, reached the Nine Lives Causeway and began to traverse it. The tide was dropping back steadily, the sky was a uniform, pearly grey, the air moist and cold but still, after the storm. The marshes lay dull, misty and drear all about us, and, ahead, the flat countryside was dripping and gloomy, without colour, without leaf, without undulation. The pony went steadily and quietly and Mr Daily hummed in a low, tuneless sort of way. I sat as one in a trance, numb, unaware of very much except the movement of the pony trap and the dankness of the air.

But, as we reached the lanes and left the marsh and the estuary behind, I did glance back once over my shoulder. Eel Marsh House stood iron-grey and grim, looming up like a crag, its windows blank and shuttered. There was no sign of any shape or shadow, no living or dead soul. I thought that no one watched us go. Then, the pony's hooves began to clip-clop briskly on the tarmac of the narrow lane between the ditches and straggling blackthorn hedges. I turned my eyes away from that dreadful place for what I fervently prayed was the last time.

From the moment I had climbed into the pony trap, Mr Samuel Daily had treated me as gently and with as much care and concern as an invalid and his efforts to make me feel rested and at ease were redoubled upon arrival at his house. A room had been prepared, a large quiet room with a small balcony overlooking the garden and the open fields beyond. A servant was dispatched at once to the Gifford Arms for the rest of my belongings and, after being given a light breakfast, I was left alone to sleep through the morning. Spider was bathed and groomed and then brought to me, 'since you've got used to her'. And she lay contentedly beside my chair, apparently none the worse for her unpleasant experience early that morning.

I rested but I could not sleep, my brain was still in a confusion and a fever, my nerves all on edge. I was deeply grateful for the peace and tranquillity, but above all for the knowledge that, although I was quite alone and undisturbed here, nevertheless in the house below and the outbuildings beyond there were people, plenty of people, going about their everyday affairs, the reassurance I so badly needed that the normal world still moved through its appointed course.

I tried very hard not to let my mind dwell upon what had happened to me. But I wrote a somewhat guarded letter to Mr Bentley and a fuller one to Stella – though to neither of them did I tell everything nor confess the extent of my distress.

After this, I went outside and took a few turns of the large lawn but the air was cold and raw and I soon returned to my room. There was no sign of Samuel Daily. For an hour or so before noon I dozed fitfully in my chair and, strangely enough, though my body jerked upright once or twice in sudden alarm, after a short time I was able to relax, and so refresh myself more than I would have expected.

At one o'clock there was a knock upon my door and a maid inquired as to whether I would like my luncheon to be served here or if I felt like going down to the dining room.

'Tell Mrs Daily I will join them directly, thank you.'

I washed and tidied myself, called to the dog and walked downstairs.

The Dailys were attentiveness and kindness itself and insistent that I remain with them a day or two longer, before I returned to London. For I had fully decided to go back: nothing on earth would have induced me to pass another hour in Eel Marsh House; I had been as bold and determined as a man could be but I had been defeated and I was not afraid to admit as much, nor did I feel any sense of shame. A man may be accused of cowardice for fleeing away from all manner of physical dangers but when things supernatural, insubstantial and inexplicable threaten not only his safety and well-being but his sanity, his innermost soul, then retreat is not a sign of weakness but the most prudent course.

But I was angry nonetheless, not with myself but with whatever haunted Eel Marsh House, angry at the wild and pointless behaviour of that disturbed creature and angry that it had prevented me, as it would no doubt prevent any other human being, from doing my job. Perhaps I was also angry with those people – Mr Jerome, Keckwick, the landlord, Samuel Daily – who had been proven right about the place. I was young and arrogant enough to feel dashed. I had learned a hard lesson.

That afternoon, left to my own devices again after an excellent luncheon – Mr Daily was soon gone to visit one of his outlying farms – I took out the packet of Mrs Drablow's papers which I had brought with me, for I was still curious about the story I had begun to piece together from my initial reading of the letters and I thought I would divert myself further by trying to complete it. The difficulty was, of course, that I did not know who the young woman – J for Jennet, who had written the letters – was, whether she might have been a relative of Mrs Drablow, or her husband, or merely a friend. But it seemed most likely that only a blood relation would have given or, rather, been forced to give her illegitimate child for adoption to another woman, in the way the letters and legal documents revealed.

I felt sorry for J, as I read her short, emotional letters over again. Her passionate love for her child and her isolation with it, her anger and the way she at first fought bitterly against and, finally, gave despairingly in to the course proposed to her, filled me with sadness and sympathy. A girl from the servant class, living in a closely bound community, might perhaps have fared better, sixty or so years before, than this daughter of genteel parentage, who had been so coldly rejected and whose feelings were so totally left out of the count. Yet servant girls in Victorian England had, I knew, often been driven to murder or abandon their misconceived children. At least Jennet had known that her son was alive and had been given a good home.

And then I opened the other documents that were bound together with the letters. They were three death certificates. The first was of the boy, Nathaniel Drablow, at the age of six years. The cause of death was given as drowning. After that, and bearing exactly the same date, was a similar certificate, stating that Rose Judd had also died by drowning.

I felt a terrible, cold, sickening sensation that began in the pit of my stomach and seemed to rise up through my chest into my throat, so that I was sure I would either vomit or choke. But I did not, I only got up and paced in agitation and distress about the room, clutching the two sheets of creased paper in my hand.

After a while, I forced myself to look at the last document also. That too was a death certificate, but dated some twelve years after the other two.

It was for Jennet Eliza Humfrye, spinster, aged thirty-six years. The cause of death was given simply as 'heart failure'.

I sat down heavily in my chair. But I was too agitated to remain there for long and in the end I called to Spider and went out again into the November afternoon that was already closing in to an early twilight, and began to walk, away from Mr Daily's house and garden, past the barns and stables and sheds and off across some stubble. I felt better for the exercise. Around me there was only the countryside, ploughed brown in ridges, with low hedges and, here and there, two or three elm trees, their bare branches full of rooks' nests, from which those ugly black birds flew up in a raucous, flapping flock, every now and then, to reel about, cawing, in the leaden sky. There was a chill wind blowing over the fields driving a spatter of hard rain before it. Spider seemed pleased to be out.

As I walked, my thoughts were all concentrated upon the papers I had just read and the story they had told and which was now becoming clear and complete. I had found out, more or less by chance, the solution – or much of it – to the identity of the woman in black, as well as the answer to many other questions. But, although I now knew more, I was not satisfied by the discovery, only upset and alarmed – and afraid too. I knew – and yet I did not know, I was bewildered and nothing had truly been explained. For how can such things be? I have already stated that I had no more believed in ghosts than does any healthy young man of sound education, reasonable intelligence and matter-of-fact inclinations. But ghosts I had seen. An event, and that a dreadful, tragic one, of many years ago, which had taken place and been done with, was somehow taking place over and over again, repeating itself in some dimension other than the normal, present one. A pony trap, carrying a boy of six called Nathaniel, the adopted son of Mr and Mrs Drablow, and also his nursemaid, had somehow taken a wrong path in the sea mist and veered off the safety of the causeway and onto the marshes, where it had been sucked into the quicksands and swallowed up by the mud and rising waters of the estuary. The child and the nursemaid had been drowned and so presumably had the pony and whoever had been driving the trap. And now, out on those same marshes, the whole episode, or a ghost, a shadow, a memory of it, somehow happened again and again – how often I did not know. But nothing could be seen now, only heard.

The only other things I knew were that the boy's mother, Jennet Humfrye had died of a wasting disease twelve years after her son, that they were both buried in the now disused and tumbledown graveyard beyond Eel Marsh House; that the child's nursery had been preserved in that house as he had left it, with his bed, his clothes, his toys, all undisturbed, and that his mother haunted the place. Moreover, that the intensity of her grief and distress together with her pent-up hatred and desire for revenge permeated the air all around.

And it was that which so troubled me, the force of those emotions, for those were what I believed had power to harm. But to harm who? Was not everyone connected with that sad story now dead? For presumably Mrs Drablow had been the very last of them.

Eventually, I began to be tired and turned back but although I could not find any solution to the business – or perhaps because it was all so inexplicable – I could not put it from my mind, I worried at it all the way home and brooded upon it as I sat in my quiet room, looking out into the evening darkness.

By the time the gong was sounded for dinner I had worked myself up into such a fever of agitation that I determined to pour the whole story out to Mr Samuel Daily and to demand to hear anything whatever that he knew or had ever heard about the business.

The scene was as before, the study of Mr Daily's house after dinner, with the two of us in the comfortable wing chairs, the decanter and glasses between us on the small table. I was feeling considerably better after another good dinner.

I had just come to the end of my story. Mr Daily had sat, listening without interruption, his face turned away from me, as I had relived, though with surprising calm, all the events of my short stay at Eel Marsh House, leading up to the time when he had found me in a faint outside early that morning. And I had also told him of my conclusions, drawn from my perusal of the packet of letters and the death certificates.

He did not speak for some minutes. The clock ticked. The fire burned evenly and sweetly in the grate. The dog Spider lay in front of it on the hearth-rug. Telling the story had been like a purgation and now my head felt curiously light, my body in that limp state such as follows upon a fever or a fright. But I reflected that I could, from this moment on, only get better, because I could only move step by steady step away from those awful happenings, as surely as time went on.

'Well,' he said at last. 'You have come a long way since the night I met you on the late train.

'It feels like a hundred years ago. I feel like another man.'

'You've gone through some rough seas.'

'Well, I'm in the calm after the storm now and there's an end of it.'

I saw that his face was troubled.

'Come,' I said bravely, 'you don't think any more harm can come of it surely?' I never intend to go back there. Nothing would persuade me.'

'No.'

'Then all is well.'

He did not answer, but leaned forward and poured himself another small tot of whisky.

'Though I do wonder what will happen to the house,' I said. 'I'm sure no one local is ever going to want to live there and I can't imagine anyone who might come from outside staying for long, once they get to know what the place is really like – and even if they manage not to hear any of the stories about it in advance. Besides, it's a rambling inconvenient sort of spot. Whoever would want it?'

Samuel Daily shook his head.

'Do you suppose,' I asked, after a few moments in which we sat in silence with our own thoughts, 'that the poor old woman was haunted night and day by the ghost of her sister and that she had to endure those dreadful noises out there?' – for Mr Daily had told me that the two had been sisters – 'if such was the case, I wonder how she could have endured it without going out of her mind?'

'Perhaps she did not.'

'Perhaps.'

I was growing more and more sensible of the fact that he was holding something back from me, some explanation or information about Eel Marsh House and the Drablow family and, because I knew that, I would not rest or be quite easy in my mind until I had found out everything there was to know. I decided to urge him strongly to tell it to me.

'Was there something I still did not see? If I had stayed there any longer would I have encountered yet more horrors?'

'That I cannot tell.'

'But you could tell me something.'

He sighed and shifted about uneasily in his chair avoiding my eye and looking into the fire, then stretching out his leg to rub at the dog's belly with the toe of his boot.

'Come, we're a good way from the place and my nerves are quite steady again. I must know. It can't hurt me now.'

'Not you,' he said. 'No, not you maybe.'

'For God's sake, what is it you are holding back, man? What are you so afraid of telling me?'

'You, Arthur,' he said, 'will be away from here tomorrow or the next day. You, if you are lucky, will neither hear nor see nor know of anything to do with that damned place again. The rest of us have to stay. We've to live with it.'

'With *what*? Stories – rumours? With the sight of that woman in black from time to time? With *what*?'

'With whatever will surely follow. Sometime or other. Crythin Gifford has lived with that for fifty years. It's changed people. They don't speak of it, you found that out. Those who have suffered worst say least – Jerome, Keckwick.'

I felt my heart-beat increase, I put a hand to my collar to loosen it a little, drew my chair back from the fire. Now that the moment had come, I did not know after all whether I wanted to hear what Daily had to say.

'Jennet Humfrye gave up her child, the boy, to her sister, Alice Drablow, and Alice's husband, because she'd no choice. At first she stayed away – hundreds of miles away – and the boy was brought up a Drablow and was never intended to know his mother. But, in the end, the pain of being parted from him, instead of easing, grew worse and she returned to Crythin. She was not welcome at her parents' house and the man – the child's father – had gone abroad for good. She got rooms in the town. She'd no money. She took in sewing, she acted as a companion to a lady. At first, apparently, Alice Drablow would not let her see the boy at all. But Jennet was so distressed that she threatened violence and in the end the sister relented – just so far. Jennet could visit very occasionally, but never see the boy alone nor ever disclose who she was or that she had any relationship to him. No one ever foresaw that he'd turn out to look so like her, nor that the natural affinity between them would grow out. He became more and more attached to the woman who was, when all was said and done, his own mother, more and more fond, and as he did so he began to be colder towards Alice Drablow. Jennet planned to take him away, that much I do know. Before she could do so, the accident happened, just as you heard. The boy ... the nursemaid, the pony trap and its driver Keckwick ...'

'*Keckwick?*'

'Yes. His father. And there was the boy's little dog too. That's a treacherous place, as you've found out to your own cost. The sea fret sweeps over the marshes suddenly, the quicksands are hidden.'

'So they all drowned.'

'And Jennet watched. She was at the house, watching from an upper window, waiting for them to return.'

I caught my breath, horrified.

'The bodies were recovered but they left the pony trap, it was held too fast by the mud. From that day Jennet Humfrye began to go mad.'

'Was there any wonder?'

'No. Mad with grief and mad with anger and a desire for revenge. She blamed her sister who had let them go out that day, though it was no one's fault, the mist comes without warning.'

'Out of a clear sky.'

'Whether because of her loss and her madness or what, she also contracted a disease which caused her to begin to waste away. The flesh shrank from her bones, the colour was drained from her, she looked like a walking skeleton – a living spectre. When she went about the streets, people drew back. Children were terrified of her. She died eventually. She died in hatred and misery. And as soon as ever she died the hauntings began. And so they have gone on.'

'What, all the time? Ever since?'

'No. Now and again. Less, these past few years. But still she is seen and the sounds are heard by someone chancing to be out on the marsh.'

'And presumably by old Mrs Drablow?'

'Who knows?'

'Well, Mrs Drablow is dead. There, surely, the whole matter will rest.'

But Mr Daily had not finished. He was just coming to the climax of his story.

'And whenever she has been seen,' he said in a low voice, 'in the graveyard, on the marsh, in the streets of the town, however briefly, and whoever by, there has been one sure and certain result.'

'Yes?' I whispered.

'In some violent or dreadful circumstance, a child has died.'

'What – you mean by accident?'

'Generally in an accident. But once or twice it has been after an illness, which has struck them down within a day or a night or less.'

'You mean any child? A child of the town?'

'Any child. Jerome's child.'

I had a sudden vision of that row of small, solemn faces, with hands all gripping the railings, that surrounded the school yard, on the day of Mrs Drablow's funeral.

'But surely ... well ... children sometimes do die.'

'They do.'

'And is there anything more than chance to connect these deaths with the appearance of that woman?'

'You may find it hard to believe. You may doubt it.'

'Well, I ...'

'We know.'

After a few moments, looking at his set and resolute face, I said quietly, 'I do not doubt, Mr Daily.'

Then, for a very long time, neither of us said anything more.

I knew that I had suffered a considerable shock that morning, after several days and nights of agitation and nervous tension, consequent upon the hauntings of Eel Marsh House. But I did not altogether realize how deeply and badly the whole experience had affected me, both in mind and body.

I went to bed that night, as I supposed for the last time under the Dailys' roof. On the next morning I planned to catch the first available train back to London. When I told Mr Daily of my decision, he did not argue with me.

That night, I slept wretchedly, waking every hour or so out of turbulent nightmares, my entire body in a sweat of anxiety, and when I did not sleep I lay awake and tense in every limb, listening, remembering and going over and over it all in my mind. I asked myself unanswerable questions about life and death and the borderlands between and I prayed, direct and simple, passionate prayers.

I had been brought up, like most children, to a belief in the Deity, brought up within the Christian church but although I still believed that its teachings were probably the best form of guidance on living a good life, I had found the Deity rather remote and my prayers were not anything but formal and dutiful. Not so now. Now, I prayed fervently and with a newly awakened zeal. Now, I realized that there were forces for good and those for evil doing battle together and that a man might range himself on one side or the other.

The morning was long in arriving and, when it did, it was again an overcast and wet one – dank, drear November. I got up, my head aching and eyes burning, my legs heavy, and somehow managed to get dressed and drag myself downstairs to the breakfast table. But I could not face food, though I had an extreme thirst and drank cup after cup of tea. Mr and Mrs Daily glanced at me anxiously now and again, as I talked of my arrangements. I thought that I would not feel well again until I was sitting in the train, watching this countryside slide away out of sight, and I said as much, though at the same time endeavouring to express my great gratitude to them both, because they had indeed been saviours, of my life and of my sanity.

Then I got up from the table and began to make my way to the dining room, but the door receded as I went, I seemed to be fighting towards it through a mist which was closing in upon me, so that I could not get my breath and felt as if I was pushing against a heavy weight which I must remove before I could go any further.

Samuel Daily caught me as I fell and I was dimly aware that, for the second time, though in very different circumstances, he was half-carrying, half-dragging me, this time up the stairs to my bedroom. There, he helped me to undress, there he left me, my head throbbing and my mind confused, and there I remained, having frequent visits from an anxious-looking doctor, for five days. After that, the worst of the fever and the delirium passed, leaving me exhausted and weak beyond belief, and I was able to sit up in an armchair, at first in my room and later downstairs. The Dailys were kindness and solicitude itself. The worst of it all was not the physical illness, the aching, the tiredness, the fever, but the mental turmoil I passed through.

The woman in black seemed to haunt me, even here, to sit on the end of my bed, to push her face suddenly down close to mine as I lay asleep, so I awoke crying out in terror. And my head rang with the sound of the child crying out on the marsh and of the rocking chair and the drowning whinny of the pony. I could not break free of any of them and, when I was not having feverish delusions and nightmares, I was remembering every word of the letters and death certificates, as if I could see the pages held up before my mind's eye.

But at last I began to be better, the fears died down, the visions faded and I found myself again, I was exhausted, drained, but well. There was nothing else the woman could do to me, surely, I had endured and survived.

After twelve days I was feeling almost completely recovered. It was a day of winter sunshine but there had been one of the first frosts of the year. I was sitting at the open French windows of the drawing room, a rug over my knees, looking at the bare bushes and trees, silvery-white and stiff with rime, stark against the sky. It was after lunch. I might sleep a little or not but, in any case, no one would disturb me. Spider lay contentedly at my feet, as she had done throughout the days and nights of my illness. I had grown more fond of the little dog than I would ever have imagined possible, feeling that we shared a bond, because we had been through our time of trial together.

A robin was perched on one of the stone urns at the top of the balustrade, head up, eyes bead-bright, and I watched him happily, while he hopped a foot or two and then paused again, to listen and to sing. I reflected that, before coming here, I would never have been able to concentrate on such an ordinary thing so completely but would have been restless to be up and off, doing this or that busily. Now, I appreciated the bird's presence, enjoyed simply watching his movements for as long as he chose to remain outside my window, with an intensity I had never before experienced.

I heard some sounds outside, the engine of a motor car, voices round at the front of the house, but paid them little attention, so wrapped up was I in my observation of the bird. Besides, they would have nothing to do with me.

There were footsteps along the corridor and they stopped outside the door of the drawing room, and then after a hesitation it opened. Perhaps it was later than I thought, and someone had come to see how I was and whether I wanted a cup of tea.

'Arthur?'

I turned, startled, and then jumped from my chair in amazement, disbelief, and delight. Stella, my own dear Stella, was coming towards me across the room.

The Woman in Black

The following morning, I left the house. We were taken, in Mr Samuel Daily's motor, directly to the railway station. I had settled my account at the Gifford Arms by messenger, and I did not go into the town of Crythin Gifford again; it seemed altogether wise to take medical advice, for the doctor had been particularly anxious that I should not do anything, or go anywhere, to upset my still delicately balanced equilibrium. And, in truth, I did not *want* to see the town, or to risk meeting Mr Jerome or Keckwick, or, most of all, to catch so much as a glimpse of the distant Marsh. All that was behind me, it might have happened, I thought, to another person. The doctor had told me to put the whole thing from my mind, and I resolved to try and do so. With Stella beside me, I did not see how I could fail.

The only regret I had at leaving the place was a genuine sadness at parting company with Mr and Mrs Samuel Daily, and, when we shook hands, I made him promise that he would visit us, when he next came to London – which he did, he said, once or, at most, twice a year. Moreover, a puppy was booked for us, as soon as Spider should produce any. I was going to miss the little dog a great deal.

But there was one last question I had to ask, though I found it hard to bring the matter up.

'I must know,' I burst out at last, while Stella was safely out of earshot and deep in conversation with Mrs Daily, whom she had been able to draw out, with her own natural friendliness and warmth.

Samuel Daily looked at me sharply.

'You told me that night – ' I took a deep breath to try and calm myself. 'A child – a child in Crythin Gifford has always died.'

'Yes.'

I could not go on but my expression was enough, I knew, my desperate anxiety to be told the truth was evident.

'Nothing,' Daily said quickly. 'Nothing has happened …'

I was sure he had been going to add 'Yet', but he stopped and so I added it for him. But he only shook his head silently.

'Oh, pray God it may not – that the chain is broken – that her power is at an end – that she has gone – and I was the last ever to see her.'

He put a hand reassuringly on my arm. 'Yes, yes.'

I wanted above all for it to be so, for the time that had elapsed since I had last seen the woman in black – the ghost of Jennet Humfrye – to be long enough now, for it to be proof positive that the curse had quite gone. She had been a poor, crazed, troubled woman, dead of grief and distress, filled with hatred and desire for revenge. Her bitterness was understandable, the wickedness that led her to take away other women's children because she had lost her own, understandable too but not forgivable.

There was nothing anyone could do to help her, except perhaps pray for her soul, I thought. Mrs Drablow, the sister she blamed for the death of her child, was dead herself and in her grave, and, now that the house was empty at last, perhaps the hauntings and their terrible consequences for the innocent would cease forever.

The car was waiting in the drive. I shook hands with the Dailys and, taking Stella's arm and keeping tightly hold of it, climbed in and leaned back against the seat. With a sigh – indeed almost a sob – of relief, I was driven away from Crythin Gifford.

*

My story is almost done. There is only the last thing left to tell. And that I can scarcely bring myself to write about. I have sat here at my desk, day after day, night after night, a blank sheet of paper before me, unable to lift my pen, trembling and weeping too. I have gone out and walked in the old orchard and further, across the country beyond Monk's Piece, for mile after mile, but seen nothing of my surroundings, noticing neither animal nor bird, unable to tell even the state of the weather, so that several times I have come home soaked through to the skin, to Esmé's considerable distress. And that has been another cause of anguish: she has watched me and wondered and been too sensitive to ask questions. I have seen the worry and distress on her face and sensed her restlessness, as we have sat together in the late evenings. I have been quite unable to tell her anything at all, she has no idea what I have been going through or why: she will have no idea until she reads this manuscript and at that time I shall be dead and beyond her.

But, now at last, I have summoned up sufficient courage, I will use the very last of my strength that has been so depleted by the reliving of those past horrors, to write the end of the story.

*

Stella and I returned to London and within six weeks we had married. Our original plan had been to wait at least until the following spring but my experiences had changed me greatly, so that I now had an urgent sense of time, a certainty that we should not delay, but seize upon any joy, and good fortune, any opportunity, at once, and hold fast to it. Why should we wait? What was there beyond the mundane considerations of money, property and possessions to keep us from marrying? Nothing. And so we married, quietly and without fuss, and lived in my old rooms, with another room added, which the landlady had been more than willing to rent to us, until such time as we could afford a small house of our own. We were as happy as a young man and his bride may possibly be, content in each other's company, not rich but not poor either, busy and looking forward to the future. Mr Bentley gave me a little more responsibility and a consequent increase in salary as time went on. About Eel Marsh House and the Drablow estate and papers I had expressly begged him that I be told nothing and so I was not; the names were never mentioned to me again.

A little over a year after our marriage, Stella gave birth to our child, a son, whom we called Joseph Arthur Samuel, and Mr Samuel Daily was his godfather, for he was our sole remaining tie with that place, that time. But, although we saw him occasionally in London, he never once spoke of the past; indeed, I was so filled with joy and contentment in my life, that I never so much as thought of those things, and the nightmares quite ceased to trouble me.

I was in a particularly peaceful, happy frame of mind one Sunday afternoon in the summer of the year following our son's birth. I could not have been less prepared for what was to come.

We had gone to a large park, ten miles or so outside London, which formed the grounds of a noble house and, in the summer season, stood open to the general public at weekends. There was a festive, holiday air about the place, a lake, on which small boats were being rowed, a bandstand, with a band playing jolly tunes, stalls selling ices and fruit. Families strolled in the sunshine, children tumbled about upon the grass. Stella and

I walked happily, with young Joseph taking a few unsteady steps, holding on to our hands while we watched him, as proud as any parents could be.

Then, Stella noticed that one of the attractions upon offer was a donkey, and a pony and trap, on both of which rides could be taken, down an avenue of great horse-chestnut trees, and, thinking that the boy would find such a treat to his liking, we led him to the docile grey donkey and I endeavoured to lift him up into the saddle. But he shrieked and pulled away at once, and clung to me, while at the same time pointing to the pony trap, and gesturing excitedly. So, because there was only room for two passengers, Stella took Joseph, and I stood, watching them bowl merrily away down the ride, between the handsome old trees, which were in full, glorious leaf.

For a while, they went out of sight, away round a bend, and I began to look idly about me, at the other enjoyers of the afternoon. And then, quite suddenly, I saw her. She was standing away from any of the people, close up to the trunk of one of the trees.

I looked directly at her and she at me. There was no mistake. My eyes were not deceiving me. It was she, the woman in black with the wasted face, the ghost of Jennet Humfrye. For a second, I simply stared in in- credulity and astonishment, then in cold fear. I was paralysed, rooted to the spot on which I stood, and all the world went dark around me and the shouts and happy cries of all the children faded. I was quite unable to take my eyes away from her. There was no expression on her face and yet I felt all over again the renewed power emanating from her, the malevolence and hatred and passionate bitterness. It pierced me through.

At that same moment, to my intense relief, the pony cart came trot- ting back down the avenue, through the shaft of sunlight that lay across the grass, with my dear Stella sitting in it and holding up the baby, who was bouncing and calling and waving his little arms with delight. They were almost back, they had almost reached me, I would retrieve them and then we would go, for I didn't want to stay here for a second longer. I made ready. They had almost come to a halt when they passed the tree beside which the woman in black was still standing and, as they did so, she moved quickly, her skirts rustling as if to step into the pony's path. The animal swerved violently and then reared a little, its eyes filled with sudden fright, and then it took off and went careering away through the glade between the trees, whinnying and quite out of control. There was a moment of dreadful confusion, with several people starting off after it, and women and children shrieking. I began to run crazily and then I heard it, the sickening crack and thud as the pony and its cart collided with one of the huge tree trunks. And then silence – a terrible silence which can only have lasted for seconds, and seemed to last for years. As I raced towards where it had fallen, I glanced back over my shoulder. The woman in black had disappeared.

They lifted Stella gently from the cart. Her body was broken, her neck and legs fractured, though she was still conscious. The pony had only stunned itself but the cart was overturned and its harness tangled, so that it could not move, but lay on the ground whinnying and snorting in fright.

Our baby son had been thrown clear, clear against another tree. He lay crumpled on the grass below it, dead.

This time, there was no merciful loss of consciousness, I was forced to live through it all, every minute and then every day thereafter, for ten long months, until Stella, too, died from her terrible injuries.

I had seen the ghost of Jennet Humfrye and she had had her revenge.

They asked for my story. I have told it. Enough.

Dolly

Iyot Lock

An autumn night and the fens stretch for miles, open and still. It is dark, until the full moon slides from behind a cloud and over the huddle of grey stone which is Iyot Lock. The hamlet straddles a cross roads between flat field and flat field, with its squat church on the east side, hard by Iyot House and the graveyard in between. On the west side, a straggle of cottages leads to Iyot Farm, whose flat fields bleed into the flat fens with no apparent boundary.

It is rare for a night here to be so still. The wind from the sea keens and whistles, though that sea is some miles away. Birds cry their eerie cries.

And then, a slight, thin movement of the air, from inland. It skims over the low dykes and watery ditches, rattles the dry reeds and rushes, rustles the grasses along the roadside.

It strengthens to a low wind and the wind weaves through the few trees in the churchyard and taps the branches of the creeper against the windows of Iyot House.

Nobody hears, for the house is empty and surely the sleepers in the churchyard are not disturbed.

The grasses whisper, the wind moves among the gravestones. And somewhere just about here, by the low wall, another sound, not like the grass but like paper rustling. But there is no paper.

The creeper scrapes the windowpanes. The moon slips out, silvering the glass.

The wind prowls around Iyot Lock, shifting the branches, stirring the grasses, swaying faintly, and from somewhere nearby, hidden or even buried, the sound of rustling.

PART ONE

One

It was a November afternoon when I returned to Iyot Lock and saw that nothing had changed. It was as I recalled it from forty years earlier, the sky as vast, the fen as flat, the river as dark and secretly flowing as it had been in my mind and memory. There had sometimes been sunshine, the river had gleamed and glinted, the larks had soared and sung on a June day, but this was how I knew it best, this landscape of dun and steel, with the sky falling in on my head and the wind keening and the ghosts and will-o'-the-wisps haunting my childhood nights.

I drove over Hoggett's bridge, seeing the water flow sluggishly beneath, and across the flat straight road, past the old lock keeper's cottage, abandoned now, but then the home of the lock keeper with a wen on his nose and one glass eye, who looked after his sluices and his eel traps in sullen silence. I used to steer clear of Mr Norry, of whom I was mortally, superstitiously afraid. But the blackened wood and brick cottage was empty and the roof fallen in. As I went by, a great bird with ragged wings rose out of it and flapped away, low over the water.

I could see far ahead to where the fen met the sky and the tower of Iyot Church, and then the house itself shimmered into view, hazy at first in the veils of rain, then larger, clearer, darker. The only trees for miles were the trees around the churchyard and those close to Iyot House, shading it from sight of the road, though few people, now as ever, were likely to pass by.

I parked beside the church wall and got out. The rain was a fine drizzle lying like cobwebs on my hair and the shoulders of my coat. Mine was the only car, so unless she had parked at the house, I was the first to arrive. That did not surprise me.

I pushed open the heavy greened wood of the gate and walked up the path to the church door. Crumpled chicken wire had been used to cover the arch and keep out birds, but it had loosened and old twigs and bits of blackened straw poked through where they had still managed to nest. I lifted the iron handle, twisted it and the door creaked open. The cold inside the porch made me catch my breath. Beyond the inner door, inside the church itself, it was more intense still and smelled of damp stone and mould. It seemed to be the cold of centuries and to seep into my bones as I stood there.

I did not remember anything about the church, though I was sure I must have been there on Sundays, with my aunt – I had a folk memory of the hard polished pews against my bony little backside and legs, for I had been a thin child. It was dull and pale, with uninteresting memorial tablets and clear glass windows that let the silvery daylight in onto the grey floor. Even the Lion and Unicorn, the only touch of colour in the church, painted in red and faded gold and blue on a wooden panel, and which might have taken the attention of a small boy, was quite unfamiliar. Perhaps my memories had been of another church altogether.

I wandered about, half expecting to hear the door open and see her standing there, but no one came and my footsteps were solitary on the stone floor.

The lights did not come on when I clicked the switch and the church was dim in the sullen November afternoon. I made my way out again, but as I stood looking out at the path and the graveyard, I had a strange and quite urgent sense that I ought to do something, that I was needed, that I was the one person who could rescue – rescue what? Who? I could not remember when I had had such an anxious feeling and as I walked out, it became stronger, almost as if someone were tugging at my sleeve and begging me to help them. But there was no one. The churchyard was empty and it felt desolate in the gathering dusk, with the brooding sky overhead, though it was only just after three o'clock.

I shook myself, to be rid of the inexplicable feeling and walked briskly to the car and drove the short distance to the house, the back and chimneys of which were hard to the road. There were the wooden gates, which I remembered well. If I opened them I could swing into the yard and park behind the scullery and outhouses, but the gate was locked and seemingly barred on the inside, so I returned to the lay-by beside the church and set out to walk back along the deserted lane to Iyot House. I glanced down the road but there was no sight of a car, even far away, no moving dot in the distance.

And then, it was as if something were tugging at my sleeve, though I felt nothing. I was being urged to return to the churchyard and I could not disobey, whatever was asking me to go there needed something – needed me? What did it want me to do and why? Where exactly was I to go?

I turned again, feeling considerably annoyed but unable to resist, and the moment I set off I sensed that this was right, and that who or whatever wanted me there was relieved and pleased with me. We all like to please by doing the thing we are being asked, in spite of our misgivings, and so I retraced my steps briskly the hundred yards to the lych gate. That was not quite far enough. I must go through and into the churchyard. By now the dark was gathering fast and I could barely see my way, but there were still streaks of light in the sky to the west and it was not a large area. I moved slowly among the gravestones. It was almost as if I were playing the old childhood game of Hide and Seek, one in which the inner sense was saying 'Cold' 'Cold' 'Warm' 'Very Warm'.

It was as I neared three gravestones that were set against the low wall at the back that the sense of urgency became very strong. I went to each one. All were ancient, moss and lichen-covered and the names and dates were no longer visible. Even as I got near to the first I felt a peculiar electric shock of heat, followed immediately by a sense of release. This was it. I was there. But where? Wherever I was meant to be? Then by whom, and why?

I stood still. The wind was keening, the darkness shrinking in to swallow me. I was not exactly afraid but I was uneasy and bewildered. And then I heard it. It seemed to be coming from the ground in front of a gravestone. I squatted down and listened. The moan of the wind was blocked out by the wall there, and it was very still. At first I could not make it out but after a few moments, I thought it sounded as if something was rustling, a dry sound, like that made by the wind in the reed beds, but softer and fainter. It came from under the grass, under the earth. A rustling, as if someone were . . .

No, I could not tell. I stayed for some minutes and the rustling came again and again, and each time it made me feel as one feels when a name one has forgotten is almost, almost on the tip of the tongue. I knew the sound, I knew what was making it, I knew why . . . but it hovered just out of reach, like the elusive name. I knew and then did not know, I remembered – but then it was gone. I waited for a few more minutes. Nothing else happened, I heard nothing else and not least because by this time I was thoroughly chilled. The east wind was whistling across the fen even more strongly and I left the churchyard and returned to Iyot House.

It was in pitch darkness and the wind had got up even more in that short time and was dashing the trees against the walls and rattling the ivy. Stupidly I had not brought a torch and had to edge my way through the gate and up the narrow path between thickly overgrown shrubs to the front door. I had the key ready and to my surprise the lock was smooth and opened at a turn. I felt about for a switch – there was none in the porch but once inside the hall I found the panel of them to my left. The hall, staircase and narrow passageway were lit, though the bulbs were quite dim. But at once, the past came rushing towards me as I not only saw but smelled the inside of the house where I had once been a small boy on occasional and always strange visits. The pictures on the wall, one of a half-draped woman by a rock pool, another of sheep in the snow, and two portraits whose eyes pierced me and then seemed to follow me, as they always had, reminded me of the past, the feel of the polished floor beneath the rug at my feet, the great brass dinner gong, the once-polished and gleaming banister, now filmed and dull, reminded me, and the silent grandfather clock, the frieze of brown carnations running along the wallpaper, the dark velveteen curtain hanging on a rod across the drawing room door, all these things reminded me . . . As I looked round I was eight years old again and in Iyot House for the first time, anxious, wary, full of half-fears, jumping at my own shadow as it glided beside me up the stairs.

But I was not afraid of anything there that late afternoon, merely affected by the atmosphere of sadness and emptiness. Iyot House had never been full of light and fun but it was not a gloomy house either and people who had lived there had looked after me as best they knew, and even loved me – though perhaps I had little sense of it as a boy. I had been afraid of shadows and darkness, of sudden sounds, of spiders and bats but I had never believed Iyot House had any ghosts or malign forces hanging about within its walls, at least not until . . .

I stopped with one foot on the stairs . . . until what? It was teasing me again, that sense of something just out of reach, almost remembered but then fluttering off just as I grasped it.

Until something had happened? Or was it to do with some*one*?

It was no good. I could not remember, it had danced away, to tantalise me yet again.

I went round the house, putting on the lights as I did so, and each room came alive at the touch of the switch, bedrooms, dressing rooms, bathrooms, their furniture and curtains and carpets exactly as I had known them, faded now and dusty, with the smell of all rooms into which fresh air had not come through an opened window, for years. I did not feel anything much, not sadness or fondness, just a certain muted nostalgia.

And then I climbed the last steep, short flight of stairs to the attics and at once I felt an odd fluttering sensation in my chest, as though I were reaching somewhere important, where I might at last be able to recall the incident that was nudging at my memory.

This was familiar. This had been my territory. These small rooms with their tiny, iron-latched windows, the narrow single bed, the bare floor-boards, had been where I slept, dreamed, thought, played . . . and where I had first encountered Leonora.

I made my way to the room that had been mine. It was the same, and yet quite different, because though the furniture was as I recalled, there were, of course, none of my clothes, toys, games or books, nothing that had made it personal to me, brought it alive. It also seemed far smaller than I had remembered – but, of course, I am a man of six feet two and I was a small boy when I had been here last. I sat on the bed. The mattress was the same, soft but with the springs beneath poking through here and there. I felt them again, digging into my thinly fleshed young back. The wicker chair was almost too small for me to sit in, the window seat narrow and hard. I remembered the wallpaper with its frieze of beige roses, the iron fireplace with the scrolled canopy, the tall cupboard set deep into the wall.

The cupboard. It was something about the cupboard; something in it or that had happened beside it?

I did not want to open it, and though I felt foolish, my hand hovered on the latch for several seconds, and my heart started to beat fast. I did not remember anything except that my mounting distress meant the game was over, I was 'hot'.

I did open it, of course. It was empty, the shelves dusty. It went some way back and as I took a couple of deep breaths and felt calmer, I reached up and ran my hand along the shelves. Nothing. There was nothing there at all, nothing until I reached the top shelf, so far from me when I was a boy that I had to stand on the stool to reach it, but now easily accessible. Still nothing.

I shook myself, and was about to close the cupboard door when I heard it – a very soft rustling, as if someone were stirring their hand about in crisp tissue paper, perhaps as they unpacked a parcel. It stopped. I opened the door wide again. The rustling was a little louder. I got the old stool, stood on it and felt the top shelf of the cupboard to the very back, where my hand touched the wall. Nothing. It was totally and completely empty.

Nevertheless, there was the sound again, and although it was no louder, it seemed more urgent and agitated.

I lost my nerve, closed the cupboard and fled, running down the stairs to the hall. When I stopped and got my breath back, I listened. The wind was whistling down the chimney and lifting the rug on the floor, but I could no longer hear even the faintest sound of paper rustling.

I went into the sitting room, thinking to wait for her there but it had such a damp and chill, and the fireplace was full of rubble, so I retreated, switched out the lights and locked the front door. The wind seemed to pare the skin off my face as I turned into the lane and I hastened to get into the car. I would drive back to the market town and my small, warm, comfortable hotel. It was obvious that she was not going to come to Iyot House – perhaps she had never intended it.

But I knew that even if she did come, she would not remember anything. We blot out bad things from our minds and especially when they have been bad things we ourselves have done, in childhood perhaps most of all.

A chill mist was smothering the fen and veils of it writhed in front of the headlights as I drove away. I would be glad to get to the Lion at Cold Eeyle, and a good malt whisky by the fire, even more glad to have the whole thing done with at the solicitor's the next morning. Would Leonora turn up there? I had no doubt that she would. The prospect of inheriting something was just what would bring her up here, as nothing else had ever done – I knew she had not visited Aunt Kestrel in forty years, but then she had lived abroad for the most part, following her mother's example in marrying several times. I did not know if she had any children but I doubted it.

The Lion was snug and welcoming, after an unpleasant ten-mile drive through the swirling fog. My room was at the top of the house, down some winding corridors. I spruced up and returned to the bar, a whisky and the log fire.

I ate a good dinner and went to bed early. The place was quiet and when I had got my key, the receptionist said that I was the only person staying. The meeting at the solicitor's was at ten, in his Cold Eeyle office.

I thought about Aunt Kestrel that night, after I had read a dozen pages and put out the light. I had barely known her, wished I had talked to her more about the family and the past she could have told me so much about. She had housed a stiff, shy small boy and a wayward girl when she had no knowledge of children, what they wanted or needed. She could have refused but she had not, feeling strongly, as her generation did, about family ties and family duty. Of course, it had never occurred to me as a boy that she was probably lonely, widowed young, childless, and living in that bleak and isolated house with only the moaning wind, the fogs and rain for company, other than sour Mrs Mullen.

I fell asleep thinking about the two of them, and about Leonora and how anxious I had been about the way she behaved, when we were children, how she had seemed so careless about bringing wrath down on her own head and curses on the house in general.

I woke and put on the bedside lamp. It was deathly quiet. Obviously the fog had not lifted but was swaddling the land, deadening every sound. Not that there would be many. Cars did not drive around Cold Eeyle at night, people did not walk the streets.

I was about to pick up my book and read a few more pages to lull myself off again, when my ears picked up a slight and distant sound. I knew what it was at once, and it acted like a pick stabbing through the ice of memory. It was the sound of crying. I got up and opened the window. The taste of the fog came into my mouth and its damp web touched my skin. But through its felted layers, from far away, I heard it again, half in my own head, half out there, and then everything came vividly back, the scene with Leonora in Aunt Kestrel's sitting room, her rage, the crack of the china head against the fireplace, my own fear, prompting my heart to leap in my chest. All, all of it I remembered – no, I re-lived, my heart pounding again, as I stood at the window and through the fog-blanketed darkness heard the sound again.

Deep under the earth, inside its cardboard coffin, shrouded in the layers of white paper, the china doll with the jagged open crevasse in its skull was crying.

PART TWO

Two

Two children were travelling, separately from different directions, to Iyot House, Iyot Lock, one hot afternoon in late June.

'Where am I to put them?' Mrs Mullen had asked, to whom children were anathema. 'Where will they sleep?'

Kestrel, the aunt, knew better than to make any suggestion, the housekeeper being certain to object and overrule.

'I wonder where seems best to you?' Images of the bedrooms flicked in a slide show through Aunt Kestrel's mind, each one seeming less suitable than the last – too dark, too large, too full of precious small objects. She had no experience of young children, though she was perfectly well disposed to the thought of having her great nephew and niece to stay, and had a vague idea that they were easily frightened of the dark or broke things. And were they to sleep in adjacent rooms or with a communicating door? On separate floors?

'The attics would suit best, in my view,' Mrs Mullen said.

Shadowy images chased across Kestrel's mind, troubling her enough to make her get up from her writing desk. 'I think we had better look. I can't remember when I was last up there.'

She went through the house, three flights of wide stairs, one of steep and narrow. Mrs Mullen did not trouble to follow, knowing it would all be decided satisfactorily.

The summer wind beat at the small latched windows but daylight changed its nature, making it seem a soft wind, and benign. The floorboards were dusty. Kestrel opened a cupboard set deep into the wall. The shelves were lined with newspaper and smelled of nothing worse than mothballs and old fluff. One of the rooms was completely empty, the second contained only a cracked leather trunk, but the two rooms next to one another, in the middle of the row, had furniture – an iron bed in each, a chest of drawers, a mirror. One had a wicker chair, one a musty velvet stool. And cupboards, more cupboards. She had lived here for over forty years and remembered a time when the attic rooms had been for maids. Now, there was Mrs Mullen, who had the basement, and a woman who came on a bicycle from a village on the other side of the fen.

The rooms could be made right, she thought, though vague as to exactly what children might need to make them so. Curtains? Rugs? Toys?

Well, linen at least.

'The attics,' she said, coming down from them, 'will do nicely.'

Kestrel Dickinson had been an only child for fourteen years before two sisters were born, Dora first and then Violet. Dora was plain and brown-eyed with brown straight hair and placid under the spotlight of every-one's attention. Their mother tried to conceal her disappointment, firstly that Dora was not a boy and secondly that she was not beautiful, though her love for both girls was never in doubt. Violet was born two years and two days after Dora and grew into a pert and extremely pretty child, with blonde bubble curls and intensely blue eyes, and was adored. She smiled, lisped, talked early, looked beautiful in frills, never got her clothes dirty, and laughed with delight at everyone who looked in her direction.

From the first Dora hated her and Violet learned quickly to meet like with like. As they grew into children and then young women, they quar-relled and despised one another. From the beginning the root of it all was Dora's jealousy, but Violet, who had had her head turned early, quickly turned proud, self-absorbed and boastful. In her turn, Dora behaved with pettiness and spite. Their feud became life-long. Violet married when she was eighteen, and again, at twenty-five and thirty-three. After that she had a succession of lovers but did not bother to marry them. When she was forty-two, she had her first and only child, Leonora, by a rich man called Philip van Vorst, before she embarked on eight years of restless travel, from Kenya to Paris, Peking to Los Angeles, Las Vegas to Hong Kong. Her daughter travelled with her, growing quickly used both to their nomadic life, a succession of substitute fathers, hotels, money and, like her mother, being pretty, spoilt, admired and both lonely and dissatisfied.

Violet rarely returned home, but whenever she did, she and Dora picked up their animosity where it had been left, always finding fresh things about which to quarrel. Violet's frivolous, amoral, butterfly nature infuriated her sister. She knew she behaved better, led a more wholesome life, but never managed to feel that these counted for anything when her sister arrived home showering presents out of her suitcases. The

adoration she had always received shone out again from parents, servants, friends, everything that had been complained of was set aside. Dora,
plain and brown, simmered in corners and, long into adult life, plotted
obscure revenge. Violet had had three husbands, innumerable lovers –
usually handsome, always rich – and a daughter with enviable looks.
Dora had had one rather anonymous suitor who had never confessed any
feelings for her and who had eventually faded from her life over a period
of several months, while she remained waiting in hope.

By this time, Kestrel was long married and living at Iyot House,
though she did not have children of her own and had detached herself
from her feuding sisters, but had never stopped feeling guilt that she had
not somehow succeeded in uniting them.

And then, in the flurry of less than three months, Dora had met and
married George Cayley, a local widower almost thirty years her senior. A
year later she had produced her small, frail son, Edward. Two years later
both she and George were dead.

Kestrel inherited Iyot House from her own husband after a short marriage. At first she had disliked it and the expanse of dun-coloured fens,
their watery aspect and huge oppressive skies, the isolation and lack of
friends, the oddness of the villagers. In time, though, she grew used to
it and found some sort of spirit half-hidden there. She had people to stay
in the spring and summer and for the rest of the year was happy with her
own company and her painstaking work as a botanical illustrator.

From Violet there came the occasional, erratic postcard which rarely
mentioned her daughter Leonora but she heard nothing of her orphaned
nephew until a letter had come asking if he might spend the summer at
Iyot House. In some desperation she wrote to Violet.

'They are cousins after all and he will need a companion.'

It was settled.

Three

'Edward Cayley,' he wrote in the steamed-up train window. 'Edward Laurence Cayley.' Then rubbed it out with his sleeve.

He had been driven from the house by his half-brother's business chauffeur and hurried across the concourse of Liverpool Street as if he must be bundled out of sight as quickly as possible. The driver carried his case; he carried a small hold-all. The station smelled of smoke, which tasted on his tongue and caught the back of his throat. His hold-all and suitcase had labels tied on with his name and the station to which he was travelling. He was put in charge of the guard, inspected, turned round, and then put into the van.

'Two hours.' The guard had several missing teeth and the rest were brown.

After that, there was nothing. No one looked at or spoke to him, he had nothing to eat or drink. The train steamed on. He saw cows and churches, fields and houses, dykes and people on bicycles. He did not think and he did not feel, he simply accepted, having learned that accepting was the best and safest way.

He was neither happy nor unhappy: he was a frozen child, as he had been since he had arrived at the house of a half-brother who neither loved nor wanted him but who, with his wife, had looked after him dutifully, without fault or favour.

He was a pale, fair, thin boy, small for his age but fit and wiry now and with a sensitive and intelligent face. He was liked. It was taken for granted that he would find his way easily in life, that excuses would never need to be made for him.

But, looking out at the cows and sheep and churches and dykes and people on bicycles, he was unaware of any of this. He wrapped himself in a bubble of unknowing.

Leonora van Vorst travelled alone from Geneva the same day, with her

name on a badge pinned to her coat and a brown suitcase covered in ship-
ping line labels, thrown from porter to porter and, finally, to the driver
of a hire car which was to take her from Dover to Iyot Lock. To anyone
watching her follow the last porter with her case on his shoulder and her
round overnight bag in his left hand, across the dock from the boat, she
looked small, solemn and lost, but within herself, she was tall, confident
and superior. She had money inside her glove for the last tip. The driver
loaded her cases and pinched her cheek, feeling sorry for what he thought
of as 'the little mite'. Leonora frowned and climbed into the back of the
car without speaking. She was self-possessed, calm, haughty, and without
any sense that there was such a thing as love, or vulnerability.

The car sped east and after only a few miles she began to feel sick,
but fearing to mention it, and seem weak, she closed her eyes and imagined a sheet of smooth black paper, as her mother had once taught her,
and eventually the nausea faded and she slept. Through the rear mirror
the driver saw a white-faced child with a halo of red hair spread behind
her on the back of the seat, lips pinched together and an expression he
could not exactly make out, partly of detachment, partly of something
like defiance.

Four

'How do you do?' The boy put out his hand, Aunt . . .' But his voice wavered on the 'Kestrel.'

'Lord, I'm not your aunt. You'd better come in.' Mrs Mullen looked down at the boy's bags, both small. The taxi had already turned and started down the long straight road twelve miles back to the station.

'Well, pick them up.' She had no intention of waiting on two children.

'Oh. Yes.'

She did not know how a boy of eight should look but Edward Cayley seemed thin, his knee-caps protruding awkwardly from bony little legs. His hair was freshly cut, too short, leaving a fringe of bristle on his neck.

'Put them down there.'

'Yes.'

They stood in the dimness of the hall staring at one another in silence for a full minute, Mrs Mullen struck by an unfamiliar sympathy for a child who was not like the few children she had known, who had been sturdy, loud, greedy, grubby and disrespectful. That was how village children were. Edward Cayley was the opposite of all those things and though she did not yet know about his appetite, no boy so thin, and pale as a peeled willow, could surely be a big eater.

Edward looked at Mrs Mullen, and then at his own feet, knowing that staring round a strange house was impolite. He could think of nothing to say, though he wondered who the woman was and where his Aunt Kestrel was, while knowing that the behaviour of adults was generally inexplicable.

The house smelled strange, half of living, breathing smells, half of age and damp.

'Wait there.'

'Yes.'

The woman disappeared into the dimness and a door bumped softly shut. He waited. All he knew was that Aunt Kestrel was related to the dead mother he did not remember and that he was to stay with her at Iyot for some weeks of this summer. He supposed that was enough.

In her dressing room, Kestrel adjusted her necklace, wondered if she should change it for another, put up her hands to the clasp and froze. The boy was here, and she was anxious. She had seen him once, as a baby of a month old, she did not know what he would be like and she was unused to children, but she was not innately hostile to them like Mrs Mullen. She wanted to make the boy comfortable, for him to talk to her, find entertainment, not be homesick or bored and now that he was here, her nerve failed her. But at least he would not be lonely.

The house was silent. Mrs Mullen had announced Edward's arrival and then disappeared. Aunt Kestrel, as she must now think of herself, replaced the necklace and went downstairs.

They had lunch in the dining room, he and the aunt, and he sat quiet, pale and watchful, eating everything he was offered quite slowly, made nervous by the room itself, with its heavy red curtains held back by brass rods, and large portraits of men with horses and dogs and women with hats and distant children.

'Are you enjoying your lunch? Is there anything else you would like?' He sensed with surprise that his aunt was as nervous as he was, and far more anxious to please. His own wish was more negative – not to annoy anyone, not to provoke irritation, not to be chastised, not to break anything. He had been warned so many times about the breaking of objects, of china and ornaments and even windows, that he was in a state of suspended terror, passing by the dresser with its huge dishes, small tables with glass paperweights and gilded figurines.

'Is your drink too strong?'

'It's very nice, thank you.'

It was lemon squash diluted so much that the water was barely tinted.

'Do you like lamb chop?'

'Yes, thank you.'

'And how was your train journey? Were you properly looked after?'

'Yes, thank you. I travelled in the guard's van with the guard.'

'Quite right. But was that uncomfortable?'

It had been. He had been forced to sit on someone's leather trunk, next to cardboard boxes of live chicks which chirped and rustled about and then went still, until they were put out onto a station platform somewhere.

But the guard had shared a chocolate bar with him and told him stories about famous railway murders and ghosts in tunnels.

'It was very nice, thank you.'

He looked up from his plate at Aunt Kestrel just as she looked straight at him. They took one another in. She looked old to him, with a tweedy skirt and a buttoned blouse, and several rings on her left hand, but her face was soft and not at all unkind.

To her, the boy was alarmingly like his mother in profile, with the same long straight nose and small mouth, but his full face was like no one she recognised. He was nervous, polite and private, his true thoughts and feelings all his own and kept hidden. His manner deterred any questions other than those about the food and drink and his journey.

'Your cousin Leonora will come tomorrow. Have you met her before?'

He shook his head, his mouth full of pears and custard.

'I thought not. She is your Aunt Violet's only child – Violet and your mother were sisters and . . . well, and I was sister to them both, of course. But older. Much older.'

He said nothing.

'So you are quite close in age. I hope you'll get on.'

He did not know what to say, having no sense at all of what it might be like to spend a whole summer with a girl cousin he had never seen.

'What would you like to do now? Do you have a rest after lunch? I'm afraid I'm not used to – to what children . . . boys . . . do. Have you brought any books to read or do you play with . . . Or you could go into the garden.'

He followed her into the hall. 'But I expect you'd like to see your room and so on now.'

'Thank you.'

Mrs Mullen appeared from behind a baize-covered door.

'I'll take him up then shall I?'

He did not want her to but could not have said and they all three stood about uncertainly for a moment.

'Well, perhaps I should . . . you carry on with the dining room, Mrs Mullen.'

He noted the name.

'Pick those up then,' Mrs Mullen said, pointing to his bags, the small one and the very small.

'Yes.'

Edward picked them up and followed his aunt to the stairs.

Five

'At what time should you go up?'

Edward looked up from the solitaire board. Aunt Kestrel had unlocked a cupboard in the drawing room, whose blinds were pulled down all day as well as at night, and found the solitaire, a shove ha'penny board and a pile of jigsaw puzzles which he taken up to the attics. He examined the glass marbles again. They were wonderful colours, deep sea green, brilliant blue, blood red, and clear glass enclosing swirls of misty grey. The board was carved out of rosewood with green velvet covering the underside.

'Do you have something to eat first, or . . .'

'I have milk and two biscuits at seven and then I go to bed.'

'Of course, these are the holidays; I daresay rules should be stretched. When would you like to go up?'

The idea that he could choose his own time, that routine was not made of iron but could be broken, was not only new but alarming.

'I am quite tired,' he said, moving a blue marble over a clear glass one, to leave only seven on the board. His aunt had shown him how to play and as it had been raining, he had done so, sitting beside the window, for most of the afternoon. Seven was the smallest number he had got down to without being unable to move again.

'You have had a rather dull day.'

'It has been very nice, thank you.'

Kestrel was taken aback again by the opaque politeness of the child.

'You will have more fun when Leonora arrives. And this miserable rain. We don't get a lot of rain at Iyot but we do get wind. Wind and skies.'

He thought everyone had sky, or skies, but perhaps this was not the case. He didn't ask.

'Five!' he said under his breath, removing another blue.

'Excellent.'

Mrs Mullen brought in a small glass of milk and two garibaldi biscuits on a lacquer tray.

'Thank you very much,' he said, stopping in the doorway. 'I have had a very nice day.'

His earnest, unformed face stayed with Kestrel for a long time after he had gone. He was her own flesh and blood, he was part of her. She did not know him, as she had not known Dora after she had grown up and married, and yet she felt connected to him and his words touched her deeply, his vulnerability impressed itself on her so that she felt suddenly afraid on his behalf and had an urge to protect him. But he had gone, his footsteps mounting the stairs carefully until they went away to the fourth flight and the attics.

Once he was there, Edward put his milk and the hated garibaldi biscuits carefully on the table beside his bed, and went to look out of the window. It was very high. The sky was huge and full of sagging leaden clouds, making the night seem closer than it was by the clock. Ragged jackdaws whirled about on the wind like scraps of torn burned paper. He could see the church tower, the churchyard, the road, and the flat acres of fen with deep dykes criss-crossing them. A small stone bridge. A brick cottage beside a lock, though he did not yet know that was what it was called.

He drank the milk in small sips and wondered what he could do with the biscuits that he could not have swallowed any more than he could have swallowed a live spider. In the end, he opened the cupboard in the wall. It was completely empty. He broke off a corner of the biscuit and crumbled it onto the plate, and climbed up and put the rest far back on the highest shelf he could reach. Perhaps mice would find it. He was not afraid of mice.

And then, as he turned round, he felt something strange, like a rustle of chill across his face, or someone blowing towards him. It was sound-less but something in the cupboard caught his eye and he thought that the paper lining the shelves had lifted slightly, as if the movement of air had caught that too.

He went back to the window but it was closed tightly, and the latch was across. It was the same with the window on the other side. He touched the door but it was closed firmly and it did not move. The room was still again.

Five minutes later, he was in bed, lying flat on his back with the sheet just below his chin, both hands holding it. The wind had got up now. The windows rattled, the sound round the rooftop above him grew louder and then wild, as the gale came roaring across the fen to hit the old house and beat it about the head.

Edward did not remember such a wind but it was outside and could not get in, and so he was not in the least afraid, any more than he was afraid of the sound of rain, or the rattle of hail on a pane. He had left the wall cupboard slightly open but the lining paper did not lift, and there was no chill breeze across his face. This was just weather. This was different.

He went to sleep rocked by the storm, and it howled through his dreams and made him turn over and over in the narrow bed, and in her own room, Kestrel lay troubled by it not for herself, well used to it as she was, but for the boy. At one point when the gale was at its height she almost got up and went to him, but surely, if he were alarmed he would call out, and she felt shy of indicating her feelings or of transmitting alarm. High winds were part of the warp and weft of the place and the old house absorbed them without complaint.

He would get used to them, and when Violet's child came tomorrow, so would she, whatever she was like.

A vision of her sister came into Kestrel's mind as she fell asleep, of the bubble curls and pretty mouth and the coquettish charm she had been mistress of at birth. Leonora. Leonora van Vorst. What sort of a child would Leonora be?

Six

He was sitting on the edge of his bed reading and as he still did not find reading easy, although he loved what he discovered in a book when he found the key to it, he had to concentrate hard and so he did not hear the footsteps on the last flights of uncarpeted stairs or their voices. He read on and one set of footsteps went away again and it was quiet, late afternoon. It had stopped raining, the wind had dropped and there was an uncertain sun on the watery fens.

And then he was aware of her, standing just inside the doorway, and looked up with a start.

'You seem to be very easily frightened,' she said.

Edward stared at the girl. She had dark red hair, long and standing out from her head as if she had an electric shock running through her, and dark blue eyes in a china white face.

'I'm not frightened at all.'

She smiled a small superior smile and came right into the room to stand a yard or two away from him.

He slid off the bed, remembering manners he had been taught almost from the cradle, and put out his hand.

'I am Edward Cayley,' he said. 'I suppose you're my cousin Leonora.'

She looked at the hand but did not take it.

'How do you do?'

She smiled again, then turned abruptly and went to the window.

'This is a dreadful place,' she said. 'What are we supposed to do?'

'It isn't actually terrible. It is quiet though.'

'Who is that woman?'

'Our aunt. Aunt Kestrel.'

Leonora tossed her hair. 'The other one, with the sour face.'

He smiled. 'Mrs Mullen.'

'She doesn't like us.'

'Doesn't she?'

'Don't be stupid, can't you tell? But what does it matter?' She looked round his room, summing its contents up quickly, then sat down on the bed.

'Where have you come from?' He opened his mouth to say 'London' but she carried on without waiting to hear. 'I came from Geneva this time,' she said, 'but before that from Hong Kong and before that from Rome. Not that way round.'

'How did you do that?'

'Well on a ship and a train, of course. I might have flown but it seemed better.'

'Not on your own.'

'Of course on my own, why not? Did you have to have someone to bring you, like an escort.'

'I came in charge of the guard.'

'Oh yes, I've done that. I came in charge of stewards and so on.' She bounced off the bed. 'Your mother's dead.'

'I know.'

'What did she die of?'

'I'm not sure. No one has ever said.'

'Goodness. My mother's alive, so is my father, but somewhere else. At the moment my stepfather is called Claude. I hope he stays, I quite like Claude, but, of course, he won't, they never do for long.'

He caught sight of her face then and it was strange and sad and distant.

'We could go out into the garden.'

'Why? Is it interesting? I don't expect so. Gardens aren't usually.'

'Our aunt found some jigsaw puzzles.'

Leonora was at the window.

'Shall I get them out?'

'I don't want to do one but you can.'

'No, it's all right. How long did it take you to get here?'

'Two days. I slept on the boat train.'

'Were you sick?'

He had gone to stand beside her at the window and he saw that he had made her angry.

'I am never sick. I am an excellent sailor. I suppose you're sick.'

'Anyway, it doesn't matter. Some people are, some aren't and you can't die of being sick.'

Her eyes seemed to darken and the centres to grow smaller. 'Where do you think people go when they die?'

Edward hesitated. He did not know how to behave towards her, whether she wanted to be friendly or hostile, if she was worried about something or about nothing.

'They go to heaven. Or . . . to God.'

'Or to hell.'

'I'm not sure.'

'Hell isn't fire you know.'

'Isn't it?'

'Oh no. Hell is a curse. You're forced to wander this world and you can never escape.'

'That sounds all right. It's what – you wander this world. You've wandered to all those places.'

He could sense something in her that needed reassurance and could not ask for it. He did not know, because he was too young and had never before encountered it, that what he sensed in Leonora was pride. Later, he was to understand, though still without having a word for it.

'Do you remember your mother?'

'No. Aunt Kestrel does but she didn't want to talk about her.'

'What, because it might upset you? How could you be upset about a mother you don't remember?'

'No. I think it – it might have upset her.'

'Oh.'

That was something else he would come to know well, the tone of her voice that signified boredom.

'Tomorrow we'll play a trick on that woman,' she said next. 'I'll think of something she won't like at all.' She sounded so full of a sort of evil glee at the idea that she alarmed him.

'I don't think we ought to do that.'

Leonora turned on him in scorn. 'Why? Do you want to be her favourite and have her pet you?'

He flushed. 'No. I just think it would be a bad thing to do. And mean.'

'Of course it would be a bad thing to do. And mean. How silly you are.'

'I don't think she's very nice but perhaps it's because she hasn't any children of her own or doesn't know any.'

'Aunt Kestrel hasn't any children but she doesn't hate us.'

'I don't think Mrs Mullen would hate us.'

'Of course she hates us. And I am going now to think about what trick to play.'

'Where are you going?'

But she had already gone. She came and went so silently and completely that he wondered if she did not move at all but simply knew how to just appear and disappear.

He did not see her again until the bell rang for supper and then, just as he was going across the hall, she was there, when she had not been there a second before.

From now on, he determined to watch her.

'Have you thought?'

But Leonora stared at him blankly across the table.

'I wish the weather would improve,' Aunt Kestrel said, slicing a teacake and buttering half for each of them. 'You would find so many good things to do out of doors.'

'What things?'

Aunt Kestrel looked like someone caught out in a lie. That is how Leonora makes me feel, Edward realised, as if she can see through me to my soul and know what I am thinking and if I am telling the truth, or trying to bluff my way out of something.

She had not yet been here for a whole day and already the mood of the house had been changed entirely.

'My mother is said to be the most beautiful woman who has ever lived,' Leonora said now. 'Did you know that?'

'How ridiculous,' Aunt Kestrel said, spluttering out some little droplets of tea. 'Of course she is not. Violet was a pretty little girl and grew up to be a pretty woman, though she was helped by clothes and having people to bring out the best in her.'

'What people?'

'Oh, hairdressers and . . . you know, those people.. But as to being the most beautiful woman who ever lived . . . besides, who could know?'

'It was written in a magazine of fashion.' Leonora's face had changed as a blush of annoyance rose through the paleness and her eyes darkened. 'It was written under her photograph so it would have to be true. Of course it is true. She is very, very beautiful. She is.' Edward watched in horror as Leonora stood up and picked up a small silver cake fork. 'She is, she is, she is.' As she said it, she stabbed the fork down into the cloth and through to the table, one hard stab for each word. Aunt Kestrel's mouth was half open, her arm slightly outstretched as if she meant to stop the dreadful stabbing, but was unable to make any movement.

'And no one is allowed to say it is not true.'

She dropped the fork on the floor and it spun away from her, and then she was gone, the skirt of her blue cotton frock seeming to flick out behind her and then disappear as she disappeared. The door closed slowly of its own accord. Edward sat, wishing that he was able to disappear too but forced to wait for Aunt Kestrel's anger to break over him and take whatever punishment there might be, for them both.

There was none. His aunt sat silent for a moment then said, 'I wonder if you can find out what is wrong, Edward?'

He sped to the door. 'She is like her mother,' she said as he went, but he thought that she was speaking to herself, not to him.

'She is too like her mother.'

Seven

He did not see Leonora and the door of her room was shut. He hesitated, listening. The wind had dropped. There was no sound from her and he opened his mouth to say her name, then did not, afraid that her anger was still raging and that she might turn it on him. He thought of the cake fork stabbing into the table.

The house no longer felt strange to him but he did not like it greatly and he was disappointed that his cousin seemed unlikely to become a friend. She was strange, if Iyot House and their Aunt Kestrel were not. She belonged with Mrs Mullen, he thought, turning on his left side. The last of the light was purple and pale blue in a long thread across the sky, seen through the window opposite his bed. It had not been like this before. Perhaps there would be sun tomorrow and they could explore the world outside. Perhaps things would improve, as in Edward's experience they often did. His school had improved, his eczema had improved, his dog had improved with age after being disobedient and running away all through puppy-hood.

He went to sleep optimistically.

There was moonlight and so he could see her when he woke very suddenly.

Leonora was standing in the doorway, her nightgown as white as her skin, her red hair standing out from her head. She was absolutely still, her eyes oddly blank and for several moments Edward thought that she was an apparition. Or a ghost. What was the difference?

'Hello?'

She didn't reply.

'Are you quite all right?'

She did not move. He saw that her feet were bare. Long pale feet. He did not know what to do.

And then she came further into the room, silently on the long pale feet, her hair glowing against the whiteness of her skin and long nightgown.

'Leonora?'

She had walked to the window and was looking out, washed by the moonlight.

Edward got up and went to stand beside her. At first he did not touch her, hardly dared to look directly at her. He had the odd sense that if he did touch her she would feel cold.

'Are you still asleep?'

She turned her head and stared at him out of the blank unseeing eyes.

'You should go back to your own room now. You could hurt yourself.'

Stories of people walking out of windows and far from home across fields and into woods while they were deeply asleep came into his mind.

You should not try to wake a sleepwalker, the shock could kill them. You should not touch a sleepwalker, or they may stay that way and never wake again.

He began to panic when Leonora sat on the ledge and started to undo the window latch, and then he did reach out and touch her shoulder. She stopped but did not look at him.

'Come on. We're going back now.'

He nudged her gently and she got up and let him guide her out of his room and back to her own. He steered her to the bed, pulled back the covers and she climbed in obediently, and turned on her side. Her eyes closed. Edward spread the covers over her with care and watched her until he was sure she was fully asleep, then crept out.

Eight

'Oh do hurry up, hurry up . . .'

Aunt Kestrel came into the hall. 'If you are going out you need stout shoes. The grass is very wet.'

Leonora ignored her, hand on the front door.

Edward looked at his feet. Were the shoes 'stout'?

'Well, perhaps you'll be all right. Don't go too far.'

'Hurry up,' Leonora said again. The inner door opened and she went to the heavy outer one, which had a large iron key and a bolt and chain.

'Anyone would suppose ravening beasts and highwaymen would be wanting to burst in,' she said, laughing a small laugh.

Mrs Mullen was in the dark recesses of the hall watching, lips pinched together.

Aunt Kestrel sighed as she closed both doors. She was confused by the children, and bewildered. Leonora was like Violet, which boded ill though perhaps not in quite the same way, who knew? Edward was simply opaque. Had they taken to one another? Were they settling?

She went into her sitting room with the morning paper.

Mrs Mullen did not ask the same questions because she had made up her mind from seeing both children, Edward, the little namby-pamby, too sweet-tongued to trust, and Leonora. She had looked into Leonora's eyes when she had first arrived, and seen the devil there and her judgment was made and snapped shut on the instant.

'Where are you going?' Edward watched his cousin going to the double gates. 'The garden is on this side.'

Leonora gave her usual short laugh. 'Who wants to go in a garden?'

She lifted the latch of a small gate within the gate and stepped through. He went after her because he thought he should look after her and persuade her to come back, but by the time he had clambered over the bottom strut she was walking fast down the road and a minute later, had crossed it and started up the path that led to the open fens.

'Leonora, we'd better not . . .'

She tossed her red hair and went on.

When he caught her up she was standing on the bank looking down into the river. It was inky and slick and ran quite slowly.

'Be careful.'

'Can you swim?'

'No, can you?'

'I wonder what you can do. Of course I can swim, one of my stepfathers taught me in . . . I think it was Italy.'

'How many have you had? Stepfathers?'

She did not answer, but moved away and followed a rivulet that led away from the main course deep into the fen. They looked back. Iyot House reared up, higher than the other huddled houses, dark behind its trees. The church rose like a small ship towards the west.

It was very still, not cold. The reeds stood like guardsmen.

'Where are we going?'

'Anywhere.'

But it was only a little further on when she stopped again. The rivulet had petered out and widened to form a pool, which reflected the sky, the clouds which were barely moving.

'There might be newts here,' Edward said.

'Are they like lizards?'

'I think so.'

'There are lizards everywhere in hot countries. On stones. On walls. They slither into the cracks. Are you afraid of things like that?'

'I've never seen one.'

She faced him, her eyes challenging, dark as sloes in her face.

'Are you afraid of hell? Or snakes or mad bulls or fire coming out of people's mouths?'

Edward laughed.

'You should be careful,' she said softly. 'Mind what you laugh at. See if there are any of your newt things in there.'

They bent over and, instinctively, Edward reached out to take her hand in case she went too near to the edge. Leonora snatched it away as if his own had burned her, making him almost lose his balance.

'Don't you ever dare to do that again.'

He wanted to weep with frustration at this girl who made him feel stupid, and so as not to show his face to her, he knelt down and stared into the water, trying hopelessly to see newts, or frogs – any living, moving creature.

'Oh. How strange.'

Leonora was pointing to the smooth, still surface of the water. At first, Edward could not see anything except the sky, which now had patches of blue behind the white clouds. He looked harder and saw what he thought was – must be – Leonora's face reflected in the water, and there was his own, wavery but recognisably him.

Leonora's red hair spread out in the water like weed, and the collar of her blue frock was clear, and a little of her long pale neck. But her face was not the same. Or rather, it was the same but . . .

'Oh,' he said.

'Who is it?' Leonora whispered.

He could not tell her. He could not say, because he did not really know, who he saw or what. He reached out his hand to her and she held it fast in her own, so tight that it seemed to hurt his bones.

'What is it? What can you see?'

She went on staring, still gripping his hand, but even when he bent down, Edward could only make out the blurred reflection of both their faces upside down. There was nothing behind them and you could not see below.

'You're hurting my hand.'

And then, she was scrabbling in the earth for small stones, and clods of turf, and then larger stones. She threw them into the water and then hurled the largest one and their images splintered and the water rocked and in a moment, stilled again and there they were, the boy Edward, the girl Leonora. Nothing else.

'I don't understand,' Edward said. But she had gone, racing away from him along the path. He watched her, troubled, but he knew he ought not to let her be by herself, sensing that she was quixotic and unsafe, and followed her from a distance but always keeping her in sight as she ran in the direction of Iyot Church.

Nine

'What did you see?' Edward asked.

He had found her wandering round the side aisles looking at memorial tablets set into the walls and brasses into the floor, running her hand over the carved pew ends and the steps of the pulpit, lifting the hassocks off their hooks and dropping them onto the pews, going restlessly, pointlessly from one to the other.

She did not answer. He was worried, felt responsible.

'I think we should go now. Maybe we aren't allowed in here at all.'

Leonora came to his side, smiling. 'What do you think would happen to us?'

'We'd get into trouble.'

'Who from?'

'The parson.'

She shook her head. Her hair lifted and seemed to float out from her head, then settle back.

'God?'

'Or the devil.'

'Why would the devil care? It isn't his place.'

'Do you believe in them?'

'Of course I do,' Edward said. 'Look – that is God, in that window.'

'And there is the devil, at the bottom of that picture.' Her voice was scornful.

'No, that's a snake.'

'The devil is a serpent, which is what a snake is in the Bible. I know a lot about it.'

'I still think we should go.'

But before he could move, Leonora had taken hold of his hand again and was pressing her fingernails into the palm. She was staring at a large silver plate that stood on a dark wooden chest against the wall beside them.

'What's the matter? I think it's for collecting money. You know, when they go round.'

But she seemed not to hear him, only went on looking at the shining circle, her face pale as paper, eyes coal-dark.

He got up and went to the dish. His own face reflected shimmering in the surface though it was distorted and hard to make out.

'Don't look,' Leonora said. 'Move away from it, don't look.'

'Why? It isn't dangerous.'

He was about to bend right over and put his face very close to the silver, when Leonora leaped up, lifted the plate and hurled it away from her down the aisle. It crashed against the stone flags and then went rolling crazily until it spun and fell flat in a corner.

'Why did you do that?'

But she was gone again, out of the church, leaving the door wide open, and away down the path before jumping off between two high grave-stones. The wind had got up again and was bending the tall uncut grasses and the branches of the yew.

This time, Edward did not race after her. He was tired of what he decided was some sort of game which she would not explain to him and in which he had no part, but he also thought that she was trying to frighten him and he was not going to allow it.

He came slowly out of the church and down the path to the gate. Then he looked round but could not see her. She had gone back to the house then. He would see her racing down the road.

As he put his hand on the gate, the heavy wooden door of the church banged loudly shut behind him in the wind.

Leonora was nowhere ahead. He turned, and then caught a glimpse of her, low down behind the stone wall among the gravestones. The wind caught the edge of her blue frock and lifted it a little.

'Leonora . . .'

What he saw on her face when she glanced round was a look so full of malice and evil, so twisted and distorted with dislike and scorn and a sort of laughing hatred, that he wanted to be the one to run, to get away as fast as he could, back to what he now thought of as the safety and shelter of Iyot House. But as long as she looked at him, he could not move, his limbs, his body, even his breath, seemed to be paralysed. He could not even cry out or speak because his lungs and his mouth felt full of heavy sand. Her look lasted for hours, for years; he was struck dumb and mo-tionless for a lifetime, while Leonora held his gaze.

But he was just as suddenly free and light as air and full of almost electric energy, and he ran.

The hands of the clock on the church tower had not moved.

For the rest of that day and several days more they fell under the spell of Bagatelle, after Aunt Kestrel had unearthed the old set and taught the game to them.

'And if you grow tired of that, here are the cards. I will teach you Piquet.'

But they did not grow tired. The weather changed and became hot, with clear, blue skies that paled to white on the horizon and a baking sun. The streams dried, the pond was lower, the river ran sluggishly. The air smelled of heat, heat seemed to fill their mouths and scratch at their eyes. They went into the garden under the shade of a huge copper beech and set the Bagatelle board out on an old table. Mrs Mullen brought a jug of lukewarm lemon barley and the despised garibaldi biscuits and they played game after game, mainly in silence. At first, Leonora won. She was quicker and slyer and saw her chances. Edward was cautious and steady. At home he played chess with his half-brother.

There was a small fish pond over which dragonflies hovered, their blue sheen catching the sun, and the flower beds were seething with bees.

'At last,' Aunt Kestrel said, as Mrs Mullen brought in her coffee. 'They have settled down together perfectly well.'

Mrs Mullen went to the window and saw the table, the game, the boy and girl bent over the board, one fair head, one brilliant red. She mistrusted the girl and thought the boy a namby-pamby. Either way, having children to stay in the house had not altered her opinion, except to harden it against them.

'I agree with you that Leonora behaved very badly, but we have to forgive her. It is all so strange and odd for them. Don't bear a grudge, Mrs Mullen.'

After the housekeeper had gone out of the room, Kestrel sat thinking about her, wondering why she was so very hostile, so clearly unable to warm to either child in any way, so readily seeing the bad and fearing worse. She knew little of her background and former life, other than that she had no children and her husband worked as a bargeman. Why she was so embittered she could not fathom.

The heat continued until the air grew stale and every morning was more oppressive than the last. The sun filmed over with a haze and midges jazzed above the waterways.

'Time we had a storm,' Aunt Kestrel said over supper at the beginning of the third week of heat.

Edward looked apprehensive. Leonora, on the other side of the table, saw his face and frowned. The previous day he had beaten her three times at Bagatelle and now she played with an angry concentration, determined to win and breathless with silent fury when, time after time, she did not.

The heat formed a heavy cloud that hung low over the garden, obscuring any sun. Edward's skin itched inside his clothes.

'Let's stop.'

'No. I have to win first.'

'You can win another time. It's too hot.'

'Stupid. I said I want to win first, then we can stop.'

'You might not win for another ten games. I'm going to read indoors by the window.'

In a single flash of movement, Leonora stood up, overturned the Bagatelle board, sending it flying onto the grass and scattering its pieces, and then she screamed, a terrible, violent scream, so loud that Edward ran from her and from the awful sound of it, across the garden, up the steps and into the house, slamming the heavy door behind him.

Mrs Mullen was in the shadows of the hall, making him start.

'I said everything would be turned upside down and we would have nothing but upset and disturbance, but never did I expect what came here.'

Edward dared not move.

'Listen to it.'

She was still screaming without apparently needing to pause for breath.

'It will turn you as well. In the end, there'll be not a pin to put between you. Can you not feel it?'

'Feel it?' Edward could scarcely hear his own voice speaking into the dark hall.

'What possesses her? Can you not feel it creeping over you too? No child could come within sight of her and not be turned.' She came out of the shadows and went smartly to the door, turned the key and slid the bolt.

'What are you doing?'

'Shutting the door against her,' Mrs Mullen said. 'Now you get off upstairs out of the sight and sound of her while you've a chance.'

'But how will she get in?'

'Maybe she won't and that would be no bad thing.'

She left him.

For several minutes, Edward stood wondering what he should do but in the end, after listening for any sound of Mrs Mullen's return, he went to the drawing room, in which they had only been allowed to step once and where there were French windows opening onto the side terrace and the wide stone steps to the garden below. The air was sultry, the sky gathering into a yellowish mass like a boil over the house. He went to where they had been sitting earlier. The Bagatelle was still scattered over the grass and the table upturned.

'Ah, she's sent the good little boy to tidy up.' He spun round. Leonora had appeared from nowhere and was standing a few yards from him.

'I came to find you. She locked the door to keep you out but she shouldn't have done that. I think there is going to be a storm.'

'Are you frightened of storms?'

'No. But you might have been.'

Leonora laughed the dry little laugh 'I'm not afraid of anything at all.'

'You were frightened of something. You were frightened of something down in the water.'

She lunged forward, grabbed his arm and bent it backwards so that he cried out. 'You must never ever say that again and I didn't see anything and I was not afraid. I am never afraid. Say it. "Leonora is never afraid."' She twisted his arm a little further back.

'Leonora is never afraid let go of my arm you're hurting.'

'Manners, little boy. "Please."'

'Please.'

She almost tossed his arm away from her, turned and went round to the side of the house. Edward followed her, angry that he had bothered to worry about her and feel worried enough to come and find her.

She ran up the steps, and through the French windows which he had left ajar, but as he came up behind her, shut them quickly and turned the key. Then she stood, her face close to the glass, looking out at him, smiling.

Ten

Edward woke when his room flared white and then for a split second, vivid blue. The thunder came almost simultaneously, seeming to crack the attic roof open like an axe splitting a log. He sat up watching it through the curtainless window for a while, until hail spattered so fiercely onto the glass that sudden light and sudden dark were all he could see. He lay down and listened. He had been two or three years old when his half-brother had taken him on a boat and out to sea; they had huddled together in the small cabin as a storm flared and crashed all round them. His brother had been bright-eyed with excitement and Edward had sensed that this was something to revel in, knowing no danger, only the drama and heightened atmosphere. He had loved storms from then, though there had never been one so momentous. Now, this was almost as good, vast and overpowering across the fens and around Iyot House.

The lightning flickered vividly across the sky again and in the flash, he saw Leonora standing in the doorway of his room, her eyes wide, face stark white.

Edward sat up. 'It's amazing! I love storms.'

She went to his window. 'Yes.' She spoke in a whisper, as if she were afraid speaking aloud might change it.

Edward got up and stood beside her.

'You should see the storms in the East. A storm across the water in Hong Kong. A storm over the mountains. They race through your blood, such storms.'

He understood her at once and for the first time they shared something completely, bound up together in the excitement and pleasure of the storm, so that he clasped hold of her hand when a thunderclap made the house shake and the walls of the attics shudder and her nails dug into his palm at a blue-green zigzag of lightning.

'I thought you would be crying,' Leonora said, glancing at him sideways.

'Oh no, oh no!'

'We could go out.'

'Don't be silly, it's like a monsoon, we'd be soaked in a minute.'

'Have you been in a monsoon? I have. The earth steams and you could boil a pan of water on the ground. It brings down whole trees.'

'I want to go there.'

They were linked in a passion to soar from this storm to that one.

'My mother is there now,' Leonora said.

'Where? In a monsoon?'

'In India, I think. Or Burma. Or perhaps she is back in Hong Kong. They move about so.'

He was unsure whether to be envious or sorry for her.

'When will she come back for you?'

Leonora shrugged and flicked her hair about her shoulders. The storm was receding, the lightning moving away to the east and the sea, the rain easing to a steady, dull downpour.

'I hope she'll come before too long,' Edward said. 'You must miss her very much.'

'I don't,' Leonora said, 'and I don't.' And sailed out of the room on her bare and silent feet.

The next morning, the parcels began to arrive. There were two, one very large, one small, and after that, as the post from abroad caught up, one or two almost every day. Leonora took them upstairs, ignoring the remarks made by Mrs Mullen about spoilt children and the concern of Aunt Kestrel that perhaps some should be put away until later.

'They are my parcels,' she said, dragging a heavy one behind her, refusing help.

'But you,' she said to Edward, 'may look if you like.'

Most of the parcels contained clothes, few of which fitted, dresses made of bright silk embroidered with gold thread and decorated with little mirrors, trailing fine scarves and long skirts with several floating panels. Leonora glanced at each one, held it up to herself, then tossed it away, to fall on the floor or her bed. Once or twice she put on a scarf and twirled round in it and kept it on. There were silver boxes and carved wooden animals, brass bells and on one day a huge box of pale green and pink

Turkish delight that smelled of scent and sent a puff of white sugar into the air when she lifted the wooden lid. They ate several pieces, one small, sticky bite at a time, and the intense sweetness set their teeth on edge.

'My mother never sends what I really want. She just doesn't.'

'But the sweets are nice. What do you really want?'

'One thing.'

'What thing?'

'And she knows and she never sends it.'

'When is your birthday?'

'August the tenth; I am a Leo.'

'That is quite soon. So I think she is going to send it for then.'

Leonora ripped open the thin brown paper on her last parcel. It contained a black satin cushion covered in gold and silver beads.

'How horrible, horrible, *horrible*.' The cushion bumped against the far wall and fell.

Edward wiped the sugar powder off his mouth. 'What is it that you do really want?'

'A doll,' Leonora said. 'You would think she could easily send me a doll but she never, never, never does. I hate my mother.'

'No, you should never say that.'

'Why? I do.'

'No.'

'Why?'

'Because – you just shouldn't.'

'You don't know anything about it. You don't know anything about mothers because you haven't got one.'

'I know,' Edward said. 'But I did once have one.'

'If she sent me what I wanted I would be able to love her.'

He wondered if that could be true, that someone made you love them by giving you what you wanted, or, that you would not love them until they did. It was confusing.

'I think that she will send you a doll. I think you will get it on your birthday.'

But the birthday came and she did not.

Aunt Kestrel gave her an ivory carved chess set in a wooden casket, a set of hairbrushes and a jar of sweets, which she had handed to Edward the night before, to hand over as from himself. Leonora's face had been pinched and sallow and when she had taken her things upstairs, with the handkerchief embroidered with her initial from Mrs Mullen, Edward had gone in to their aunt's sitting room.

'She doesn't mean to be ungrateful.'

'No. It is hard to know what to give but I thought you might teach her chess as you are so fond of it.' The Bagatelle board had been damaged beyond repair by being left outside in the storm.

'Yes. It is her mother.'

Aunt Kestrel sighed.

'She sends her so many parcels with nice things but never what she really wants.'

'The trouble is, Violet barely knows her own child and always had more interest in herself than anyone else. You will please never repeat that, Edward.'

'No.'

He explained about the doll.

'It seems an obvious thing to send. But I am going to London next week. If Violet has not had the sense to send a doll, I must find one.'

Eleven

Another storm was building for the whole day Aunt Kestrel was away. The fen was dun green with the river like an oil slick where it ran deep between its banks. Edward watched the lock keeper pace slowly along, peering into the water, cross the bridge, then walk back. The thunder rumbled round the edges of the sky.

Leonora was sullen and silent, not wanting to learn chess, not wanting to have him anywhere near her. In the end, he found a book about adventures in the diamond mines of South Africa, and read it sitting on the windowsill. Mrs Mullen rang them down for lunch, which was cold beef, cold potatoes and hard boiled eggs, with custard to follow, and they ate it silently in the dining room as the rain began to teem down the windows.

Mrs Mullen did not come near to them for the rest of the day. She rang the supper bell, told them they must be in bed by eight o'clock, and disappeared behind her door.

Eight came and the attics were pitch dark. The storm had fizzled out but the rain was so loud they could not hear themselves speak, but did a jigsaw in silence. Leonora was bored and lost interest. Edward went to bed and read his book. He was not unhappy at Iyot House. He was a boy of equable temperament and no strong passions, who was never seriously unhappy anywhere, but tonight, he wished strongly that he could be at home in his own London bed. How long he and Leonora were staying here no one had said.

He usually slept deeply and dreamed little, but tonight, he fell into a restless, uncomfortable doze, skidding along the surface of strange dreams and hearing sounds that half woke him. He had an odd sense that something was about to happen, as if Iyot House and everyone in it were a bubbling pan about to boil over and hiss out onto a stove. In the middle of the night, he woke yet again, to the sound of crying, but it was not coming from his cousin's room, it came from somewhere near at hand and the crying was of a baby not a girl like Leonora.

He sat up. Everything was still. There was very little wind but clouds slid in front of a full moon now and again.

Nothing stirred. No one cried.

He lay down again but the strange sensation of foreboding did not leave him, even in sleep.

And then, a different sort of crying woke him, and this time he recognised it.

He went to Leonora. She had her head half underneath her pillow, which lifted and fell occasionally.

'It's all right.'

He pretended not to hear her when she told him to go away. It had been a miserable birthday and he was sorry for her.

'I want you to tell me something.'

She flung her pillow off her face. 'I said to . . .'

'I know but I'm not going to. I want you to tell me.'

Leonora turned her back on him.

'What kind of doll would you like best? I want you to tell me what it would look like, tell me everything.'

'Why? You can't get it for me so why would I tell you?'

'I can't get it for you but I can do something else.'

Silence. Then she sat up and pushed her hair out of her eyes. Edward was careful not to stare at her.

'I've got paper and some pencils and paints and I can draw it for you.'

She made a scornful sound in her throat.

'Isn't it better than no doll? And Aunt Kestrel is bringing you one.'

'She wouldn't find anything like this.'

'But she will find something nice.'

She described the doll she wanted very well, so that Edward could draw and then paint it with the greatest care. It was an Indian royal bride, with elaborate clothes and jewels and braiding in her hair, which Leonora knew in every tiny detail, every colour and shading and texture.

'Have you wanted one like it for a very long time?'

'Since I was about two or three. It is the only thing I ever ever wanted and my mother knows that and she has never got it for me.'

'Perhaps she tried hard and couldn't. Perhaps there has never been one like it in any shop.'

'Of course there hasn't, she should have had it made for me.'

He went on painting the doll, wondering as he did so why Leonora did not know that it was impolite to demand and want and order presents.

'I think it's finished but I shall put it here to dry.'

He was afraid to wait until she had looked at it and went back quietly to bed, and slept at once.

The following morning, he went by himself out to the garden early, before breakfast. Leonora did not follow him for a long time but eventually she came, carrying the picture he had painted.

'I'm sorry it's not a doll,' Edward said.

'Yes. But there will be a doll. Just exactly like this. I know there will.'

She put the painting down on the grass. She had not thanked him for it and he was not very surprised that she left it there when they had to run in from the heavy rain.

She asked a hundred times when Aunt Kestrel would be back from London. Mrs Mullen said, 'When she's ready.' Edward said cautiously that it might be after they were asleep.

'I won't go to sleep until I see the doll.'

She did not. It was after eleven o'clock when she woke Edward to say that she had heard the station taxi.

'Get up, get up, I'm going downstairs.'

Her eyes were wild with excitement and she had two small spots of colour burning in the pale of her face. She raced down the stairs so fast he was afraid she would trip but her feet seemed not to touch the ground. She burst into Aunt Kestrel's sitting room but then some sense of how to behave touched her enough to make her stop and say, 'I am sorry. I should have knocked on the door.' But her eyes had travelled straight to a large box, wrapped in brown paper, on the round table.

'You should both be in bed. It is very very late.'

Edward was about to defend his cousin by pointing out that she should be excused because she was so excited about her birthday present, but Leonora had already gone to the table and put her hand on the box.

'Is this for me, is this it?'

There was a silence. Kestrel was tired, and wanted only to give the child her present and have them all go to bed but she saw Violet in the greedy little face, a carelessness about anyone or anything except herself, let alone even the most ordinary politeness. She knew that she ought to reprimand, to withhold the box until the next morning, to start however belatedly to control this strange, proud, self-centred child to whom she felt she had a vague responsibility.

But this was not the time and besides, she could not face whatever scene might follow.

'Yes, you may open it but after that you must go to bed or you will make yourself overwrought and ill.'

Leonora gave her a swift, ecstatic smile and then started to open the parcel but the string had difficult knots, so that Aunt Kestrel was obliged to find her small scissors. The child's eyes did not leave the parcel. Edward held his breath. He prayed for the doll to be like to the one he had painted for her, as like as possible and if not, then every bit as grand.

The doll was in a plain oblong white box, tied with red ribbon. Now Leonora held her breath too, her small fingers trembling as she unpicked the bow. Edward moved closer, wanting to see, wanting to close his eyes.

There was the rustle of layer after layer of tissue paper as she unwrapped each sheet very carefully. And then she came to the doll.

It was a baby doll, large and made of china, with staring blue eyes and a rosebud mouth in a smooth, expressionless face. It wore a white cotton nightdress and beside it was a glass feeding bottle.

Neither Edward nor Kestrel ever forgot the next moments. Leonora looked at the doll, her body rigid, her hands clenched. Then, with what sounded like a growl which rose in pitch from deep in her throat into her mouth and became a dreadful animal howl, she lifted it out of the box, turned and hurled it at the huge marble fireplace. It hit a carved pillar and there was a crack as it fell, one large piece and a few shards broken from the head to leave a jagged hollow, so that in his shock Edward wondered crazily if brains and blood might spill out and spread over the hearth tiles.

There was a silence so absolute and terrible that it seemed anything might have happened next, the house split down the middle or the ground open into a fiery pit, or one of them to drop down dead.

Twelve

Leonora ran. Her footsteps went thundering up the stairs and they could hear them, even louder, even faster, as she reached the top flights. The door of her bedroom slammed shut.

Aunt Kestrel seemed to have difficulty catching her breath and at last Edward said, 'I'm sure she didn't mean to be hurtful.'

She looked at him out of eyes whose centres were like brilliant pin-points of light but said nothing. Edward went to the doll in the hearth, picked it up, together with the broken pieces of china head, and trailed out, afraid to speak, even to glance at Aunt Kestrel.

The attic floor was dark and silent. He hesitated at Leonora's door and listened. She must have heard him come upstairs and stop and did not want to see him. He went into his own room, carrying the doll, switched his bedside lamp on and sat down with it on his bed. The single large piece of china from its damaged head could probably be glued back, but the shards and fragments he thought were far too small. He sat holding it, wondering what he could do.

'Poor Dolly,' he said, holding it in his arms, rocking and stroking it.

The doll stared blankly, the crevasse in its china skull jagged, with cracks now running from it down the face like the spider cracks in walls. But he was bleary with tiredness and returned the doll to its box, put the lid back on and pushed it under his bed.

He slept restlessly, as if he had a fever, hearing the crack of the china doll hitting the fireplace and seeing Leonora's twisted, furious little face as she hurled it, and the wind howling through a crack in the window frame mingled with her scream. It was not yet midnight by his small travelling clock when he woke again. The wind still howled but in between he heard something else, fainter, and not so alarming.

He went out onto the landing. The wind was muffled and now he heard it more clearly he thought it was the sound of Leonora's crying. Her door was closed. Edward put his ear close to the wood. Silence. He waited. Still silence. He turned the handle slowly and eased open the door a very little. He could hear Leonora's very soft breathing but nothing else, no sobbing, no snuffling, nothing at all to show that she was crying now or had just been crying.

He could not go back to sleep, because of the wind and remembering the scene earlier, and because, when he lay down, he could hear the faint sound again. It was coming from beneath his bed, where the doll lay in its box. He sat bolt upright and shook his head to and fro hard to clear the sound but it had not gone away when he stopped. The wind was dying down and before long it died altogether and then his room was frighteningly silent except for the crying.

He was not a cowardly boy, though he had a natural cautiousness, but for a long time he lay, not daring to lean over and pull the box out from under the bed. He had no doubt that the sound came from it and he knew that he was awake, no longer in the middle of a nightmare, and that a china doll could not cry.

The crying went on.

When he gathered enough courage to open the box, taking the lid off slowly and moving each layer of tissue paper round the doll with great caution, he looked at the broken face and saw nothing, no fresh cracks or marks and above all, no tears and no changed expression to one of sadness or distress. The doll still stared out sightlessly and when he touched it the china was cold as cold.

He waited. Nothing. He covered the doll and moved it back out of sight. He lay down. The soft crying began again at once.

Edward got out of bed and switched on his lamp, took the box and without opening it again, carried it over to the deep cupboard and climbed onto a wooden stool. He put the box on the top shelf and pushed it as far to the back as he could, into the pitch darkness and dust.

'Now be quiet,' he said, 'please stop crying and be quiet.'

He lay still for a long time, his ears straining to hear the faintest sound from the cupboard. But there was none. The doll was silent.

Thirteen

For the next three nights the doll cried until Aunt Kestrel asked Edward why he was white-faced with dark stains beneath his eyes, from lack of sleep. He said nothing to anyone and Leonora had spent little time with him. She had been in disgrace, forbidden to go outside, forbidden to have toys, kept to her room until she gave what Aunt Kestrel called 'a heartfelt apology'. Edward had crept in a couple of times and found her sitting staring out of the window, or lying on her back on the bed, not reading, not sleeping, just looking up at the ceiling. He had offered to stay, told her he was sorry, that he would ask Aunt Kestrel to let her come outside, suggested this or that he could bring to her. She had either not replied or shaken her head, but once, she had looked at him and said, 'Mrs Mullen said I was possessed by a demon. I think that may be true.'

He had told her demons did not exist, that she simply had a bad temper and would learn to overcome it, but she said it was not just a bad temper, it was an evil one. Mrs Mullen had brought her boiled fish, peas and a glass of water on a tray and told her she was bringing badness upon the house.

'I am, I am.'

'Don't be silly. I'm very bored. I wish you would apologise and then you could come out and we could do something, walk along the river and watch the lock open or look for herons.'

But she had yawned and turned away.

The doll cried for a fourth night and this time he climbed up to the shelf and took it down. It lay in its box, stiff and still, looking like a body in a coffin.

And realising that, he knew what he should do.

He was sure he should do it by himself. Leonora was likely to scream or have a fright, behave stupidly or tell Aunt Kestrel. The prospect only frightened him a little.

Leonora was allowed downstairs, though because she had stood in front of Aunt Kestrel with a mutinous face and refused to apologise, she was still forbidden the outside world.

It was hot again, the sun blazing out of an enamel blue sky, the fens baked and the channels running dry but when Edward woke at five the air still had a morning damp and freshness. He dressed in shorts and shirt, and put on his plimsolls which made no noise.

He looked in the box. Dolly lay still in her tissue paper shroud, though he had heard the crying as he went to sleep and when he woke once in the night.

Someone would hear him, the stairs would creak, the door key would make a clink, the door would stick, as it did after rain. He waited, holding his breath, for Mrs Mullen to appear and ask what he was doing, or Aunt Kestrel to take the box and order him back to bed.

But he went stealthily, made no sound. No one heard him, no one came.

The road to the church was dusty under the early morning sun. Smoke curled from the chimney of the lock keeper's cottage beside the water. The dog barked. A heron rose from the river close beside him, a great pale ghost flapping away low over the fen.

He was afraid of the churchyard, afraid of the gnarled trunks of the yew trees and the soft swish of tall grasses against his legs. At the back, against the wall, the gravestones were half sunken into the earth, their stone lettering too worn away or moss-covered to read. No one left flowers here, no one cleared and tidied. No one remembered these ancient dead. He wondered about what was under the soil and inside the coffins, imagined skulls and bones stretched out.

He had brought a tin spade he had found in a cupboard. Its edge was rough and the wooden handle wobbled in its shaft and when he started trying to dig with it into the tussocks of grass he realised it would break before he had broken into the ground. But further along the grass petered out to thin soil and pine needles and using the spade and his hands, he dug out enough. It took a long time. His hands blistered quickly and the blisters split open and his arms tired. A thrush came and pecked at the soil he had uncovered and a wagon went down the road. He ducked behind the broad tree trunk.

When he came to bury the doll in its small cardboard coffin he thought he should say a prayer, as people always did at funerals, but it was not easy to think of suitable words.

'Oh God, let Dolly lie in peace without crying.'

He bowed his head. The thrush went on pecking at the soil, even after he had dragged it over the coffin and the grave with his tin spade.

When he slipped back into the house, he heard Mrs Mullen from the kitchen, and his aunt moving about her room. It was after seven o'clock.

No one found out. No one took the slightest notice of him, he was of no account. A telegram had arrived saying that Leonora's mother was in London and waiting for her, she should be put on the train as soon as possible that day.

'I long for her,' Aunt Kestrel said, as she finished reading the telegram out.

Mrs Mullen, setting down the silver pot of coffee on its stand, made a derisive sound under her breath.

The morning was a scramble of boxes and trunks and people flying up and down the stairs. Edward went outside, afraid to be told that he was getting underfoot, the image of the silent, buried doll filling his mind. He did not know what he might do if Leonora asked for it.

She did not. She stood in the hall surrounded by her luggage, her hair tied back in a ribbon which made her look unfamiliar, already someone he did not know. He could not picture where she was going to, or imagine her mother and the latest stepfather.

'I will probably never see you again,' she said. The station taxi was at the door and Aunt Kestrel was putting on her hat, looking in her bag. She would see Leonora onto the train.

'You might,' Edward said. 'We are cousins.'

'No. Our mothers hated one another. I think we will be strangers.'

She put out a slender, cool hand and he shook it. He wanted to say something more, remind her of things they had said to one another, what had happened, what they had shared, to hold onto this strange, interesting holiday. But Leonora was already somewhere else and he sensed that she would not welcome such reminders.

He watched her walk, stiff-backed, down the path, her luggage stowed away in the taxi, Aunt Kestrel fussing behind her.

'Goodbye, Leonora,' he said quietly.

She did not look round, only climbed in to the taxi and sat staring straight ahead as the car moved off. She did not glance back at him, or at

Iyot House, which he understood was for her already part of the past and moving farther and farther away as the taxi wheels turned.

The sound of the motor died away.

'And good riddance,' Mrs Mullen said from the hall. 'That's a bad one and brought nothing but bad with her, so be glad she's gone and pray she's left none of it behind her.'

Edward woke in the middle of the night to a deathly stillness, in the house and outside, and remembered that he was alone in the attics. Aunt Kestrel was two floors below, Mrs Mullen in the basement. Leonora had gone.

He closed his eyes and tried to picture a sea of black velvet, which he had once been told was the way to bring on sleep, and after a time he did fall into drowsiness, but through it, in the distance, he heard the sound of paper rustling and the muffled crying of Dolly, buried beneath the earth.

PART THREE

Fourteen

I was abroad when I had the letter telling of my Aunt Kestrel's death. She was over ninety and had been in a nursing home and failing for some time. I had always sent her birthday and Christmas cards and presents but I had seen her very little since the holidays I spent at Iyot as a boy and now, as one always does, I felt guilty that I had not made more effort to visit her in her old age. I am sure she must have been lonely. She was an intelligent woman with many interests and one who was happy in her own company. She was not a natural companion for a small boy but she had always done her best to ensure that I was happy when I stayed there and as I grew older I had been able to talk to her more about the things that interested her and which I was beginning to learn a little about – medieval history, military biography, the Fenlands, and her impeccable botanical illustrating.

I was saddened by her death and planned to return for her funeral but the day after I received the news, I had a letter from her solicitor informing me that Aunt Kestrel had given him strict and clear instructions that it was to be entirely private, followed by cremation, and so anxious had she been not to have any mourners that the day and time were being kept from everyone save those immediately involved and the lawyer himself. But he concluded:

'However, I have Mrs Dickinson's instructions that she wishes you and your cousin, Mrs Leonora Sebastian to attend my office, on a day to be arranged to your convenience, to be told the contents of her Will, of which I am the executor.'

I wrote to Leonora at the last address I had but I had had no contact with her for some years. I knew that she had married and been divorced and thought she sounded like her mother's daughter, but she had not replied to my last two cards and had apparently dropped out of sight.

Then, the evening I received the solicitor's letter, she telephoned me.

I had just arrived back in London. She sounded as I might have expected, haughty and somewhat brusque.

'I suppose this is necessary, Edward? It's not convenient and I hate those bloody fens.'

'He wouldn't have asked us if he could have dealt with it any other way – he is almost certainly acting on Aunt Kestrel's instructions. I shall drive up. Would you like me to take you?'

'No, I'm not sure what arrangements I shall make. I want to see the house, do you? I presume we are the only legatees and we'll get everything? Though as I am older and my mother was older than yours, it would seem fairer that I get the lion's share.'

She left me speechless. We agreed to meet at Iyot House, and then again at the solicitor's the following morning. I wondered what she would look like now, whether she still had the wonderful flaring red hair, if she still had a temper, if she had married again and borne any children. I knew almost nothing about Leonora's adult life, as I imagined she knew little about mine. She would not have had enough interest in me to find out.

She had not, of course, turned up the previous evening at the house, and left no message. I daresay she couldn't be bothered. But that she would bother to attend the reading of our aunt's Will I had no doubt.

Fifteen

The solicitor's office was everything one would have expected, housed in a small building in the Market Square of Cold Eeyle, which was probably Elizabethan and little changed, but the solicitor himself, a Mr James Maundeville, was quite unlike the person I had pictured. He had worked for his father and uncle, and then taken over the firm when both had retired. He was only in his late thirties, at a guess, and had a woman as junior partner.

'Mrs Sebastian is not here yet. Can I get you some coffee or would you prefer to wait until she arrives?'

I said that I would wait and we chatted about my aunt and Iyot House, while we looked out onto the Square, which was small, with shops and banks and businesses on two sides, the Town Hall and an open cobbled market on the other. It was a cold, windy morning with clouds scudding past the rooftops, but the fog had quite gone.

We chatted for perhaps ten minutes, and then Maundeville went out, saying he had something to sign. Another ten minutes went by. I was not surprised. It fitted in with everything I had known of Leonora that she should be so late and it was forty minutes after ten when I finally heard voices and footsteps on the stairs. Maundeville's secretary opened the door and said that he was on the telephone, apologised, and said that she would bring coffee in a couple of minutes.

I had wondered how much my cousin might have changed but as she walked into the room, I knew her at once. Her flaring red hair had softened in colour a little, but still sprang from her head in the old, commanding way; her face was as pale, though now made up and with a tautness at the sides of her eyes and jaw that indicated she had probably had a face lift. Her eyes were as scornful as ever, her hand as cool when she put it briefly into mine.

'Why are we being dragged to this godforsaken place when everything could easily have been sent in the post?'

She did not ask me how I was, tell me where she had come from, mention Aunt Kestrel.

I said I supposed the solicitor was following our aunt's instructions and I heard again the short, hard little laugh I had got to know so well.

She sat down and glanced at me with little interest.

'God I hated that place,' she said. 'What on earth am I going to do with it? Sell it, that's the only possible thing, though whoever would be mad enough to want it? Do you remember those awful poky little rooms she gave us in the attics?'

'Yes. Do you . . .'

'And that woman . . . Mrs . . . pinch-face . . .'

'Mullen.'

'You were a very meek little boy.'

I did not remember myself as that, though I knew I had been intimidated by Leonora, and also quite careful in manner and behaviour, anxious not to cause any trouble.

'Quite the goody-goody.'

'Whereas you . . .'

The laugh again.

'God I hated it. Nothing to do, the wind howling, boring books, no games.'

'Oh but there were games – don't you remember playing endless Bagatelle?'

'No. I remember there was nothing to do at all.'

'You had your birthday while we were there.'

'Did I? What, eight, nine, something like that?'

'Nine.'

'Do you have children?'

'No, I'm afraid . . .'

'Nor do I yet but I'm expecting one, God help me.'

I must have looked startled.

'Yes, yes, I know, I'm forty-three, stupid thing to do.'

'Your husband . . .'

'Archer? American, of course. He's twenty years younger, so I suppose he ought to have a family but this will be it, he's lucky to get one.'

She told me that he was her third husband, an international hotelier, that they had flats in New York and Paris but spent most of the time travelling.

'I live in grand hotels, out of a suitcase. Where is the man?'

Every so often I caught sight of the child Leonora inside this brittle, well-dressed woman, but she was more or less completely masked by what, oddly, seemed to me a falsely adult air. I wondered if she still had terrors and a temper. I was about to find out.

James Maundeville came back, full of apologies. Leonora made a gesture of annoyance. He picked up a file on his desk, and took out the usual long envelope in which solicitors file Last Will and Testaments.

'I won't read the preamble; it's just the familiar disclaimers. Mrs Dickinson had savings and investments which formed the capital on whose interest she lived for many years but that capital was considerably eroded by the needs of her last year in a nursing home. The remainder amounts to some twelve thousand pounds. There are no valuables – a few items of personal jewellery worth perhaps a thousand pounds all told. But she expressly asked that you should both, as her sole legatees, come here to learn not so much what she has left but the somewhat – er – eccentric – conditions attached. I did not draw up Mrs Dickinson's will, my father did and I'm afraid he has been suffering from dementia for the last eighteen months and so I wasn't able to discuss this with him.'

He looked up at us both. His face was serious but there was a flicker of amusement there too. He was a good looking, pleasant man with a strong trace of the local accent in his educated voice.

Leonora sat with one stockinged leg crossed tightly over the other. I tried to imagine her as the mother of a child, but simply could not. I felt sorry for any offspring she might produce.

'Mrs Dickinson left her entire estate, which includes everything I mentioned above – the money, pieces of jewellery and so on, plus Iyot House, with all its contents – with an exception which I will come to –' He cleared his throat nervously, and hesitated a moment before continuing, 'to Mr Edward Cayley. . .' A glance at me.

'The exception . . .'

But before he could read on, Leonora let out an animal cry of rage and distress. I had heard it once before. The voice was older, the tone a little deeper, but otherwise her furious howl was exactly the same as the one she had uttered the night of her birthday when she had opened the doll Aunt Kestrel had brought for her from London.

Mr Maundeville looked alarmed. I got up, and took Leonora's arm but she shook me off and raged at us both, her words difficult to make out but not difficult to guess at. He proffered water, but then simply sat waiting for the outburst to run its course.

Leonora was like someone possessed. She raged against Aunt Kestrel, me, the solicitor, raged about unfairness and deceit and hinted at fraud and collusion. The house should have been hers, the estate hers, though we could not discover why she was so sure. Desire, want, getting what she believed ought to be hers – simple greed, these were what drove her, as they had driven her in childhood and, I saw now, throughout her life.

In the end, I persuaded her to calm and quieten by saying that whatever Aunt Kestrel had willed, once the estate was mine I could do what I liked and there was no question of not sharing things with her fairly. This stopped her.

Mr Maundeville had clearly formed a poor impression of Leonora and wanted her out of his sight. He went back to the Will.

'Mrs Dickinson has left one item to you, Mrs Sebastian. I confess I do not fully understand the wording.

'My niece Leonora should have the china doll which was my 9th birthday gift to her and for which she was so ungrateful, in the hope that she will learn to treat it, as she should treat everyone, with more kindness and care.'

He sat back and laid down the paper. Leonora's hands were shaking, her face horribly pale and contorted with fury. But she said no word. She got up and walked out, leaving me to smooth things over, explain and apologise as best I could and follow her into the square.

She was nowhere to be seen. I wandered about for some time looking for her but in the end I gave up, and drove back out to Iyot House. Of course, I intended to share my inheritance with Leonora. I could not in conscience have done anything else, though she had made me angry and tempted me to change my mind and keep everything, simply out of frustration at her behavior. She was the child she had been and if no one else could bring her face to face with her unpleasant character, perhaps I could.

But whatever I decided, I was determined that she should have the wretched doll. As I drove across the fen something was hovering just under the surface of my mind, as it had been hovering all the previous night, but when I had heard Maundeville read out the clause about the doll, something had bubbled nearer to the surface, and I had remembered Leonora's outburst that terrible evening, Aunt Kestrel's hurt and annoyance, and then something else, something closer to me, or rather, to my eight-year-old self.

The sun was shining and there was a brisk breeze. As I went towards the gates to the yard, I saw that they had been opened already and that a large car was parked there. Leonora was ahead of me.

The house felt cold and bleak, and smelled more strongly of dust and emptiness than I had remembered from the previous day. I went inside and called out. At first, there was no reply, but as I went up the stairs, calling again, I heard Leonora's voice.

She was in the attics, standing at the window of her old room, looking down.

'How weird,' she said. 'It's smaller and dingier than I remember and it reeks of unhappiness.'

'Not mine,' I said, 'I was never unhappy here though I was sometimes bored and sometimes lonely. But I thought you and I had quite a happy time that summer.'

She shook her head, not so much in disagreement as if she were puzzled.

'Did you understand that nonsense about a doll?' She spoke dismissively.

'Anyhow, why should I care tuppence about it, whatever she meant? The old woman was obviously demented. But now, I suggest the only thing to be done here is for you to sell the house and divide the money between us. God knows, I wouldn't want to come back again and I doubt if you do.'

But I had stopped listening to her. We were in my old attic room now and I had seen the cupboard in the wall again. And I remembered I had first hidden the doll there. I stood transfixed, a small boy lying in the bed and hearing the rustle of the tissue paper. I was looking again inside the white cardboard box and seeing the smashed china head and the blue, sightless yet staring eyes, and feeling sorry for the doll even though, like my cousin, I did not care for it very much. I had been frightened too, for what doll could cry, let alone move so that its tissue covering rustled?

She had gone back down the stairs and I could hear her snapping up one of the blinds in Aunt Kestrel's sitting room.

'Come on,' I said, 'I know where it is.'

'What are you babbling about now?'

But I was out and down the path to the gate. I called back to her over my shoulder. 'I'm going to get it for you.'

I was not in control of myself. I felt pushed on by the urge to find out if I was right, get the doll and give it back to Leonora, as if I could never rest again until I did. It seemed to be the doll that was urging me, demanding to be rescued and returned to its owner, but I knew now that it, or perhaps, the memory of it, had possessed me for all those years. I felt partly that I wanted to be rid of all trace of it, partly responsible because only I knew where it was and could rescue it. I did not pause to consider how sane this all was, or that I was behaving bizarrely, a man in his forties who had never before been under the influence of something I could only fear was other than human.

Sixteen

'Edward? Where are you? What in God's name are you doing?'

'Here. Over here.'

Dusk was rapidly gathering now, the sky still light on the horizon, but the land darkening. I had reached the churchyard and was clambering over the hassocks of thick grass and the prone gravestones, to reach the low stone wall. I could hear Leonora calling after me and then her footsteps coming down the path but I did not wait. I knew what I must do and she was no longer any part of it. I was acting alone and under the urging of something quite other.

I found what I thought was the nearest gravestone and then, to my surprise, the patch of soil that no grass had managed to invade. There were pine needles and a few small fir cones. It was hard and bone dry there and I had nothing with which to dig but my own bare hands. But I knelt down and started to scrabble away at the surface.

Leonora appeared beside me, breathing hard, as if she had been running, but more out of fear than exertion I knew.

'Edward?'

'I have to do this. I have to do it.'

'Do what? Dig a hole? Find something down there?'

'Both.' I sat back on my heels. 'But it's hopeless; I can make no impression at all. I need a spade.' And I remembered the feel of the small tin spade in my hands, the blunted, rusty edge with which I had dug into this same ground. I cannot have gone down far.

I got up and went round the side of the church, finding what I needed almost at once – the shed in which whoever maintained the churchyard and dug the occasional grave kept his things. The padlock was undone. I found what I needed easily enough, wondering how much it was used; Iyot Lock was a hamlet of so few houses – there cannot have been many burials.

Leonora had followed me, obviously not wanting to be alone, and now was beside the wall, looking down. I pushed the blade into the earth with all my strength but it was extremely hard ground and yielded little. I scraped away as best I could, and after a short time the soil loosened. There were some tree roots which must have spread in the many years since I was last here and which made my task harder but I did not have to go very deep before I bumped against something caught beneath one of them. It was not hard, but felt compressed. I threw down the space and knelt on the grass. Leonora was standing nearby, and as I glanced up I saw that she was looking with alarm at me, as if she feared I had gone mad.

'It's all right,' I said, in a falsely cheerful voice, 'I told you I would find it for you.'

'Find what? What on earth are you doing, Edward, and should you be digging about in a churchyard? Isn't that wickedness or illegal or some such thing? You could be digging up someone's grave.'

'I am,' I said.

It seems insane indeed, now I look back, but at the time I was possessed by the need to find out if I was right, and get Leonora what my aunt had willed her. She was right, as she had screeched in the solicitor's office, she had been cut out of the rest of the inheritance and only left the wretched doll in what was perhaps the one mean-spirited gesture our aunt had ever made. Her childhood behaviour over the birthday doll, her spoilt tantrum and violent rejection of it, when Kestrel had gone to buy it especially, to make up for disappointment, must have rankled for years – unless she had written her will shortly after it had all happened. Either way, she intended Leonora to be taught a lesson but I was not going to indulge in that sort of tit-for-tat gesture. I would tell Leonora that I planned to give her exactly half the money we eventually achieved.

This had all become some sort of game that had gone too far. I knew that well enough as I knelt on the ground and felt around with both my hands in the space under the tree root. I soon came upon a damp lump of something and gradually used my fingers to ease it away from the soil.

The white cardboard box had rotted away over the years and then adhered like clay to the contents, and as I took it in my hands, I could feel the shape beneath. It was a slimy grey mess.

It was also almost completely dark and I laid the object on the ground while I hastily covered the soil back over the shallow place I had cleared.

'Come on, back to the house. I can't see anything here.'

'Edward, what have you done?'

'I told you – I have retrieved your inheritance.'

I carried it carefully down the dark road back to Iyot House. It felt unpleasant, slimy and with clots of soil adhering to the wet mush of cardboard.

I do not know that I had thought particularly about the state the doll would be in after being buried for so long. Certainly the way the box had disintegrated was no surprise – the very fact that it was there at all was remarkable. If you had asked me I suppose I would have said the doll would be very dirty, perhaps unrecognisable as a doll, but undamaged – china or pot or plastic, whatever it was actually made of, would not have rotted like the box.

I went into the old kitchen, found a dust sheet and laid it on the deal table. Leonora seemed to be as intrigued as I was, though also distinctly alarmed.

'How did you know where to look? What on earth was it doing buried there in the churchyard?'

I half remembered that something had happened to startle me and make me want the wretched thing out of the house but the details were hazy now.

'I think I had a dream about it.'

'Don't be ridiculous.'

But now we were both looking at the filthy soil-coated object on the table. I found a bowl of cold water, an ancient cloth and a blunt kitchen knife and began to rinse and scrape away carefully.

'I don't know why you are doing this. Is it full of money?'

'I doubt it.'

'No, of course it isn't. I don't want it, can't you understand Edward? This is a stupid game. For God's sake, throw it in a bin and let's get out of this awful house.'

All the same, she could not help watching me intently as I worked patiently away. It did not take me long to get rid of the wet sodden mush of soil and cardboard and then my fingers touched the hard object beneath. I emptied and re-filled the bowl of water and rinsed and re-rinsed. First the body of the china doll appeared, dirty but apparently intact.

'I know Aunt Kestrel would have wanted you to have it in as near perfect condition as we can get it, Leonora!'

She was transfixed by the sight. 'I remember it,' she said after a moment. 'It's coming back to me – that awful night. I remember expecting it to be something so special, so beautiful, and this hideous china baby came out of the box.'

'Do you remember what kind of a doll you had wanted? I drew a picture of it for you.'

She told me, though some of the detail was inaccurate, but the bridal princess came to life as she spoke.

I was anxious not to damage this doll, so I worked even more slowly as I got most of the outer dirt away and then I carried it to the tap and rinsed it under a trickle of water. If I had stopped to think how ridiculous I must have looked – how oddly we were both behaving indeed, perhaps I would not have gone on. I wish now that indeed I had not, that I had left the doll covered and buried under the earth in its sorry grave. But it was too late for that.

'There,' I said at last. 'Let us see your treasure, Leonora!' I spoke in a light and jocular tone, the last time I was to do so that night and for many others.

I carried the doll, still wet but clean, to the table and laid it down directly under the light. I had pushed all the rubbish into a bin so there was now just the scrubbed, pale wooden table top and the doll lying on it.

We both looked. And then Leonora's hand flew to her mouth as she made a dreadful low sound, not a cry, not a wail, hardly a human sound but something almost animal.

I looked into the face of the doll and then I too saw what she had seen.

When we had both looked at it last we were children and the doll was a baby doll, with staring bright blue eyes, a painted rosebud mouth and a smooth china face, neck, arms, legs and body. It was an artificial-looking thing but it was as like a human baby as any doll can ever be.

Now, we both stared in horror at the thing on table in front of us. It was not a baby, but a wizened old woman, a crone, with a few wisps of twisted greasy grey hair, a mouth slightly open to reveal a single black tooth, and the face gnarled and wrinkled like a tree trunk, with lines and pockmarks. It was sallow, the eyes were sunken and the lids creased with age, the lips thin and hard.

I let out a small cry, and then said, 'But of course. This isn't your doll. Someone has changed it for this hideous thing.'

'How ' Leonora asked in a whisper, 'When? Why? Whoever knew it had been buried there?'

I would have tried to come up with a thousand explanations but I could not even begin. For as I looked at the dreadful, aged doll, I realised that the crack in the skull and the hollow beneath it, which had come when Leonora had hurled it at the wall, were exactly the same, still jagged like a broken egg, though dirty round the edges from being in the earth.

This was not a replacement doll, put there by someone – though God knows who – with a sick sense of humour. This was the first doll, the bland-faced baby. The crack in its skull was exactly as it had been, I was sure of that. The body was the same size and shape though oddly crooked and with chicken-claw hands and feet and a yellow, loose-skinned neck. This was the doll Aunt Kestrel had given Leonora. It was the same doll.

But the doll had grown old.

I managed to find some brandy in Aunt Kestrel's old sitting-room cupboard, and poured us both a generous glassful. After that, I locked up the house, leaving everything as it was, and drove Leonora back to Cold Eeyle and the hotel, for she was in no state to do anything for herself. She sat beside me shaking and occasionally letting out a little cry, after which her body would give a long convulsive shudder. I insisted that a doctor be called out, as she was in the early stages of pregnancy, and stayed until he had left, saying that she needed sleep and peace but that she and the child were essentially unharmed.

I spent a terrible night, full of nightmares in which dolls, old ones and young ones mixed together, came at me out of thick fog, alternately laughing and crying. I woke at six and went straight out, driving fast to Iyot House through a drear, cold morning.

The doll which had grown old was where we had left it, on the kitchen table, and still old and wizened, like a witch from a fairy tale. I had half expected to find that it had all been some dreadful illusion and that the doll was still a baby, just filthy and distorted by having been buried in the damp earth for so long.

But the earth had done nothing to the doll, other than ruining its cardboard coffin. The doll was a crone, looking a hundred years old or a thousand, ancient and repulsive.

I did as I had done before, went alone to the churchyard and buried it, this time wrapped in an old piece of sheeting. I dug as deep as I could and replaced the earth firmly on top. When I had finished I felt a sense of release. Whatever had happened, the wretched, hideous thing would never emerge again and there was an end.

But she had power to haunt me. I dreamed of the aged doll for many nights, many months. I worried over what had happened and how. Sometimes, I half convinced myself that we had both imagined it, Leonora and I, for, of course, an inanimate object, a doll made of pot, could not age. The dirt and soil, added to years in the damp ground, had changed the features – that was quite understandable.

In the end, the image faded from my mind and reason took over.

Leonora disappeared from my life once more, though I heard in a roundabout way that she had returned to the Far East and her hotelier husband.

As for me, I was about to pack up Iyot House and put it up for sale, when I was asked to go abroad myself, to do a special job for a foreign government and it was such a major and exciting challenge that the house in the fens and everything to do with it went from my mind.

PART FOUR

Seventeen

I was to spend three or four months in the city of Szargesti, a once-handsome place in the old Eastern Europe. It had an old and beautiful centre, but much of that had been demolished during the 1970s, to make way for wide roads on which only presidential and official cars could travel, vast, ugly new civic buildings and a monstrous presidential palace. The Old Town was medieval, and had once housed a jewellery quarter, bookbinders and small printers, leather workers, and various tradesmen who kept the ancient buildings upright. Many had been wood and lathe, with astonishing painted panels on their façades. There had been a cathedral and other old churches, as well as a synagogue, for a large section of the original population of Szargesti had been Jewish. The place had been vandalised and the demolition had proceeded in a brutal and haphazard fashion, alongside the hurried erection of a new civic centre. But the Prague Spring had come to Szargesti, the president had been exiled, many of his cronies executed, and both demolition and building had come to an abrupt halt. Huge craters stood in the middle of streets, blocks of flats were left half in ruins, the machinery which had been pulling them down left rusting in their midst. It was a testament to grand designs and the lust for power of ignorant men. I am an adviser on the conservation of ancient buildings and sometimes, on whole areas, as in the case of Szargesti. My task was to identify and catalogue what was left, photograph it and make certain that nothing else was destroyed, and then to give the city advice on how to shore up, preserve, rebuild with care.

I knew that the Old Town, with its medieval buildings – houses, shops, workshops – was the most important area and in urgent need of conservation and repair. I had quickly come to love the place, with its small, intimate squares, narrow cobbled alleyways, beautiful, often ramshackle four-storey buildings with their neglected but still beautiful frescoes and wall paintings. The best way of getting to know a place is simply to wander and this is almost all I did for the first couple of weeks, taking dozens of photographs. Every evening I returned to my hotel to make copious notes, but after I had come to know the city a little better I would often stay out late, find a café in the back streets, drink a beer or a coffee and watch what little street life there was. People were still uncertain, ground down by years of a brutal dictatorship and most of them kept safely inside their homes after dark. But one warm summer evening I went into the Old Town and a square I had chanced upon earlier in the day, and which had some of the most beautiful and undamaged houses I had so far discovered. It would once have housed traders and craftsmen in precious metals whose workshops were situated beneath their houses. On the corner I passed an old stone water trough with an elaborately carved iron tap stood beside it. Horses would have drunk here, but the water had probably also been carried away in buckets, for use in smelting.

Now, the heavy wooden doors and iron shutters of the workshops were closed and some were padlocked, and those padlocks were rusty and broken. Many of the upper rooms had gaping dark spaces where windows had fallen out.

There was a small café with a few tables on the cobbles. The barman appeared the moment I sat down, brought my drink and a small dish of smoked sausage, but then returned to the doorway and watched me until I began to feel uneasy. I had no need to be, I knew, and I tried to enjoy the quietness, the last of the sunshine and the way the shadows lengthened, slipping across the cobbles towards me. The old women who had been sitting on a bench chatting, left. The tobacconist came out with a long pole and rattled down his shutters. The beer was good. The sausage tasted of woodsmoke.

I continued to feel uneasy and strangely restless, alone in the darkening square. So far as I knew, only the waiter was looking at me but I had the odd sense that there were others, watching from the blanked-out windows and hidden corners. I have always believed that places with a long history, especially those in which terrible events have taken place, retain something of those times, some trace in the air, just as I have been in many a cathedral all over the world and sensed the impress of centuries of prayers and devotions. Places are often filled with their own pasts and exude a sense of them, an atmosphere of great good or great evil, which can be picked up by anyone sensitive to their surroundings. Even a dog's hackles can rise in places reputed to be haunted. I am not an especially credulous man but I believe in these things because I have experienced them. I am not afraid of the dark and it was not the evening shadows that were making me nervous now. Certainly I had no fear of potential attackers or of spies leftover from the city's past. Thank God those days were over and Szargesti was struggling to come to terms with the new freedoms.

I finished my beer and got up.

The air was still warm and the stars were beginning to brighten in the silky sky as I walked slowly round the square, where the cobbles gave way to stone paving. Every window was dark and shuttered. The only sound was that of my own footsteps.

Here and there an old stable door stood ajar, revealing cobbles on which straw was still scattered though the horses had long gone. I passed a music shop, a cobbler's, and one tiny frontage displaying pens and parchment. All were locked up, and dark. Then, in the middle of the narrowest, dimmest alley, where the walls of the houses bulged across almost to meet one another, I saw a yellowish light coming from one of the windows and nearing it, I found a curious shop.

The window was dusty, making it difficult to see much of what was inside but I could make out shelves and an ancient counter. No attempt had been made to display goods attractively – the window held a jumble of objects piled together. I put my hand on the latch and at once heard the ring of an old-fashioned bell.

A very small old man was behind the mahogany counter, his skin paper pale and almost transparent over the bones of his cheeks and skull. He had tufts of yellow-white hair, yellow-white eyebrows and a jeweller's glass screwed into one eye, with which he was examining a round silver box, dulled and stained with verdigris.

He raised a finger in recognition of my entrance, but continued to peer down at the object, and so I looked round me at the stock, which was crammed onto the shelves, spilled out of drawers, displayed in glass cabinets. The floor was of uncovered oak boards, polished and worn by the passage of feet over years.

The lower shelves contained small leather bound books, boxes of various sizes with metal hasps, dulled by the same verdigris as the box being scrutinised, wooden trays with what looked like puzzles fitted into them, a couple of musical boxes. Higher up, I saw wooden cabinets with sets of narrow drawers, each labelled in the old Cyrillic alphabet which had not been used in the country for almost a century. A doll's house stood on the floor beside me, its eaves and roof modelled on those of the buildings in the square, its front hanging half-off its single hinge. Beside it was a child-sized leather trunk, the leather rubbed and lifting here and there. I glanced at the old man but now he had set the box on a scrap of dark blue velvet set down on the counter and was peering at it even more intently through his eyeglass, I thought perhaps trying to make out some pattern or inscription.

I turned back to the doll's house and trunk and as I did so, I heard a sound which at first I took to be the scratching of a mouse in the skirting somewhere – I hoped a mouse, and not a rat. It stopped and then, as I put out my hand to touch the front of the wooden house, started again, and though it was still very soft, I knew that it was not the noise made by any sort of rodent. I could not tell exactly where it originated – it seemed to be coming from the darkness somewhere, behind me, or to one side – I could not quite pin down the direction. It was a rustling of some kind – perhaps the sound made when the wind blows through branches or reeds, perhaps the movement of long grass. Yet it was not altogether like those sounds. It stopped again. I looked at the old man but he was crouching over his box, his narrow back half bent, shoulders hunched.

I waited. It came again. A soft, insistent, rustling sound. Like paper. Someone was rustling paper – perhaps sheets of tissue paper. I turned my head to one corner, then the other but the sound did not quite come from there, or there, or from anywhere.

Perhaps it was inside my own head.

The old man sat up abruptly, put down the eyeglass and looked directly at me. His eyes were the watery grey of the sea on a dull day, dilute and pale.

'Good evening,' he said in English. 'Is it something special you look for, because in a moment, I close.'

'Thank you, no. I was just interested to find a shop here and open at this time.'

'Ah.'

'You sell many different things. What do you call yourself?'

'A restorer.'

'But so am I!'

'Toys?'

'No, ancient buildings. Like those in this quarter. I'm an architectural conservator.'

He nodded.

'Little is beyond repair but my job is more easy than yours.'

He gestured round. I had begun to notice that many of the objects on his shelves and even standing around the floor were old toys, mostly of wood, some painted elaborately, some simply carved. As well as the dolls' house I had already seen, there were others, and then a fort, many soldiers in the original military uniforms of the country's past, a wooden truck, a railway engine and many boxes of different sizes and shapes. A lot of them had clearly been gathering dust for years. I looked down at the cloth on which the miniature silver box was standing.

'This has been chased by hand, the most expert hand.' He offered the eyeglass for me to examine it. 'The work of a fine craftsman. It was found on the dresser of a dolls' house – but I think it was not a toy item. Please, look.'

I did so. There was some intricate patterning forming the border and in the centre, a night sky with moon and stars and clouds, with a swirl of movement suggesting a wild wind.

'Certainly not a toy.' I handed back the eyeglass. 'Marvellous workmanship.'

'This old part of Szargesti, were craftsmen who worked in silver many years past, special craftsmen who passed down their skill to younger ones. Now . . .' he sighed. 'Almost none left. Skills in danger of death. I do not have these skills. I am only repairer of toys. Please, look round. You have some children?'

I shook my head. I assumed that everything here was waiting for repair and not for sale but even old toys, like many other domestic artefacts, tell a conservator something about the times in which they were made and even of the buildings in which they belonged and I poked about a little more, finding treasures behind treasures. But I wondered how long some of them had been lying here and how much longer they would have to wait for the mender's attention. And then I wondered if some of the children who had owned and played with them were now grown-up or even dead, the toys were so old-fashioned.

The old man let me look around, poke into corners, touch and even pick things up without taking any notice of me and I was at the very back of the shop, where it was even darker and dustier, when I heard it again. The faint rustling sound seemed to be coming from something close to me but when I turned, became softer as if it were moving away. I stood very still. The shop was quiet. I heard the rustling again, as if tissue paper were being scrumpled up or unfolded, and now I thought I could trace the sound to somewhere on the floor and quite close to my feet. I bent down but it was very dark and I saw nothing unusual, and there was no quick movement of a rodent scuttling away. It stopped. Started again, more softly. Stopped. I took a step or two forwards and my foot bumped up against something. I bent down. A cardboard box, about the size to contain a pair of boots, was just in front of me, the lid apparently tied on with stout string. It was as I put my hand out to touch it that I felt an iciness down my spine, and a sudden moment of fear. I was sure that I was remembering something but I had no idea what. Deep in my subconscious mind a cardboard box like this one had a place but in what way or from what stage of my life I did not know.

I stood up hastily and as I did so, the rustling began again. It was coming from inside the box.

But I did not have a chance to try to trace the source of the sound, even if I was sure that I wanted to do so, because the old man unnerved me by saying:

'You are looking for a doll I think.'

I opened my mouth to say that I was not, had just been drawn into the shop out of curiosity, but I realised that was not true.

'Look there.'

I looked. In a cabinet just above my head was the doll, the exact, the same doll, which Leonora had yearned for all those years ago, the doll she had described in such detail and which I had tried to draw for her as some sort of compensation.

The Indian Princess, in her rich garments, shining jewels, sequins, beads, embroidery, sparkling with gold and silver, ruby and emerald, pearl and diamond, was sitting on some sort of velvet chair with a high, crested back, her face bland and serene, her veil sprinkled with silver and gold suns, moons and stars. She was not a doll for a child, not a doll to be played with, dressed and undressed, fed and pushed about in an old pram, she was far too fine, too regal, too formal. But I knew that this was the doll my cousin had yearned for so desperately and that I had no choice but to buy it – it had been placed here for just that reason. Even as the thought flashed across my mind, I was almost embarrassed, it was so ridiculous, and yet some part of me believed that it was true.

The old man was still tapping away calmly, smiling a little.

'Are your dolls for sale?'

'You wish to buy that one.' It was not a question.

He glanced at me, the very centres of his eyes steel-bright, fixed and all-seeing.

Now, he had come round the counter and was unlocking the cabinet. A shiver rippled down my back as he reached inside and took hold of the Indian Princess. He did not ask me if this was the one I wanted, simply took it down, locked the cabinet again and then laid the doll on the counter.

'I have the exact box.' He retreated into the shadows where I could just make out a door that stood ajar. My back was icy cold now. The shop was very quiet and somewhere in that quietness, I heard the rustling sound again.

He came back with the doll, boxed, lidded, tied with string and handed it over to me. I paid him and fled, out into the alley under the tallow light of the gas lamp, the coffin-like box under my arm. Through the window, I could make out the old man, behind the counter. He did not look up.

When I got back to the hotel, I pushed the doll under the bed in my room and went down to the cheerful bar, with its red shaded lamps and buzz of talk, and had a couple of brandies to try to rid myself of the unpleasant chill through my body, and a general sense of malaise. Gradually, I calmed. I began to try to work out why I had heard the rustling sound and what it had meant, but soon gave up. It could not have had anything to do with any of the similar sounds I had heard before. I was in another country, a different place.

I went to bed, fortified by the brandy, and was on the very cusp of sleep when I sat straight up, my heart thumping in my chest. The rustling sound had started up again and as I listened in horror, I realised that it was coming from close to hand. I lay down again and then it was louder. I sat up, and it faded.

Either the rustling was in my own head – or rather, in my ears, some sort of tinnitus – or it was coming from underneath the bed.

That night my dreams were full of cascading images of dolls, broken, damaged, buried, covered in dirt, labelled, lying on shelves, being hammered and glued and tapped. In the middle of it all, the memory of Leonora's twisted and angry face as she hurled the unwanted doll at the fireplace, and floating somewhere behind, the old man with the gimlet eyes.

I woke in a sweat around dawn and pulled the box from under the bed where I had left it, the string still carefully knotted. I did not want it in my sight, but I was sure that if I disposed of the doll I would have cause to regret it and first thing the next morning I took it to the post office. I had addressed it to myself in London but changed my mind at the last moment, and sent it instead to Iyot House. The reasons were mainly practical yet I was also sending the doll there because it seemed right and where it naturally belonged.

I felt relief when it was out of my hands. I had kept it and yet I had not.

Eighteen

Some months passed, during which I heard via an announcement in *The Times* that Leonora had given birth to a daughter. I returned to England, but for the next year or so I was constantly travelling between London and Szargesti, absorbed in my work and I gave thought to little else.

And then I received a letter from the solicitor, telling me that Leonora wished to be in touch with me urgently. She had written via Iyot House but received no reply. Might he forward my address to her?

By the time I did receive a letter, I was married, I had finished my work in Szargesti, and embarked on a new project connected with English cathedrals. Leonora was far from my mind.

Dear Edward

I write to you from the depths of despair. I am unsure how much you know of what has happened to me since we last met. Briefly, I have a daughter, who is now two years old, and named Frederica, after her father and my beloved husband, Frederic, who died very suddenly. We were in Switzerland. In short, he has left me penniless; the hotels are on the verge of bankruptcy thanks to bad advice. I did not know a thing. How could I have known when Frederic protected me from everything? And now my daughter has a grave illness.

I have nowhere to go, nowhere to live. I am staying with friends out of their kindness and pity but that must come to an end.

In short, I am throwing myself on your generosity and asking if you would allow me to have Iyot House in which to live, though God knows I hate the place and would not want to set foot inside it again, if this were not my only possible home. Perhaps we could make it habitable.

If you have already disposed of it then I ask if you could share some of the proceeds with me so that I can buy a place in which my sick child and I can live.

Please reply c/o the poste restante address and tell me urgently what you can do. We are cousins, after all,

Affectionately
Leonora.

I had done nothing about Iyot House and after I told my wife the gist of the story she agreed at once that, of course, Leonora and her daughter should live there for as long as they wished.

'It's been locked up for years. I don't know what state it will be in and it was never the most – welcoming of houses anyway.'

'But surely you can get people to go in and make sure it is clean and that there hasn't been any damage . . . that the place isn't flooded? Then she can make the best of it . . . Anything other than being homeless.'

I agreed but wondered as I did so if Leonora had told me the full truth, if she had indeed been left literally penniless and without the means to put a roof over her head. Her letter was melodramatic and slightly hysterical, entirely in character. Catherine chided me with heartlessness when I tried to explain and perhaps she was right. But then, she did not know Leonora.

Nevertheless, I wrote and said that she could have the house, that I would put anything to rights before she arrived, and would come to see her when I could manage it.

I had to travel to Cambridge a few days later, and I arranged to make a detour via Iyot House. It was September, the weather golden, the corn ripe in the fields, the vast skies blue with mare's tail clouds streaked high. At this time of year the area is so open, so fresh-faced, with nothing hidden for miles, everything was spread out before me as I drove. It is still an isolated place. No one has developed new housing clusters and the villages and hamlets remain quite self-contained, not spreading, not even seeming to relate to one another. Apart from some drainage, square miles had not changed since I was an eight-year-old boy being driven from the railway station on my first visit to Iyot House. I remembered how I had felt – interested and alert to my surroundings, and yet also lonely and apprehensive, determined but fearful. And when I had first glimpsed the place, I had shivered, though I had not known why. It was as though nothing was exactly as it seemed to be, like a place in a story, there were other dimensions, shadows, secrets, the walls seemed to be very slightly crooked. I was not an especially imaginative child, so I was even more aware of what I felt.

The house smelled of dust and emptiness but not, to my surprise, of damp or mould, and although everything seemed a little more faded and neglected, there was no interior damage. I pulled up some of the blinds and opened a couple of windows. A bird had fallen down one of the chimneys and its body lay in the empty fireplace, grass sprouted on window ledges. But the place was just habitable, if I found someone to clean and reorder it. Leonora would at least have a roof over her head for however long she and the child needed it.

I had noticed that the box I had sent from Szargesti was in the porch, tucked safely out of the weather. I took it inside and decided that I would place it upstairs in the small room off the main bedroom which Leonora might well choose for her daughter. The attics were too far away and lonely for a small child.

I put the box on the shelf, hesitating about whether to take the doll out and display it, or leave it as a surprise. In the end I removed all the outer wrapping and string, but left the box closed, so that the little girl could have the fun of opening it.

Nineteen

I have written this account in a reasonably calm, even detached frame of mind. I have remembered that first strange childhood visit to Iyot House in some detail without anxiety and although it distressed me a little to recall the unpleasantness over the doll with the aged face, its burial and exhumation, and Leonora's violent tempers, I have written with a steady hand. Events were peculiar, strange things happened, and yet I have looked back steadily and without falling prey to superstitions and night terrors. I have always believed that the odd happenings could be put down to coincidence or perhaps the effects of mood and atmosphere. I suppose I believed myself to be a rational man.

But reason does not help me now that I come to the climax of the story, and as I remember and as I write, I feel as if there is no ground beneath my feet, that I might disintegrate at any moment, that my flesh will dissolve. I feel afraid but I do not know of what. I feel helpless and at the mercy of strange events and forces which not only can I not explain away but in which I do not believe.

Yet what happened, happened, all of it, and the end lies in the beginning, in our childhood. But the blame is not mine, the blame is all Leonora's.

Work preoccupied me and then Catherine and I took a trip to New York, so that I was not in touch with Leonora until she had been living in Iyot House for some weeks.

It was one day in December when I had finished some more work in Cambridge earlier than I had expected, and I decided to drive across to Iyot House and either beg a bed for the night there or carry on to the inn at Cold Eeyle. I tried to telephone my cousin in advance but there was no reply and so I simply set off. It was early dusk and the sun was flame and ruby red in the clearest of skies as I went towards the fens. Once off the trunk roads, it was as quiet as ever. There were few lock keeper's cottages occupied now – that had been the one major change since my boyhood – but here and there a light glowed through windows, and the glint of these or of the low sun touched the black deep slow-running waters in river and dyke. The church at Iyot Lock stood out as a beacon in the flat landscape for miles ahead, the last of the sun touching its gilded flying angels on all four corners of the tower.

It was beautiful and seemed so serene an aspect that I was moved and felt happier to be coming here than ever before. So much of what we imagine is a product of an ill mood, a restless night, indigestion, or the vagaries of the weather and I began to feel certain that all the previous events at Iyot House had been caused by one or other of these, or by other equally fleeting outside circumstances. Empty houses breed fantasies, bleak landscapes lend themselves to fearful imaginings. Only lie awake on a windy night and hear a branch tap-tap-tapping on a casement to understand at once what I mean.

I drew up outside the house – the gate to the back entrance was locked and barred, so I parked in the road and got out. There was a light on in the sitting room, behind drawn curtains, one upstairs and possibly one at the very back. I did not want to startle Leonora, for she would presumably not expect callers on an early December evening, so I banged the door of the car shut a couple of times, and made some noise opening the gate and tramping up the path to the front door. I pulled the bell out hard and heard it jangle through the house.

Those few moments I stood waiting outside in the cold darkness were, I now realise, the last truly calm and untroubled ones I was ever to spend. Never again did I feel so steady and equable, never again did I anticipate nothing ahead of me of a frightening, unnerving and inexplicable kind. After this, I would be anxious and apprehensive no matter where I was or what I did. That something terrible, though I never knew what, was about to happen, in the next few moments, or hours, or days, I was always certain. I did not sleep well again, and if I feared for my own health and sanity, how much more did I fear for those of my family.

The front door opened. Leonora was standing there and in the poor light of the hall she looked far older, less smart, less assured, than she had ever been. When she held the door open for me in silence, and I stepped inside, I could see her better and my first impression was strengthened. The old Leonora had been well-dressed and groomed, elegant, sophisticated, hard, someone whose expression veered between fury and defiance, with an occasional prolonged sulkiness.

Tonight, she looked ten years older, was without make-up and her hair rolled into a loose bun at the back of her neck was thickly banded with grey. She seemed exhausted, her eyes oddly without expression, and her dress was plain, black, unbecoming.

'I hope I haven't startled you. I don't imagine you get many night callers. I did try to call you.'

'The phone is out of service. You'd better come into the kitchen. I can make tea. Or there might be a drink in the house somewhere.'

I followed her across the hall. Nothing seemed to have changed. The old furniture, pictures, curtains, carpet were still in place, as if they were everlasting and could never be worn out.

'Frederica is in here. It's the warmest room. I can't afford to heat the whole house.'

We went down the short passageway to the kitchen. It was dimly lit. Electricity was expensive.

'Frederica, stand up please. Here is a visitor.'

The child was seated at the kitchen table with her back to me. I saw that she looked tall for her age but extremely thin and that she had no hair and inevitably, the word 'cancer' came to me. She had had some terrible version of it and the treatment had made her bald and I felt sorry beyond expression, for her and for my cousin.

And then she got down from her chair, and turned to face me.

For a moment, I felt drained of all energy and consciousness, and almost reached out and grabbed the table to steady myself. But I knew that Leonora's eyes were on me, watching, watching, for just such a reaction, and so I managed to stay upright and clear-headed.

Frederica was about three years old but the face she presented to me now was the face of a wizened old woman. She had a long neck, and her mouth was misshapen, sucked inwards like that of an old person without teeth. Her eyes protruded slightly, and she had almost no lashes. Her hands were wrinkled and gnarled at the joints, as if she were ninety years old.

'There is no treatment and no cure.'

Leonora's voice was as matter-of-fact as if she had been giving me the name of a plant.

I did not want to stare at the child, but I shuddered to look at her. There was something alien about her. I have never had any reaction to a human being with a disfigurement or disease other than extreme sympathy and it has always seemed best to try to ignore the outward signs as quickly as possible and address the human being within. But this was so very different. I felt the usual recoil, shock, pity but far, far more strongly, I felt fear, fear and horror. Because this small child had aged in the way the china doll had aged. And insane and irrational as it seemed, I had no doubt she had aged because of it. The consequences of Leonora's violent temper and cruel, spiteful, destructive action all those years ago had come home to her now.

I did not want to stay at Iyot House. I had a drink and read a picture book to the little girl, saddened when Leonora told me in bitterness that she would not live beyond the age of ten or so. She was a happy, friendly child with the happy chatter of a three year old coming so oddly out of that wizened little body.

As I was leaving, Leonora asked me to wait in the porch. The child had been left playing with a jigsaw in the kitchen, where I gathered they spent much of their time, because the rest of the house was so cold and unwelcoming, though I thought that she might have made it more cheerful if she had tried.

She came downstairs and handed me the cardboard box which I had left.

'Take it,' she said, 'hideous thing. What possessed you to leave such a thing here?'

'I – It seemed the right place for it, now there is a child here. Could Frederica not play with it?'

Leonora's face was pinched with a mixture of anger and scorn.

'Get rid of it, for God's sake. Haven't you done enough harm?'

'I? What harm have I done? You were the one who hurled the doll against the fireplace and smashed its head open, you were the one who caused . . .'

I stopped. Whatever crazy imaginings I had ever had, I could not conceivably blame my cousin for bringing such a dreadful fate upon her own child. I had no idea how the face of the broken doll had apparently aged but it was inanimate. It could not extract revenge.

I took the box which Leonora was pushing at me, and went. The front door was slammed and bolted before I had reached the gate.

The inn at Cold Eeyle was as comfortable and snug as ever. I was given my old room, and after a stiff whisky, I dined and then slept well and left a happier man to drive back home the next morning.

Twenty

How to tell the rest of my story? How to explain any of it? I prided myself on being a rational man, on having explained things clearly to myself and come to some understanding of the phenomenon of coincidence. I even studied it a little, via the books of those whose life's work it is, and discovered just how much that was once thought mystical, magical, mysterious, is perfectly easily explained by coincidence, whose arm stretches far further than most people would guess.

Is that how I explain away the hideous events of the next few years? Am I convinced by putting it all down to likely chance?

Of course I am not. Things had happened to me in the past which I had pushed out of mind, buried deep so that I did not need to remember them. I had known then that they were not easily explained away and that the emotions and fears, the forebodings and anxieties that overwhelmed me from time to time were fully justified. Strange and inexplicable things had happened, and hidden forces had shaped events for reasons I did not understand. I also remained certain that Leonora was the lightning conductor for all of them.

A little over a year after my last visit to Iyot House my wife Catherine gave birth to a daughter, whom we christened Viola Kestrel. When she was almost three my work took me to India, which I loved, but about which Catherine had mixed feelings. She found the heat and humidity intolerable and the extreme poverty distressed her. But she loved the inhabitants at once, and found much to do helping women and their children in a remote village, where there were no medical facilities and where clothes and people were washed in the great river that flowed through the area. Viola was adored by everyone, and was an easy, smiling child, content to be petted and fussed by a dozen people in succession.

And then she was struck down within a few hours by one of the terrible diseases that ravage this beautiful country. Poor sanitation, contaminated water, easy spread of infection, any or all of them were to blame and in spite of Catherine's care and strict precautions it was perhaps a miracle that the child had not suffered from anything serious earlier.

Viola was very ill indeed, with a high fever, pains in her limbs and an intolerance of light. She was delirious and in great distress and we were in an agony of fear that we would lose her. On the fourth day, she woke with a rash of pox-like spots, raised, and red, all over her face and body. The spots were inflamed and became infected and scabbed, so that her fresh skin and beautiful features were hidden. After a week, handfuls of her beautiful corn-coloured hair began to fall out and did not regrow. She was a distressing sight and I think I was the one who felt the loss of her beauty the most. Catherine was absorbed in trying to nurse her, help her struggle through the fevers and relieve her symptoms, and so far as she was concerned that Viola should live, no matter what her eventual condition, was all she asked.

She did live. Slowly the fevers subsided and then ceased, her pain and discomfort eased, and she lay, limp and exhausted but out of danger, on a bed as cool as could be made for her, in a darkened corner. Her rash was less red and raised, but the hideous spots crusted and when they fell off left ugly pockmarks which were deep and unlikely ever to disappear. Her beautiful eyes were dimmed and lost their wonderful colour and translucence and seemed to have receded deep into their sockets.

Weeks and then three months went by before she began to regain energy and a little weight, to laugh sometimes and clap her hands when the Indian women who had agonised over her clapped theirs.

We returned home exhausted and chastened, wondering what the future held for our once-perfect daughter, still perfect to us, still overwhelmingly loved, but nevertheless, sadly disfigured. In London we consulted a specialist in tropical diseases, who in turn passed us to a dermatologist, and thence to a plastic surgeon. None of them held out any hope that Viola's scars would ever fade very much. It might be possible for her to have a skin graft when she was older but success was by no means certain and there were risks.

Weeks went by while all this was attended to and we settled back with some difficulty into our old life in England.

It was then that I started to search for some particular files and in hunting, found both these and a white cardboard box. At first I did not recognise it and assumed it belonged to Catherine. I set it down on my work table, beside some drawings, but then forgot it until the following day, when I walked into my office early in the morning and as I saw it, remembered immediately where it had come from and what it held.

I saw Leonora again, in the semi-darkness outside Iyot House, thrusting the box into my hands and telling me, almost screaming at me to take it away. Well, my Viola might enjoy the Indian Princess doll, would recognise it as one of her friends and playmates from the country she still remembered vividly.I untied the loosely knotted string and lifted the lid. The rustle of the tissue paper brought goose flesh up on the back of my neck. It was not a sound I would ever again find pleasant and I pushed it aside quickly, not even liking the feel of it against my fingers.

The Indian Princess doll lay as I remembered her in the bottom of the coffin-like cardboard box. Her elaborate, richly embroidered and be-jewelled clothes, her rings, earrings, bracelets and bangles and beads, her satin and lace and gold and silver braid and trim, were all as I had remembered them. There were just two things that were so very different.

Her thick long black hair had come away here and there, leaving ugly bald patches, and the fallen hair was lying in tufts at the bottom of the box.

And her face and hands, which were all that showed of her skin, were covered in deep and hideous pockmarks and scars. She was no longer a beauty, she was no longer about to be a bride, she was a pariah, a sufferer from a disfiguring disease which would mark her for life, someone from whom everyone turned away, their eyes downcast.

The Man in the Picture

Prologue

The story was told to me by my old tutor, Theo Parmitter, as we sat beside the fire in his college rooms one bitterly cold January night. There were still real fires in those days, the coals brought up by the servant in huge brass scuttles. I had travelled down from London to see my old friend, who was by then well into his eighties, hale and hearty and with a mind as sharp as ever, but crippled by severe arthritis so that he had difficulty leaving his rooms. The college looked after him well. He was one of a dying breed, the old Cambridge bachelor for whom his college was his family. He had lived in this handsome set for over fifty years and he would be content to die here. Meanwhile a number of us, his old pupils from several generations back, made a point of visiting him from time to time, to bring news and a breath of the outside world. For he loved that world. He no longer went out into it much but he loved the gossip – to hear who had got what job, who was succeeding, who was tipped for this or that high office, who was involved in some scandal.

I had done my best to entertain him most of the afternoon and through dinner, which was served to us in his rooms. I would stay the night, see a couple of other people and take a brisk walk round my old stamping grounds, before returning to London the following day.

But I should not like to give the impression that this was a sympathy visit to an old man from whom I gained little in return. On the contrary, Theo was tremendous company, witty, acerbic, shrewd, a fund of stories which were not merely the rambling reminiscences of an old man. He was a wonderful conversationalist – people, even the youngest Fellows, had always vied to sit next to him at dinner in hall.

Now, it was the last week of the vacation and the college was quiet. We had eaten a good dinner, drunk a bottle of good claret, and we were stretched out comfortably in our chairs before a good fire. But the winter wind, coming as always straight off the Fens, howled round and occasionally a burst of hail rattled against the glass.

Our talk had been winding down gently for the past hour. I had told all my news, we had set the world to rights between us, and now, with the fire blazing up, the edge of our conversation had blunted. It was delightfully cozy sitting in the pools of light from a couple of lamps and for a few moments I had fancied that Theo was dozing.

But then he said, 'I wonder if you would care to hear a strange story?'

'Very much.'

'Strange and somewhat disturbing.' He shifted in his chair. He never complained of it but I suspected that the arthritis gave him considerable pain. 'The right sort of tale for such a night.'

I glanced across at him. His face, caught in the flicker of the firelight, had an expression so serious – I would almost say deathly serious – that I was startled. 'Make of it what you will, Oliver,' he said quietly, 'but I assure you of this, the story is true.' He leaned forward. 'Before I begin, could I trouble you to fetch the whisky decanter nearer?'

I got up and went to the shelf of drinks, and as I did so, Theo said, 'My story concerns the picture to your left. Do you remember it at all?'

He was indicating a narrow strip of wall between two bookcases. It was in heavy shadow. Theo had always been known as something of a shrewd art collector with some quite valuable old-master drawings and eighteenth-century watercolours, all picked, he had once told me, for modest sums when he was a young man. I do not know much about paintings, and his taste was not really mine. But I went over to the picture he was pointing out.

'Switch on the lamp there.'

Although it was a somewhat dark oil painting, I now saw it quite well and looked at it with interest. It was of a Venetian carnival scene. On a landing stage beside the Grand Canal and in the square behind it, a crowd in masks and cloaks milled around among entertainers – jugglers and tumblers and musicians and more people were climbing into gondolas, others already out on the water, the boats bunched together, with the gondoliers clashing poles. The picture was typical of those whose scenes are lit by flares and torches which throw an uncanny glow here and there, illuminating faces and patches of bright clothing and the silver ripples on the water, leaving other parts in deep shadow. I thought it had an artificial air but it was certainly an accomplished work, at least to my inexpert eye.

I switched off the lamp and the picture, with its slightly sinister revellers, retreated into its corner of darkness again.

'I don't think I ever took any notice of it before,' I said now, pouring myself a whisky. 'Have you had it long?'

'Longer than I have had the right to it.'

Theo leaned back into his deep chair so that he too was now in shadow. 'It will be a relief to tell someone. I have never done so and it has been a burden. Perhaps you would not mind taking a share of the load?'

I had never heard him speak in this way, never known him sound so deathly serious, but of course I did not hesitate to say that I would do anything he wished, never imagining what taking, as he called it, 'a share of the load' would cost me.

One

My story really begins some seventy years ago, in my boyhood. I was an only child and my mother died when I was three. I have no memory of her. Nowadays, of course, my father might well have made a decent fist of bringing me up himself, at least until he met a second wife, but times were very different then, and although he cared greatly for me, he had no idea how to look after a boy scarcely out of nappies, and so a series of nurses and then nannies were employed. I have no tale of woe, of cruelty and harm at their hands. They were all kindly and well-meaning enough, all efficient, and though I remember little of them, I feel a general warmth towards them and the way they steered me into young boyhood. But my mother had had a sister, married to a wealthy man with considerable land and properties in Devon, and from the age of seven or so I spent many holidays with them and idyllic times they were. I was allowed to roam free, I enjoyed the company of local boys – my aunt and uncle had no children but my uncle had an adult son from his first marriage, his wife having died giving birth – and of the surrounding tenant farmers, the villagers, the ploughmen and blacksmiths, grooms and hedgers and ditchers. I grew up healthy and robust as a result of spending so much time outdoors. But when I was not about the countryside, I was enjoying a very different sort of education indoors. My aunt and uncle were cultured people, surprisingly widely and well read and with a splendid library. I was allowed the run of this as much as I was allowed the run of the estate and I followed their example and became a voracious reader. But my aunt was also a great connoisseur of pictures. She loved English watercolours but also had a broad, albeit traditional, taste for the old masters, and though she could not afford to buy paintings by the great names, she had acquired a good collection of minor artists. Her husband took little interest in this area, but he was more than happy to fund her passion, and seeing that I showed an early liking for certain pictures about the place, Aunt Mary jumped at the chance of bringing someone else up to share her enthusiasm. She began to talk to me about the pictures and to encourage me to read about the artists, and I very quickly understood the delight she took in them and had my own particular favourites among them. I loved some of the great seascapes and also the watercolours of the East Anglia school, the wonderful skies and flat fens – I think my taste in art had a good deal to do with my pleasure in the outside world. I could not warm to portraits or still lifes – but nor did Aunt Mary and there were few of them about. Interiors and pictures of churches left me cold and a young boy does not understand the charms of the human figure. But she encouraged me to be open to everything, not to copy her taste but to develop my own and always to wait to be surprised and challenged as well as delighted by what I saw.

I owe my subsequent love of pictures entirely to Aunt Mary and those happy, formative years. When she died, just as I was coming up to Cambridge, she left me many of the pictures you see around you now and others, too, some of which I sold in order to buy different ones – as I know she would have wished me to do. She was an unsentimental woman and she would have wanted me to keep my collection alive, to enjoy the business of acquiring new when I had tired of the old.

In short, for some twenty years or more I became quite a picture dealer, going to auctions regularly and in the process of having fun at the whole business building up more capital than I could ever have enjoyed on my academic salary. In between my forays into the art world, of course, I worked my way slowly up the academic ladder, establishing myself here in the college and publishing the books you know. I missed my regular visits to Devon once my aunt and uncle were dead, and I could only make sure I maintained my ties to a country way of life by regular walking holidays.

I have sketched in my background and you now know a little more about my love of pictures. But what happened one day you could never guess and perhaps you will never believe the story. I can only repeat what I assured you of at the start. It is true.

Two

It was a beautiful day at the beginning of the Easter vacation and I had gone up to London for a couple of weeks, to work in the Reading Room of the British Museum and to do some picture dealing. On this particular day there was an auction, with viewing in the morning, and from the catalogue I had picked out a couple of old-master drawings and one major painting which I particularly wanted to see. I guessed that the painting would go for a price far higher than I could afford but I was hopeful of the drawings and I felt buoyant as I walked from Bloomsbury down to St James's, in the spring sunshine. The magnolias were out, as were the cherry blossom, and set against the white stucco of the eighteenth-century terraces they were gay enough to lift the heart. Not that my heart was ever down. I was cheerful and optimistic when I was younger – indeed, in general I have been blessed with a sunny and equable temperament – and I enjoyed my walk and was keenly anticipating the viewing and the subsequent sale. There was no cloud in the sky, real or metaphorical.

The painting was not, in fact, as good as had been made out and I did not want to bid for it, but I was keen to buy at least one of the drawings, and I also saw a couple of watercolours which I knew I could sell on and I thought it likely that they would not fetch high prices because they were not the kind of pictures for which many of the dealers would be coming to this particular sale. I marked them off in the catalogue and went on wandering round.

Then, slightly hidden by a rather overpowering pair of religious panels, that Venetian oil of the carnival scene caught my eye. It was in poor condition, it badly needed cleaning and the frame was chipped in several places. It was not, indeed, the sort of picture I generally liked, but there was a strange, almost hallucinatory quality about it and I found myself looking at it for a long time and coming back to it, several times. It seemed to draw me into itself so that I felt a part of the night-time scene, lit by the torches and lanterns, one of the crowd of masked revellers, or of the party boarding a gondola and sailing over the moonlit canal and off into the darkness under an ancient bridge. I stood in front of it for a long time, peering into every nook and cranny of the palazzi with their shutters opening here and there on to rooms dark save for the light of a branch of candles here, a lamp there, the odd shadowy figure just glimpsed in the reflected light. The faces of the revellers were many of them the classic Venetian, with prominent noses, the same faces that could be seen as Magi and angels, saints and popes, in the great paintings that filled Venice's churches. Others, though, were recognizably of different nationalities and there was the occasional Ethiopian and Arab. I absorbed the picture in a way I had not done for a long time.

The sale began at two and I went out into the spring sunshine to find some refreshment before returning to the auction rooms, but as I sat in the dim bar of a quiet pub, through the windows of which the sun lanced here and there, I was still immersed in that Venetian scene. I knew of course that I had to buy the picture. I could barely enjoy my lunch and became agitated in case something happened to prevent my getting back to the rooms to bid, so I was one of the first there. But for some reason, I wanted to be standing at the back, away from the rostrum, and I hovered close to the door as the room began to fill. There were some important pictures and I caught sight of several well-known dealers who would be there on behalf of well-to-do clients. No one knew me.

The painting I had at first come to bid for was sold for more than I had expected, and the drawings went quickly beyond my means, but I was almost successful in obtaining a fine Cotman watercolour which came immediately after them when some of the buyers for the lots in the first half had left. I secured a small group of good seascapes and then sat through one stodgy sporting oil after another – fat men on horseback, huntsmen, horses with docked tails giving them an odd, unbalanced air, horses rearing, horses being held by bored grooms, on and on they went and up and up went the sea of hands. I almost dozed off. But then, as the sale was petering out, there was the Venetian carnival scene, looking dark and unattractive now that it was out in the open. There were a couple of half-hearted bids and then a pause. I raised my hand. No one took me on. The hammer was just coming down when there was a slight flurry behind me and a voice called out. I glanced round, surprised and dismayed that I should have last-minute competition for the Venetian picture, but the auctioneer took the view that the hammer had indeed fallen on my bid and there was an end to it. It was mine for a very modest sum.

The palms of my hands were damp and my heart was pounding. I have never felt such an anxiety – indeed, it was close to a desperation to obtain anything and I felt oddly shaken, with relief and also with some other emotion I could not identify. Why did I want the picture so badly? What was its hold over me?

As I went out of the saleroom towards the cashier's office to pay for my purchases, someone tapped me on the shoulder. I turned and saw a stout, sweating man carrying a large leather portfolio case.

'Mr …?' he asked.

I hesitated.

'I need to speak with you urgently.'

'If you will forgive me, I want to get to the cashier's office ahead of the usual queue …'

'No. Please do not.'

'I beg your pardon?'

'You must listen to what I have to say first. Is there somewhere we can go so as not to be overheard?' He was glancing around him as if he expected a dozen eavesdroppers to be closing in on us and I felt annoyed. I did not know the man and had no wish to scurry off with him to some corner.

'Anything you have to say to me can surely be said here. Everyone is busy about their own affairs. Why should they be interested in us?' I wanted to secure my purchases, arrange for them to be delivered to me, and be done.

'Mr …' he paused again.

'Parmitter,' I said curtly.

'Thank you. My name is not relevant – I am acting on behalf of a client. I should have been here far earlier but I encountered a road accident, some unfortunate knocked over and badly injured by a speeding car and I was obliged to stay and speak to the police, it made me too late, I …' He took out a large handkerchief and wiped his brow and upper lip but the beads of sweat popped up again at once. 'I have a commission. There is a picture … I have to acquire it. It is absolutely vital that I take it back with me.'

'But you were too late. Bad luck. Still, it was hardly your fault – your client cannot reasonably blame you for witnessing a road accident.'

He looked increasingly uncomfortable and was sweating even more. I made to move away but he grabbed me and held me by the arm so fiercely that it was painful.

'The last picture,' he said, his breath foetid in my face, 'the Venetian scene. You obtained it and I must have it. I will pay you what you ask, with a good profit, you will not lose. It is in your interests after all, you would only sell it on later. What is your price?'

I wrenched my arm from his grip. 'There is none. The picture is not for sale.'

'Don't be absurd man, my client is wealthy, you can name your price. Don't you understand me – I *have to have that picture*.'

I had heard enough. Without troubling about good manners, I turned on my heel and walked away from him.

But he was there again, pawing at me, keeping close to my side. 'You have to sell the picture to me.'

'If you do not take your hands off I will be obliged to call the porters.'

'My client gave me instructions … I was not to go back without the picture. It has taken years to track it down. I have to have it.'

We had reached the cashier's office, where there was now, of course, a considerable queue of buyers waiting to pay. 'For the last time,' I hissed at him, 'let me alone. I have told you. I want the picture. I bought it and I intend to keep it.'

He took a step back and, for a moment, I thought that was that, but then he leaned close to me and said, 'You will regret it. I have to warn you. You will not want to keep that picture.'

His eyes bulged, and the sweat was running down his face now. 'Do you understand? Sell me the picture. It is for your own good.'

It was all I could do not to laugh in his face but, instead, I merely shook my head and turned away from him, to stare at the grey cloth of the jacket belonging to the man in front of me as if it were the most fascinating thing in the world.

I dared not look round again but by the time I had left the cashier's window having paid for my purchases, including the Venetian picture, the man was nowhere to be seen.

I was relieved and dismissed the incident from my mind as I went out into the sunshine of St James's.

It was only later that evening, as I was settling down to work at my desk, that I felt a sudden, strange frisson, a chill down my spine. I had not been in the least troubled by the man – he had clearly been trying to make up some tale about the picture to convince me I should let him have it. Nevertheless, I felt uneasy.

Everything I had bought at the auction was delivered the next day and the first thing I did was take the Venetian picture across London to a firm of restorers. They would clean it expertly, and either repair the old frame or find another. I also took one of the others to have a small chip made good and because picture restorers work slowly, as they should, I did not see the paintings again for some weeks, by which time I had returned here to the Cambridge summer term that was in full swing.

I brought all the new pictures with me. I was in my London rooms too infrequently to leave anything of much value or interest there. I placed the rest with ease but wherever I put the Venetian picture it looked wrong. I have never had such trouble hanging a painting. And about one thing I was adamant. I did not want it in the room where I slept. I did not even take it into the bedroom. Yet I am not a superstitious man, and up until that time had only ever suffered nightmares if I was ill and had a fever. Because I had such trouble finding the right place for it, in the end I left the painting propped up there, against the bookcase. And I could not stop looking at it. Every time I came back into these rooms, it drew me. I spent more time looking at it – no, into it – than I did with pictures of far greater beauty and merit. I seemed to need it, to spend far too much time looking into every corner, every single face.

I did not hear any more from the tiresome pest in the auction rooms, and I soon forgot about him entirely.

Just one curious thing happened around that time. It was in the autumn of the same year, the first week of Michaelmas term and a night when the first chills of autumn had me ring for a fire. It was blazing up well, and I was working at my desk, in the circle of lamplight, when I happened to glance up for a second. The Venetian painting was directly in my sight and something about it made me look more closely. Cleaning had revealed fresh depths to the picture, and much more detail was now clear. I could see far more people who were crowded on the path beside the water, several rows deep in places, and gondolas and other craft laden with revellers, some masked, others not, on the canal. I had studied the faces over and over again, and each time I found more. People hung out of windows and over balconies, more were in the dim recesses of rooms in the palazzi. But now, it was only one person, one figure, which caught my eye and stood out from all the rest, and although he was near the front of the picture, I did not think I had noticed the man before. He was not looking at the lagoon or the boats, but rather away from them and out of the scene – he seemed, in fact, to be looking at me, and into this room.

He wore clothes of the day but plain ones, not the elaborate fancy dress of many of the carnival-goers, and he was not masked. But two of the revellers close to him wore masks and both appeared to have their hands upon him, one on his shoulder, the other round his left wrist, almost as if they were trying to keep a hold of him or even pull him back. His face had a strange expression, as if he were at once astonished and afraid. He was looking away from the scene because he did not want to be part of it and into my room, at me – at anyone in front of the picture – with what I can only describe as pleading. But for what? What was he asking? The shock was seeing a man's figure there at all when I had previously not noticed it. I supposed that the lamplight, cast on the painting at a particular angle, had revealed the figure clearly for the first time. Whatever the reason, his expression distressed me and I could not work with my former deep concentration. In the night, I woke several times, and, once, out of a strange dream in which the man in the picture was drowning in the canal and stretching out his arms for me to save him, and so vivid was the dream that I got out of bed and came in here, switched on the lamp and looked at the picture. Of course nothing had changed. The man was not drowning though he still looked at me, still pleaded, and I felt that he had been depicted trying to get away from the two men who had their hands on him.

I went back to bed.

And that, for a very long time, was that. Nothing more happened. The picture stayed propped up on the bookcase for months until eventually I found a space for it there, where you see it now.

I did not dream about it again. But it never lessened its hold on me, its presence was never anything but powerful, as if the ghosts of all those people in that weirdly lit, artificial scene were present with me, forever in the room.

Some years passed. The painting did not lose any of its strange force but of course everyday life goes on and I became used to it. I often spent time looking at it though, staring at the faces, the shadows, the buildings, the dark rippling waters of the Grand Canal, and I also vowed that one day I would go to Venice. I have never been a great traveller, as you know; I love the English countryside too much and never wanted to venture far from it during vacations. Besides, in those days I was busy teaching here, performing more and more duties within the college, researching and publishing a number of books and continuing to buy and sell some pictures, though my time for that was limited.

Only one odd thing happened concerning the picture during that period. An old friend, Brammer, came to visit me here. I had not seen him for some years and we had a great deal to talk about but at one point, soon after his arrival and while I was out of the room, he started to look round at the pictures. When I returned, he was standing in front of the Venetian scene and peering closely at it.

'Where did you come by this, Theo?'

'Oh, in a saleroom some years ago. Why?'

'It is quite extraordinary. If I hadn't ...' He shook his head. 'No.'

I went to stand beside him. 'What?'

'You know about all this sort of thing. When do you suppose it was painted?'

'It's late eighteenth century.'

He shook his head. 'Then I can't make it out. You see, that man there ...' He pointed to one of the figures in the nearest gondola. 'I ... I know – knew him. That's to say it is the absolute likeness of someone I knew well. We were young men together. Of course it cannot be him ... but everything – the way he holds his head, the expression ... it is quite uncanny.'

'With so many billions of people born and all of us only having two eyes, one nose, one mouth, I suppose it is even more remarkable that there are not more identical.'

But Brammer was not paying me any attention. He was too absorbed in studying the painting, and in scrutinizing that one face. It took me a while to draw him away from it and to divert him back to the topics of our earlier conversation, and several times over the next twenty-four hours he went back to the picture and would stand there, an expression of concern and disbelief on his face, shaking his head from time to time.

There was no further incident and, after a while, I put Brammer's strange discovery if not out of, then well to the back of my mind.

Perhaps, if I had not been the subject of an article in a magazine more general than academic, some years later, there would have been nothing else and so the story, such as it was until then, would have petered out.

I had completed a long work on Chaucer and it happened that there was a major anniversary which included an exhibition at the British Museum. There had also been an important manuscript discovery relating to his life, about which we have always known so little. The general press took an interest and there was a gratifying amount of attention given to my beloved poet. I was delighted of course. I had long wanted to share the delights his work afforded with a wider public and my publisher was pleased when I agreed to be interviewed here and there.

One of the interviewers who came to see me brought a photographer and he took several pictures in these rooms. If you would care to go to the bureau and open the second drawer, you will find the magazine article filed there.

Three

Theo was a meticulous man — everything was filed and ordered. I had always been impressed, coming in here to tutorials, and seeing the exemplary tidiness of his desk by comparison with that of most other fellows — not to mention with my own. It was a clue to the man. He had an ordered mind. In another life, he ought to have been a lawyer.

The cutting was exactly where he had indicated. It was a large spread about Theo, Chaucer, the exhib-ition and the new discovery, highly informed and informative, and the photograph of him, which took up a full page, was not only an excellent likeness of him as he had been some thirty years previously, but a fine composition in its own right. He was sitting in an armchair, with a pile of books on a small table beside him, his spectacles on top. The sun was slanting through the high window onto him and lighting the whole scene quite dramatically.

'This is a fine photograph, Theo.'

'Look though — look at where the sun falls.'

It fell onto the Venetian picture, which hung behind him, illuminating it vividly and in a strange harmony of light and dark. It seemed to be far more than a mere background.

'Extraordinary.'

'Yes. I confess I was quite taken aback when I saw it. I suppose by then I had grown used to the picture and I had no idea it had such presence in the room.'

I looked round. Now, the painting was half hidden, half in shade, and seemed a small thing, not attracting any attention. The figures were a little stiff and distant, the light rippling on the water dulled. It was like someone in a group who is so retiring and plain that he or she merges into the background unnoticed. What I saw in the magazine photograph was almost a different canvas, not in its content, which was of course the same, but in — I might almost say, in its attitude.

'Odd, is it not?' Theo was watching me intently.

'Did the photographer remark on the picture? Did he deliberately arrange it behind you and light it in some particular way?'

'No. It was never mentioned. He fussed a little with the table of books, I remember … making the pile regular, then irregular … and he had me shift about in the chair. That was all. I recall that when I saw the results – and there were quite a number of shots of course – I was very surprised. I had not even realized the painting was there. Indeed …' He paused.

'Yes?'

He shook his head. 'It is something, to be frank, that has played on my mind ever since, especially in the light of … subsequent events.'

'What is that?'

But he did not answer. I waited. His eyes were closed and he was quite motionless. I realized that the evening had exhausted him, and after waiting a little longer in the silence of those rooms, I got up and left, trying to make my exit soundless, and went away down the dark stone staircase and out into the court.

Four

It was a still, clear and bitter night with a frost and a sky thick and brilliant with stars and I went quickly across to my own staircase to fetch my coat. It was late but I felt like fresh air and a brisk walk. The court was deserted and there were only one or two lights shining out from sets of rooms here and there.

The night porter was already installed in his lodge with a fire in the grate and a great brown pot of tea.

'You mind your step, sir, the pavements have a rime on them even now.'

I thanked him and went out through the great gate. King's Parade was deserted, the shops shuttered. A solitary policeman on the beat nodded to me as I passed him. I was intent on both keeping warm and staying upright as the porter had been right that the pavements were slippery here and there.

But quite without warning, I stopped because a sense of fear and oppression came over me like a wave of fever, so that a shudder ran through my body. I glanced round but the lane was empty and still. The fear I felt was not of anyone or anything, it was just an anonymous, unattached fear and I was in its grip. It was combined with a sense of impending doom, a dread, and also with a terrible sadness, as if someone close to me was suffering and I was feeling that suffering with them.

I am not given to premonitions and, so far as I was aware, no one close to me, no friend or family member, was in trouble. I felt quite well. The only thing that was in my mind was Theo Parmitter's strange story, but why should that have me, who had merely sat by the fire listening to it, so seized by fear? I felt weak and unwell so that I no longer wanted to be out tramping the streets alone and I turned sharply. There must have been a patch of frost exactly there for I felt my feet slither away from under me and fell heavily on the pavement. I lay winded and shaken but not in pain and it was at that moment that I heard, from a little distance away to my left, the cry and a couple of low voices. After that came the sound of a scuffle and then another desperate cry. It seemed to be coming from the direction of the Backs and yet, in some strange sense which is hard to explain, to be not *away* from me at all but here, at my hand, next to me. It is very difficult to convey a clear impression because nothing was clear, and I was also lying on a frozen pavement and anxious in case I had injured myself.

If what I had heard was someone being set upon in the dark and robbed – and that was as near to what it all sounded like as I could describe – then I should get up and either find the victim and go to his aid, or warn the policeman I had seen a few minutes before. Yet no one had been about. It was just after midnight, not a night for strollers, other than fools like me. It then came to me that I was in danger of being attacked myself. I had my wallet in my inner pocket, and a gold watch on my chain. I was worth a villain's attack. I pulled myself to my feet hastily. I was unhurt apart from a bash to the knee – I would be stiff the next day – and looked quickly round but there was no one about and no sound of footsteps. Had I imagined the noises? No, I had not. In a quiet street on a still and frosty night, when every sound carries, I could not have mistaken what I heard for wind in the trees, or in my own ears. I had heard a cry, and voices, and even a splash of water, yet although the sounds had come from the riverside, that was some distance away and hidden by the walls and gardens of the colleges.

I went back to the main thoroughfare and caught sight of the policeman again, trying the doorhandles of shops to check that they were secure. Should I go up to him and alert him that I had almost certainly heard a street robbery? But if I had heard the robbers, he, only a few yards away in a nearby street, must surely have heard them too, yet he was not rushing away but merely continuing down King's Parade with his steady, measured tread.

A car turned down from the direction of Trinity Street and glided past me. A cat streaked away into a dark slit between two buildings. My breath smoked on the frosty air. There was nothing untoward about and the town was settled for the night.

The oppression and dread that had enshrouded me a few minutes earlier had lifted, almost as a consequence of what I had heard and of my fall but I was puzzled and I did not feel comfortable in my own skin, and by now I was also thoroughly chilled so I made my way back to the college gate as briskly as I could, my coat collar turned up against the freezing night air.

The porter, still ensconced by his glowing fire, wished me goodnight. I replied, and turned into the court.

All was dark and quiet but light shone from one of the same two windows I had noticed when I went out, and now from another on the far left-hand row. Someone must just have returned. In a couple of weeks term would have begun and then lights would be on all round – undergraduates do not turn in early. I stood for a moment looking round, remembering the good years I had spent within these walls, the conversations late into the night, the japes, the hours spent sweating over an essay and boning up for Part One. I would never want to be like Theo, spending all my years here, however comfortable the college life might be, but I had a pang of longing for the freedoms and the friendships. It was then that my eye was caught by one light, the original one, going out, so that now there was only one room with a light on, on the far side, and it was automatic for me to glance up there.

What I saw made my blood freeze. Whereas before there had been a blank, now a figure was in the room and close to the window. The lamp was to one side of him and its beam was thrown onto his face, and the effect was startlingly like that of the Venetian picture. Well, there was nothing strange about that – lamplight and torchlight will always highlight and provide sharply contrasting shadows in this way. No, it was the face at the window by which I was transfixed. The man was looking directly at me and I could have sworn I recognized him, not from life but from the picture, because he bore such an uncanny resemblance to one of the faces that I would have sworn in any court that they were one and the same. But how could this possibly be? It could not, and besides, I had merely glanced at the one and it was at a window some distance from me, whereas the other was in a picture and I had studied it closely for some time. There are only so many combinations of features, as Theo himself had said.

But it was not the mere resemblance which struck so, it was the expression on the face at the window that had the impact upon me and produced such a violent reaction. The face was one I had particularly noticed in the picture because it was a fine depiction of decadence, of greed and depravity, of malice and loathing, of every sort of inhuman feeling and intent. The eyes were piercing and intense, the mouth full and sardonic, the whole face set into a sneer of arrogance and concupiscence. It was a mesmerizingly unpleasant face and it had repelled me in the picture as much as it horrified me now. I had glanced away, shocked, from the window, but now I looked up again. The face had gone and after another couple of seconds the light went out and the room was black. The whole court was now in darkness, save for the lamps at each corner, which cast a comforting pool of tallow light onto the gravel path.

I came to, feeling numb with cold and chilled with fear. I was shivering and the sense of dread and imminent doom had returned and seemed to wrap me round in place of my coat. But at the same time I was determined not to let these feelings get the better of me and I went across the court and up the staircase of the rooms from which the light had been shining. I remembered them as being the set a friend of mine had occupied in our time and found them without trouble. I stood outside the door and listened closely. There was a silence so absolute that it was uncanny. Old buildings generally make some sound, creaking and settling back, but here it was as still and quiet as the grave. After a moment, I knocked on the outer door, though without expecting any reply, as the occupant would now be in the bedroom and might well not have heard me. I knocked again more loudly, and when again there was no answer, I turned the door handle and stepped inside the small outer lobby. The air was bitterly cold here, which was strange as no one would be occupying rooms on such a night without having heated them. I hesitated, then went into the study.

'Hello,' I said in a low voice.

There was no response and after I had repeated my 'Hello' I felt along the wall for the light switch. The room was empty, and not only empty of any person, but empty of any thing, apart from a desk and chair, one armchair beside the cold and empty grate, and a bookcase without any books in it. There was an overhead light but no lamp of any kind. I went through to the bedroom. There was a bed, stripped of all linen. Nothing else.

Obviously, I had mistaken the rooms and I left, and made my way to the second set adjacent to them, the only others on the upper level of this staircase – each one had two sets up and a single, much larger set, on the ground floor and the pattern was the same on three sides of this, the Great Court. (The Inner Court was smaller and arranged quite differently.)

I knocked and, hearing only silence in response again, went into this set of rooms too. They were as empty as the first – emptier indeed since here there was no furniture other than the bookcases which were built into the wall. There was also a smell of plaster and paint.

I thought that I would go across to the night porter and ask who normally occupied this staircase. But what purpose would that serve? There were no undergraduates in residence, these sets had not been used by fellows for many years and clearly, decoration and maintenance were underway.

I cannot possibly have seen a lamp lit and a figure in any of these windows.

But I knew that I had.

I went, thoroughly shaken now, down the staircase, and across the court to the guest set in which I was staying. There, I had a bottle of whisky and a soda siphon. Ignoring the latter, I poured myself a large slug of the scotch and downed it in one, followed by another, which I took more slowly. I then went to bed and, in spite of the whisky, lay shivering for some time before falling into a heavy sleep. It was filled with the most appalling nightmares, through which I tossed and turned and sweated in horror, nightmares filled with strange flaring lights and fires and the shouts of people drowning.

I woke hearing myself cry out, and as I gathered my senses, I heard something else, a tremendous crash, as of something heavy falling. It was followed by a distant and muffled cry, as if someone had been hit and injured.

My heart was pounding so loudly in my ears and my brain still so swirling with the dreadful pictures that it took me a moment to separate nightmare from reality, but when I had been sitting upright with the lamp switched on for a few moments, I knew that what I had seen and the voices of the people drowning had been unreal and parts of a disturbing nightmare, but that the crashing sound and the subsequent cry most certainly had not. Everything was quiet now but I got out of bed and went into the sitting room. All was in order. I returned for my dressing gown, and then went out onto the staircase but here, too, all was still and silent. No one was occupying the adjacent set but I did not know if a fellow was in residence below. Theo Parmitter's rooms were on a different staircase.

I went down in the dark and icy cold and listened at the doors below but there was absolutely no sound.

'Is anyone there? Is everything all right?' I called but my voice echoed oddly up the stone stairwell and there was no answering call.

I went back to bed, and slept fitfully until morning, mainly because I was half frozen and found it difficult to get warm and comfortable again.

When I looked out of the windows a little after eight, I saw that a light snow had fallen and that the fountain in the centre of the court had frozen solid.

I was dressing when there was a hurried knock on the outer door and the college servant came in looking troubled.

'I thought you would want to know at once, sir, that there's been an accident. It's Mr Parmitter …'

Five

There is really no need to trouble a doctor. I am a little shaken but unhurt. I will be perfectly all right.'

The servant had managed to get Theo into his chair in the sitting room, where I found him, looking pale and with an odd look about his eyes which I could not read.

'The doctor is on his way so there's an end to it,' I said, nodding approvingly at the servant, who had brought in a tray of tea and was refilling a water jug. 'Now tell me what happened.'

Theo leaned back and sighed, but I could tell that he was not going to argue further. 'You fell? You must have slipped on something. We must get the maintenance people to check ...'

'No. It is not their concern.' He spoke quite sharply.

I poured us both tea and waited until the servant had left. I had already noticed that the Venetian picture was no longer in its former place.

'Something happened,' I said. 'And you must tell me, Theo.'

He took up his cup and I noticed that his hand was shaking slightly.

'I did not sleep well,' he said at last. 'That is not unusual. But last night it was well after two before I got off and I slept very fitfully, with nightmares and general disturbance.'

'I had nightmares,' I said. 'Which is most unusual for me.'

'It is my fault. I should never have started on that wretched story.'

'Of course it is not – I went for a brisk walk to clear my head and woke myself up too thoroughly. It was also damned cold.'

'No. It was more than that, as it was with me. I am certain of it now. I was in such discomfort and sleeping so wretchedly that I knew I would be better off up and sitting in this chair. It takes me some time to get myself out of bed and stirring and I had heard the clock strike four when I made my way in here. As I came up to that wall on which the picture hung, I hesitated for a split second – something made me hesitate. The wire holding the painting snapped and the whole thing crashed down, glancing my shoulder so that I lost my balance and fell. If I had not paused, it would have hit me on the head. There is no question about it.'

'What made you pause? A premonition surely.'

'No, no. I daresay I was aware, subliminally, of the wire straining and being about to break. But the whole incident has shaken me a little.'

'I'm sorry – sorry for you, of course, but I confess I am sorry that I will not hear the rest of the story.'

Theo looked alarmed. 'Why? Of course, if you have to leave, or you prefer not to … but I wish that you would stay, Oliver. I wish that you would hear me out.'

'Of course I will. I could hardly bear to be left dangling like this but perhaps it would be better for your peace of mind if we let the whole thing drop.'

'Most emphatically it would not! If I do not tell you the rest I fear I shall never sleep well again. Now that it is buzzing in my mind it is as disturbing as a hive of angry bees. I must somehow lay them to rest. But do you now have to return to London?'

'I can stay another night – indeed it would be time well spent. There are some things I can usefully look at in the library while I am here.'

There was a tap on the door. The doctor arrived and I told Theo I would see him later that day, if he was up to talking – but that he must on no account disobey any 'doctor's orders' – the tale could wait. It was of no consequence. But I did not mean that. It was of more consequence now than I dared admit. Enough things had happened both to unnerve me and also to convince me that they were connected though each one taken alone meant little. I should say that I am by no means a man who jumps readily to outlandish conclusions. I am a scholar and I have been trained to require evidence, though as I am not a lawyer, circumstantial evidence will sometimes satisfy me well enough. I am also a man of strong nerve and sanguine temperament, so the fact that I had been disturbed by events is noteworthy. And I now knew that Theo Parmitter too was disturbed and, above all, that he had begun to tell me the story of the Venetian picture not to entertain me as we sat by the fire, but to unburden himself, to share his misgivings and fears with another human being, not unlike him in temperament, one who would bring a calm rational mind to bear upon them.

At least my mind, like my nervous state, had been calm until the previous night. Now, although my reason told me that the falling picture was a straightforward event and readily explained, my shadowy sense of foreboding and unease told me otherwise. I knew and often applied the principle of Occam's razor but, here, my intuition ruled my reason.

I spent most of the day in the library working on a medieval psalter and then went into the town to have tea in the Trumpington Street café I had often frequented and which was generally full of steam and the buzz of conversation. But that, of course, was in term-time. Now it was almost deserted and I sat eating my buttered crumpets in a somewhat chill and gloomy atmosphere. I had hoped to be cheered up by plenty of human company but even the shopping streets were quiet – it was too cold for strollers and anyone who had needed to buy something had done so speedily and returned to the warmth and snugness of home.

I would be doing the same tomorrow, and although I loved this town which had been of such benefit to me and in which I had spent some supremely happy years, I would not be sorry when this particular visit was over. It had been an unhappy and an unsettling one. I longed for the bustle of London and for my own comfortable house.

I returned to the college and, because I felt in need of company, went to dine in hall with half a dozen of the fellows. We made cheerful conversation and finished off a good bottle of port in the combination room in typical Cambridge fashion, so that it was rather late by the time I went across the court and up the staircase to my rooms. I found an anxious message awaiting me from Theo asking me to go and see him as soon as I was free.

I sat down for a few moments before doing so. I had, it was true, avoided going to see him since the morning, though I had of course enquired and been told that he was none the worse, physically, for the morning's incident, though still a little unnerved. I had managed to blow away the clinging cobwebs of my low and anxious mood and I was apprehensive about hearing any more of Theo's story. Yet he had all but begged me to go and hear him out, for his peace of mind depended upon it, and I felt badly about leaving him alone all day.

I hurried out and down the staircase.

Theo was looking better. He had a small glass of malt whisky beside him, a good fire and a cheerful face and he enquired about my day in a perfectly easy manner.

'I'm sorry I was occupied and didn't get along here earlier.'

'My dear fellow, you're not in Cambridge to sit with me day and night.'

'All the same ...'

I sat down and accepted a glass of the Macallan. 'I have come to hear the rest of the story,' I said, 'if you feel up to it and still wish to tell me.'

Theo smiled.

The first thing I had looked for on coming into the room was the picture. It had been re-hung in its original position but it was in full shadow, the lamp turned away and shining on the opposite wall. I thought the change must have been made deliberately.

'What point had I reached?' Theo asked. 'I can't for the life of me remember.'

'Come, Theo,' I said quietly, 'I rather think that you remember very clearly, for all that you dropped off to sleep and I left you to your slumbers. You were coming to an important part of the story.'

'Perhaps my falling asleep was a gesture of self-defence.'

'At any rate, you need to tell me the rest or both of us will sleep badly again tonight. You had just shown me the article in the magazine, in which the picture appeared too prominently. I asked you if the photographer had placed it deliberately.'

'And he had not. So far as I was aware he had paid it no attention and I certainly had not done so. But there it was one might say dominating the photograph and the room. I was surprised but nothing more. And then, a couple of weeks after the magazine appeared, I received a letter. I have it still and I looked it out this morning. I had filed it away. It is there, on the table beside you.'

He pointed to a stiff, ivory-coloured envelope. I picked it up. It was addressed to him here in college and postmarked Yorkshire, some thirty years previously. It was written in violet ink and in an elaborate, old-style hand.

Hawdon by Eskby
North Riding of Yorkshire

Dear Dr Parmitter,
I am writing to you on behalf of the Countess of Hawdon, who has seen an article about you and your work in the —Journal and wishes to make contact with you in regard to a painting in the room in which you appear photographed. The painting, an oil of a Venetian carnival scene, hangs immediately behind you and is of most particular and personal interest to her Ladyship.

Lady Hawdon has asked me to invite you here as there are matters to do with the picture that she needs most urgently to discuss.

The house is situated to the north of Eskby and a car will meet your train from the railway station at any time. Please communicate with me as to your willingness to visit her Ladyship and offer a date, at your convenience. I would stress again that because of her Ladyship's frail health and considerable agitation on this matter, an immediate visit would suit.

Yours etc

John Thurlby
Secretary.

'And did you go?' I asked, setting the letter down.

'Oh yes. Yes, I went to Yorkshire. Something in the tone of the letter meant that I felt I had no choice. Besides, I was intrigued. I was younger then and up for an adventure. I went off with a pretty light heart, as soon as term ended, within a couple of weeks.'

He leaned forward and poured himself another glass of whisky and indicated that I should do the same. I caught his expression in the light from the fire as he did so. He spoke lightly, of a jaunt to the north. But a haunted and troubled look had settled on his features that belied the conscious cheerfulness of his words.

'I do not know what I expected to find,' he said, after sipping his whisky. 'I had no preconceived ideas of the place called Hawdon or of this Countess. If I had … You think mine is a strange story, Oliver. But my story is nothing, it is merely a prelude to the story told me by an extraordinary old woman.'

Six

Yorkshire proved dismal and overcast on the day I made my journey. I changed trains in the early afternoon when rain had set in, and although the scenery through which we passed was clearly magnificent in decent weather, now I scarcely saw a hundred yards beyond the windows – no great hills and valleys and open moors were visible but merely lowering clouds over dun countryside. It was December, and dark by the time the slow train arrived, panting uphill, at Eskby station. A handful of other passengers got out and disappeared quickly into the darkness of the station passageway. The air was raw and a damp chill wind blew into my face as I came out into the forecourt, where two taxis and, at a little distance away, a large black car were drawn up. The moment I emerged, a man in a tweed cap slid up to me through the murk.

'Dr Parmitter.' It was not a question. 'Harold, sir. I'm to take you to Hawby.'

Those were the only words he spoke voluntarily, the entire way, after he had put my bag in the boot and started up. He had automatically put me in the back seat, though I would have preferred to sit beside him, and as it was pitch dark once we had left the small town, which sat snugly on the side of a hill, it was a dreary journey.

'How much farther?' I asked at one point.

'Four mile.'

'Have you worked for Lady Hawdon many years?'

'I have.'

'I gather she is in poor health?'

'She is.'

I gave up, put my head back against the cold seat leather and waited, without saying any more, for the end of our journey.

What had I expected? A bleak and lonely house set above a ravine, with ivy clinging to damp walls, a moat half empty, the sides slippery with

green slime and the bottom black with stagnant water? An aged and skel-
etal butler, wizened and bent, and a shadowy, ravaged figure gliding past
me on the stairs?

Well, the house was certainly isolated. We left the main country road
and drove well over a mile, at a guess, over a rough single track but, at the
end, it broadened out suddenly and I saw a gateway ahead with great iron
gates standing open. The drive bent round so that at first there was only
darkness ahead, but then we veered quite sharply to the right and over a
low stone bridge, and peering through the darkness, I could see an imposing house with lights shining out from several of the high upper windows.
We drew up on the gravel and I saw that the front door, at the top of a
flight of stone steps, stood open. Light shone out from here too. It was
altogether more welcoming than I had expected, and although a grand
house it had a pleasing aspect and bore not the slightest resemblance to
the House of Usher, whose fearsome situation I had been remembering.

I was greeted by a pleasant-faced butler, who introduced himself as
Stephens, and taken up two flights of stairs to a splendid room whose
long dark-red curtains were drawn against the dismal night and in which I
found everything I could have wanted to pass a comfortable night. It was
a little after six o'clock.

'Her Ladyship would like you to join her in the blue drawing room
at seven thirty, sir. If you would ring the bell when you are ready I will
escort you down.'

'Does Lady Hawdon dress for dinner?'

'Oh yes, sir.' The butler's face was impassive but I heard a frisson of
disdain in his voice. 'If you do not have a dinner jacket ...'

'Yes, thank you, I do. But I thought it best to enquire.'

It had been only as an afterthought that I had packed the jacket and
black tie, as I have always found it best to be over- rather than under-pre-
pared. But I had now no idea at all what to expect from the evening ahead.

Stephens came promptly to lead me down the stairs and along a wide
corridor, lined with many large oil paintings, some sporting prints, and
cabinets full of curiosities, including masks, fossils and shells, silver and
enamel. We walked too quickly for me to do more than glance eagerly
from side to side but my spirits had lifted at the thought of what treasures
there must be in the house and which I might be allowed to see.

'Dr Parmitter, m'Lady.'

It was an extremely grand room, with a magnificent fireplace, in front of which were three large sofas forming a group and on which lamplight and the light of the fire were focused. There were lamps elsewhere in the room, on small tables and illuminating pictures, but they were turned low. There were a number of fine paintings on the walls, Edwardian family portraits, hunting scenes, groups of small oils. At the far end of the room I saw a grand piano with a harpsichord nearby.

There was nothing decaying, dilapidated or chilling about such a drawing room. But the woman who sat on an upright chair with her face turned away from the fire did not match the room in warmth and welcome. She was extremely old, with the pale-parchment textured skin that goes with great age, a skin like the paper petals of dried Honesty. Her hair was white and thin, but elaborately combed up onto her head and set with a couple of glittering ornaments. She wore a long frock of some green material on which a splendid diamond brooch was set, and there were diamonds about her long, sinewy neck. Her eyes were deep set but not the washed-out eyes of an old woman. They were a piercing, unnerving blue.

She did not move except to reach out her left hand to me, her eyes scrutinizing my face. I took the cold, bony fingers, which were heavily, even grotesquely jewelled, principally with diamonds again but also with a single large chunk of emerald.

'Dr Parmitter, please sit down. Thank you for coming here.'

As I sat, the butler appeared and offered champagne. I noticed that it was an extremely fine vintage and that the Countess was not drinking it.

'This is a very splendid house and you have some wonderful works of art,' I said.

She waved her hand slightly.

'I presume this is a family home of some generations?'

'It is.' There was a dreadful silence and I felt a miasma of gloom descend on me. This was going to be a tricky evening. The Countess was clearly not one for small talk, I still did not know exactly why I had been summoned, and in spite of the comfort and beauty surrounding me I felt awkward.

I wondered if we were to be alone for dinner.

Then she said, 'You cannot know what a shock I received on seeing the picture.'

'The Venetian picture? Your secretary mentioned in his letter to me …'

'I know nothing of you. I do not customarily look at picture papers. It was Stephens who chanced upon it and naturally brought it to my attention. I was considerably shaken, as I say.'

'May I ask why? What the picture has to do with you – or perhaps with your family? Clearly it is of some importance for you to ask me here.'

'It is of more importance than I can say. Nothing else in life matters to me more. *Nothing else.*'

Her gaze held mine as a hand might hold another in a grip of steel. I could not look away and it was only the voice of the silent-footed butler, who now appeared behind us and announced dinner, which broke the dreadful spell.

The dining room was high-ceilinged and chill and we sat together at one end of the long table, with silver candlesticks before us and the full paraphernalia of china, silver and glassware as for an elaborate dinner. I wondered if the Countess sat in such state when she dined alone. I had offered her my arm across the polished floors into the dining room and it had been like having the claw of a bird resting there. Her back was bent and she had no flesh on her bones. I guessed that she must be well into her nineties. Sitting next to me, she seemed more like a moth than a bird, with the brilliant blue eyes glinting at me out of the pale skin, but I noticed that she was made up with rouge and powder and that her nails were painted. She had a high forehead behind which the hair was puffed out, and a beaky, bony nose, a thin line of mouth. Her cheekbones were high, too, and I thought that, with the blue of her eyes and with flesh on her distinguished bones, she might well have been a considerable beauty in her youth.

A plate of smoked fish was offered, together with thinly sliced bread and chunks of lemon, and a bowl of salad was set in front of us. I filled my mouth full, partly because I was hungry, but also in order not to have to talk for a few moments. A fine white Burgundy was poured, though, again, the Countess drank nothing, save from the glass of water beside her. The dinner proceeded in a stately way and the Countess spoke little, save to give me some scraps of dullish information about the history of the house and estate and the surrounding area, and to ask me a couple of cursory questions about my own work. There was no liveliness at all in her manner. She ate little, broke up a piece of bread into small fragments and left them on her plate, and seemed tired and distant. I was gloomy at the thought of spending the rest of a long slow evening with her and frustrated that the point of my journey had not been reached.

At the end of dinner, the butler came to announce that coffee was

served in the 'blue room'. The Countess took my arm and we followed
him down the long corridor again and through a door into a small, wood-
panelled room. I barely felt the weight of her hand but the fingers were
pale bones resting on my jacket and the huge emerald ring looked like a
carbuncle.

The blue room was partly a library, though I doubt if any of the heavy,
leather-bound sets of books had been taken down from the shelves for
years, and partly lined with dull maps of the county and legal documents
with seals, framed behind glass. But there was a long polished table, on
which were set out several large albums, and also the magazine with
the article and the Venetian picture behind me, spread open. The butler
poured coffee for me and a further glass of water for the Countess, helped
her to a chair at the table before the books, and left us. As he did so, he
turned the main lights down a little. Two lamps shone onto the table at
either side of us and the Countess motioned for me to sit beside her.

She opened one of the albums, and I saw that it contained photographs, carefully placed and with names, places, dates, in neat ink. She
turned several pages over carefully without explanation or inviting me to
look, but at last came to a double spread of wedding photographs from
seventy or more years ago, sepia pictures with the bridegroom seated,
the bride standing, others with parents, the women draped in lace and
wearing huge hats, the men moustached.

'My wedding, Dr Parmitter. Please look carefully.'

She turned the album round. I studied the various groups. The Countess had indeed been a very beautiful young woman, even as she stood
unsmiling, as was the way in such photographs then, and I admired her
long face with its clear skin, straight nose, small and pretty mouth, pert
chin. Her eyes were large and deeply set and, even though these pictures
were in sepia, I could imagine their astonishing blue.

'Does nothing strike you?'

It did not. I looked for a long time but knew no one, recognized
nothing.

'Look at my husband.'

I did so. He was a dark-haired young man, the only male who was
clean-shaven. His hair was slightly waved at the sides, his mouth rather
full. He had a handsome face of character but not, I would say, rare
character.

'I confess I do not know him – I recognize no one save yourself, of
course.'

She turned her eyes on me now and her face wore a curious expression, partly of hauteur but also, I saw, of a distress I could not fathom.

'Please ...'

I glanced down again and, in that split second, had an extraordinary flash of – what? Shock? Recognition? Revelation?

Whatever it was, it must have shown clearly on my face, for the Countess said, 'Ah. Now you see.'

I was groping in the dark for a moment. I had seen and yet what had I seen? I now knew that there was something very familiar, I might almost say intimately familiar, about a face – but which face? Not hers, not that of ... No. His face. Her young husband's face. I knew it, or someone very like it. It was as though I knew it so well that it was the face of a member of my own family, a face I saw every day, a face with which I was so very familiar that I was, if you understand me, no longer aware of it.

Something was in the shadows of my mind, out of reach, out of my grasp, hovering but incomprehensible.

I shook my head.

'Look.' She had taken up the magazine and was gazing at it – for a moment, I thought she was gazing at the photograph of myself, sitting in my college rooms. But then she slid the paper across the table to me, one long thin finger pointing down.

There was a brief instant when what I saw made me experience a wave of shock so tremendous that I felt rising nausea and the room seemed to lurch crazily from side to side. What had been at the back of my mind came to the very front of it and clicked into place. Yet how could I believe what I was seeing? How could this be?

The Venetian picture was very clear in the magazine photograph, but even if it had not been, I knew it so well, so thoroughly and intimately, I was so familiar with every detail of it, that I could not have been mistaken. There was, you remember, one particular scene within the scene. A young man was being held by the arm and threatened by another person, on the point of stepping into one of the boats, and his head was turned to look into the eyes of whoever was viewing the picture, with an expression of strange, desperate terror and of pleading. Now, I looked at it and it was vivid, even at one stage removed, through a photograph. The face of the young man being persuaded into the boat was the face of the Countess's husband. There was no doubt about it. The resemblance was absolute. This was not a near-likeness. The two young men did not share a similar physiognomy. They were one and the same. I saw it in the eyes, on the lips, in the set of the forehead, the jut of the jaw. Everything came together in a moment of recognition.

She was staring at me intently.

'My God,' I whispered. But I struggled for words, tried to grab hold of sanity. There was, of course, a sensible, an ordinary, a rational explanation.

'So your husband was a sitter for the artist.' As I said it, I knew how ridiculous it was.

'The picture was painted in the late eighteenth century.'

'Then – this is a relative? One you perhaps have only just discovered? This is an extraordinary family likeness.'

'No. It is my husband. It is Lawrence.'

'Then I do not understand.'

She was leaning over the photograph now, gazing at the picture and at the face of her young husband, with an intensity of longing and distress such as I had never seen.

I waited for some time. Then she said, 'I would like to return to the drawing room. Now that you have seen this, now that you know … I can tell you what there is to tell.'

'I would like to hear it. But I have no idea how I can help you.'

She put out her hand for me to assist her up.

'We can make our own way. We have no need of Stephens.'

Once more, the thin, weightless hand rested on my arm and we walked the length of the corridor, now in shadow as the wall lamps had been dimmed, so that the pictures and cabinets receded into darkness except when the gilt corner of a frame or a panel of glass glowed eerily in the tallow light.

The Countess's Story

I was married when I was twenty. I met my husband at a ball and we experienced a *coup de foudre*. Few people are lucky enough to know that thing commonly called love at first sight. Few people really know and understand its utterly transforming power. We are the fortunate ones. Such an experience changes one entirely and for ever.

It was such an ordinary place to meet. That is how young people all met one another in those days, is it not? I daresay they still do. But how many of them know such instant, such blinding love? He was several years older, in his early thirties. But that did not matter. Nothing mattered. My parents were a little concerned – I was young, and I had an elder sister who should, in the natural order of these things, have been married before me. But they looked upon Lawrence with favour, nevertheless. There was only one thing to trouble us. He had been on the verge of an engagement. He had not proposed but there was an understanding. If he and I had not met that evening, it is sure that there would have been an engagement and a marriage and naturally the young woman in question was bitterly hurt. These things happen, Dr Parmitter. I had no reason to feel in any way to blame. Nor, perhaps, had he. But of course he felt a great concern for the girl and I – when I was eventually told – I felt as great a guilt and sorrow as a girl of twenty in the throes of such a love could be expected to feel. What happens in these cases? What usually happens is that one party suffers for a certain period of time from hurt pride and a broken heart, both of which are eventually healed, generally by the arrival of another suitor.

In this instance, it was otherwise. The young woman, whose name was Clarissa Vigo, suffered so greatly that I believe it turned her mind. I had not known her at all prior to this but I had been assured, and had no reason to doubt it, that she had been a charming, gentle, generous young woman. She became a bitter, angry, tormented one whose only thought was of the injury she had suffered and how she could obtain revenge. Of course, the best way was to destroy our happiness. That is what she set her mind to and what consumed her time and energy and passion. Much of this was kept from me, at least at first, but I learned afterwards that her family despaired of her sanity to the extent that they had her visited by a priest!

This was not the parish vicar, Dr Parmitter. This was a priest who undertook exorcisms. He was called both to houses under the influence of unhappy spirits and to persons behaving as if they were possessed. I believe that is how the young woman was treated. But he came away, he said, in despair. He felt unable to help her because she would not allow herself to be helped. Her bitterness and desire for retribution had become so strong that they possessed her entirely. They became her reason for living. Whether that is what you would class as demonic possession I do not know. I do know that she set out to destroy. And she succeeded. She succeeded in the most terrible way. I have always believed that if the priest could have exorcised her demons then, all would have been well, but as he could not things grew worse, her determination grew stronger and with it her power to do harm. She was indeed possessed. Anger and jealousy are terrible forces when united together with an iron will.

But to begin with I was unaware of any of this. Lawrence referred only briefly and somewhat obliquely to her, and of course I was obsessed and possessed in my turn – by an equally single-minded and powerful love.

My time and energies were entirely consumed by Lawrence and by our forthcoming marriage, preparations for our new home and so forth. All that is perfectly usual of course. I was not an unusual young woman, you know. Two things happened in the weeks before our marriage. I received an anonymous letter. Anonymous? It was unsigned and I did not know who had sent it. Not then. It was full of poison. Poison against me, against Lawrence, bitter, vindictive poison. It contained a threat, too, to destroy our future. To bring about pain and shock and devastating loss. I was terrified by it. I had never known hatred in my happy young life and here it was, directed at me, hatred and the desire – no, more, the determination to harm. For several days I kept the letter locked in a drawer of my writing desk. It seemed to sear through the wood. I seemed to smell it, to feel the hatred that emanated from it, every time I went near, so that in the end I tore it into shreds and burned it in the hearth. After that I tried to put it out of my mind.

We were to be married the following month and naturally wedding presents began to arrive at my parents' house – silver, china and so forth – and I was happily occupied in unpacking and looking at it all, and in writing little notes of thanks. And one day – I remember it very clearly – along with some handsome antique tables and a footstool, a picture arrived. There was a card with it, on which was written the name of the painter, and a date, 1797. There was also a message To the Bride and Bridegroom. Let what is begun be completed in the same hand as the malign letter.

I hated the picture from the moment I first saw it. Partly, of course, that was because it came from someone unknown, the same someone who had sent me the letter and who wished us harm. But it was more than that. I did not know much about art but I had grown up among delightful pictures which had come down through my family on my mother's side, charming English pastoral scenes and paintings of families with horses and dogs, still-life oils of flowers and fruit, innocent, happy things which pleased me. This was a dark, sinister painting in my eyes. If I had known the words 'corrupt' and 'decadent' then I would have used them to describe it. As I looked at the faces of those people, at the eyes behind the masks and the strange smiles, the suggestions of figures in windows, figures in shadows, I shuddered. I felt uneasy, I felt afraid.

But when Lawrence saw the picture he had nothing but praise for it. He found it interesting. When he asked me who had sent it I lied. I said that I had mislaid the card, muddled it with others in so much unwrapping. I could certainly not have expressed to him any of my feelings about the picture – they were so odd, even to me, so unlike anything I had ever experienced. I could not have found the right words for them and, in any case, I would have been afraid of being ridiculed. Two secrets. Not a good way to begin a marriage, you may feel. But what else should I have done?

I had had so little experience of the world and of different kinds of people. I had led a happy and a sheltered upbringing. So it was not until a day or two before our wedding that I understood who had sent both the anonymous letter and the picture, and then only when I chanced to see an envelope addressed to Lawrence in the same handwriting. I asked him who had sent it and he told me, of course, that it was from the young woman he might have married. I remember his tone of voice, as if he were holding something back from me, as if he were trying not to make anything of the letter. It was just some snippet of information he had asked for many months before, he said, and changed the subject. I was not worried that he had any feelings for her. I was worried because I knew at once that he, too, had received a letter full of hatred and ill-will, that he wanted to protect me and keep it from me, that the woman was the sender of the picture. I did not ask him. I did not need to ask him. But once all of these things fell into place, I was more than ever afraid. Yet of what I was afraid – how could I know? I disliked the picture – it repelled me, made me shudder. But it was just a picture. We could hang it in some distant corner of our house, or even leave it wrapped and put it away.

Our wedding was a happy occasion, of course. Everyone was happy – our families, our friends. We were happy. Only one person in the world was not but naturally she did not attend and on that day no one could have been further from our thoughts.

I did as best I could to put the incidents and the painting out of my mind and we began our married life. Six weeks after the wedding, Lawrence's father, the Earl of Hawdon, died very suddenly. Lawrence was the eldest son and I found myself, not yet even twenty-one years old, the mistress of this large house and with a husband thrust into the running of a huge estate. We had taken a short honeymoon on the south coast and planned a longer tour the following spring. Now, perhaps we would never undertake it.

I have said that my father-in-law died suddenly – quite suddenly and unexpectedly. He had been in the best of health – he was an energetic man, and he was found dead at his desk one evening after dinner. A stroke. Of course we believed the medical men. One must. What reason was there to doubt them?

I have now to tell you something which I expect you to disbelieve. At first, that is to say, you will disbelieve it. I would ask you to go across to the bureau in the far corner of this room and look at the framed photograph which stands there.

I crossed the long, silent room, leaving the Countess, a tiny, wraithlike figure hunched into her chair in the circle of lamplight, and entering the shadows. But there was a lamp on the bureau, which I switched on. As I did so, I caught my breath.

I saw a photograph in a plain silver frame. It was of a man in middle age, sitting at this same desk and half turning to the camera. His hands rested on the blotter which was in front of me now. He had a high forehead, a thick head of hair, a full mouth, heavy lids. It was a good face, a strong, resolute face of character, and a handsome one too. But I was transfixed by the face because I knew it. I had seen it before, many times. I was familiar with it.

I had lived with that face.

I looked back to the old woman sitting once again with her head back, eyes closed, a husk.

But she said, her voice making me start, 'So now you see.'

My throat was dry and I had to clear it a couple of times before I could answer her, and even when I did so, my own voice sounded strange and unfamiliar.

'I see but I scarcely know what it is that I do see.'

But I did know. Even as I spoke, of course I knew. I had known the instant I set eyes on the photograph. And yet … I did not understand.

I returned to my chair opposite the old woman.

'Please refill your glass.'

I did so thankfully. After I had downed my whisky and poured a second, I said, 'Now, I confess I do not understand but I can only suppose this is some hoax … the painting cannot be of its date, of course, there is some trick, some faking? I hope you will explain.'

I had spoken in a falsely amused and over-loud tone and as the words dropped into the silent space between us, I felt foolish. Whatever the explanation, it was not a matter for jest.

The Countess looked at me with disdain.

'There is no question of either a hoax or a mistake. But you know it.'

'I know it.'

Silence. I wondered how this great house could be so silent. In my experience old houses are never so, they speak, they have movements and soft voices and odd footfalls, they have a life of their own, but this house had none.

Nothing happened immediately. My father-in-law was dead and we were thrown into the usual business which surrounds a death – and my husband found himself pitched into a wholly new life with all its responsibilities. We had not even moved into the small house at the far side of the estate which was to have been our married home, and now we found ourselves forced to take over this house instead. We had barely unpacked our wedding presents and there was no place for most of them here. It was a week after we had moved in. Lawrence and his mother of course were shocked and still in deep mourning. I was sad but I had known my father-in-law so little. I wandered about this great place like a lost soul, trying to get to know each room, to find a role for myself, to keep out of everyone's way. It was on these wanderings that I finally came upon the Venetian picture. It had been put with some other items into one of the small sitting rooms on the first floor – a room that I think was rarely used. It smelled of damp and had an empty, purposeless air. The curtains hung heavy, the furniture seemed ill-chosen.

The picture was propped up on a half-empty bookcase. It faced me as I went into the room. And … and it seemed to me that it drew me to it and that every face within it looked into mine. I cannot describe it better. Every face. I wanted to leave the room at once, but I could not, the picture drew me to itself as if every person painted there had the strength to reach out and pull me towards it. As I approached it, some of the faces receded, some disappeared completely into the shadows and were no longer there after all. But one face was there. It was a face at a window. There is a palazzo with two lighted windows and with open shutters and a balcony overlooking the Grand Canal. In one of those lighted rooms, but looking out as if desperate to escape, even to fling himself over the balcony into the waters below to get away, there was a man, turned towards me. His body was not clearly depicted – his clothes seem to be only sketched in hastily, almost as an afterthought. But his face … It was the face of my father-in-law, so lately, so suddenly dead. It was his exact likeness save that it wore an expression I had never seen him wear, one full of fear and desperation, of panic. Horror? Yes, even horror. I knew that I had not only never noticed his face, his likeness, in the picture before but that, absolutely and unmistakably, *it had not been there.*

You can imagine that scene, Dr Parmitter. I was a very young woman who had already been subjected to a number of great changes in my life. I had encountered passionate and single-minded hatred and jealousy for the first time, come face to face with sudden death for the first time, and now I was alone in a remote room of this house which was home and yet could not have felt less like a home to me, and looking into the terrified face of my dead father-in-law trapped inside a picture.

I felt nauseous and faint and I remember grabbing hold of a chair and holding on to it while the ground dipped and swayed beneath me. I was terrified and bewildered. What should I do? Who could I speak to about this? How could I bring my husband here to see the picture? How could I begin to tell him what I had so far kept entirely to myself? Only two people knew anything of this – I myself and the woman, Clarrisa Vigo. I was faced with something I did not understand and was poorly equipped to deal with.

I dared not touch the picture, or I would have taken it down and turned it face to the wall, or carried it up to one of the farthest attics and hidden it there. But I doubted if many people came into this fusty little room. On leaving it, I discovered that the key was in the lock, so I turned it and put the key in my pocket. Later, I slipped it into a drawer of my dressing table.

The following weeks were too busy and too exhausting, too strange, for me to think much about the picture, though I had nightmares about it and I preferred not to go down the corridor leading to the small sitting room but would always take a long detour. My mother-in-law was in mourning and great distress and I had to spend much time with her, as of course Lawrence was occupied from dawn till dusk in taking up the reins of the estate. She was a kindly but not very communicative woman and my memories of this time are mainly of sitting in this drawing room or in her own small boudoir, turning the pages of a book which I never managed to read, or glancing through country magazines, while she sat with crochet on her lap, her hands still, staring ahead of her. And I carried a dreadful and bewildering secret within me, knowledge I did not want and could not share. I had never before quite understood that once a thing is known it cannot be unknown. Now I did. Oh, I did.

I became even thinner and Lawrence once or twice commented that I looked pale or tired. He came to me one day saying that he wanted us to get away, though it could only be for a week or ten days at most, and that we would travel down through France and Italy by train to Venice. He was so pleased, so anxious for me to be well and happy. I should have welcomed it all. We had barely spent any time alone together and I had never travelled. But when he told me that we were to visit Venice I felt a terrible sensation, as if someone's hand had squeezed my heart so tightly that for a moment I could not breathe.

But there was nothing I dared say, nothing I could do. I had to endure in silence.

One thing happened before we left. We were invited to a very large dinner at the house of a neighbour in the county, and as we were seated, I looked up to see that opposite me, exactly opposite, so that I could not avoid her gaze, was Clarissa Vigo. I do not think I have said that she was a remarkably beautiful woman and she was also beautifully dressed. I was not clever at dressing. I wore simple clothes, which Lawrence always preferred, and did not like to stand out. Clarissa stood out and I sat across the table feeling both inferior and afraid. Her eyes kept finding me out, looking over the silver and the flowers, challenging me to meet her gaze. When I did it made me tremble. I have never known such hatred, such malevolence. I tried to ignore it, to talk to my neighbours and bend my head to my plate, but she was there, watching, filled with loathing and a terrible sort of power. She knew. She knew that she had power over me, over us. I felt ill that evening, ill with fear.

But it passed. She did not speak a word to me. It was over.

A week later, we left for our trip to Europe.

I will not take you step by step with us down through France and the northern part of Italy. We were happy, we were together, and the strains and responsibilities of the past months receded. We could pretend to be a carefree, recently married couple. But a dark shadow hung over me, and even as I was happy, I dreaded our arrival in Venice. I did not know what would or could happen. Many times, I told myself severely that my fears were groundless and that Clarissa Vigo had no power, no power over either of us.

Dr Parmitter, I have read that everyone who visits Venice falls in love with that city, that Venice puts everyone under her spell. Perhaps

I was never going to be happy there, because of the painting and of what I had seen, but I was taken aback by how much I disliked it from the moment we arrived. I marvelled at the buildings, the canals, and the lagoon astonished me. And yet I hated it. I feared it. It seemed to be a city of corruption and excess, an artificial place, full of darkness and foul odours. I looked over my shoulder. I saw everything as sinister and threatening and, as I did so, I knew that an unbridgeable chasm had opened between Lawrence and myself, for he loved the city, adored it, said he was never happier.

I could only follow him and smile and remain silent. It was a hard, a bitter week, the days passed so slowly, and all the time, I was in a state of dread. I felt isolated within an invisible cell, where I suffered and feared and could only wait, helplessly. My love for my dear husband had turned to a terrible thing, a desperation, a passionate, fearful clinging desire to possess and hold and keep. I did not want to let him out of my sight, and when he was within it, I looked and looked at him in case I forgot him. How strange that must sound. But it is true. I was possessed by fear and dread.

We were to be there for five nights and the blow fell on the third. I fell asleep in the afternoon. I found Venice enervating and my fear exhausting. I could not help myself and while I slept Lawrence went out. He liked simply to wander in and out of the squares and over the bridges, looking, enjoying. When I woke he was in the room and smiling with delight. He had bumped into friends, he said, I would never believe it, except that one always did meet everyone one knew in Venice. They lived here for several months of the year, and had a palazzo on the Grand Canal. Tomorrow night, there was a mini-Carnival, with a masked ball. They were to go, they would be taking a party. We were to join them. Costumiers would be visited, costumes and masks hired, he had arranged an appointment in an hour's time.

How can I convey to you the fearfulness of that place? It was a narrow dark shop in one of the innumerable alleyways and reached a long way back. The walls were festooned with costumes, masks and hats, all of them, I was told, traditional to carnivals and balls in Venice for hundreds of years and none of them to me pretty or beautiful or fun, every one sinister and strange. One could dress as a weeping Jew, a satyr, a butcher, a king with his sceptre or a man with a monkey on his shoulder; as a peasant girl with a baby, a street ruffian or a masquerader on stilts; as Pantaloon, Pulcinello, or the plague doctor. As a woman I had less choice and Lawrence wanted me to wear silk and lace and taffeta with an ornate jewelled mask, but I preferred to go as the peasant girl with her child in a basket: I could not have borne to dress up any more elaborately, though I was still obliged to take a mask on its ribboned stick. Lawrence hired a great black cloak and tricorn hat, and his mask was black and covered in mother of pearl buttons. He had long shining boots too. He was thrilled, excited, he was like a child going off to a party. I could not bear to see him and by now I was in a fever of dread. I could not prevent my bouts of sudden trembling and I saw that my face was deathly pale. I prayed for the whole thing to come and go quickly, because I somehow felt sure that when it had gone, so would whatever it was that I feared be gone too.

It was a hot night and I was nauseated by the smell of the foetid canals, whose slimy black water seemed to me full of all the filth and scum of the city. There were the smells of oil and smoke from the flares, and from street food vendors, smells of hot charred meat and peculiar spices. The ballroom of the palazzo was packed with people and noise and I found it strange and sinister not being able to see faces, not to know if people were old or young or even man or woman. But there was good food and drink to which one helped oneself and I revived myself by eating fruit and sweetmeats and drinking some sparkling wine, and then I danced with Lawrence and the evening seemed, if not very pleasurable, at least less frightening than I had feared. The time passed.

I was almost enjoying myself, almost relaxed, when it was announced that we were to leave the palazzo and go down into the streets, to parade through the squares to the light of flares, watched by the citizens from all their windows, joined by passers-by – the whole celebration would move out to become part of the city. Apparently this was usual. The people expected it. There was then a great exodus, a rush and general confusion, during which I became separated from my husband. I found myself pushed along among the other revellers, beside a Pulcinello and a priest and a wicked old witch, as we crowded down the great staircase and streamed outside. The torches were flaring. I can see them now, orange and smoking against the night sky. You can see the scene, Dr Parmitter. You have seen it often enough. The light glancing on the dark waters. The waiting gondolas. The crowds pressing forward. The masks. The eyes gleaming. The lights in the other buildings along the Grand Canal. You have seen it all.

What happened next I can barely believe or bring myself to tell. You may dismiss it. Any sane person would. I would not believe it. I do not believe it. But I know it to be true.

We were outside the Palazzo on the landing stage. Some of the crowd had already gone on into the streets on that side of the canal – we could hear the laughter and the cries. People were leaning out of windows now, looking down on us all. The gondolas were lining up waiting to take us out onto the canal, over to the other side, up to the Rialto Bridge ... occasionally they bumped together and rocked and the reflection of their lamps also rocked wildly, sickeningly, in the churning water. I was standing a yard or two from Lawrence when suddenly I heard my name called. Of course, I turned my head. The strange thing was that I responded even though it was my old name I heard, my maiden name. Who here knew my former name? The voice had come from behind me, but when I looked round I saw no one I knew – not everyone was still masked, but every face was strange in one way or another. And then I thought I saw not a face, but only the eyes, of someone I recognized. They were the eyes of Clarissa Vigo, looking out from a white silk mask with silver beads below a great plume of white feathers. How could I know? I knew.

I tried to move through the throng on the landing stage to get closer to her, but someone swung towards me and I had to avoid them or I would have been knocked over. When I looked again the white-masked woman had gone.

The gondoliers were crying out and the water was splashing over the wooden stage and someone was trying to get me to go on board. I would not go alone, of course, I wanted only to go if my husband would too – and indeed, I would infinitely have preferred not to embark on one of the gondolas and slink off across that dark and sinister water. I drew back and then I started to look for Lawrence. I searched for him there, and then I made my way down the side of the building and over the narrow bridge which led into a square. But the revellers had moved far on, I could not even hear them now, and the cobbled square was in almost total darkness. I retreated and now there was panic in my search. Lawrence was not on the landing stage and I was as certain as I could be that he would never have crossed the canal without me. I thought I should return inside the palazzo and look for him there. I was frightened. I had seen the woman, I had heard her whisper my name. I had dreaded this night, this place, and now I was dry-mouthed with fear.

But as I tried to make my way to the open doors of the palazzo, I heard a commotion behind me and then a shout. It was my husband who was shouting to me but I had never heard his voice sound like it. He was shouting in alarm – no, in terror, in horrible fear. I pushed forward and managed to reach the edge of the wooden landing stage. The last gondola laden with revellers was pulling away and I searched it in vain for a glimpse of my husband but there was no one like him or dressed like him. Most of the people had gone. A few stood, apparently uncertain if another gondola would come up and unable to decide if they wanted to go aboard if it did. I went back into the palazzo. The great rooms were deserted apart from some servants who were clearing the last of the feast. I spoke no Italian, but I asked if they had seen my husband and went on asking. They smiled, or gestured, but did not understand. Everyone else had gone. I found my cape and left. I ran through the squares, into the main piazza, ran like a mad demented creature, calling Lawrence's name. No one was about. A beggar was lying in an alleyway and snarled at me, a dog barked and snapped as I ran past. I reached our hotel in a state of frenzy yet I was sure there might still be an innocent explanation, that Lawrence would be there, waiting. But he was not. I roused the entire hotel, and was in such distress that after pressing a glass of brandy to my lips, the proprietor called the police.

Lawrence was never found. I stayed on in Venice for sixteen days beyond the original date for our departure. The police search could hardly have been more thorough but nothing came to light. No one had seen him, no one else had heard his voice that last time. No one remembered anything. It was concluded that he had accidentally slipped into the canal and drowned but his body was never discovered. He was not washed up. He had simply vanished.

I returned home. Home? This great hollow barren place? But yes, it was my home.

I was in such a state of distress that I fell ill and for two or three weeks the doctors feared for my life. I remember almost nothing of that terrible time but sometimes, in the midst of feverish dreams, I heard my husband crying out, sometimes I felt that he was just beside me, that if I reached out my hand I could save him. All through this time, something would slide towards my conscious mind but then dodge out of my grasp, as happens when a particular name eludes one. Through feverish days and the storms of my nightmares, it was there, just out of reach, this piece of information, this knowledge – I did not even know what it was.

I recovered slowly. I was able to sit up in a chair, then to be taken into the garden room to benefit from the sunshine during the afternoon. I asked time and time again for news of Lawrence but there never was any. My mother-in-law, who had received a double blow in such a few months, was sunk into a profound, silent depression and I barely saw her.

And then I discovered, as I was beginning to feel stronger, that I was expecting a child. My husband was the last of the line and the title would have died out with his death – if indeed he were dead. Now, and if I had a son, title, estates, house, would be secure. I had a reason to live. My mother-in-law rallied too.

The nightmares loosened their hold and became strange dreams with only intermittent horrors. But in the middle of one night I woke suddenly, because what had been hovering just out of reach had come cleanly into my mind. It was not a thought or a name, it was an image, and as I recognized it, I felt icy cold. My hands were stiff so that I could hardly move my fingers but I managed to get into my dressing robe, to find the key in my dressing table and to leave my bedroom, and make my way slowly down the long, dark, silent corridors of the house. The portraits and the sporting prints seemed to loom towards me. The cabinets of artifacts – there are endless collections in this place – gleamed in the light of the small torch I had brought, for I did not want to switch on any lights and, indeed, did not know where half of the switches might be found. Odd shapes, stones and dead birds and moths and bits of bronze, pieces of bone, feathers, even tiny skulls – Lawrence's family had been travellers, collectors and hoarders, everything came back here to Hawdon and was found a place. I wondered fleetingly how a tiny child would view these old, musty, hideous things. The further I walked down through this little-used end of the house, the stronger was the image in my mind. I felt ill, I felt weak, I felt afraid yet I had no choice but to see this dreadful thing through. If I did so, perhaps I would rid myself of the horrible image once and for all.

There were no sounds at all. My slippered feet barely seemed to make any impression on the long runner of carpet down the middle of the corridor. I had a sensation of being watched and not so much followed as accompanied, as if someone were close to my side the whole way, making sure I did not weaken and turn back. Oh it was a dreadful journey. I shudder when I remember it, as I often, so often, do.

I reached the door of the small sitting room and turned the key. It smelled of old furniture and fabrics which had been sealed in against any fresh air and light. But I did not want to be here with only my torch, and when I found the switch, the two lamps, with their thin light, came on and then I saw the picture again. And as I saw it, I realized that in the mustiness I could smell something else, a hint of something sharp and very distinctive. It took me a second or two to work out that it was paint, fresh oil paint. I looked around everywhere. Perhaps this room was used after all, perhaps one of the servants had been here to repair or repaint something, though I could see no sign of it. Nor were there any painting materials or brushes lying about.

The picture was as I had left it, with its face to the wall, and once I had located it I stood for long moments, hearing my heart pound in my ears and shaking with fear. But I knew that I would never rest until I had satisfied myself that I was in the grip of fancies and nightmares, caused by the shocks, distress and illness I had suffered.

In a single moment of determination, I took hold of the painting, turned it, and then looked at it with wide-open eyes.

At first, it seemed exactly as before. It reminded me starkly of that horrible evening and of the masks and costumes, the noise, the smell, the light from the torches and of losing my husband among the crowd. Some of the costumes and masks were familiar but, of course, they are traditional, they have been on display on such occasions in Venice for hundreds of years.

And then I saw. First, I saw, in one corner, almost hidden in the crowd, the head of someone wearing a white silk mask and with white plumes in the hair and the eyes of Clarissa Vigo. It was the eyes that convinced me I was not imagining anything. They were the same staring, brilliant, malevolent eyes, wishing me harm, full of hatred but also now with a dreadful gloating in them. They seemed to be both looking straight at me, into me almost, and to be directing me elsewhere. How could eyes look in two places at once, at me and at …

I followed them. I saw.

Standing up at the back of a gondola was a man wearing a black cloak and a tricorn hat. He was between two other heavily masked figures. One had a hand on his arm, the other was somehow propelling him forwards. The black water was choppy beneath the slightly rocking gondola. The man had his head turned to me. The expression on his face was ghastly to see – it was one of abject terror and of desperate pleading. He was trying to get away. He was asking to be saved. He did not want to be on the gondola, in the clutches of those others.

It was unmistakably a picture of my husband and the last time I had seen the Venetian painting, *it had not been there* – of that I was as sure as I was of my own self. My husband had become someone in a picture painted two hundred years before. I touched the canvas with one finger but it was clean and dry. There was no sign that anything had been painted onto it or changed at all within it at any recent time, and in any case, I could no longer smell the oil paint that had been so pungent moments before.

I was faint with shock and distress, so that I was forced to sit down in that dim little room. I could not explain what had happened or how but I knew that an evil force had caused it and knew who was responsible. Yet it made no sense. It still makes no sense.

One thing I did know, and it was with a certain relief, was that Lawrence was dead – however, wherever, in whatever way dead, whether 'buried alive' in this picture or buried in the Grand Canal, he was dead. Until now I had hoped against hope that one day I would receive a message telling me that he had been found alive. Now I knew that no such message could ever come.

I remember little more. I must have made my way back to my room and slept, but the next day I woke to the picture before my eyes again and I made myself go back to look at it. Nothing had changed. In such daylight as filtered between the heavy curtains and half-barred windows of the sitting room, which overlooked an inner courtyard, I saw the painting where I had left it and the face of my husband looking out at me, beseeching me to help him.

She was silent for a long time. I think she had exhausted herself. We sat on opposite one another not speaking, but I felt a closeness of understanding and I wanted to tell her of my own small experiences in the presence of the Venetian picture, of how it often troubled me.

I was wondering if I should simply get up and make my way to my room, leaving any further conversation until the following day when she would be more refreshed, but then the blue eyes were open and on my face as the Countess said, 'I must have that picture,' in such a fierce and desperate tone, that I started.

'I do not understand,' I replied, 'how it left your hands and eventually came into mine.'

Her old face crumpled and tears came then, softening the glare of those brilliant blue eyes.

'I am tired,' she said. 'I must ask you to wait until tomorrow. I do not think I have the strength to tell you any more of this terrible story tonight. But I am spurred on by the thought that it will soon be over and I will be able to rest. It has been a long, long search, an apparently hopeless journey but now it is almost at an end. It can wait a few more hours.'

I was unsure exactly what she meant but I agreed that she should rest as long as she wished and that I was at her disposal at any time the next day. She asked me to ring the bell for Stephens, who appeared at once to show me to my room. I took her hand for a moment as she sat, like a little bird, deep in the great chair, and, on a strange impulse, lifted it to my lips. It was like kissing a feather.

I slept badly. The wind blew, rattling the catches every so often, and episodes of the strange story the Countess had told me came back to me and I tried hopelessly to work out some rational explanation for it all. I would have dismissed her as old and with a failing mind had it not been for my own experiences with the picture. I was uneasy in that house and her story had disturbed me profoundly. I knew only too well the fierce power of jealousy which fuels a passion to be avenged. It does not happen very often but when it does and a person has their love rejected and all their future hopes betrayed for another, rage, pride and jealousy are terrible forces and can do immeasurable harm. Who knows that they could not do even these evil supernatural deeds?

But my own part in all of this was innocent. I had nothing to fear from the jilted woman who in any case was presumably long dead, or, I imagined, from the Countess. Yet as I lay tossing and turning through that long night, it seemed as if I was indeed being possessed by something unusual – for there grew in me an absolute determination to keep the Venetian picture. Why I should now so desperately want it, I did not know. It was of value but not priceless. It had caused me some trouble and anxiety. I did not need it. But just as, when I had been approached by the sweating, breathless man after the sale, desperate that I sell it to him for any amount of money I cared to name, I again felt a stubbornness I had never known. I would not sell then, and I would neither sell nor give back the painting to the Countess now. I felt almost frightened of my resolution, which made no sense and which seemed to have taken hold of me by dint of some outside force. For of course she had brought me here to ask for the painting. What other reason could there be? She could not have simply wanted to tell her story to a stranger.

I did not see her until late the following morning and occupied myself by taking a long walk around the very fine parkland and then by enjoying the excellent and I thought little-used library. I met no one other than a few groundsmen and maids cleaning the house and the latter scurried away like mice into holes on seeing me. But a little after eleven the silken-footed Stephens materialized and told me that coffee and the Countess awaited me in the morning room.

He led me there. It was a delightful room, furnished in spring yellows and light greens and with long windows onto the gardens, through which the sun was now shining. It is extraordinary how a little sunshine and brightness will lift both the aspect of any room, and of one's spirits on entering it. My tiredness and staleness from the sleepless night lifted and I was glad to see the old Countess, looking still small and frail but with rather more colour and liveliness than by the light of evening lamps.

I began to make remarks about the grounds and so on but she cut me short.

There is only a little more to tell. I will complete the story.

I gave birth to a son, Henry. This family has always alternated the names of the male heirs – Lawrence and Henry, for many generations. All was well. I kept the door of the small sitting room locked and the key in its turn locked in my dressing table and from that first terrible night I did not go into it again.

My mother-in-law lived here and my son grew up. Gradually, I became used to my state and to this house as being my home – and naturally I adored my only son, who looked so very like his father.

At his coming-of-age, we gave a great party – neighbours, tenants, staff. That is traditional. It would have been a happy occasion – had it not been for the arrival, with a party from another house, of the woman Clarissa Vigo. When I set eyes on her … well, you may imagine. But one has to be civil. I was not going to spoil my only son's most important day.

And so far as I was aware, nothing untoward occurred. The party proceeded. Everyone enjoyed it. My son was a fine young man and took over his duties with pride.

But I had reckoned without the powers of evil. On that evening, Clarissa Vigo took my son. I mean that. She took him by force of persuasion, she seduced him, however you wish to describe what happened. He was lost to me and to everything else here. He was under her influence and her sway and he married her.

Clearly she had been planning this for years. Within six months of that terrible day, my mother-in-law was dead and I had been dismissed from here, given a small farmhouse on the farthest side of the estate and a few sticks of furniture. I had an inheritance of a personal income from my husband which could not be taken from me but otherwise I had nothing. Nothing. This house was barred to me. I did not see my son. Her reign was absolute. And then the plunder began – things were removed, sold, thrown away and otherwise disposed of, things she did not care for, and without a word of protest from my son. She took charge of everything. She had what she had wanted and schemed for, for so many years. In the midst of it all, the Venetian picture was among the things she got rid of and I knew nothing. I knew nothing until later. The final tragedy came five years later. She and my son went out hunting, as they did almost every day throughout the winter. My husband had never hunted – he loathed field sports, though he allowed shooting of vermin on the estate. He was a gentle man but she stamped upon any streak of gentleness there may have been in his son. As they hunted one November day, in jumping a fence in the wood, she fell and was killed outright, and in the crashing fall disturbed a decayed tree, which was uprooted and came down, killing another horseman and injuring my son. He lived, Dr Parmitter. He lived, paralysed in every limb, for seven years. He lived to regret bitterly what he had done, to regret his marriage, to come out from under her possession and to ask me to forgive him. Of course I did so without hesitation and I returned to live here and to care for him until he died.

And I made it my work to restore the house and everything in it to the way it had been and to undo every single change she had made, to throw out every hideous modern thing with which she had filled this place. I brought back the servants she had dismissed. It was my single-minded determination to obliterate her from Hawdon and to leave it in as near the state in which I had first seen it as I could.

I succeeded very well. I was helped by the loyal people here, who flocked back, and by friends and neighbours who sought out so many items and brought them back here, over time.

But one thing I could never trace. The Venetian picture mattered to me because … because my husband was trapped there. My husband lived – lives, lives – within that picture.

'I sought after it for years', the Countess continued, 'and then it was found for me in an auctioneer's catalogue. I commissioned someone to attend the sale and buy it for me no matter what it cost. But as you know, things went wrong at the last minute, you bought it because my representative was not there and you would not sell it to him afterwards. That was your privilege. But I was angry, Dr Parmitter. I was angry and distressed and frustrated. I wanted that picture, my picture, and I have continued to want it for all these years. But you had disappeared. We could not trace the buyer of the picture.'

'No. In those days, I dealt rather a lot and I bid and bought under aliases – all dealers do. The auction houses of course know one's true identity but they never disclose that sort of information.'

'You were Mr Thomas Joiner and Mr Joiner was never to be found. And so the matter rested. Of course I continued to hope, and friends and searchers continued to keep their eyes and ears open, but my picture had vanished together with Mr Joiner.'

'Until you chanced to see my photograph in a magazine.'

'Indeed. I cannot begin to describe to you my feelings on seeing the picture there – the sense of an ending, the realization that at last, at long last, my husband would in a very real sense return home to me.'

In a macabre comparison, it flashed through my mind that, to the Countess, wanting the picture back was like wanting to receive an urn full of his cremated ashes. Whatever had happened, to her he was as present in the Venetian painting as he would have been in some funereal jar.

'I invited you here with the greatest of pleasure,' she said now. 'And I felt that you had every right to hear the full story and to meet me, to see this place. I could have employed some envoy – and hope that it was a more efficient one than the last time – but that was not the way I wanted to bring about a conclusion to this most important business.'

'A conclusion?' I said with feigned innocence. Inside me I could feel determination, that absolute and steadfast steel resolve. It was unlike me. The man you know as Theo Parmitter would most likely have not so much sold back but given back the Venetian painting. But something had possessed me there. I was not the man you knew and know.

'I mean to have my picture. You may name your price, Dr Parmitter.'

'But it is not for sale.'

'Of course it is for sale. Only a fool would refuse to sell when he could name his price. You have been a dealer in pictures.'

'No longer. The Venetian picture and all the others I have chosen to keep are my permanent collection. I value them quite beyond money. As I said, it is not for sale. I would be happy to provide you with a very good photograph. I would be glad for you to visit me in Cambridge to see it at any time to suit you. But I will never sell.'

Two points of bright colour had appeared on her high cheekbones and two points of brightness in the centre of her already piercing blue eyes. She was sitting upright, straight-backed, her face a white mask of anger.

'I think that perhaps you do not understand me clearly,' she said now. 'I will have my picture. I mean it to come to me.'

'Then I am sorry.'

'You do not need it. It means nothing to you. Or only in the sense that it pleases you as a decoration on your wall.'

'No. It means more than that. You must remember that I have had it for some years.'

'That is of no consequence.'

'It is to me.'

There was a long silence, during which she stared at me unflinchingly. Her expression was quite terrifying. She had not struck me in any case as a warm woman, though she had spoken of her sufferings and her feelings and I had sympathized with her. But there was a cold ruthlessness, a passionate single-mindedness about her now which alarmed me.

258 ☀ SUSAN HILL

'If you do not let me have the picture, you will live to regret your decision, regret it more than you have ever regretted anything.'

'Oh, there is little in my life that I regret, Countess.' I kept a tone of lightness and good humour in my voice which I most assuredly did not feel.

'The picture is better here. It will be quite harmless.'

'How on earth could it be anything else?'

'You have heard my story.'

I stood up. 'I regret that I must leave here today, Countess, and leave without acceding to your request. I found your story interesting and curious and I am grateful to you for your hospitality. I hope you may live out your days in this beautiful spot with the peace of mind you deserve after your sufferings.'

'I will never have peace of mind, never rest, never be content, until the picture is returned to me.'

I turned away. But as I walked towards the door, the Countess said quietly, 'And nor will you, Dr Parmitter. Nor will you.'

Seven

'You will feel better for having told all this to me,' I said to Theo. He had his head back, his eyes closed, and when he had finished speaking, he had drained his whisky glass and set it down.

It was late. He looked suddenly much older, I thought, but when he opened his eyes again and looked at me there was something new there, an expression of relief. He seemed very calm.

'Thank you, Oliver. I am grateful to you. You have done me more good than you may know.'

I left him with a light heart and took a turn or two around the college court. But tonight, all was quiet and still, there were no shadows, no whisperings, no footsteps, no faces at any lighted windows. No fear.

I slept at once and deeply, and I remember, as I dropped down into the soft cushions of oblivion, praying that Theo would do the same. I thought it most likely.

I woke in the small hours of the morning. It was pitch black and silent but as I came to, I heard the chapel clock strike three. I was sweating and my heart was racing. I had had no nightmares – no dreams of any kind – but I was in a state of abject fear. I could barely take deep breaths to calm myself. I got up and drank water, lay down again, but immediately, I was seized with the need to go down and check on Theo. The message in my head would not be ignored or dismissed. I rinsed my head under the cold tap and rubbed it vigorously dry to try and get some grip on myself and think rationally, but I could not. I was terrified, not for myself but for Theo. The story he had told me was vivid in my mind and although unburdening himself of it had clearly eased his mind greatly, I sensed that, in some terrible way, it was unfinished, that there would be more strange, dark happenings which made no sense, could not be, yet were.

I could not rest. I went down the dark staircase and along to Theo's set. All was quiet. I put my head to the door and listened intently but there was no sound at all. I waited, wondering if I should knock, but it was bitterly cold and I had only a thin dressing gown. I turned to go but, as I did so, it occurred to me that Theo might well not lock his door. He was old and unable to move far, and looked after well by the college. I did not know how he would summon help if he were ill and could not reach the telephone.

I reached my hand out to try the door. As I touched it, there was a harsh and horrible cry from within followed by a single loud crash.

I turned the knob and found that the door was indeed unlocked. I pushed my way in and switched on the lights.

Theo was lying on his back in the entrance to the sitting room, in his night clothes. His face was twisted slightly to the left, his mouth looked as if he were about to speak. His eyes were wide open and staring and they had in them a look I will never forget to my dying day, a look of such horror, such terror, such appalled realization and recognition that it was dreadful to see. I knelt down and touched him. There was no breath, no pulse. He was dead. For a second, I assumed that the crash I had heard was of his own fall, but then I saw that on the floor a few yards away from him lay the Venetian picture. The wire, which I knew had been strong and firm the previous evening, was intact, the hook on the wall in its place. Nothing had snapped or broken, sending it crashing down and Theo had not knocked against it, he had not reached it before he fell.

There were two things I knew I had to do. Obviously, I had to call the lodge, wake the college, set the usual business in motion. But before I did that, I had to do another thing. I dreaded it but I would never be able to rest again until I had, and, also, I felt I owed this last favour to my old tutor. I had to find out.I lifted up the picture and took it into the study where I propped it against the bookcase and turned the lamp directly onto it.

I drew in my breath and looked at the picture, knowing what I would find there.

But I did not. I searched every inch of that canvas. I looked at every face, in the crowd, in the gondolas, in the windows of the houses, in corners, down alleyways, barely visible. There was no Theo. No face remotely resembled his. I saw the young man I took to be the Countess's young husband, and the figure in the white silk mask with the plume of white feathers in her hair which I supposed was Clarissa Vigo. But of Theo, thank God, thank God, there was no image. I realized that in all probability, he had woken, felt unwell, got up and had his fatal stroke or heart attack. In crashing to the ground, he had shaken floor and walls – he was a heavy man – and the picture had been disturbed and fallen also.

Breaking out in a sweat again, but this time of relief, I went to the telephone on Theo's desk and dialled the night porter.

It was a desperately sad few days and I missed Theo greatly. The college chapel was packed and overflowing for his funeral, the oration one of the best I had ever heard and afterwards everyone spoke fondly of him. I was still shocked, my mind still full of our last hours together. From time to time, one thing came to my mind to trouble me. I had satisfied myself, I am pretty sure, that Theo's death had had nothing to do with the story he had told me, with the Venetian picture or indeed with anything shocking or unexplained. Yet I could not forget the look of terror on his dead face, the horrified expression in his open eyes, the way his arm was outstretched. The picture had fallen, and although there was a perfectly sensible explanation for that, it worried me.

I left Cambridge with a heavy heart. I would never again sit in those comfortable rooms, talking over a fire and a whisky, hearing his sound views on so many subjects, his humorous asides and his sharp but never cruel comments on his fellows.

But I could not remain overly sad or troubled for long. I had work to get back to, but even more I had Anne. I had told Theo in the first few minutes after my arrival that I was engaged to be married to Anne Fernleigh – not a fellow scholar in medieval English but a barrister – beautiful, accomplished, fun, a few years younger than I was. The perfect wife. Theo had wished me well and asked that I would take her to meet him soon. I had said that I would. And now I could not. It cast a shadow. Of course, one wants two people one cares for to meet and to care for one another in turn.

I had told her of Theo's death, of course – the reason that I had stayed on longer than planned, and now, as we sat in her flat after a good dinner, I told her in turn the story of the Venetian picture and of the old Countess. She listened intently, but at the end, smiled and said, 'I'm sorry I won't meet your old tutor for I have a feeling I would have liked him, but I can't say I'm sorry not to be meeting the picture. It sounds horrible.'

'It's rather fine, actually.'

'Not the art – I'm sure you may be right. The story. The whole business of …' she shuddered.

'It's a tale. A good one, but just a tale. It needn't trouble you.'

'It troubled him.'

'Oh, not so very much. It was a story he wanted to tell over a whisky and a good fire on a cold night. Forget it. We've more important things to discuss. I have something I want to ask you.'

Since my days with Theo and his sudden death, I had had one thought. I do not know why, but it seemed very important to me that instead of marrying the following summer, planning everything in a leisurely way and making a fuss of it, we should marry now, straight away.

'I know it will mean we marry quietly, without all the razzmatazz and perhaps that will disappoint you. But I don't want us to wait. Theo's death made me realize that we should seize life – and he was a lonely man, you know. No family other than a Cambridge college. Oh, he was contented enough but he was lonely and a college full of strangers, however warmly disposed, is not a wife and children.'

But to my surprise, Anne said she had no problem at all in giving up plans for a lavish wedding and in being married quietly, with just our family and closest friends, as soon as it could be arranged.

'It isn't the money you spend and the fuss you make – a marriage is about other things that are far more serious and lasting. Think of that poor old Countess – think of the wretched other woman. We are very fortunate. We should never forget it.'

I never would. I never will. I could not have been happier and I had a good feeling that Theo would have agreed, and approved. I felt his blessing upon us and his benign presence hovering about us as we made our preparations.

The only hesitation I had was when Anne determined that, even though work meant we could not now take the long honeymoon in Kenya that we had planned, we should manage a long weekend away and asked if we might spend it in Venice.

'I went once when I was fourteen,' she said, 'and I sensed something magical but I was too young to know what it was – I think one can be too young for Venice.'

'Well perhaps we should save it for a longer visit in that case,' I said, 'and go down to the south of France.'

'No, it won't be warm enough there yet. Venice. Please?'

I shook off any forebodings and made the booking. Superstitions and stories were not going to cast their long shadow over the first days of our marriage and I realized that in fact I was greatly looking forward to visiting the city again. Venice is beautiful. Venice is magical. Venice is like nowhere else, in the real world or the worlds of invention. I remembered the first time I visited it, as a young man taking a few months out to travel, and emerging from the railway station to that astonishing sight – streets which were water. The first ride on the vaporetto down the Grand Canal, the first glimpse of San Giorgio Maggiore rising out of the mist, the first sight of the pigeons rising like a ghostly cloud above the cathedral in St Mark's Square, and of those turrets and spires touched with gold and gleaming in the sun. Walks through squares where all you hear are the sounds of many footsteps on stone, because there are no motor vehicles, hours spent at café tables on the quiet Giudecca, the cry of the fishsellers in the early morning, the graceful arch of the Rialto Bridge, the faces of the locals, old and young men and women with those memorable, ancient Venetian features – the prominent nose, the hauteur of expression, the red hair.

The more I thought about the city in those days leading up to the wedding, the more my pulse quickened with the anticipation of seeing it again, and this time with Anne. Venice filled my dreams and was there when I woke. I found myself searching out books about her – the novels by Henry James and Edith Wharton and others which caught the moods so vividly. Once or twice, I thought about Theo's picture and its strange story, but now I was merely intrigued, wondering where the tale had originated and how long ago. When we got back, I meant to look up Hawdon and the Countess's family. Perhaps we would even take a few days in Yorkshire later in the year. The real settings of stories always hold a fascination.

Anne and I were married two weeks later, on a day of brilliant, warm sunshine – surely a good omen for our happiness. We had a celebratory lunch with our families and a couple of friends – I wished Theo could have been there – and by late afternoon, we were en route for our honey-moon in Venice.

Eight

To give myself something to do while I wait here, I write what I am beginning to fear must be the end of this story, and with such grief and anguish, such bewilderment and fear, that I can barely hold the pen. I am writing to give myself something, something to do in these long and dreadful hours when all hope is lost and yet I still must hope, for once hope is extinguished, there is nothing else left.

I am sitting in the room of our hotel. The balcony windows are open wide onto this quiet corner of the city. Just now, through the darkness, from one of the houses opposite the hotel I heard a man singing arias from Puccini and Mozart. Cats yowl suddenly. I write and I do not understand what I am writing or why but they say that a fear, like a nightmare, written down is exorcised. Writing should calm me as I wait. When I stop writing, I pace up and down the room, before returning to this small table in front of the window. The telephone is at my right hand. Any moment, any moment now, it will ring with the news I am desperate to hear.

How do I describe what happened when I barely know? How to explain something for which there is no explanation? I can as soon convey the pain I am feeling.

But I must, I have to. I cannot let the story remain unfinished or I shall go mad. For now it is my story, mine and Anne's, we have somehow become a part of this horrible nightmare.

We had been less than twenty-four hours in the city when Anne discovered that there was, as there so often is, a festival in honour of one of Venice's hundreds of saints, with a procession, fireworks, dancing in the square.

I said that we would go but that I was adamant that if there was to be any dressing-up, any tradition of wearing masks, we would not join in. I did not believe in Theo's story and yet it, together with the strange things that had happened to me in Cambridge and his subsequent death, had made me anxious nevertheless, anxious and suspicious. It was irrational but I felt that I needed to stay on the side of good luck, not court the bad.

The first hour or two of the festival was tremendous fun. The streets were full of people on their way to join the procession, the shops had some sort of special cakes baking and the smell filled the night air. There were drummers and dancers and people playing pipes on every corner, and many of the balconies had flags and garlands hanging from them. I am trying to remember how it felt, to be lighthearted, to be full of happiness, walking through the city with Anne, such a short time ago.

St Mark's Square was thronged and there was music coming from every side. We walked along the Riva degli Schiavoni and back, moving slowly with the long procession, and as we returned, the fireworks began over the water, lighting the sky and the ancient buildings and the canal itself in greens and blues, reds and golds in turn. Showers of crystals and silver and gold dust shot up into the air, the rockets soared. It was spectacular. I was so happy to be a part of it.

We walked along the canal, in and out of the alleys and squares, until we came down between high buildings again to a spot facing the bridge.

The jetty was thronged with people. All of those who had been processing must have been there and we were pushed and jostled by people trying to get to the front beside the canal, where the gondolas were lined up waiting to take people to the festivities on the opposite bank. The fireworks were still exploding in all directions so that every few minutes there was a collective cry or sigh of wonder from the crowd. And then I noticed that some of them were wearing the costumes of the carnival: the ancient Venetian figures of the Old Woman, the Fortune Teller, the Doctor, the Barber, the Man with the Monkey, Pulcinello, and Death with his scythe mingled among us, their faces concealed by low hats and masks and paint, eyes gleaming here and there. I was suddenly stricken with panic. I had not meant to be here. I wanted to leave, urgently, to go back to our quiet square and sit at the café over a drink in the balmy evening. I turned to Anne.

But she was not at my side. Somehow, she had been hidden from me by the ever-changing crowd. I pushed my way between bodies urgently, calling her name. I turned to see if she was behind me. And as I turned, the blood stopped in my veins. My heart itself seemed to cease beating. My mouth was dry and my tongue felt swollen and I could not speak Anne's name.

I glimpsed, a yard or two away, a figure wearing a white silk mask studded with sequins and with a white plume of feathers in her dark hair. I caught her eyes, dark and huge and full of hatred.

I struggled to my left, towards the alleyway, away from the water, away from the gondolas rocking and swaying, away from the masks and the figures and the brilliant lights of the fireworks that kept exploding and cascading down again towards the dark water. I lost sight of the woman and when I looked back again she had gone.

I ran then, ran and ran, calling out to Anne, shouting for help, screaming in the end as I searched frantically through all the twists and turns of Venice for my wife.

I came back to the hotel. I alerted the police. I was forced to wait to give them Anne's description. They said that visitors to Venice get lost every day, especially in a crowd, that until it was daylight they had little hope of finding her but that she would be most likely to return here on her own, or perhaps in the care of someone local, that perhaps she had fallen or become ill. They were stolid. They tried to reassure me. They left, telling me to wait here for Anne.

But I cannot wait.

I have to leave this wretched story and go out again, I will go mad until I find her. Because I saw the woman, the woman in the white silk mask with the white plumes in her hair, the woman in the story, the woman desperate for revenge. I believe in her now. I have seen. Why she would want to harm Anne I have no idea, but she is a destroyer of happiness, one whom even death cannot stop in her desire to haunt and hurt.

I will do whatever is necessary – and perhaps I am the only person who can – to put an end to it all.

Nine

It is left to me, Anne, to end this story. Will there be an ending? Oh, there has to be, there must. Such evil surely cannot retain its power for ever?

In the crowd of people on the landing stage beside the water, I had felt myself at first jostled and pushed by a number of people who were trying to surge forward – indeed, I feared for a child at the very edge of the canal and pulled her away in case she fell in. I almost lost my own balance, but I felt a hand on my arm, helping me to right myself. The only unnerving thing was that the hand gripped me so hard it was painful and I had to wrench myself hard to get away. I caught a glimpse of someone, of a malevolent glance that made me shudder, and saw a hand reached out again towards me. But then I was being taken forward by the crowd trying to go in the opposite direction, away from the crowd by the water and I let myself go with them, up the narrow walk between the high houses and onto one of the small bridges over a side canal.

Then, the procession, which I had thought disbanded, re-formed, a band began to play and we were all walking together to the music, towards the Rialto and over it and on and on, and I felt myself caught up in the scene, laughing and clapping and occasionally looking back at the fireworks still bursting into the night sky. It was exhilarating, it was fun. I was unaware of where we were walking but quite happy, confident that, in a short time, I would separate myself from the others, and turn back.

But for one reason or another I did not and then we were far away, the band still playing, children banging toy drums, through streets, across bridges, into squares. The Venice I knew was left far behind. And then I slipped on an uneven stretch of the pavement, and fell, and in doing so, put my weight on my arm. I heard a crack and felt the pain, I let out a cry. Someone stopped. Someone else shouted. People bent over me. I was surrounded, helped, admonished, and everyone was jabbering in fast Italian which I could not understand. I was suddenly and violently sick and the sky whirled and then it was coming down on my head.

There is little else to tell. I was taken into a nearby house and a doctor was fetched. I had not, he decided, broken my arm, I had bruised it badly and cut my hand and they looked after me very kindly. I was bandaged, given an injection against infections, swallowed painkillers. By now, it was two in the morning and I wrote down and gave to one of those looking after me my name and the telephone number of the hotel. But I felt nauseous again and the doctor insisted that I should lie down and sleep, that everything would be done. I would be moved the next morning.

I did sleep. The pain in my arm and hand did not wake me for some hours, and by then I was feeling better in myself and able to drink some good strong coffee and eat a soft bread roll with butter.

What happened next made me laugh. I wonder, when I will laugh again?

I was coaxed into a wheelchair belonging to the grandmother of the family, and trundled through the morning streets of Venice in the sunshine, my bandaged arm resting proudly on my lap, back to our hotel and my husband.

Except that Oliver was not there. He had gone out to search for me again, they said, he had slipped past the night porter in the early hours, distraught. At first, no one reported having seen him but, later that day, the police, who had switched from looking for me to looking for him with some irritation at accident-prone visitors, told me that a gondolier, up early to wash out his craft, reported having seen a man answering to Oliver's description. But at first I dismissed it, saying that it could not have been Oliver. He had been reported as walking between two men who had their hands on his arms and seemed to be making him get into another gondola, farther up the jetty, against his will. Oliver would have been alone.

The police took it more seriously but could see no reason at all, if it had been Oliver with two men, why he should have been taken anywhere against his will. He did not look rich, our hotel was not one of the grandest, his wallet was still in the room and the watch he always wore was a plain steel one without great value.

I did not buy any theories of kidnap, ransom or the mafia. Italian police seem obsessed with all three but I knew they were far from the mark.

I knew. I know.

I read the story Oliver had left. I read everything twice, slowly and carefully, I crawled over it, if you like, looking for a message, an explanation.

I came back to London alone.

That was a fortnight ago. Nothing happened. There was no news. In the first few days the Venetian police telephoned me. The Inspector spoke good English.

'Signora, we have revised our opinion. This man the _gondoliere_ saw with the others … we think it is not probable to be your husband, after all. Our theory is now, he slip and fall into the Grande Canale. He was out in the dark, the ground there is often wet.'

'But you would have found his body?'

'Not yet, not found yet. But yes, the body will be washed up later or sooner and we will call you at once.'

'Will I have to come to identify him?'

'_Si_. I am very sorry but yes, it is necessary.'

I thanked him and then I wept. I wept for what felt like hours, until my body ached, my throat was sore and I had no tears left. And I dreaded having to travel back to Venice to see Oliver's dead – his drowned – body, when the time came. I had been told about the look of death by water.

I decided I must go back to work, if only in the office. I must have something to occupy my mind and it was a relief to sit reading through complex, dry, legal phraseology for hours at a time. If my thoughts turned to Venice, the black filthy waters of the Grand Canal, the next flight I would take there, I went out and walked for miles through London, trying to tire myself out.

Two days ago, I had walked from Lincoln's Inn back to our flat. My arm still ached a little and I thought I would take some strong painkillers and try to sleep. The phone was switched through to my office, and when I left there, to my mobile, so I knew I had not missed a call from the police.

The porter in our mansion block told me that he had taken in a parcel and put it upstairs outside the door. I was not expecting anything and it was with some distress that I saw the label addressed to Oliver. Taped to the outside of the parcel was an envelope – the whole had been delivered by courier.

I took it inside. The sun was shining in through the tall windows. I opened one of them and heard a blackbird singing its heart out on the plane tree outside. I took off my coat and riffled through the other post, which was of no interest. There was nothing for Oliver.

And so I peeled the envelope from the parcel and opened it. I did not believe, by then, you see, that Oliver would ever return to open it. Oliver was dead. Drowned. Before long I would see that, with my own eyes.

The letter was from a firm of solicitors in Cambridge. It enclosed a cheque for a thousand pounds, left to Oliver by his old tutor, Theo, 'to buy himself a present'. I had to wipe the tears out of my eyes before reading on, to learn that the letter came with an item which Dr Parmitter had also left to Oliver in his will.

It is very strange, but as I began to cut off the brown paper, I had no idea as to what the item could possibly be. I should have known, of course I should. I should have taken the whole package, unopened, down to the incinerator and burned it, or taken a knife and slashed it to shreds.

Instead, I simply undid the last of the wrapping paper and looked down at the Venetian picture.

And as I did so, as my heart contracted and my fingers became numb, I smelled, quite unmistakably, the faintest smell of fresh oil paint.

Then, I began the frantic search for my husband.

He was not hard to find. Behind the crowd in their masks and cloaks and tricorn hats, behind the gleaming canal and the rocking gondolas and the flaring torches, I saw the dark alley leading away, and the backs of two large men, heavy and broad-shouldered, cloaked in black, their hands on a man's arms, gripping them. The man was turning his head to look back and to look out, to look beyond the world of the picture, to look at me and his expression was one of terror and of dread. His eyes were begging and imploring me to find him, follow him, rescue him. Get him back.

But it was too late. He was like the others. He had turned into a picture. It took me a little longer to find the woman and then it was only the smallest image, almost hidden in one corner, the gleam of white silk, the sparkle of a sequin, the edge of a white-plumed feather. But she was there. Her arm was outstretched, her finger pointed in Oliver's direction, but her eyes were looking, like his, at me, directly at me, in hideous triumph.

I dropped into a chair before my legs gave way. I had only one hope left. That by taking Oliver, as she had taken the others, surely, surely to God the woman had satisfied her desire for revenge. Who is left? What more can she do? Has she not done enough?

I do not know. I will not know though I cannot say, 'never'. I will live with this fear, this dread, this threat, during all the years ahead until the child I have learned I am expecting, grows up. All I do now is pray and it is always the same prayer – a foolish prayer, of course, since the die is already cast.

I pray that I will not have a son.

Printer's Devil Court

Temple, Farley and Freeman. Solicitors
2 Delvers Court
St James's SW1

Dear Sir

The enclosed item has been sent on to me by Messrs. Geo Rickwell, Antiquarian Bookseller, with the instruction that it be passed on to the beneficiaries of the estate of the late Dr Hugh Meredith. As you know, the library in which it was found was entrusted for sale to Messrs Rickwell. Of a few items not included in the sale, mainly for reasons of poor physical condition, the enclosed was deemed to have no commercial value. I am therefore sending it to you to deal with in any way you see fit. I would be grateful for acknowledgement of its receipt in due course,

Yours etc.

The book in question measures some eight inches square and the sheets, of a pleasing cream paper, had been folded and hand-sewn together with heavy card backing – a neat and careful piece of amateur bookbinding. Apparently this, together with botanical illustration and embroidery, was one of the soothing hobbies taken up by Dr Meredith in old age, when he had long ceased to practice medicine, not only because of his advancing years, the family story has it, but because he suffered from a sort of intermittent nervous condition.

The book has no title on the cover or the spine but on the first page is written:

The Wrong Life.

Hugh Meredith MD

THE BOOK

In my first year as a junior doctor I moved into lodgings in a small court close by Fleet Street, an area which could not at the time have changed greatly since the days of Dickens. The court was small and the tall, narrow, grimy houses faced into a dismal yard, at one end of which a passageway led into the main thoroughfare. At the other end, a similar snicket led to the graveyard and thence to the church of St Luke-by-the-Gate. The church was pressed in on either side by two warehouse buildings and most of the graveyard was ancient and no longer in use. Old stones leaned this way and that, monuments and tombs were greened and yellowed over with moss and lichen. One or two trees struggled upwards to find what little light they could, and at their bases, more gravestones, sunken flat to the earth, were almost entirely obscured by weeds, ivy and rank grasses. In between was a mulch of dead leaves. I sometimes took a short cut through the churchyard on my way – often late – to the hospital. Once, when my sister was visiting me and I took her that way, she said that she could not understand why I was not frightened out of my wits when walking.

'Frightened of what?'

'Ghosts ... the dead.'

'As to ghosts, my dear Clara, I do not believe in them for a moment and dead bodies I see in the hospital every day so why would either of those things frighten me? The only thing to be wary of in these dark hidden corners of London are living thieves and pickpockets. Even the vagrants can be threatening after they have been drinking illicit cider.' I laughed, as nevertheless, Clara pulled me by the arm to hasten our way to the main gate.

When this story begins it's late and dismal autumn. Every morning mist rose and hung over the river after a cold night and when it turned milder for a day or two, the choking fog rolled over the city, muffling sounds, blurring the outlines of buildings and tasting foul in the mouth and nostrils, so that everyone went about with their faces half-covered in mufflers. Braziers burned at the street corners, where the hot chestnut and potato sellers rubbed hands stiff and blue with cold. Traffic crawled along the Strand to Fleet Street, headlamps looming like great hazy moons out of the mist. Fleet Street was a din of hot metal presses turning out the daily and evening newspapers. Open a small wooden door in a wall and you saw down into a bedlam of huge iron machines and the clatter of chutes, down which rolled the *Evening News* and *Standard*, *The Times* and the *Chronicle*, by the mile. Men at work below were dwarfed by the presses, faces grimy with oil and the air was thick with the smell of it and of fresh ink and hot paper. I loved it and wandered these old streets whenever I had a half hour to spare, venturing up unfamiliar passages and alleys into Courts and Buildings, discovering hidden churches and little gardens. But best of all I liked to walk beside the river, or to stand on the terrace of the medical school which overlooked its great flowing expanse, now treacle black, now sparkling in the sun and carrying so many and various craft on its tide. Such idle moments were rare, however. I was usually attending patients, following great physicians on their ward rounds, learning from the surgeons in theatre and the pathologists in the mortuary. I loved my work as I had loved every moment of my studies. I suppose the latest in a line of doctors would either take to medicine as a duck to water or rebel and become a bank manager.

Three other doctors lived at number two, Printer's Devil Court, at the time of which I write. Walter Powell, a year ahead of the rest, James Kent and Rafe McAllister. James and I occupied one floor, Walter and Rafe the other. It was a dark house, with steep, narrow stairs and we each had a miserably small bedroom and shared bathroom, with temperamental plumbing. But we had one large sitting room which stretched the width of the house and had a coal fire with a chimney that drew well, a reasonably comfortable sofa and three armchairs. There was a handsome mahogany table at which we ate and sometimes worked. The room had two windows, one at either end, in each of which stood a desk. There was precious little natural light and the outlook was of the opposite buildings. By now it was dark at four o'clock and lamps and fire were lit early. We kept irregular hours, sometimes working all day and all night, so that we only met to eat or relax together a couple of times a week. The landlady, Mrs Ratchet, rarely spoke a word but she looked after us well enough in her way, cleaning and clearing, making the beds and the fire and providing food at odd hours. We were fortunate, hard-working and innocent – or so I thought. I got on well with my fellows. James was a simple, easygoing man, with little imagination but a great deal of human sensibility. He was a plain-speaking and compassionate doctor in the making. Rafe was serious, studious and silent. He was never unfriendly and yet I could not get to know him – he presented a closed-off front and seemed to live in a world of test tubes and apparently dreamed only of finding cures for rare and obscure conditions. He had little to do with patients, which was probably for the best but I judged that one day he would make some remarkable medical breakthrough, in his own, intense and purposeful way.

Walter Powell was an even more complex character. If ever I felt a dislike or approval of any of my fellows, it was of him. He was jovial and friendly enough but he had a sly way with him and something shadowy in his personality though I could not have put a finger on quite what – at least not then. The only way I can give any idea of how he – and indeed, Rafe – affected me is to say that I would happily have entrusted my life to James but to Walter and Rafe, never.

PART TWO

One

It was a murky November evening with a fog off the river and a fuzzy halo round every street lamp, when the conversation, which had such a hideous outcome, took place. We had all four of us returned to our lodging house earlier than usual and eaten our lamb stew and treacle pudding together at the big table – Mrs Ratchet knew how to line the stomachs of hungry young doctors in such bleak weather. Everything had been cleared away and we sat with the precious bottle of port, generously provided by James's wine merchant brother, around a good fire. James and Walter had lit their pipes and the sweet smell of Old Holborn tobacco was pleasing to the two of us who did not smoke.

We had begun to talk in an idle way about the day's work. I had been following an eminent thoracic specialist on his ward round, taking in as much as I could – he kept up a brisk pace – about rare lung diseases, and then working in the crowded outpatient clinics. Walter had been in the mortuary, assisting at the post mortems of bodies washed up or pulled out of the River Thames. One had been trapped under the hull of an abandoned barge for several weeks, he told us with a certain relish. I shuddered but he merely smiled his tight little smile.

'You will have to acquire a stronger stomach for the game, Hugh.'

'Hardly a game.'

He shrugged and for a moment we all fell silent. The fire shifted down. James bent forward and threw on another couple of coals. And then Walter said, 'What opinions do we all have about the story of the raising of Lazarus?'

I suppose the leap from bodies drowned in the River Thames to the New Testament story of the man miraculously raised from the dead by Jesus, was not such a great one but the question silenced us again.

'I'm not sure I remember many of the details,' I said at last. 'I rather switched off the chapel sermons in my senior school years.'

James said that he knew the story. Rafe did not speak.

'Or that of the centurion's daughter?' Walter continued, taking the pipe from his mouth to smile again. I remember noticing what a pale complexion he had, even in the ruddy glow from the fire, which gave the others a more cheerful aspect. Walter's hair was already receding, showing his high forehead and oddly large skull.

'Come, you must all have some theory.'

'I am no biblical scholar,' James said, 'but for what it is worth, I believe fully in the stories. They have the ring of truth.'

'Of course,' Walter nodded. 'You, as a conscientious Christian would. But as a medical man?'

Rafe got up abruptly and went out. We heard his footsteps going up the stairs two at a time. He returned to the room carrying a Bible.

'Let us read the exact accounts before we express any further opinions.'

I noted that it took him almost no time to find the relevant pages, which surprised me as I had not put Rafe down as a religious man. We settled quietly while he read first, in two of the Gospels, the account of the raising of Jairus's daughter.

'Well, that seems quite straightforward,' James said. 'One line is con-clusive and repeated in each gospel account. "The maid is not dead but sleepeth." As Jesus saw.'

'Yes, plenty of that sort of thing,' I said, 'we have all seen it – the deep coma resembling death. People have been pronounced dead and taken to the mortuary or even to the undertaker and consigned to their coffin, only to have woken again.'

'Perhaps that would take care of Luke, Chapter 7?'

Walter took up the Bible and, like Rafe, found the page almost immediately.

'When he came to the gate of the city, behold, there was a dead man carried out … And Jesus came and touched the bier and said "Young man, I say to thee, arise. And he that was dead sat up and began to speak."'

'More problematic all the same. The man was on the bier being taken for burial, which has to take place very quickly in hot countries,' Walter said. 'I vote that this was another case of the deep coma – the man had a lucky escape.'

James looked perturbed. Walter flipped the pages and found the story of the raising of Lazarus. 'Here,' he said, a slight smugness in his tone, 'this is unequivocal, I think.'

'Now he had been in the grave for four days …'

'Can we be sure of that ?' I asked.

'No, but the story is quite detailed – why would they lie? His sister says, "by this time he stinketh for he hath been dead four days."'

Rafe looked blank yet I thought I caught the glint of something like excitement in his eyes.

'Listen then,' Walter continued, 'Jesus cried with a loud voice, "Lazarus, come forth." And he that was dead came forth, bound hand and foot with grave cloths and his face was bound about with a napkin.'

James sat back. 'And that,' he said, 'I do believe.'

Thinking to lighten the atmosphere, I knelt on the hearth rug and made up the fire, poking at it to loosen the ashes below, then adding more coals. The whole flared up so quickly that I started back and as I did so, I glanced round the room. James sat very still, his demeanour very calm. Rafe's face was closed and expressionless, his eyes down. Walter was looking directly at me with an expression I could not wholly read, but which seemed almost rapacious, so that I felt distinctly uncomfortable.

'I vote for another glass of port,' I said, 'if James would allow.'

He jumped up at once and busied himself over refilling the glasses. When he had seated himself again, Walter said, 'You two were not here when Rafe and I began discussions on this subject.'

'Discussion about the miracles of Jesus Christ?' I said, surprised.

'Not exactly,' Walter leaned forward and I caught the same glint in his eyes as I had noticed in Rafe's.

'Oh, it was nothing but some macabre joking,' he said now, giving Walter a quick look, as if in warning. 'We had both had some encounters with death in its various forms that day and you know as well as I that we need a touch of gallows humour to see us through. That is why medical students traditionally play such ghoulish tricks on one another.'

James laughed. 'Like Anderson in the dissecting room and ...'

Walter held out his hand. 'Yes, yes.' Something in his tone doused our mirth of the incident. 'But other than in those remote biblical times – and who knows how reliable the witnesses were after all? – Have any of us heard of men – or women, for that matter – being raised from the dead? By dead I mean exactly that. Dead.'

'Well of course not,' James said.

'Yet you are ready to believe in incidents recorded more than two thousand years ago.'

James nodded but said nothing.

'Let's leave biblical times. Do any of us believe that this miracle could be performed now? Though clearly not by the man Jesus.'

'So what are you talking about?' I asked. 'Do you mean by those who serve in His ministry now?'

'No. By men like us – doctors and scientists that we are.' I saw that he and Walter exchanged another glance.

'Is this some fantasy you have been beguiling yourselves with on your walks to and from the hospital?' I asked, for Walter and Rafe generally went together. Now, Rafe leaned forwards with some eagerness.

'It is far more than that, and we are not men to waste time on fantasies.'

James looked troubled but I simply laughed.

'Enough teasing,' I said, 'you had better tell us, as it's the time of a dismal evening for a good tale.' My voice sounded over-loud and hearty in the room.

'I assure you that I am deadly serious and so is Rafe. But if you cannot be, let us say no more on the subject.' Walter tamped and fidgeted away with his pipe.

'Come now,' I said, 'I will take you at your word. Let us hear what you have to say and we can make up our own minds.'

Walter continued to work away at the pipe, like an actor confident that he has his audience and can keep them waiting. Eventually it was lit to his satisfaction and he drew on it a few times before beginning.

'As you may have guessed by now, I have been considering our subject for some time. And because I am no more than a basic scientist, whereas Rafe here is a scientific genius, I have discussed it all with him. I have put difficult questions to him and he to me and we have each played devil's advocate. Now we have reached the point where we think we should bring you two into the secret. On one condition.'

He took the pipe from his mouth again and paused, enjoying the melodrama of the moment.

'So what is your condition, Walter?'

'That you must want to know, and know everything. If you do not – perhaps I will say "dare not" – we will continue to share these agreeable lodgings with you both as usual and never mention the matter again.'

Walter looked steadfastly at me and then at James and I was so mesmerised by the look in his eyes as he stared that I could not glance away.

'That is all very well,' I said, 'but how on earth can I tell you I don't want to hear a word more when I don't know what it is all about?'

'But you do. You have been given more than a hint – quite enough on which to base a decision.'

'The subject being the miracles of raising the dead?'

'Not precisely. As I said, we are not biblical scholars and those times are long past. It was a convenient way of introducing the nature of the business, that is all.'

'Well for my part,' James said, 'I don't understand any of it.' He looked at me. 'I must say that my instincts tell me to remain in ignorance – even in innocence.'

I paused. I was still more or less convinced that the whole thing was an elaborate game on Walter's part. Rafe's chair was pulled back into the shadows so that his face was hidden, only his spectacles occasionally gleaming in the firelight. Now he said quietly, 'Just remember that what you know you can never unknow. If you are afraid …'

'Of course not. What trick could you two cook up that would be so alarming?'

Rafe did not reply.

'Make your decision,' Walter said.

'Before I reply,' I said, 'tell us why it is so important to make us party to whatever game you propose to play.'

'Because you may find it more interesting and remarkable than you suppose. Because you will be entirely impartial witnesses. And because we may need your help. It would not be easy to find two other men we know so well and more importantly, whom we trust.'

'Is this enterprise dangerous?'

'To you? I am not sure. But I can see no reason why you would be at serious risk of harm.'

'Is it legal?'

'I have no idea. I suspect that the law has never been tested in the matter.'

Suddenly, my mind was made up. I slapped the arm of the chair. 'Then, dammit …'

But Walter held up his hand. 'Just one more thing, though I suspect I know what you have decided. If you are with us, you must swear solemnly that you will tell no one – no one. Now or at any time. If you are ever questioned, which is improbable, you must deny all knowledge or involvement.' His expression was as serious as a man's could be.

'Then I swear it,' I said, and as I did so, I felt an odd nervous lurch in my belly. 'I swear it and I am with you.'

Walter did not reply but turned to look at James, who had gone horribly pale.

'I cannot swear,' he said. 'I am not with you, whatever this nonsense is about and so I would rather not hear more.'

He got up quickly and nodding us 'good night', he left the room. We heard his footsteps and his door close. It was disconcerting. I liked and trusted James and for a moment, I thought of changing my mind. I looked at Walter and as I did so, I felt a flicker of alarm. Something in his eyes gave out a warning and a threat.

'Another glass of port,' I said hastily. 'I'm sure James would not object.'

Walter frowned. 'No, we need clear heads.'

I let the port stand but I tried to keep my tone light as I asked, 'Now – what is this all about? What are you proposing?'

'We are proposing,' Walter replied, 'to bring the dead back to life.'

Two

I slept soundly that night perhaps because I still believed that Walter's proposed experiment was nothing more than a jape. At first, nothing else happened, though I caught James looking at me anxiously once or twice. But then there were some subtle changes to our household routine. Rafe had apparently discovered some time earlier that the house had a basement room – no more than a cellar – which was empty and unused, and he persuaded our landlady to let it to him for a pittance. I returned home early one day with a feverish cold, to find him unloading what looked like half the contents of a laboratory and lugging it down the area steps. He certainly did not speak and I was feeling too rotten to ask any questions or offer him help.

The next time I saw him he was coming up from the basement, slipping a key into his pocket. He rarely joined us at supper now and when he did, he ate quickly and immediately made off downstairs. There were no more leisurely, companionable evenings when we four sat talking round the fire. Walter seemed to spend longer hours at the hospital, especially at night and when he was home, kept to his own room. Shortly afterwards, I forgot about the whole secret episode because my head cold descended onto my lungs and the subsequent bronchitis put me first to bed for a week and then sent me away from London's foul winter air to the home of my family in coastal Norfolk. There, I regained my health and strength, albeit slowly, until I could take walks along the seashore and across the marshes. Nothing could have been better calculated to restore me.

Christmas came and went and we saw in the New Year merrily. I was preparing to return to London when on 2 January I received a telegram from Walter.

Enterprise critical stage.
Urgent you return and witness.

After the fogs and damp of late autumn, London had come in for one of the worst winters for decades. Snow had fallen thickly for several days and then frozen hard to the ground every night. Temperatures remained below freezing and twice plummeted to depths barely known since the Great Frost, when the Thames had frozen over.

The fire made little impression on the air of the sitting room and our windows were ferned and feathered over with ice, on the inside. The hospital, of course, was full to bursting point: vagrants and beggars died on the streets in shameful numbers and we were all working round the clock. I had hurried back as requested but for over two weeks Walter had no time to talk to me and Rafe was unable to work in his cellar laboratory, the cold was so intense. James I almost never saw and when I did, I felt that he had withdrawn from me as well as from the others and was wary of conversation.

On a night in early March, when at last the thermometer hovered just above freezing, Walter knocked on my door well after one o'clock in the morning. He was wearing his outdoor clothes and there was something almost akin to an electrical charge about him, so that I jumped up from my desk in alarm.

'What has happened?'

'Nothing yet. But it is time. Come – Rafe is waiting.'

'Where are we going?'

'To the hospital. But we must go stealthily and take great care.'

The pavements were treacherous and piles of dirty, frozen snow lay in the gutters. The half-moon was hazy, so that we had to watch our every step, and a raw and bitter wind blowing off the river scoured our faces.

The lamps at the hospital entrance gates glowed out but much of the building was dimmed, as people slept. We entered by the front doors and at once turned along a covered way to the old East Wing and then down three flights of stairs that led to the basement corridors. Walter's footsteps made barely a sound and I thought that he must have walked this way at night many times before. Once or twice he stopped, raised his hand, and listened, before continuing. I followed in his footsteps, barely able to breathe, I was so tense. We turned a corner into a short passageway with an unmarked double-door at the end. No one else was about. This part of the hospital was little used, though the old wards had been hastily re-commissioned to cope with the overflow of patients. The whole place smelled cold and slightly damp. We stopped and Walter tapped on the door, though not on the panel but on the frame, presumably so that the sound was muffled. At once, it was opened by Rafe. He so rarely gave any-thing away on his impassive features but now he wore an expression of scarcely concealed excitement and I felt the same strange electrical charge coming off him as I had noticed with Walter.

The second we were both inside, Rafe turned the key in the lock. The two did not speak as they moved into the centre of the small room. It was windowless, save for a row of rectangular panes high up along one side, and the walls were tiled to the ceiling. Two lamps stood on a laboratory bench, only one of which was lit and that dimly but it was enough for me to see about me.

Next to the lamps stood a small array of laboratory paraphernalia – test tubes, rubber piping, glass phials. A bunsen burner gave out a low, steady blue flame and there were a couple of items of medical equip-ment. In the body of the room stood a hospital trolley, levered to its full height and with the metal sides raised. On it was a still figure covered in a single grey blanket. I went closer, and saw that it was the body of an old man. His head was covered in grey stubble, with the same forming a close beard. His skin was bruise coloured and grime enseamed the neck, the skin below his eyes, and around the nose and ears. Clearly, though he looked to have been given a cursory wash, the dirt was ingrained so as to have become almost a part of the scheme itself. One hand was uncovered, the nails had recently been cut but more dirt was wedged beneath them and in the creases of the fingers.

At first glance, I took this to be a corpse but then I saw the faintest of movements as the breath rose and fell in the man's chest. Walter bent down and put a finger under the nostrils and nodded. The man's breath-ing was laboured and as we stood looking at him a rattle came from his throat. Walter glanced at Rafe and it was as if a flint had been struck and the quick spark passed between them.

'Yes,' Walter said, 'not long. A moment or two only but the old ones put up a brave fight. Life has been hard to them and they are used to battling.'

I started to say something but at first my voice refused to come out and I could only make a hoarse croaking sound, as if it was I and not the old man fighting for breath. But eventually, I managed to speak.

'Who is he?'

Walter shrugged. 'Brought in from the street a couple of nights ago, half frozen to death and full of pneumonia. He had nothing on him but his clothes. His pockets were full of chestnut husks – he had probably been living off the scraps of nuts that fell onto the pavement and perhaps tossed a whole one now and again by the seller.'

'No name?'

'No name, no home, no family, no friends, no hope. He is not long for this world and will be better out of it.'

I had an uprush of terror as he said it, and took a quick step nearer to the trolley on which the old man lay.

'You are surely not thinking of hastening his end, for some foul purpose? The man is dying and will be at peace soon enough. I will not stand by and watch you commit murder.'

Walter put a hand on my arm. 'No, my friend, we are doctors in the business of saving life, not disposing of it.'

'You swear?'

'I swear.'

I turned to Rafe, who nodded.

'Then I have done you an injustice.'

'No matter. But I am puzzled as to why you should think either Rafe or myself likely to be common murderers.'

I did not know. I could not say that something about their manner had been troubling me sorely and that this urgent journey to the bowels of the hospital at the dead of night had thoroughly unnerved me.

'Nevertheless, I think I am entitled to some explanation of all this.'

'You are and before long you will be our witness and I swear to you that we plan nothing nefarious and nothing to endanger a life which is about to draw up to a peaceful end.'

Walter stepped forward and put his hand out to the man who lay there, breathing with more and more difficulty. The rattle in his throat was more pronounced and once or twice, the grimy fingers and hand twitched. Once the eyelids seemed about to open but then did not. The gas in Rafe's burners hissed and popped softly, otherwise the room was quite silent.

Had Walter and Rafe succumbed to some sort of madness? But what sort would grip two men together yet not also cause them to appear feverish and raving? Insanity is not infectious unless it comes about as the result of some rabies-like infection and they both seemed eminently well.

They could simply have been two doctors paying close attention to a patient for whom all hope had gone. What was I doing there, I as sane as any other, for all that I felt nervous and baffled? Walter had said that I was their witness but what was I witnessing? Only an old man dying.

In the next moment something happened, his raucous breathing changed, slowed and quietened.

'Now!' Walter said in an urgent tone and at once, Rafe crossed to the bench and took up a glass phial, a length of narrow tubing and a test-tube, together with what resembled an oxygen mask, but with a couple of alterations. He went up to the dying man and put the mask over his face. It sat loosely and he appeared quite unaware of it – indeed, I thought that the man was unaware of everything now. One end of the tubing was fixed to the mask and the other into the top of the phial and secured by a clip. The phial had two small holes in the side. Rafe held the test tube up and I saw some clear liquid, perhaps to a depth of half an inch, in the bottom. We were now all standing in such silence and stillness that our own breathing seemed to slow almost to a stop. There was no sound.

The old man's face was sunken in, the flesh already waxen. He breathed two more shallow breaths, then a third. I thought that I could hear the pounding not only of my own heart but that of Walter and Rafe's, too.

There came one more, unsteady breath and Walter said again 'Now!' But in a voice so faint that I barely heard him. On the same instant, Rafe poured the clear liquid out of the test tube into the phial. The old man exhaled for the last time and the breath travelled down from the mask over his face into the tubing. For a split second I saw it mist the inside of the glass. He breathed no more and at the very second that he was still, and in death, the liquid in the phial seemed to catch fire and to turn not into an ordinary flame but a sort of phosphorescent gas that crept up the inside of the glass, a very slightly pulsating substance, semi-transparent and astonishingly beautiful. I gazed at it in amazement and in disbelief. It remained when Rafe disconnected the tubing and quickly stopped the aperture. He held up the phial. I glanced at Walter and saw that he was transfixed by it and that his face wore an almost beatific expression – partly of triumph and partly what I can only call joy. Then he gave a small sigh and we all looked at the old man. His chest did not rise. He was utterly still and his face was changed by a look of utter tranquillity. Walter bent and lifted each of his eyelids and then beckoned me to move closer. He handed me his ophthalmic torch and I bent to examine the corpse's pupils.

'Fixed and dilated,' I said.

'Pulse?'

I held first one wrist then the other, for a full minute and put my finger to the carotid artery. I took the stethoscope and listened closely to the chest. There was nothing – no breath, no heartbeat, no sign of life at all.

'To the best of my knowledge and observation, this man is dead.'

There was an almost reverential hush. Rafe stood on the other side of the trolley, holding the glass. The beautiful light contained within it gleamed silver white and still phosphorescent and as we stared at it we saw that it still pulsed faintly in time with the beating of our hearts.

'So – there we have it,' Walter said.

I managed to pull myself out of my half-trance.

'I suppose you call whatever is in that phial "the spark of life" and I presume you now have plans to replace it into the dead body and wait for a resurrection?' I shuddered. The room was deathly cold, though I had been quite unconscious of the fact until now. I was badly frightened and completely out of my depth medically, ethically and simply as a human being. Walter touched my arm and I jumped back. His eyes were still sparking with excitement but his voice was full of concern.

'No,' he said. 'This man, whoever he is, will now be left to rest in peace and accorded a proper burial, by the Christian church – for which, by the way, though not a member, I have a profound respect.'

'Close by,' Rafe said, still holding the phial, which continued to gleam and pulsate, 'is the hospital mortuary, to which our friend here will now be taken. And then we plan to conduct the next and most vital phase of our experiment. I am warning you now, as I have warned Walter many times, it is the part most is likely to fail, though I have a flicker of confidence, based on experiments I have already conducted in my laboratory.'

'The cat!'

'Indeed, but after all, one ginger cat may easily be confused with another and besides, the cat is a living organism but it is not a human being. It lacks many attributes of the human and many religious people would say that a cat has no soul.'

I felt giddy and put my hand to my head. 'Is this night never to end? Will there be no conclusion to the strange events?'

As I swayed, Walter took firm hold of me and held me, while letting me slide gently to the floor. He propped me up with my back against the wall and then pushed me forwards with my head between my knees.

'If you still feel unsteady in five minutes, I will take you home. You are a robust man but you were gravely ill at the end of last year and you have just been subjected to a severe nervous strain.'

'No,' I said, as the swirling sensation behind my eyes gradually slowed, like a fairground carousel coming to a standstill. 'No, I intend to see this through. I am your witness and I won't let you down.'

'Good man. Now drink this.' He held a small flask. 'No no, it is simply a good brandy, it will do you nothing but good. I intend to have a dram myself.'

I took a good mouthful and the liquid fire of it re-invigorated me in seconds. I stood up. Walter was ready with a hand but I did not need it.

'I am quite well,' I said, 'and quite ready.'

Three

We covered the face and body of the old vagrant with a sheet and Walter and Rafe left the small room, Rafe pushing the trolley, Walter walking a step or two ahead. The corridors were empty and silent – any sounds from the main body of the hospital did not penetrate this subterranean annex. The old mortuary – there was a much newer one in the East Wing – was close by and unattended because it was now little used, but because of the recent influx of mortally ill patients, it was fully equipped and functioning. Walter had a key – I did not ask how he had obtained it.

'Is Rafe not coming with us?'

'We have things to attend to in readiness. You will stay here and guard our departed friend.' He glanced almost fondly at the sheeted body.

'Where are you going?'

'You seem nervous – surely you are accustomed to death by now?'

'I am agitated about what you and Rafe are doing. You must agree that it is hardly regular or normal.'

'It is unique,' Walter said.

'Perhaps, but as to remaining alone here with our friend – of course I am not nervous.'

'I am pleased to hear it,' Walter smiled and I realised what had always perturbed me about that smile. It was not sinister, though it was not especially pleasant but it had an odd effect. It changed his face from that of a young, fresh-faced man into one far older. It was uncanny. He was twenty-six but instantly became ancient, his features showing briefly the ravages of old age and bitter, even terrible experience. He glanced at me as he closed the mortuary door, leaving me alone and as the smile had faded his face was young again, the face on which few cares or troubles had made any mark. How peculiar, that the change should be wrought by a smile.

Being alone with a dead man did not perturb me in the least and I lifted the sheet to look again at his face. It still wore the expression of great calm and acceptance. I could discern, beneath the ravages of a hard lived life, and of ageing, that the man had once been handsome, with a broad brow and a well-shaped and resolute mouth. There was a gentleness about him which was delightful and strangely comforting. Whatever his life had been, death had resolved all suffering and troubles. I covered his face. No, I was not in the least afraid of a corpse which could do me no harm, but I was terrified of what living men might be about. The phrase 'playing with fire' came to mind, followed by remembrance of horrible stories, so that I was relieved when I heard the key being turned in the lock.

Rafe came in first, still carrying the glass phial, as if it contained a rare and precious oil. Walter was at his heels, pulling another trolley into the room, upon which another figure lay. He locked the door behind him.

'What –?'

He did not answer but stationed the trolley under the lamp.

'I need to call upon you again,' he said to me. 'You are my witness.'

He drew down the sheet and I caught my breath. The body was that of a young woman of eighteen or twenty years, wearing a green cotton hospital gown. Her hair was a rich brown, with the reddish tinge of a chestnut fresh from its carapace. Her skin was flawless. She was beautiful.

'Again,' Walter said at my side, 'as with our other body, we do not know her identity. She was brought into the hospital two days ago, found gravely ill with hypothermia on the river embankment. I attended to her and saw at once that here was the other half of the equation – if that does not put it too crudely. We made strenuous efforts to save her but when it became clear that we would not do so, I called Rafe. When I arrived here with you earlier, I hastened to find our old man and ascertain how much longer he had to live.'

All three of us looked down at the young woman. She was still breathing in a shallow and faltering rhythm. Walter felt her pulse.

'Weak and very slow.' His voice dropped to a whisper so that I felt he was talking to himself. 'If only she knew. If only …'

'I hope you do not intend to do her any injury or harm. Leave her to slip away peacefully, for God's sake. Leave your shabby experiments at least to the old and hopeless.'

Walter simply shook his head and did not reply. All gazed silently at the dying girl. There was no harsh rattle this time, merely a few sounds in her throat, as if she was trying to cough. Walter turned urgently to Rafe, who held the phial containing the pulsating phosphorescence, and a fresh oxygen mask which he quickly attached to the girl's face.

'Careful – wait – be very careful,' Walter said urgently. My mouth was dry, my eyes staring so that I scarcely blinked.

On the instant and without further warning, the girl's breathing stopped and at once the shadow of death, invisible yet almost tangible, crept over her face.

'Now!'

A split second and Rafe had started to squeeze the tube attached by one end to the phial and the other to the girl's mouth beneath the mask. The liquid flared up and became radiant as it travelled at great speed out of the phial until the glass was empty. We all held our breath and then I felt as if the air in the whole room had somehow lightened and taken on a life of its own. I felt my heart leap, I felt jubilant, joyous, more alive than I had ever been. I felt new-born. When I looked at the others, I saw by a strange pearlescence on their skin and light in their eyes that they experienced it too. It all lasted only a thousandth of a second and yet it seemed to last for all eternity, and when it faded, I felt as if I had been let down from the air, to land softly, safely, on the ground by Rafe's side. I did not dare to think, speculate, hope. I let my mind go blank. My body seemed held together by the finest of wires, which was taut but quite painless. And then I looked down.

The girl was breathing. Her pallor had the faintest colouring as the blood re-filled arteries, veins, capillaries, just below the skin. Her fingernails were flushed pink. She did not open her eyes, her body did not stir. Walter passed me the stethoscope and I could feel the trembling in his hand. I bent over the now living girl and listened to her heartbeat, heard the sound of air passing in and out of her lungs. I felt her pulse and lifted each eyelid in turn. The pupils were bright but unseeing. She was not conscious but as I removed the stethoscope, I said, 'I have no doubt that she is alive.'

Walter grabbed Rafe's hand in a grip so tight that the man winced.

'You have succeeded!'

Rafe was deathly pale.

'You have raised the dead!'

'No!' I said, and was startled to hear how loud and emphatic my voice sounded in the quiet room. 'You go too far. Your claim is too immense – it is not credible. It defies everything I know, or I have been taught – it defies human experience.'

'Yes,' Walter said, 'it does indeed. But now we must be practical. The young woman must be taken back to an acute ward and put under close observation. I will take her myself and instruct the nursing staff. Rafe must attend to the dead man. We will meet again at Printer's Devil Court where my prescription is a glass each of good brandy.'

We watched Walter wheel away the still-breathing young woman. Our own work was quickly done. We left the old mortuary and locked the door. Rafe took possession of the key and we went, neither of us speaking, out of the hospital and up through the dark and deserted streets in the bitter cold, to our lodgings.

Four

'One thing I do not understand and that is why? What possible reason could you have for performing this whole charade?'

We were all three of us sitting round the fire, which was smoking and sulking dismally in the grate, in spite of our best efforts. None of us was calm enough to sleep. I had said nothing on the way home or for some time after we had all our brandy and battled with the fire but I had been thinking hard, my brain trying to produce a plausible explanation for what had happened, which had shocked and unnerved me until, as if some piece finally clicked into place, I saw what should have been clear all along. Walter and Rafe had performed an elaborately staged series of clever conjuring tricks.

'You went to a good deal of trouble,' I said now. 'You prepared the way carefully and prepared me too for that matter and at some considerable risk. I see it all but I still do not see a reason, so perhaps before we retire please, Walter and Rafe, an explanation.'

Then I saw that Walter was angry. His mouth was tight, his eyes narrowed.

'You do not understand – *you*? Correct me, Hugh, but I think *we* are the ones owed an explanation and an apology.'

'How so?'

'Do you not believe the evidence of your own eyes? How can what you witnessed tonight be some kind of trick or charade? If it had been, then I agree you would be fully entitled to ask for a reason and an explanation, but credit us with more intelligence and maturity. What possible reason indeed could be behind such a trick? What a puerile game we would have been playing, what a waste of our time and energy – what an offence that would have been.'

'You cannot expect me to believe that it was anything other than a fraud.'

'I do expect it. What we witnessed was a triumphant success

– the culmination of much work and strain over many months and many setbacks.'

I stood up. 'So you refuse to give me your reason – so be it. I am horrified that you should have played such macabre games with the bodies of your patients. Shame on you. I want no more part of it. I will find new lodgings. I bid you both good night and God grant you forgiveness which is better than you deserve.'

I did not go to bed, merely took off my jacket and shoes, loosened my collar and sat in my chair for the few hours that remained of the night, in a turmoil of confused and angry thoughts. I could not forget the sight of the old vagrant dying before us, and the look of release and acceptance on his face. I could not forget the sight of the beautiful young woman in her coma, in that cold basement room. I intended to scour the hospital on the following day, to find her and discover what state she was in and whether she was expected to recover. About Walter and Rafe I could do nothing. I had, of course, no evidence of their nefarious activities. I wanted nothing more to do with them and prayed that whatever the reason for their dark and secret games, they would now cease to dabble in them and let the dead and the dying alone.

I wish now that I had taken James's course. I could never *un*-know what I now knew or forget whatever it was that I had witnessed. James would be deeply troubled not the least because, in his eyes, they had spoken blasphemously in their casual talk of 'raising the dead' and even gone on to pretend that they had done so. I might almost have believed them, had the old man, who I had confidently pronounced dead, woken. He had not. He had remained dead. The young woman, of course, had never been dead at all.

Altogether, I was ashamed to have had the smallest part in it.

I felt unwell the next morning, weak and exhausted. I did not go into the hospital and on the day after that, being worse, I again took myself to Norfolk, where I became seriously ill, my nervous system shattered, and I spent many weeks recuperating. I suffered from appalling nightmares and waking terrors, so much so that our family physician questioned whether I was fit to return to the hospital and continue my medical career. This roused me, and I realised how badly my body, mind and spirits had been affected. But that was my turning point. I pulled myself up, determined to return to the practice of medicine.

A year later I left London for a hospital in the West Country. I worked hard, my interest and enthusiasm fully roused again and gradually, I forgot Walter, Rafe and all their sinister trickeries.

James wrote to me to say that he had abandoned medicine, to study for the Ministry. Of Walter and Rafe, I heard nothing.

PART THREE

Five

I travelled to London rarely. In the past twenty years, I had visited no more than half a dozen times. I had a horror of the place and I had never again ventured to my old hospital nor set foot near Fleet Street and its environs. Many people enjoy revisiting old haunts but a shadow fell on me if I so much as thought about them.

I practised as a country physician in a most beautiful and peaceful part of England for almost forty years and married a young widow, Eleanor Barnes, who brought me a fine brace of stepsons. We did not produce any children of our own but that had never troubled me. Both Eleanor's boys had grown up to be fine young men. Toby had gone into the army, Laurie had followed in my footsteps and I took a great deal of interest and pleasure in observing his progress through medical school and into his career as a doctor. He had no desire to be a family physician in a country parish – bury himself, as he put it, but went into medical research, made a pioneering study of certain genetic defects in children and became the country's leading expert in their diagnosis and treatment. He spent some time travelling abroad. Earlier in the year of which I now write, he had finally returned and came down to see us. He was in his late thirties by then, the prime of life, a tall, handsome man with his mother's deep brown eyes and sweetness of temperament.

We were only the three of us at dinner on that first night after his return and when the beef had been set on the table, Laurie said, 'That looks a fine bottle of claret you have opened, Hugh.' (He and Toby had never called me by anything other than my Christian name since childhood, in accordance with our wishes and out of respect for their late father.)

'Good enough for a toast.'

'It is indeed,' I said, touching the St Emilion from an especially fine year. 'Tell us what news you have that deserves toasting.'

Eleanor looked at her son, a slight flush coming to her cheeks. 'Are you going to be married, Laurie?'

He let out a shout of laughter. 'Whenever have I had the chance to look around for a wife? No, no, you will have to wait a long time before that happens. I have been appointed as consultant physician at St Luke's – your own hospital, Hugh!'

In the midst of the general rejoicing and congratulations, a sudden chill descended on me, so that I had to force myself to remain full of laughter and good spirits, but it passed before long. I was proud of Laurie and delighted for him but I never wanted to set foot in that hospital again. However, some six months after he had taken up his appointment, I was obliged to do so.

Laurie was presenting a paper to a learned medical society, a great honour, and of course I must attend. Eleanor was away on a visit to her aged mother so that I went up to London alone. Laurie booked me a room in St Luke's club – for past and present members of the hospital. It was well-appointed, the public rooms were delightfully comfortable, in an old-fashioned way and I went off to hear the lecture wondering why I did not come to London more often, country bumpkin that I had become.

After the event, we enjoyed a celebratory dinner and then, as Laurie wanted to stay up into the small hours talking to his colleagues, I left them to it. Just before midnight I set off to walk back to the club. My route was the old one, but this corner of London had changed a good deal. Fleet Street no longer housed the hot-metal presses and many of the old alleys and courts had long gone, most of them bombed to smithereens by the Blitz. Once or twice I took a wrong turn and ended up among new buildings I didn't recognise. At one point, I retraced my steps for a hundred yards and suddenly I was thrown back in time. I realised that the old Printer's Devil Court, where I had lodged, had been laid waste and that the hospital club was now sited on part of the same ground. I thought little of it – Printer's Devil Court held no special memories for me, other than those last peculiar and unpleasant ones.

I was about to turn into the club when I noticed that there was still a passageway to one side and saw the tower of St-Luke's-at-the-Gate rising up ahead of me in the fitful moonlight. I stood stock still. London churches are always a fine sight and I was glad that this one, with a surprising number of others, had escaped destruction. The passageway ended at the back of the old graveyard, as before, and that seemed unchanged, the tombstones still leaning this way and that and even more thickly covered in moss.

And then I saw her. She was a few yards away from me, moving among the graves, pausing here and there to bend over and peer, as if trying to make out the inscriptions, before moving on again. She wore a garment of a pale silvery grey that seemed strangely gauze-like and her long hair was loose and free. She had her back to me. I was troubled to see a young woman wandering here at this time of night and started towards her, to offer to escort her away. She must have heard me because she turned and I was startled by her beauty, her pallor and even more, by the expression of distress on her face. She came towards me quickly, holding out her hand and seeming about to plead with me, but as she drew near, I noticed a curious blank and glassy look in her eyes and a coldness increased around me, more intense than that of the night alone. I waited. The nearer she came the greater the cold but I did not – why should I? – link it in any way to the young woman, but simply to the effects of standing still in this place where sunlight rarely penetrated and which had a dankness that came from the very stones and from the cold ground.

'Are you unwell?' I asked. 'You should not be here alone at this time of night – let me see you safely to your home.'

She appeared puzzled by my voice and her body trembled beneath the pale clothes.

'You will catch your death of cold.'

She stretched out both her hands to me then but I shrank back, un-accountably loathe to take them. Her eyes had the same staring and yet vacant look now that she was close to me. But she was fully alive and breathing and I had no reason to fear.

'Please tell me what is wrong?'

There was a second only during which we both stood facing one another silently in that bleak and deserted place and something seemed to happen to the passing of time, which was now frozen still, now hurtling backwards, now propelling us into the present again, but then on, and forwards, faster and faster, so that the ground appeared to shift beneath my feet, yet nothing moved and when the church clock struck, it was only half past midnight.

'Please help me. I need someone to help me.'

I would have replied again to ask her how I could help but I was si-lenced, not by her words, but by her voice, which was not that of a girl of no more than eighteen or twenty, but of an old man, a deep, hoarse voice, cracked and wavering. It was like hearing a puppet-master accidentally speaking in the voice of one doll while pulling the strings of another. I recoiled but I also went on staring at the girl not only because of the voice but because now I knew that I had seen her before – in the basement room of the hospital some forty years earlier, lying on a trolley and subject to the vile tricks played by Walter and Rafe.

'Sir? I have been searching for so long. Please help me.'

She was walking away from me and now began to move in and out between the graves again, going to first one and then another, quickening her pace, faster and faster, so that she seemed to be floating just above the ground. At each stone she bent and peered briefly at the inscription, though most of them were so overgrown and worn away by the weather, that few were legible. I followed her every step. I could not help myself. But at each grave, she let out a low, harsh cry of disappointment.

'Tell me,' I said, 'I will try to help you. Are you looking for a particular grave? That of a parent perhaps? A loved one? Let us look together, though we had really better do it in the daylight.'

She sank to the ground then and bent her head. 'My own …' she said.

'Your own family? Or perhaps even your own child?'

She shook her head violently, as if she was angry that I did not understand.

'Taken …' She seemed to have greater difficulty in forming the words now, as if she had little breath left and her voice sounded even older.

'The … wrong … life …'

My blood felt as if it flowed more and more slowly through my veins and I felt the chill tighten around me again. I looked in horror at the young woman and as I did so, one moment she was there, kneeling on the cold ground trying desperately to speak, and the next, she seemed to be dissolving, to become absorbed, like the damp, into the rough earth in front of the grave. I closed my eyes in terror of what I was seeing and when I opened them again she had gone. She was simply no longer there before me. Nothing was there. Nothing at all.

Seconds later, I seemed to be dissolving too and then the stones around me and the walls of the church, all seemed to shimmer and fade and then go black.

I surfaced from a swirl of nightmares to find Laurie bending over me and as his features materialised from the mist, I realised that I was in my bed at the club. He told me that he and some fellows had taken a short cut home from their evening at the hospital dinner and found me lying insensible. Having checked that I was not injured but had merely fainted, they had carried me back between them.

I recovered quickly, my head cleared and after drinking some brandy and hot water, I sat beside the fire. It was then that I told the whole story to Laurie, from the events in my days at the hospital and Printer's Devil Court. When I reached the climax of the tale, with Rafe transferring the contents of the phial to the dead young woman, Laurie started up.

'Walter Powell! That name is known in the medical world – though I know you never hear a word of these things, buried as you are in the country. His name is known and so is that of his cohort, Rafe McAllister. They were apprehended in the course of stealing a body from the mortuary at St Luke's and from taking away a patient who was on the point of death, without permission or authority. A night porter gave testimony and one of his fellows swore to having seen the two men about their dreadful business more than once. He had alerted the hospital authorities but nothing was done. In fact, that porter was dismissed – I dare say he was believed to have had a breakdown. Nothing more was reported for over a year, when the two men were caught and police were called. I only know all this from hospital legend and reading up old newspapers. A macabre and distasteful business and quite inexplicable. I was mildly interested. I like to study peculiarities of human behaviour, as you know, but I came to the conclusion that it must all have been some money-making lark – that or blackmail though God knows how or what. The days of Burke and Hare are long gone.'

'Did you hear what happened to the two men? Presumably they went to jail.'

'I have no idea – I gave up reading about it – I'm far too busy. I know they were given bail on the usual conditions, that they surrender their passports and report to the police but more than that …' Laurie held out his hands.

'Meanwhile, Hugh, you are obviously sickening for something. Whatever caused you to pass out must be investigated – I am having you in St Luke's first thing tomorrow.'

It was clear that he had not taken my story seriously but put it down to the ravings of a man with a feverish illness of some kind. But I knew that the scene was no delusion. It was as real as the furniture in that club bedroom.

'I have no need of any hospitalisation, thank you Laurie. I am tired and a little chilled. A good night's sleep will sort that out and I will be right as rain tomorrow. I will return to my quiet, dull ways in the depths of the country, where no ghost has ever troubled me.'

He knew that I meant what I said and got up to leave, but at the door he turned.

'I do not believe in ghosts,' he said, 'nor in the raising of the dead to life.'

'No. Until tonight, nor did I.'

He sighed and left, saying that he would check on me in the morning before he would countenance my going home.

As soon as he had gone, I felt restless and anxious, not for myself but for the young woman, whatever – *whatever* she was. She had asked me for help. Did she linger about the churchyard night after night searching and pleading?

I dressed and went downstairs. The night porter's cubby-hole had a low light showing within and the man was leaning back in his leather arm-chair, eyes closed, snoring gently, but as soon as I started to creep towards the outer door, he woke.

'Are you well, sir? What can I do for you?'

'I need to take a turn in the air. Would you be so kind as to let me out?' He looked perturbed.

'I should not be gone long but I find this is usually the way to settle myself if I am restless.'

He unlocked a side door to the main entrance and told me it would be open and he himself awake, on my return.

'Don't stay out too long, Sir, or hang about the back streets – you never know, at this hour.'

I knew that I would see her. She was wondering anxiously among the graves, just as before, leaning down to read the inscriptions. I made no sound but she turned, as if sensing my presence. Her expression was lost, distraught and she lifted her arm up.

'Help me. I cannot find ... Find ...'

The voice was old, as before, that of an old man. It was still so very strange and unnerving but I forced myself to remain calm.

'What are you looking for? You know that if I can help you I will.' She covered her eyes with her hands.

'Don't be afraid of me.' She said nothing.

'Tell me again.'

'I have ... I am ... Nothing.'

'What are you looking for?'

'I am ... Not. I have ... Not.' She gave a long and weary sigh and her whole body shuddered. 'The wrong life.' The words came out after a great effort. 'Help me ... I must ... Must ... Find.'

What those two men had tried to do was not possible, and it was madness, terrifying and unimaginable, but that their terrible experiment had somehow succeeded in part I could not now doubt. The life force they had captured and transfused was no mere anonymous breath or spark, it was imprinted with the character – the being – the soul even – of the dead man. Was this young woman still alive or had she died a second time and this for good? Had she been unable to rest, or move on until she was rid of 'the wrong life' and re-united with her true self? Was she a ghost? But she spoke. Does a ghost speak? How could I know?

The next moment, again, she was no longer there. Had she slipped away, out of the side gate? Gone into the church perhaps? But I would have seen her, sensed some movement. She had not passed me. The moon was behind clouds, it was pitch dark but my eyes were so well adjusted to it that I could make out the graves, the wall, the church tower. I waited. I called out but my voice sounded oddly hollow and unreal, fading into the emptiness.

The next morning, I told Laurie I had changed my mind and wanted to stay another night. I needed to look up a few bits of information in the hospital records.

I found everything. The old man was listed as Patient A207. He had been certified dead by Walter Powell M.D. Touchingly, although I learned that the A stood for Anonymous, he had been given a burial name – John.

A young woman, Patient A194, was recorded a couple of days earlier, having been picked up from the street in an unconscious state. A locket had been found on her person with the name Grace barely visible on it. But there was no record of her death until several years later when again she had been found out of doors, suffering from malnutrition and hypothermia. The death certificate had been signed by a P. R. Ross M.D. but there was a pathologist's report inserted – a post-mortem had been requested by the coroner, as was by then becoming usual for those found dead on the streets of London. The body was that of a young woman aged around twenty-five to twenty-eight. She was severely malnourished, but this would not have accounted for her having the vocal cords, larynx and lungs of someone over seventy years of age, who had been a heavy tobacco smoker. 'Inconsistent with other findings' was jotted to one side in the usual pathologist's barely legible hand.

I closed the record book with a strange feeling of relief. I had to find one further piece of information and then I would have all I needed to bring the whole business to a conclusion. If I was insane, hallucinating or suffering the effects of a brain injury, then I had no symptoms. I had a clear head, a calm mind, a steady pulse and a resolution as firm as I had ever known.

I did not mention any of it to Laurie. We ate supper together, during which he was full of medical talk. He glanced at me sharply once or twice, but I thought that everything about my demeanour and easy conversation put him at ease. When I told him that I was to travel home the next day on the late morning train I saw the relief in his eyes and I understood it fully. How could he possibly have believed my story? He was, like me, a doctor and a scientist and he knew far more than I did about delusional states. Although the boundaries of what was possible in medicine had been pushed farther than I would have ever thought possible as a young doctor, they surely could never extend to raising the dead. If what Walter and Rafe had done was real, we had better throw away all our textbooks and templates and prior assumptions, for the very ground on which we stood was unstable. Whatever the truth, whatever I had seen, I knew I must make a last attempt to lay it all to rest. If I did not, I feared I would never sleep again.

Just after one o'clock in cold clear moonlight I was waiting for her again, and again she seemed to materialise on an instant and was wandering among the graves as before. When she looked up and saw me, she beckoned. She wore the same thin grey clothes, her feet were bare and her flesh had a faint blue sheen.

'Help me – please help me.'

'I can and I will,' I said, going over to her, 'but this is not the place. You must follow me.'

The old churchyard led, through an opening in the far wall, to a more recent burial ground, with some twenty identical gravestones, little worn or touched by the moss and lichen. I had discovered that the hospital had taken over the space for the burials of patients whose identities were unknown of whom there used to be many more than there are now. I led the way to two of the graves, marked simply John and Grace above a date and a simple cross.

She was standing beside the entrance and I beckoned to her. She said again, 'Help me, please help me,' in that old, croaking voice, her eyes vacant. I still shuddered to hear it as I looked at her beautiful face. Then, with steps that seemed hardly to touch the ground, she came close to me and as she did so, and for the first time, I smelled the smell of death and decay upon her. I did not shrink back. She approached the grave marked John and at once recoiled. I edged closer, speaking to her as reassuringly as I would to a child. I thought that I now understood what was wrong, though I was working more or less on blind instinct and I had a notion of how she might find her rest and resolution at last. She turned to me, looking fearful.

'No,' I said, speaking in as quiet and reassuring voice as I could. 'There is nothing for you to be frightened of. In this grave is the body of the old man whose life you were given. I can explain it no more clearly – it is beyond my understanding.'

She bent to read the inscription and I saw her whole being begin to tremble as she reached out her hand, as if to trace the outline of the lettering. I moved slowly along to the grave marked Grace and stopped beside it and as I did so I felt that same deathly chill wrap me round. She was standing very close to me and it seemed as if her breath was becoming fainter. The cold grew more intense. I was afraid myself now and felt unreal, as if I was standing beside my own body but I managed to speak, though it was hard and I could only get out a few words. 'Grace. Find. Go.' My chest seemed to be tightening and my throat about to close up.

'Back. Give. Back.' I could say no more. My brain was working slowly, in flashes of consciousness between terrible stretches of darkness. I knew what she must do, and that I was trying to help her as she had begged me. She took a couple of steps forwards. I did not see her turn again and now she was beside John's grave. I stared. Nothing happened and the bitter cold was binding me with iron bands now and the constriction in my chest was agonisingly painful. She glanced once more at her 'own' grave and I saw intense suffering and distress in her face, before she took a single further step, so that now she was standing right on the burial place. And then she had gone. She was no longer there. Nothing was there. At once, the chill that had held me lifted, and the pain and constriction were loosed.

I came to, as if I had woken from sleep but not from any dreams. I was fully conscious of where I was and of everything that had happened. Whatever help Grace had needed, I felt sure I had given it to her but I

could do no more and I made my way towards the passage. The clouds
had almost cleared and the moon shone with a soft hazy light. I looked
back. Above the grave of John was a pale mist, not visible in any other
part of the churchyard. It had no form and there was no sense of 'presence'. It was like the mist that sometimes happens over the surface of
water at dawn. As I looked, it began to dissolve and I felt an uneasy calm.
Whatever I had done, whatever had happened, I believed that the young
woman had now found her peace, and that both she and the old man were
somehow whole and restored.

Six

At home, work and country life absorbed me again and although I cannot pretend that I forgot about what had happened or that my sleep was always untroubled, on the whole I was fairly at ease.

A year passed. We saw Laurie infrequently – he was rarely free from the hospital – and when we did meet, he and I never referred to what I had told him.

One bright, clear morning in October, I opened a letter addressed to me alone, in Laurie's hand, which was somewhat surprising but I told Eleanor I had been expecting some medical information from him and, because I had a sense of foreboding, I delayed opening it until I was alone.

My dear Hugh,

In haste, but I thought this might interest you. The names caught my eye in the paper and remembering your strange stories, I looked at the records for the era at St Luke's of those two doctors you knew. As you remember, Powell and McAllister were arrested, charged and bailed on various dreadful suspicions. They were both dismissed from the hospital and subsequently struck off the medical register 'for behaviour in a manner so as to call the profession into disrepute'.

They were accused of gross misconduct in relation to the certification and preparation of deceased patients and the improper disposal of their remains but there must have been far more to it, none of which could be proved.

I confess that I doubted your tale until I came upon this and of course, I am sure you are not surprised to hear that I still believe parts of it to be entirely fanciful – you could never resist embellishing a good story, as I recall from boyhood! I wondered what had happened to Powell and McAllister – who I assumed must have been imprisoned for some years but later released. Such men often disappear abroad, where they do not find it as difficult as it should be to continue practising medicine. I asked frequently if any older members of the hospital medical staff recalled them and eventually an eminent pathologist, sometime retired, raised an eyebrow and said that such things were best forgotten but then he added, 'Their bodies were washed up just a few days after they were released on bail. I performed the post mortems. As I recall, both of the stomachs were full of strychnine and their hands and arms were held together by chains.' I asked if he had suspected murder.

'Who knows? But for my money it was a clear case of joint suicide. They were unable to live with themselves any longer and the world was well rid of them.'

The case may not be closed in police files but I am inclined to take the pathologist's view. So there you have it – a melancholy little tale but I hope you're interested to hear the end of it.

I had always known that what Walter and Rafe were dabbling in was evil and dangerous and there was no doubt in my mind now that the pathologist was correct. They had taken their own lives out of shame, guilt and terror of what they had done. It would have led to worse. They had stopped themselves in the only certain way. I felt nothing but cold contempt for them. I like to think that I am a compassionate man but in this, my heart was hard.

Postscript

Here, the small book ends. When eventually I read it, after my stepfather's death, I presumed that there was no more to be added. Whatever the truth of his story that was it –'a story'. Many a writer has told a tale in the first person and his own voice, as if he is recounting real events but I was entertained by the way Hugh had done it, presumably as a diversion from the often humdrum life of a country doctor. Why he had chosen this particular topic on which to base his fiction I had no idea but it was as good as many others and makes for a creepy tale.

At least, that was what I thought when I received the little book. I read it, put it away on the shelf and forgot all about it.

Hugh died at the age of ninety-two, pretty well and in command of his faculties until almost the end, when he became confused and not always fully aware of us or his surroundings. I thought he had suffered a small stroke, though if so, it did not cause him any physical problems and he continued to read and write letters to old colleagues, to play chess, do *The Times* crossword and to enjoy visits from Toby and myself. Toby, having retired from the Army and married, bought a small farm only half an hour from Hugh and Eleanor. I continued to work in London at St Luke's, but I drove down to the country every other weekend, now that my parents were becoming increasingly frail.

My mother died a year before Hugh and of course, not only did he miss her greatly but he seemed to have a strong sense that he was nearing his own end. He stayed in the old house tended by two wonderful women from the village and the visiting nurse, and I then went down every week. Toby or Joy, his wife and their two daughters, visited almost every day. I think that Hugh was as content as he could be and always seemed sanguine and philosophical and quite often downright cheerful.

He still took a daily walk around the village and even a little further afield when the weather was mild. He was well known and loved over a wide area, and often met with old patients and their descendants on his walks. They would stop their cars for a chat and frequently give him a lift home.

I was due to go down as usual for the weekend when, very late on a Thursday evening, I received an urgent phone call from Toby to tell me that Hugh was extremely ill. Mrs Barford had popped in to see him at half past three and he said he proposed going out for a last walk. It was early October, the sun had been shining all day and there was as yet no hint of winter frosts or chill winds. She had reminded him that it was dark by five now and that she would have his supper ready, as usual, for seven o'clock. She last saw him making his way across the garden, and through the gate which led to the orchard – a favourite walk of his. From the orchard, the path led to the church and he could then return home via the body of the village, in a circular walk.

He had not returned after well over an hour and by then it was quite dark. Mrs Barford had raised the alarm and within a few minutes several men from the village had formed a search party.

Hugh was found in the churchyard, lying on the grass among the older gravestones. It was clear that he had suffered a severe stroke. He was got home, the local doctor – Hugh had appointed him as his successor – had said that he was unlikely to live very much longer and might well suffer a second and fatal vascular incident at any time. He was to be kept at home and made comfortable – the hospital was twenty miles away and would be able to do nothing more for him. It would be a cruelty to take him there.

When I arrived, Hugh was semi-conscious, the left side of his face slightly contorted, which gave him a staring, vacant look, and I thought that he had been frightened. I imagine he felt the first symptoms and knew he was alone and might die out there. He could not speak and I sat with him, alternating with Toby, through that night. He drifted in and out of sleep and his expression did not change until just around dawn, when he struggled to sit up. I tried to settle him back comfortably again but he clawed at my hand and arm and I saw that there was a beseeching look in his eyes. His mouth moving, a few inarticulate sounds came, gravelly and hoarse, but he was not able to form any words. I tried asking him to press my hand if he wanted a drink or was in any pain but he only clawed again, several times, each time more weakly, his eyes intent on my face, as if asking, asking. But asking what? It was more than distressing to be unable to understand or to help him and I felt only a great relief when, just after six o'clock in the morning, he gave a sigh, his face changed, flickered with something I can only describe as delight for a second and then his body relaxed and he breathed his last, quiet breath.

We had already decided to sell the house. Toby was very well settled as he was, and I did not have occasion to take it over – my life and work will always be in London. We disposed of the everyday contents but we went through all the objects of value, the pictures and books, dividing them between us and sending the remainder to a saleroom. Toby entrusted me with the task of going through Hugh's papers, most of which related to his lifetime as a doctor, and it was while doing so that I came upon the pages that follow, which I presume he had intended to form the last part of his book. They were written in Hugh's own hand, legible but wavering – indeed, towards the end the writing became a wild scrawl which confirmed to me that he had suffered from more than one stroke.

I found myself greatly upset and unnerved by what I read and I could not – cannot – take it easily or lightly, as I once could the original story. I cannot get them out of my mind. I cannot sleep for asking myself endless questions relating to the whole business, from its very beginning in the old lodgings in Printer's Devil Court. Without knowing about the subsequent events, about Hugh's last walk to the churchyard at dusk and then his final hours, and the fear I saw on his face during his last moments I would still have taken it all as a tale he had cooked up himself. But as I read the ending over and over again, I became racked with doubts, troubled in my mind, unable to resolve any of it to my satisfaction. I still cannot.

I am horribly afraid that I never will.

Hugh's Final Pages

I had long forgotten all about her. But perhaps nothing is ever truly forgotten, it simply lies dormant, waiting to be re-awakened. Certainly I had not thought of her – of any of it – for many years when I took my walk through our churchyard that late evening. It is a beautiful spot, bordering orchards and meadows, and the gentle hills beyond. This was the soft end to a mellow autumn day. In a couple of weeks it would be Harvest Festival, the service I have always tried to attend. It means a great deal to us in the country. So I was in a calm and unruffled mood when I unlatched the wooden gate. Eleanor is buried here. I do not hang about her grave in a melancholy way, but I like to visit from time to time, to talk to her, to remember. I have never felt the least troubled or afraid in this sacred place. Why would I?

I turned and I saw her. There was no mistaking the young woman and I knew her at once. Everything raced in towards me as an incoming tide. I had thought her to be at rest. I had thought I had done all I could to ensure it. But now here she was and I was not only struck as if by lightning with the shock of seeing her, I was also confused. Why was she here? How did she find me? Seeing me, she stretched out both her arms and I saw the old, distraught and beseeching expression in her eyes, on her face. I felt unsteady but I also felt a sense of dread. I did not want to see her here, I did not want to remember.

'Go. Please go,' I managed to say. 'Go back. You do not belong here. You are not welcome. Leave me in peace. Go home.'

But she came quickly across the grass, barely touching the ground, as before, still holding out her hands to me, pleading. 'I can do no more for you,' I said.

She stopped a few yards away from me and began to speak – or at least, she opened her mouth, her lips moved, framing a rush of desperate words. But no sound came. No sound at all. She went on and on, gesturing to me, touching her face, her mouth, showing me what I already understood. She was dumb. She had given the old man's voice back to him but she had never found her own again and she had been searching for it, and for me, all these years.

I began to shake violently and I fled from her, stumbled away, making as quickly as I could for the gate and my own orchard.

I looked back once, hoping not to see her but she was still there, as clear as day and now she seemed to have a faint glow of phosphorescence round her. She was still holding out her hands, pleading, pleading and I could not bear it. I did not know how, but then I knew I must try and help her, as I had helped her before and I stopped and called out, 'I will come back. I will come back.' And I will go, I will go back …

(Here, the writing peters out.)

The Small Hand

One

It was a little before nine o'clock, the sun was setting into a bank of smoky violet cloud and I had lost my way. I reversed the car in a gateway and drove back half a mile to the fingerpost.

I had spent the past twenty-four hours with a client near the coast and was returning to London, but it had clearly been foolish to leave the main route and head across country.

The road had cut through the Downs, pale mounds on either side, and then run into a straight, tree-lined stretch to the crossroads. The fingerpost markings were faded and there were no recent signs. So that when the right turning came I almost shot past it, for there was no sign at all here, just a lane and high banks in which the roots of trees were set deep as ancient teeth. But I thought that this would eventually lead me back to the A road.

The lane narrowed. The sun was behind me, flaring into the rear-view mirror. Then came a sharp bend, the lane turned into a single track and the view ahead was dark beneath overhanging branches.

I slowed. This could not possibly be a way.

Was there a house? Could I find someone to put me on the right road?

I got out. Opposite me was an old sign, almost greened over. THE WHITE HOUSE. Below, someone had tacked up a piece of board. It hung loose but I could just make out the words GARDEN CLOSED in roughly painted lettering.

Well, a house was a house. There would be people. I drove slowly on down the track. The banks were even steeper, the tree trunks vast and elephantine.

Then, at the end of the lane I came out of the trees and into a wide clearing and saw that it was still light after all, the sky a pale enamelled silver-blue. There was no through road. Ahead were a wooden gate and a high hedge wound about with briars and brambles.

All I could hear were birds settling down, a thrush singing high up on the branches of a walnut tree and blackbirds pinking as they scurried in the undergrowth. I got out of the car and, as I stood there, the birdsong gradually subsided and then there was an extraordinary hush, a strange quietness into which I felt I had broken as some unwelcome intruder.

I ought to have turned back then. I ought to have retraced my way to the fingerpost and tried again to find the main road. But I did not. I was drawn on, through the gate between the overgrown bushes.

I walked cautiously and for some reason tried not to make a noise as I pushed aside low branches and strands of bramble. The gate was stuck halfway, dropped on its hinges, so that I could not push it open further and had to ease myself through the gap.

More undergrowth, rhododendron bushes, briar hedge growing through beech. The path was mossed over and grassy but I felt stones here and there beneath my feet.

After a hundred yards or so I came to a dilapidated hut which looked like the remains of an old ticket booth. The shutter was down. The roof had rotted. A rabbit, its scut bright white in the dimness of the bushes, scrabbled out of sight.

I went on. The path broadened out and swung to the right. And there was the house.

It was a solid Edwardian house, long and with a wide verandah. A flight of shallow steps led up to the front door. I was standing on what must once have been a large and well-kept forecourt – there were still some patches of gravel between the weeds and grass. To the right of the house was an archway, half obscured by rose briars, in which was set a wrought-iron gate. I glanced round. The car ticked slightly as the engine cooled.

I should have gone back then. I needed to be in London and I had already lost my way. Clearly the house was deserted and possibly derelict. I would not find anyone here to give me directions.

I went up to the gate in the arch and peered through. I could see nothing but a jungle of more shrubs and bushes, overarching trees, and the line of another path disappearing away into the darkening greenery.

I touched the cold iron latch. It lifted. I pushed. The gate was stuck fast. I put my shoulder to it and it gave a little and rust flaked away at the hinges. I pushed harder and slowly the gate moved, scraping on the ground, opening, opening. I stepped through it and I was inside. Inside a large, overgrown, empty, abandoned garden. To one side, steps led to a terrace and the house.

It was a place which had been left to the air and the weather, the wind, the sun, the rabbits and the birds, left to fall gently, sadly into decay, for stones to crack and paths to be obscured and then to disappear, for windowpanes to let in the rain and birds to nest in the roof. Gradually, it would sink in on itself and then into the earth. How old was this house? A hundred years? In another hundred there would be nothing left of it.

I turned. I could barely see ahead now. Whatever the garden, now 'closed', had been, nature had taken it back, covered it with blankets of ivy and trailing strands of creeper, thickened it over with weed, sucked the light and the air out of it so that only the toughest plants could grow and in growing invade and occupy.

I should go back.

But I wanted to know more. I wanted to see more. I wanted for some reason I did not understand to come here in the full light of day, to see everything, uncover what was concealed, reveal what had been hidden. Find out why.

I might not have returned. Most probably, by the time I had made my way back to the main road, as of course I would, and reached London and my comfortable flat, the White House and what I had found there in the dusk of that late evening would have receded to the back of my mind and before long been quite forgotten. Even if I had come this way I might well never have found it again.

And then, as I stood in the gathering stillness and soft spring dusk, something happened. I do not much care whether or not I am believed. That does not matter. I know. That is all. I know, as surely as I know that yesterday morning it rained onto the windowsill of my bedroom after I had left a window slightly open. I know as well as I know that I had a root canal filling in a tooth last Thursday and felt great pain from it when I woke in the night. I know that it happened as well as I know that I had black coffee at breakfast.

I know because if I close my eyes now I feel it happening again, the memory of it is vivid and it is a physical memory. My body feels it, this is not only something in my mind.

I stood in the dim, green-lit clearing and above my head a silver paring of moon cradled the evening star. The birds had fallen silent. There was not the slightest stirring of the air.

And as I stood I felt a small hand creep into my right one, as if a child had come up beside me in the dimness and taken hold of it. It felt cool and its fingers curled themselves trustingly into my palm and rested there, and the small thumb and forefinger tucked my own thumb between them. As a reflex, I bent it over and we stood for a time which was out of time, my own man's hand and the very small hand held as closely together as the hand of a father and his child. But I am not a father and the small child was invisible.

Two

It was after midnight when I got back to London and I was tired, but because what had happened to me was still so clear I did not go to bed until I had got out a couple of maps and tried to trace the road I had taken in error and the lane leading to the deserted house and garden. But nothing was obvious and my maps were not detailed enough. I needed several large-scale Ordnance Survey ones to have any hope of pinpointing an individual house.

I woke just before dawn and as I surfaced from a dreamless sleep I remembered the sensation of the small hand taking hold of my own. But it was a memory. The hand was not there as it had been there, I was now quite sure, in the dusk of that strange garden. There was all the difference in the world, as there was each time I dreamed of it, which I did often during the course of the next few weeks.

I am a dealer in antiquarian books and manuscripts. In the main I look for individual volumes on behalf of clients, at auction and in private sales as well as from other bookmen, though from time to time I also buy speculatively, usually with someone in mind. I do not have shop premises, I work from home. I rarely keep items for very long and I do not have a large store of books for sale at any one time because I deal at the upper end of the market, in volumes worth many thousands of pounds. I do collect books, much more modestly and in a disorganised sort of way, for my own interest and pleasure. My Chelsea flat is filled with them. My resolution every New Year is to halve the number of books I have and every year I fail to keep it. For every dozen I sell or give away, I buy twenty more.

The week after finding the White House saw me in New York and Los Angeles. I then went on trips to Berlin, Toronto and back to New York. I had several important commissions and I was completely absorbed in my undertakings. Yet always, even in the midst of a crowded auction room, or when with a client, on a plane or in a foreign hotel, always and however full my mind was of the job I was engaged upon, I seemed to have some small part of myself in which the memory of the small hand was fresh and immediate. It was almost like a room into which I could go for a moment or two during the day. I was not in the least alarmed or troubled by this. On the contrary, I found it oddly comforting.

I knew that when my present period of travel and activity was over I would return to it and try both to understand what had happened to me and if possible to return to that place to explore and to discover more about it – who had lived there, why it was empty. And whether, if I returned and stood there quietly, the small hand would seek mine again.

I had one disconcerting moment in an airport while buying a newspaper. It was extremely busy and as I queued, first of all someone pushed past me in a rush and almost sent me flying and then, as I was still recovering myself, I felt a child's hand take my own. But when I glanced down I saw that it was the real hand belonging to a real small boy who had clutched me in panic, having also been almost felled by the same precipitate traveller. Within a few seconds he had pulled away from me and was reunited with his mother. The feeling of his hand had been in a way just the same as that of the other child, but it had also been quite different – hot rather than cool, sticky rather than silky. I could not remember when a real child had last taken my hand but it must have been years before. Yet I could distinguish quite clearly between them.

It was mid-June before I had a break from travelling. I had had a profitable few weeks and among other things I had secured two rare Kelmscott Press books for my client in Sussex, together with immaculate signed first editions of all Virginia Woolf's novels, near-mint in their dust wrappers. I was excited to have them and anxious to get them out of my hands and into his. I am well insured, but no amount of money can compensate for the loss or damage of items like these.

So I arranged to drive down with them.

At the back of my mind was the idea that I would leave time to go in search of the White House again.

Three

Was there ever a June as glorious as that one? I had missed too much of the late spring but now we were in the heady days of balmy air and the first flush of roses. They were haymaking as I drove down and when I arrived at my client's house, the garden was lush and tumbling, the beds high and thick with flowers in full bloom, all was bees and honeysuckle and the smell of freshly mown grass.

I had been invited to stay the night and we dined on a terrace from which there was a distant view of the sea. Sir Edgar Merriman was elderly, modest of manner and incalculably rich. His tastes were for books and early scientific instruments and he also had a collection of rare musical boxes which, when wound and set going, charmed the evening air with their sound.

We lingered outside and Sir Edgar's blue-grey coils of cigar smoke wreathed upwards, keeping the insects at bay, the pungent smell mingling with that of the lilies and stocks in the nearby beds. His wife, Alice, sat with us, a small, grey-haired woman with a sweet voice and a shyness which I found most appealing.

At one point the servant came to call Sir Edgar to the telephone and as she and I sat companionably in the soft darkness, the moths pattering around the lamp, I thought to ask her about the White House. Did she know of it? Could she direct me to it again?

She shook her head. 'I haven't heard of such a place. How far were you from here?'

'It's hard to tell … I was hopelessly lost. I suppose I'd driven for forty-five minutes or so? Perhaps a bit longer. I took a byroad which I thought I knew but did not.'

'There are so many unsigned roads in the country. We all know our way about so well, but they are a pitfall for the unwary. I don't think I can help you. Why do you want to go back there, Mr Snow?'

I had known them both for some four or five years and stayed here overnight once or twice before, but to me they were always Sir Edgar and Lady Merriman and I was always Mr Snow, never Adam. I rather liked that.

I hesitated. What could I have said? That a deserted and half-derelict house and overgrown garden had some attraction for me, had almost put me under a spell so that I wanted to explore them further? That I was drawn back because … how could I have told her about the small hand?

'Oh – you know how some old places have a strange attractiveness. And I might want to retire to the country some day.'

She said nothing and, after a moment, her husband returned and the conversation turned back to books and to what he had a mind to buy next. He had wide-ranging tastes and came up with some unusual suggestions. I was always challenged by him, always kept on my toes. He was an exciting client because I could never second-guess him.

'Do you know,' he asked now, passing me the decanter, 'if another First Folio of Shakespeare is ever likely to come up for sale?'

I almost knocked over my glass.

It was half an hour later but the air was still warm as we gathered ourselves to go inside. I was fired with enthusiasm at the same time as I was coolly certain that no First Folio was likely to come my way for Sir Edgar. But even the speculative talk about it had made me think of his wealth in quite new terms.

As I was bidding him goodnight, Lady Merriman said suddenly, 'I think I have it, Mr Snow. I think I have the answer. Do just give me a moment if you would.' She went out of the room and I heard her footsteps going up the stairs and away into the depths of the house.

I sat in a low chair beside the open French windows. The lamp was out and a faint whiff of oil came from it. The sky was thick with stars.

And I asked in a low voice, 'Who *are* you?' For I had a strange sense of someone being there with me. But of course there was no one. I was alone and it was peaceful and calm.

Eventually, she returned carrying something.

'I am so sorry, Mr Snow. What we are looking for has always just been moved somewhere else. But this may possibly help you. It came to me as we were sitting there after dinner – the house. The name you gave, the White House, did not register with me because it was always known as Denny's House, to everyone locally – it is about twenty miles from here, but in the country that is local, you know.'

She sat down.

'You really shouldn't have gone to any trouble. It was a passing whim. I don't quite know now why it affected me.'

'There is an article about it in this magazine. It's rather old. We do keep far too much and I have quite a run of these. The house became known as Denny's House because it belonged to Denny Parsons. Have you heard the name?'

I shook my head.

'How quickly things fall away,' she said. 'You'll find everything about Denny Parsons and the garden in here.' She handed me a *Country Life* of some forty years ago. 'Something happened there but it was all hushed up. I don't know any more, I'm afraid. Now, do stay down for as long as you like, Mr Snow, but if you will excuse me, I am away to my bed.'

I went out on to the terrace for a last few moments. Everything had settled for the night, the stars were brilliant, and I thought I could just hear the faint hush of the sea as it folded itself over on the shingle.

In my room I sat beside my open window with the sweet smell of the garden drifting in and read what Lady Merriman had found for me.

The article was about a remarkable and 'important' garden created at the White House by Mrs Denisa – apparently always known as Denny – Parsons and contained photographs of its creator strolling across lawns and pointing out this or that shrub, looking up into trees. There was also one of those dewy black-and-white portrait photographs popular in such magazines then, of Mrs Parsons in twinset and pearls, and holding a few delphiniums, rather awkwardly, as if uncertain whether or not to put them down. The soft focus made her look powdery and slightly vacant, but I could see through it to a handsome woman with strong features.

The story seemed straightforward. She had been widowed suddenly when her two children were nine and eleven years old and had decided to move from the Surrey suburbs into the country. When she had found the White House it had been empty and with an overgrown wilderness round it, out of which she had gradually made what was said in the reverential article to be 'one of the great gardens of our time'.

Then came extensive descriptions of borders and walks and avenues, theatre gardens and knot gardens, of fountains and waterfalls and woodland gardens set beside cascading streams, with lists of flowers and shrubs, planting plans and diagrams and three pages of photographs. It certainly looked very splendid, but I am no gardener and was no judge of the relative 'importance' of Mrs Parsons's garden.

The place had become well known. People visited not only from miles away but from other countries. At the time the article was written it was 'open daily from Wednesday to Sunday for an entrance fee of one shilling and sixpence'.

The prose gushed on and I skimmed some of the more horticultural paragraphs. But I wanted to know more. I wanted to know what had happened next. Mrs Parsons had found a semi-derelict house in the middle of a jungle. The house in the photographs was handsome and in good order, with well-raked gravel and mown grass, fresh paint, open windows, at one of which a pale upstairs curtain blew out prettily on the breeze.

But the wheel had come full circle. When I had found the house and garden they were once again abandoned and decaying. That had happened to many a country house in the years immediately after the war but it was uncommon now.

I was not interested in the delights of herbaceous border and pleached lime. The house was handsome in the photographs, but I had seen it empty and half given over to wind and rain and the birds and was drawn by it as I would never have been by somewhere sunny and well presented.

I set the magazine down on the table. Things change after all, I thought, time does its work, houses are abandoned and sometimes nature reclaims what we have tried to make our own. The White House and garden had had their resurrection and a brief hour in the sun but their bright day was done now.

Yet as I switched out the lamp and lay listening to the soft soughing of the sea, I knew that I would have to go back. I had to find out more. I was not much interested in the garden and house. I wanted to know about the woman who had found it and rescued it yet apparently let it all slip through her fingers again. But most of all, of course, I wanted to go back because of the small hand.

Had Denny Parsons stood there in the gathering dusk, looking at the empty house, surrounded by that green wilderness, and as she made her plans for it felt the invisible small hand creep into her own?

Four

Nothing happened with any connection to the Merrimans or the part of the world in which they lived, and where I had come upon the White House, for several weeks. My trade was going through a dull patch. It happens every so often and ought not to trouble me, but after a short time without any requests from clients or phone calls about possible treasures I become nervous and irritable. If the dead patch continues for longer, I start wondering if I will have to sell some of my own few treasures, convinced that the bottom has dropped out of the business and I will never be active again. Every time it happens I remind myself that things have never failed to turn round, yet I never seem able to learn from experience.

I was not entirely idle of course. I bought and sold one or two complete library sets, including a first edition of Thomas Hardy, and even wondered whether to take up the request from an American collector to find him a full set of the James Bond first editions, mint and in dust wrappers, price immaterial. This is not my field, but I started to ask about in a desultory way, knowing I was probably the hundredth dealer the man had employed to find the Bonds and the one least likely to unearth them.

The summer began to stale. London emptied. I thought half-heartedly of visiting friends in Seattle.

And then two things happened on the same day.

In the post I received an envelope containing a card and a cutting from an old newspaper.

Mr Snow, I unearthed this clipping about the house, Denny's House, which you came upon by chance when getting lost on your way to us in June. I thought perhaps you might still be interested as it tells a little story. I am sure there is more and if I either remember or read about it again I will let you know. But please throw this away if it is no longer of interest. Just a thought.

Sincerely, Alice Merriman.

I poured a second cup of coffee and picked up the yellowed piece of newspaper.

There was a photograph of a woman whom I recognised as Denisa Parsons, standing beside a large ornamental pool with a youngish man. In the centre of the pool was a bronze statue at which they were looking in the slightly artificial manner of all posed photographs. The statue was of a young boy playing with a dolphin and a golden ball and rose quite beautifully out of the still surface of the water, on which there were one or two water lilies. There might have been fish but none was visible.

The news item was brief. The statue had been commissioned by Denisa Parsons in memory of her grandson, James Harrow, who had been drowned in what was simply described as 'a tragic accident'. The man with her was the sculptor, whose name was not familiar to me, and the statue was now in place at 'Mrs Parsons's internationally famous White House garden'. That was all, apart from a couple of lines about the sculptor's other work.

I looked at the photograph for some time but I could read nothing into the faces, with their rather public smiles, and although the sculpture looked charming to me, I am no art critic.

I put the cutting in a drawer of my desk, sent Lady Merriman a post-card of thanks and then forgot about the whole thing, because by the same post had come a letter from an old friend at the Bodleian Library telling me that he thought he might have news of a Shakespeare First Folio which could conceivably be for sale. If I would like to get in touch ...

Fifteen minutes later I was in a taxi on my way to Paddington station to catch the next train to Oxford.

Five

I haven't had an extended lunch break for, what, five years? So I'm taking one today.'

It did not surprise me. I have known quite a few librarians across the world, in major libraries and senior posts, and none has ever struck me as likely to take a long lunch, or even in some cases a lunch at all. It is not their way. So I was delighted when Fergus McCreedy, a very senior man at the Bodleian, suggested we walk from there up to lunch at the Old Parsonage. It was a warm, bright summer's day and Oxford was, as ever, crowded. But in August its crowds are different. Parties of tourists trail behind their guide, who holds up a red umbrella or a pom-pom on a stick so as not to lose any of his charges and language-school students on bicycles replace undergraduates on the same. Otherwise, Oxford is Oxford. I always enjoy returning to my old city, so long as I stay no more than a couple of days. Oxford has a way of making one feel old.

Fergus never looks old. Fergus is ageless. He will look the same when he is ninety as he did the day I met him, when we were both eighteen and in our first week at Balliol. He has never left Oxford and he never will. He married a don, Helena, a world expert on some aspect of early Islamic art, they live in a tiny, immaculate house in a lane off the lower Woodstock Road, they take their holidays in countries like Jordan and Turkistan. They have no children, but if they ever did, those children would be, as so many children of Oxford academics have always been, born old.

I had not seen Fergus for a couple of years. We had plenty to catch up on during our walk to lunch and later while we enjoyed a first glass of wine at our quiet table in the Old Parsonage's comfortable dining room. But when our plates of potted crab arrived, I asked Fergus about his letter.

'As you know, I have a very good client who has set me some difficult challenges in the past few years. I have usually found what he wanted – he's a very knowledgeable book collector. It's a pleasure to work with him.'

'Not one of the get-me-anything-so-long-as-it-costs-a-lot brigade, then.'

'Absolutely not. I have no idea how much he's worth or how he made his money, but it doesn't signify, Fergus, because he loves his books. He's a reader as well as a collector. He appreciates what I find for him. I know I have a living to earn and money is money, but there are some I could barely bring myself to work for.'

I meant it. I had had an appalling couple of years being retained by a Russian oil billionaire who only wanted a book if it was publicised as being both extremely rare and extremely expensive and who did not even want to take delivery of what I bought for him. Everything went straight into a bank vault.

'So your man wants a First Folio.'

Our rare fillet of beef, served cold with a new potato and asparagus salad, was set down and we ordered a second glass of Fleurie.

'I told him it was more or less impossible. They're all in libraries.'

'We have three,' Fergus said. 'The Folger has around eighty. Getty bought one a few years ago of course – that was sold by one of our own colleges.'

'Oriel. Yes. Great shame.'

Fergus shrugged. 'They needed the money more than the book. I can understand that. A small private library in London with a mainly theo- logical collection, Dr Williams's Library, sold its copy a year or so back for two and a half million. But that endows the rest of their collection and saves it for the foreseeable future. It's a question of balancing one thing against another.'

'If you had a First Folio would you sell it?'

Fergus smiled. 'The one I have in mind as being just possibly for sale does not belong to me. Nor to the Bodleian.'

'I thought every one of the 230 or so copies was accounted for?'

'Almost every one. It was thought for some years that apart from all those on record in libraries and colleges and a few in private hands, there was one other First Folio, somewhere in India. But almost by chance, and by follow- ing up a few leads, I think I have discovered that that is not the case.'

He helped himself to more salad. The room had filled. I looked at the walls, which were lined with an extraordinary assortment of pictures, oils and watercolours, five deep in places – none of them was of major impor- tance but every single one had merit and charm. The collection enhanced the pleasant room considerably.

'The Folio was mentioned to me in passing,' Fergus said, 'because my German colleague was emailing me about something entirely different, which we have been trying to track down for a long time – a medieval manuscript in fact. In the course of a conversation I had with Dieter, he said almost in passing something like, "They don't know half of what they do possess, including a Shakespeare First Folio."'

'They?' I said.

Fergus got up. 'Shall we have our coffee on the terrace? I see the sun has come out again.'

Sitting at a table under a large awning, we were somewhat protected from the noise of the passing traffic on the Banbury Road and the coffee was first-rate.

Fergus took three gulps of his double espresso. 'Have you ever heard of the monastery of Saint Mathieu des Etoiles?'

'I didn't so much as know there was such a saint.'

'Not many do. He's pretty obscure, though there are a couple of churches in France dedicated to him, but so far as I know only one monastery bears his name. It's Cistercian, an enclosed and silent order, and very remote indeed, a bit like La Grande Trappe – high up among mountains and forests, in its own small pocket of time. In winter it can be completely cut off. There is a village some six miles away, but otherwise it's as remote from civilisation as you can probably get anywhere in Western Europe. Oh and it also maintains the tradition of wonderful sacred music. A few people do visit – for the music, for a retreat – and the monastery is surprisingly in touch with what you might call our world.'

'Most of them are,' I said. 'I know one in the Appalachian Mountains – remote as they come, but they are on email.'

'When you think about it, the silent email suits the rule far better than the telephone. Now, a couple of years ago I had the good fortune to visit Saint Mathieu. They have one of the finest and oldest and best-preserved monastic libraries in the world. One of the ways they earn their living is in book restoration and rebinding for other libraries. We've used their skills occasionally. You're wondering what all this has to do with you? More coffee?'

We ordered. The terrace was emptying out now, as lunchtime drew to a close.

'The monastery, like so many, is in need of money for repairs. When your building dates from the twelfth century things start to wear out.

They are not a rich order and the work they do keeps them going, but without anything over and to spare. They urgently need repairs to the chapel frescoes and the roof of the great chapter house, and even though they will provide some of the labour themselves, the monks can't do it all – they don't have the skills and, besides, many of them are in their seventies and older. So, after a great deal of difficulty, they have obtained permission to sell one or two treasures – mainly items which don't have much reason to be there, and which sit rather oddly in a Cistercian monastery. For instance, for some strange reason they have one or two early Islamic items.'

'Ah – so Helena comes into the picture.'

'She does. So do we. They have a couple of medieval manuscripts, for instance – an Aelfric, a Gilbert of Hoyland. In each case it was thought only one or possibly two copies existed in the world, but Saint Mathieu turns out to have wonderful examples. They only need to sell a few things to pay for all of their repairs and rebuilding and to provide an endowment against future depredations. They're pretty prone to weather damage up there, apart from anything else. They need to protect themselves against future extreme winters.'

'It's pretty unusual for items like this to come on the market, Fergus. What else have they got? You make me want to get on the next plane.'

He held up his hand. 'No. "The market" is exactly what they do not want to know about any of this. They made contact with us under a seal of total confidentiality. I'm not supposed to be talking to you, so I'd be obliged if you said nothing either.'

I was put out. Why tell me at all if my hands were going to be tied as well as my lips sealed?

'Don't sulk.' Fergus looked at me shrewdly. 'I haven't mentioned this to anyone and I don't intend to – apart from anything else, there would be no point. But the thing is, they have a Shakespeare First Folio – one that was supposed to be somewhere in India. It has never been properly accounted for and my view is that it isn't in India at all but in the Monastery of Saint Mathieu des Etoiles.'

'How on earth did they acquire it?'

He shrugged. 'Who knows? But in the past when rich young men entered the monastery as postulants their families gave a sort of dowry and it sometimes took the form of art treasures, rare books and so on, as well as of money. That's probably what happened in this case.'

'Do they know what they've got?'

'Pretty much. They're neither fools nor innocents. And they are certainly not to be cheated. No, I know you would not, Adam, but your trade is as open to charlatans as any other.'

'I like the way you call it "my" trade.'

'Oh, don't look at me,' Fergus said, smiling slightly. 'I'm just a simple librarian.' He stood up. 'I've extended my lunch hour far enough. Are you walking back into town?'

He paid the bill and we turned out of the gate and began to walk towards St Giles.

'The thing is,' Fergus said, 'some of the items they might conceivably sell will go to America – we simply don't have the money in this country. I am talking to a couple of potential private benefactors but I don't hold out much hope – they get talked to by the world and his wife. Why should they want to give us a single priceless medieval manuscript when they could build the wing of a hospital or endow a chair in medical research? I can't blame them. We've already got First Folios. So have the other libraries. We none of us need another. But you have a client who could presumably afford three or four million to get what he wants?'

'He would never have mentioned it to me if he didn't know how unlikely I was to get one for him, how much it might cost if I ever did and that he could well afford that. He's a gentleman.'

'Ah, one of those. Would you like me to get in touch with the monastery and ask one or two discreet questions? I won't mention your name or anything of that kind – and I'll have to work up to it. I think I have the way of them now, but I don't want to pounce or the portcullis will come down.'

'And they'll be off to the Huntington Library in a trice.'

Fergus's mouth firmed slightly. I laughed.

'You'd all stab one another in the back just as surely as we dealers would,' I said. 'But thank you, Fergus. And of course, please put in a word. Whatever it takes.'

'Yes,' he said. 'Don't call us and all that.'

We parted outside Bodley, Fergus to go in to his eyrie beyond the Duke Humfrey Library, while I went on towards the High. It was a beautiful day now, the air clear and warm, a few clouds like smoke rings high in the sky. There were plenty of trains back to London but I was in no hurry. I thought I would walk down to one of my old favourite haunts, the Botanic Garden, which is surely Oxford's best-kept secret.

Six

I went in through the great gate and began to walk slowly down the wide avenue, looking about me with pleasure, remembering many a happy hour spent here. But it was the Cistercian monastery of Saint Mathieu des Etoiles and its library, as well as the possibility of acquiring a very rare book indeed, which were at the front of my mind. I knew that I could not speak a word of what Fergus had told me, not to Sir Edgar Merriman, nor to a single other soul. I was not such a fool and, besides, I rather wanted to prove to Fergus that antiquarian book dealers are not all charlatans. But I was sure that he had been half-teasing. He knew me well enough.

I wondered how long it would take him to oil his way round to mention of the First Folio in his correspondence with the monastery – presumably by email, as he had hinted. Perhaps not long at all. Perhaps in a day or so I might know whether the business was going to move a step further forward or whether the subject of the Folio would be scotched immediately. There was absolutely nothing I could do but wait.

I had come to the great round lily pond which attends at the junction of several paths. Three or four people were sitting on the benches in the semicircle beside it, enjoying the sunshine. One woman was reading a book, another was knitting. A younger one had a pram in which a baby was sound asleep.

I sat at the end of a bench, still thinking about the Folio, but as I sat, something happened. It is very hard to describe, though it is easy enough to remember. But I had never known any sensation like it and I can feel it still.

I should stress again how at ease I was. I had had a good lunch with an old friend, who had given me a piece of potentially very exciting information. I was in one of my favourite cities, which holds only happy memories for me. The sun was shining. All was right with the world, in fact.

The young woman with the pram had just got up, checked on her baby and strolled off back towards the main gate, leaving the reader, the knitter and me in front of the raised stone pool in which the water lay dark and shining and utterly still.

And at that moment I felt the most dreadful fear. It was not fear of any-thing, it was simply fear, fear and dread, like a coldness rising up through my body, gripping my chest so that I felt I might not be able to breathe, and stiffening the muscles of my face as if they were frozen. I could feel my heart pounding inside my ribcage, and the waves of its beat roaring through my ears. My mouth was dry and it seemed that my tongue was cleaving to the roof of my mouth. My upper lip and jaw, my neck and shoulder and the whole of my left side felt as if they were being squeezed in a vice and for a split second I believed that I was having a heart attack, except that I felt no pain, and after a second or two the grip eased a little, though it was still hard to breathe. I stood up and began to gasp for air, and I felt my body, which had been as if frozen cold, begin to flush and then to sweat. I was terrified. But of what, of what? Nothing had hap-pened. I had seen nothing, heard nothing. The day was as sunlit as before, the little white clouds sailed carelessly in the sky and one or two of them were reflected in the surface of the still pool.

And then I felt something else. I had an overwhelming urge to go close to the pool, to stand beside the stone rim and peer into the water. I realised what was happening to me. Some years ago, Hugo, my brother and older than me by six years, went through a mental breakdown from which it took him a couple of years to recover. He had told me that in the weeks before he was forced to seek medical help and, indeed, to be admitted to hospital, almost the worst among many dreadful experiences was of feeling an overwhelming urge to throw himself off the edge of the under-ground station platform into the path of a train. When he was so afraid of succumbing to its insistence he walked everywhere, he felt he must step off the pavement into the path of the traffic. He stayed at home, only to be overwhelmed again, this time by the urge to throw himself out of the window onto the pavement below.

And now it was happening to me. I felt as if I was being forced forward by a power outside myself. And what this power wanted me to do was throw myself face down into the great deep pool. As I felt the push from behind so I felt a powerful magnetic force pulling me forward. The draw seemed to be coming from the pool itself and between the two forces I was totally powerless. I think that I was split seconds from flinging myself forward into and under the dark water when the woman who had been knitting suddenly started up, flapping at a wasp. Her movement broke the spell and I felt everything relax, the power shrink and shrivel back, leaving me standing in the middle of the path, a yard or so from the pool. A couple were walking towards me, hand in hand. A light aircraft puttered slowly overhead. A breeze blew.

Slowly, slowly, the fear drained out of me, though I felt shaken and light-headed, so that I backed away and sat down again on the bench to recover myself.

I stayed for perhaps twenty minutes. It took as long as this for me to feel calm again. As I sat there in the sunshine, I thought of Hugo. I had never fully understood until now how terrifying his ordeal had been, and how the terrors must have taken him over, mentally and physically. No wonder he had said to me when I first visited him in the hospital that he felt safe for the first time in several years.

Was it hereditary, then? Was I about to experience these terrifying urges to throw myself out of windows or into the path of oncoming trains? I knew that Hugo had gone through a very turbulent time in his youth and I had put his condition down to a deep-seated reaction to that. So far as I knew, neither of our parents had ever suffered in the same way.

At last, I managed to get up and walk towards the gates. I felt better with every step. The fear was receding rapidly. I only shivered slightly as I looked back at the pool. Nothing more.

I was glad to be in the bustle of the High and I had no urge whatsoever to throw myself under a bus. I walked briskly to the railway station and caught the next train back to London.

That night I dreamed that I was swimming underwater, among shimmering fish with gold and silver iridescent bodies which glided past me and around me in the cool, dark water. For a while, it was beautiful. I felt soothed and lulled. I thought I heard faint music. But then I was no longer swimming, I was drowning. I had seemed to be like a fish myself, able to breathe beneath the surface, but suddenly the air was being pressed out of my lungs by a fast inflow of water and I was gasping, with a painful sensation in my chest and a dreadful pulsing behind my eyes.

I came to in the darkness of my bedroom, reached out to switch on the lamp and then sat, taking in great draughts of air. I got up and went to the window, opened it and breathed in the cool London night, and the smell of the trees and grass in the communal gardens of the square. I supposed the panic which had overcome me beside the pool in the Botanic Garden had inevitably left its traces in my subconscious, so that it was not surprising these had metamorphosed into night horrors.

But it faded quickly, just as the terror of the afternoon had faded. I am generally of an equable temperament and I was restored to my normal spirits quite easily. I was only puzzled that I should have had such an attack of panic out of the blue, followed by a nightmare from which I had surfaced thrashing in fear. I had had a pleasant day and I was excited about Fergus's possible coup. The tenor of my life was as even and pleasant as always.

The only untoward thing that had happened to me recently was the incident in the garden of the White House. Unlike the terror and the nightmare, the memory of that had not faded – indeed, if anything it was clearer. I closed my eyes and felt again the small hand in mine. I could almost fold my fingers over it, so real, so vivid was the sensation.

Without quite knowing that I was going to do so then, I did fold my fingers over as if to enclose it. But there was nothing.

Not this time. Not tonight.

Seven

My business was going through the usual summer lull and I did not have enough to occupy me. The nightmare did not return, but although I had no more attacks of fear, I could not get that experience out of my mind and, in the end, I decided that I would talk to my brother. I rang to ask if I could go to see them for a night and got his Danish wife, Benedicte, who was always welcoming. I think that so far as she was concerned I could have turned up on their doorstep at any time of the day or night and I would have been welcome. With Hugo, though, it was different.

He was now a teacher in a boys' public school situated in a pleasant market town in Suffolk. They had a Georgian house with a garden running down to the river and the slight air of being out of time that always seems to be part of such places.

They had one daughter, Katerina, who had just left to stay with her cousins in Denmark for the holiday. Hugo and Benedicte were going to the States, where he was to teach a summer school.

I have always felt a great calm and contentment as I step through their front door. The house is light and elegant and always immaculate. But if it belongs to the eighteenth century from the outside, within it is modern Scandinavian, with a lot of pale wood flooring, cream rugs, cream leather chairs, steel and chrome. It would be soulless were it not for two things. The warmth that emanates from Benedicte herself, and the richly coloured wall hangings which she weaves and sells. They make the house sing with scarlet and regal purple, deep blue and emerald.

It is a strange environment for my brother. Hugo has perhaps never quite picked up the last threads of equilibrium, which is why the house and his wife are so good for him. He has an edginess, a tendency to disappear inside himself and look into some painful distance, detached from what is going on around him. But he loves his job and his family and I do not think he is greatly troubled – for all that he has reminders of his sufferings from time to time.

I arrived in the late afternoon and caught up on news. Benedicte was going out to her orchestra practice – she plays the oboe – but left us with a delicious dinner which needed only a few final touches put to it. The kitchen opened on to the garden, with a distant glimpse of the river, and it was warm enough for us to have the doors open on to a still evening. The flames of the candles in their slender silver holders scarcely flickered.

'I need your advice,' I said to Hugo, as we began to eat our smoked fish. 'Advice, help – I'm really not sure which.'

He looked across at me. We are not alike. Hugo takes after our mother, in being tall and dark with a long oval face. I am stockier and fairer, though we are of a height. But our eyes are the same, a deep smoky blue. Looking into Hugo's eyes was oddly like looking into my own in a mirror. How much else of his depths might I see in myself, I wondered.

'Do you ever …' I looked at the fish on my fork. I did not know how to ask, what words to use that would not upset him. 'I wonder if you sometimes …'

He was looking straight at me, the blue eyes direct and as unwavering as the candle flames. But he was silent. He gave me no help.

'The thing is … something quite nasty happened to me. Nothing like it has ever happened before. Not to me. Nothing …' I heard my voice trailing off into silence.

After a moment Hugo said, 'Go on.'

As if a torrent had been unleashed, I began to tell him about the afternoon in the Botanic Garden and my terrible fear and then the overwhelming urge to fall face down into the water. I told him everything about the day, I elaborated on my feelings leading up to the fear, I went into some detail about how things were in my present life. The only thing I did not mention, because there were somehow not the words to describe it, was the small hand.

Hugo listened without interrupting. We helped ourselves to chicken pie. A salad.

I fell silent. Hugo took a piece of bread. Outside it had grown quite dark. It was warm. It was very still. I remembered the night I had sat out on the terrace at the Merrimans' house in the gathering dusk, so soon after these strange events had begun.

'And you think you are going mad,' Hugo said evenly. 'Like me.'

'No. Of course I don't.'

'Oh, come on, Adam … If you're here to get my advice or whatever it is you want, tell me the truth.'

'I'm sorry. But the truth is – well, I don't know what it is, but you didn't go mad.'

'Yes, I did. Whatever "mad" is, I went it to some degree. I was in a madhouse, for God's sake.'

I had never heard him speak so harshly.

'Sorry,' I said.

'It's fine. I hardly think about it now. It's long gone. Yet there is sometimes the shadow of a shadow, and when that happens I wonder if it could come back. And I don't know, because I don't know what caused it in the first place. My psyche was turned inside out and shaken, but they never got to the bottom of why.'

He looked at me speculatively. 'So now you.' Then, seeing my expression, he added quickly, 'Sorry, Adam. Of course not you. What you had was just a panic attack.'

'But I've never had such a thing in my life.'

He shrugged. A great, soft, pale moth had come in through the open window and was pattering round the lamp. I have never cared for moths.

'Let's go out for some air,' I said.

It was easier, strolling beside my brother down the garden. I could talk without having to see his face.

'Why would I have what you call a panic attack, out of the blue? What would cause it?'

'I've no idea. Perhaps you're not well?'

'I'm perfectly well.'

'Shouldn't you see your GP all the same, get a check?'

'I suppose I could. When you …'

'No,' he said, 'I wasn't ill either.'

We stood at the bottom of the path. A few paces away was the dark river.

'I was within a hair's breadth of throwing myself into that pool. It was terrifying. It was as if I had to do it, something was making me.'

'Yes.'

'I'm afraid it will happen again.'

He put a hand briefly on my shoulder. 'Go and see someone. But it probably won't, you know.'

'Did you ever ask if anyone else in the family had had these – attacks, these fears?'

'Yes. So far as anyone knew, they didn't.'

'Oh.'

'I think that part really is coincidence.'

'I might not be able to resist another time.'

'I'm pretty sure you will.'

'Might you have jumped in front of one of those trains?'

'I think …' he said carefully, 'that there was usually something inside me that held me back – something stronger than it, whatever "it" was. But once … once perhaps.' He shook himself. 'I'd rather not.'

'The shadow of a shadow.'

'Yes.'

We heard the sound of Benedicte's car pulling up and then the bang of the front door. Hugo turned to go back inside. I did not. I walked on, beyond the end of the garden and across the narrow path until I was standing on the riverbank. I could smell the water, and although there was only a half-moon, the surface of it shone faintly. I felt calm now, calm and relieved. Hugo seemed to have come through his own ordeal unscathed. He did not want to dwell on it and I couldn't blame him. I think I knew that whatever had happened to me was of a different order and with a quite different origin. I also knew that if ever it happened to me again, my brother would not want to help me. Nothing had been said and in all other respects I knew I would always be able to rely on him, as I hoped he would upon me. But in this, I was alone.

Or perhaps not alone.

I heard the water lap the side of the bank softly. I felt no fear of it. Why should I?

I waited for some time there in the darkness. I heard their voices from the house. A door closed. A light went on upstairs.

I waited until I felt the night chill off the water and then I turned away with what I realised was a sort of sadness, a disappointment that the small hand had not crept into mine. I was coming to expect it.

I still had the sense then that the hand belonged to someone whose intentions were wholly benign and who was well disposed towards me, who was trusting.

I was to look back on that night with longing – longing for the sense of peace I knew then, even if I also felt an odd sudden loneliness; even if I had, God help me, for some strange reason actually hoped for the presence of the small hand holding mine.

Eight

The following night I had another vivid dream. I was standing as I had stood that evening beside the broken-down gate that led into the garden of the White House, only this time it was not evening but night, a cold, clear night with a sky sown with glittering stars. I was alone and I was waiting. I knew that I was waiting but for whom I waited the dream did not tell me. I felt excited, keyed up, as if some longed-for excitement was about to happen or I was to see something very beautiful, experience some great pleasure.

After a time, I knew that someone was coming towards me from the depths of the garden beyond the gate, though I neither heard nor saw anything. But there was a small light bobbing in the darkness among the trees and bushes some way ahead and I knew that it was getting nearer. Perhaps someone was carrying a lantern.

I waited. In a moment, whoever it was would appear or call out to me. I was eager to see them. They were bringing me something – not an object but some news or information. They were going to tell me something and when they had told me, everything would fall into place. I would know a great secret.

The light disappeared now and then, as the undergrowth obscured it, but then I saw it again a little nearer to me. I moved a step or two forward, my hand on the broken gate. I can feel it now, the cool roughened wood under my palm. I can see the lamp growing a little brighter.

I felt a great wave of happiness and, at the same time, a desire to run towards the light, to push my way roughly through the branches that hung low over the path. I had to do so. I was needed. It was urgent that I should go into the garden, that I should meet the lantern-bearer, that I should not waste another moment, as I somehow felt that I had wasted so many – not moments, but months and years.

I pushed on the gate to try and free it from where it was embedded in the earth and grass, which had grown up in great coarse clumps around it.

I was not pushing hard enough. The gate did not budge. I put my shoulder to it. I had to open it and go into the garden, go quickly, because now the light was very near but going crazily from side to side, as if someone was swinging it hard.

I put my whole strength to the gate and pushed. It gave suddenly so that I was pitched forward and felt myself falling.

And as I fell, I woke.'

I thought a great deal about the dream in the course of the next couple of days and instead of fading from my mind the memory of it became stronger. Perhaps if I could find out more about the White House and its garden, and if I went there again, I would be able to loosen the strange hold it seemed to have on me.

I would pay a visit to the London Library, and if that yielded nothing the library of the RHS, and try to find anything that had been written about it. I had no interest in gardens but something had led me to the ruins of that one and something had happened to me during those few minutes I had spent there which was haunting me now.

Before I had a chance to get to any library, however, a phone call from Fergus McCreedy put the whole matter from my mind.

'I have news for you,' he said.

The monastery of Saint Mathieu des Etoiles clearly trusted Fergus. The Librarian had sent him a confidential list of the treasures they felt able to sell to raise the money they needed. They included, he said, two icons, the Islamic objects in which Helena was so interested, and three medieval manuscripts. And a Shakespeare First Folio. The Librarian had asked Fergus if he would act as go-between in the disposal of the items – they wanted someone who had an entrée to libraries, museums and collectors round the world, who could be trusted not to send out a press release, and above all a man they regarded as fair and honourable. Fergus was to visit the monastery later in the summer, to look at everything, but he had proposed that I be allowed to go there at once, specifically to look at the First Folio. He had told the Librarian about me. My credentials seemed to satisfy and Fergus suggested I make arrangements with the monastery to visit as soon as I could. If I agreed, he proposed to forward all the contact details.

'It is a silent order,' he said, 'but the Librarian and the Guest Master are allowed to talk in the course of their duties, and both speak English. I suggest you get on with it.'

I asked if that meant he thought they might change their minds.

'Not at all. It has been deliberated over for a long time. They are quite sure and the Head of the Order has approved it all. But you don't want anyone else to get wind of this and neither do I. In my experience things have a way of getting out, even from enclosed orders of silent monks.'

Nine

I started on my journey in a mood of cheerfulness and optimism. The shadows had blown away. The sun had come out. I needed a break, which was why I flew to Lyons and then hired a car, for I planned to take my time, meandering on country roads, staying for two or three nights in different small towns and villages, enjoying France. I knew parts of the country well but not the region in which the monastery of Saint Mathieu des Etoiles was situated, high up in the mountains of the Vercors. I was ready to explore, pleased to be going on what I thought of as a pleasant jaunt and with the prospect of discovering a rare and wonderful book to delight a client at the end of it.

I hardly recognise the person I was at the beginning of that journey. It is true I had had a strange encounter and been touched by some shadow, but I had pushed them to the back of my mind; they had not changed me as I was later to be changed. I was able to forget. Now, I cannot.

I see those few days in a sunlit France as being days of light before the darkness, days of tranquillity and calm before the gathering storm. Days of innocence, perhaps.

It was high summer and hot, but the air was clear and, as always in such weather, the countryside looked its best, welcoming and uplifting to the spirits. There were pastures and gentle hills, charming villages. One night I had a room above an old stable in which chickens scratched contentedly and swallows were nesting. In the morning, I woke to lie looking across a distant line of violet-coloured hills. I was heading towards them that day. They seemed like pictures in a child's book.

I ate modestly at breakfast and lunch, but always stopped in time to dine well, so that I slept seven or eight hours, deep draughts of dreamless sleep.

By the time I was on the road for the third morning, the weather had begun to change. The sun shone for the first half-hour or so, but as I climbed higher I drove into patches of thin, swirling mist. It was very humid and I could see dark and heavy clouds gathering around the mountains ahead. Earlier, I had driven through many a small and pleasant village and seen people about, in the streets, working in the fields, cycling, walking, but now I was leaving human habitations behind. Several times I passed small roadside shrines, commemorating the wartime dead of the Resistance, which had been so strong in these parts. Once, an old woman was putting fresh flowers into the metal vase clipped to one of them. I waved to her. She stared but did not respond.

The roads became steeper and the bends sharper. The clouds were darkening. I passed through several short tunnels cut from the rock. On either side of me, the cliffs began to tower up, granite grey with only the odd fern or tree root clinging to its foothold. The car stuttered once or twice and I needed all my concentration to steer round some of the bends that coiled like snakes, up and up.

But then I came out on to a narrow plateau. The sky was darkening but to my right a thin blade of sunlight shot for a second down through the valley below. Somewhere, it caught water and the water gleamed. But then great drops of rain began to fall and a zigzag of blue-white lightning ran down the side of the rock. I was unsure whether to wait or to press on, but the road was narrow and I could not safely pull in to the side. I had not seen another vehicle for several miles but if one came up behind me, especially in the darkness and now blinding rain of the storm, it would certainly crash into me. I drove on extremely slowly. The rain was slanting sideways so that my windscreen was strangely clear. More lightning and still more streaking down the sulphurous-looking sky and arcing onto the road. I could not tell whether what was roaring on the car roof was rain or thunder.

The road was still narrow but now, instead of climbing I began to descend, skirting the highest part of the mountain and heading towards several lower slopes, their sides thickly overgrown with pine trees.

The rain was at my back and seemed to be coming out of a whirlwind which drove the car forward.

I am a perfectly calm driver and I had driven in atrocious conditions before then, but now I was afraid. The narrowness of the road, the way the storm and the high rocks seemed to be pressing down upon me at once, together with the tremendous noise, combined to unnerve me almost completely. I was conscious that I was alone, perhaps for many miles, and that although I had a map I had been warned that the monastery was difficult to find. I thought I had perhaps another twenty miles to go before I turned off on the track that led to Saint Mathieu, but I might well miss it in such weather.

Two things happened then.

Once again, in the midst of that black, swirling storm, a blade of sunlight somehow pierced its way through the dense cloud. This time I almost mistook it for another flash of lightning as it slanted down the rock face to my left and across the road ahead, which had the astonishing effect of turning the teeming rain into a thousand fragments of rainbow colours. It lasted for only a second or two before the clouds overwhelmed it again, but it was during those seconds that I saw the child. I was driving slowly. The road was awash and I could not see far ahead. But the child was there. I had no doubt of that then. I have no doubt of it now.

One moment there was only rain, bouncing up off the road surface, pouring down the steep sides of the cliff beside the car. Then, in the sudden shaft of sunlight, there was the child. He seemed to run down a narrow track at the side of the road between some overhanging trees and dash across in front of me. I braked, swerved, shouted, all at the same moment. The car slid sideways and came to a halt at the roadside, nose towards the rocks. I leaped out, disregarding the rain and the storm still raging overhead. I did not see how I could have avoided hitting the child, it had been so near to me, though I had felt no impact. I had not seen him – I was sure that it was a boy – fall but surely he must have done so. Perhaps he was beneath the car, lying injured.

Such violent storms blow themselves out very quickly in the mountains and I could see the veils of rain sweeping away from the valley ahead and it grew lighter as the clouds lifted. The thunder cracked above me but the lightning was less vivid now.

One glance under the car told me that the body of the child was not lying in the road beneath it. There was no mark on the front.

I looked round. I saw the track between the pine trees down which he must have come running. So he had raced in front of the car, missing it by inches, and presumably down some path on the opposite side.

I crossed the road. The thunder grumbled away to my right. Steam began to rise from the surface of the road and wisps of cloud drifted across in front of me like ectoplasm.

'Where are you?' I shouted. 'Are you all right? Call to me.' I shouted again, this time in French.

I was standing on a patch of rough grass a few yards away from the car on the opposite side. Behind rose the jagged bare surface of rock.

I turned and looked down. I was standing on the edge of a precipice. Below me was a sheer drop to a gorge below. I glimpsed dark water and the cliffs on the far side before I stepped back in terror. As I stepped, I missed my footing and almost fell but managed to right myself and leap across the road towards the safety of the car. As I did so, I felt quite unmistakably the small hand in mine. But this time it was not nestling gently within my own, it held me in a vicious grip and as it held so I felt myself pulled towards the edge of the precipice. It is difficult to describe how determined and relentless the urging of the hand was, how powerful the force of something I could not see. The strength was that of a grown man although the hand was still that of a child and at the same time as I was pulled I felt myself in some strange way being urged, coaxed, guided to the edge. If I could not be taken by force, then it was as though I were to be seduced to the precipice and into the gorge below.

The storm had rolled away now and the air was thick with moisture which hung heavily about me so that I could hardly breathe. I could hear the sound of rushing water and the rumble of stones down the hillside not far away. The torrent must have dislodged something higher up. I was desperate to get back into the safety of the car but I could not shake off the hand. What had happened to the child I could not imagine, but I had seen no pathway and if he had leaped, then he must have fallen. But where had a child come from in this desolate and empty landscape and in the middle of such a storm, and how had he managed to avoid being hit by my car and disappear over the edge of a precipice?

I wrenched my hand as hard as I could out of the grip of the invisible one. I felt as if I were resisting a great magnetic force, but somehow I stumbled backwards across the road and then managed to free my hand and get into the car. I slammed the door behind me in panic and, as I slammed it, I heard a howl. It was a howl of pain and rage and anguish combined, and without question the howl of a furious child.

Ten

My map was inadequate and there were no signs. I was shaking as I drove and had to keep telling myself that whatever might have happened, I had not killed or injured any child nor allowed myself to be lured over the precipice to my death. The storm was over but the day did not recover its spirits. The sky remained leaden, the air vaporous. From time to time, the curtain of cloud came down, making visibility difficult. Twice I took a wrong turning and was forced to find a way of retracing my route. I saw no one except a solitary man leading a herd of goats across a remote field.

After an hour and a half, I rounded a sharp bend, drove through one of the many tunnels cut into the rock and then saw a turning to the left, beside another of the little shrines. I stopped and consulted my map. If this was not the way to the monastery, I would press on another six miles to the next village and find someone to ask.

The narrow lane ran between high banks and through gloomy pine trees whose slender trunks rose up ahead and on either side of my car, one after another after another. After being level for some way, it began to twist and climb, and then to descend before climbing again. Then, quite suddenly, I came out into a broad clearing. Ahead of me was a small wooden sign surmounted by a cross: MONASTERE DE SAINT MATHIEU DES ETOILES. VOITURES.

I switched off the engine and got out of the car. The smell of moist earth and pine needles was intense. Now and again a few raindrops rolled down the tree trunks and pattered onto the ground. Thunder grumbled but it was some distance away. Otherwise, everything was silent. And I was transported back on the instant to the evening I had stood outside the gate of the White House and its secret, overgrown garden. I had the same sense of strangeness and isolation from the rest of the world.

I was expected at the monastery. I had had email correspondence with the Librarian and been assured that a guest room would be made available for me at any time. They had very few visitors and those mainly monks from other houses. The Librarian, Dom Martin, had attached a helpful set of notes about the monastery and its way of life. I would be able to speak only to him and (although it was possible I would also be received by the Abbot), to the Guest Master, might attend the services in the chapel and would be given access to the library. But this was an enclosed and silent order and, though I was welcome, I would be kept within bounds.

'C'est probable,' the Librarian had written, 'que vous serez ici tout seul.'

Now I took my bag from the car and set off down the narrow path through the dense and silent pines. I was still suffering from the effects of what had happened, but I was glad to have arrived at a place of safety where there would be other human beings, albeit silent and for the most part unapproachable. A monastery was holy ground. Surely nothing bad could happen to me here.

The track wound on for perhaps half a mile and for most of the way it was monotonous, rows of pines giving way to yet more. At first it was level, then I began to climb, and then to climb quite steeply. The only sound was the soft crunch of my own footsteps on the pine-needle floor. There were no birds, though in the distance I could hear falling water, as if a stream were tumbling down over rocks. The air was humid but as I climbed higher it cleared and even felt chill, which was a welcome relief. I imagined this place in deep winter, when the snow would make the track impassable and muffle what few sounds there were.

I stopped a couple of times to catch my breath. I walk about London and other cities a great deal, but that is easy walking and does not prepare one for such a steep climb. I wiped my face on my jacket sleeve and carried on.

And then, quite suddenly, I was out from between the trees and looking down the slope of a stony outcrop on to the monastery of Saint Mathieu des Etoiles.

The roofs were of dark grey shingle and the whole formed an enclosed rectangle with two single buildings on the short sides, one of which had a high bell tower. The long sides were each divided into two dozen identical units. There was a second, smaller rectangle of buildings to the north. The whole was set on the level and surrounded by several small fenced pastures, but beyond these the ground was sheer, climbing to several high peaks. The slopes were pine-forested. The sun came out for a moment, bathing the whole in a pleasant and tranquil light. The sky was blue above the peaks, though there were also skeins of cloud weaving between them.

I heard the tinkle of a cowbell, of the sort that rings gently all summer through the Swiss Alps. A bee droned on a ragged purple plant at my feet. The rest was the most deep and intense silence.

I stood, getting my breath and bearings, the canvas bag slung across my shoulders, and for the first time that day I felt a slight lifting of the fear that had oppressed me. And I also recalled that somewhere in that compact group of ancient buildings below were the most extraordinary treasures, books, icons, pictures – who knew what else?

I shifted the bag on to my left shoulder and began to make my way carefully down the steep and rocky path towards the monastery.

I do not know what I expected. The place was silent save for a single bell tolling as I approached the gate. It stopped and all I could hear were those faint natural sounds, the rain dripping off roofs and trees, the stream. But when the door in the great wooden gate was opened to me and I gave my name, I was greeted by a smiling, burly monk in a black hooded habit and a large cotton apron. He greeted me in English.

'You are welcome, Monsieur Snow. I am Frère Jean-Marc, the Guest Master. Please …' – and he took my bag from me, lifting it as if it contained air and feathers.

He asked me where I had left my car and nodded approval as he led me across an inner courtyard towards a three-storey building.

Every sound had its own resonance in such a silent atmosphere. Our footsteps, separate and in rhythm, the monk's slight cough, another bell.

'You have come a long way to visit us.'

'Yes. I also came through a terrible storm just now.'

'Ah, mais oui, the rain, the rain. But our storms go as quickly as they come. It's the mountains.'

'The road is treacherous. I'm not used to such bends.'

He laughed. 'Well, you are here. You are welcome.'

We had climbed three flights of stone stairs and walked along a short corridor to the door which he now opened, standing aside to let me pass.

'Welcome,' he said again.

I felt real warmth in his greeting. Hospitality to strangers was an important part of the monastic rule, for all that these monks did not receive many.

I walked into the small, square room. The window opposite looked directly on to the pine-covered slopes and the jagged mountain peak. The sun was out, slanting towards us and lighting the deep, dark green of the

trees, catching the whitewashed stone walls of the surrounding monastery buildings.

'Ah,' the Guest Master said, beaming, 'beautiful. But you should see it
in the snow. That is a sight.'

'I imagine you have few guests in winter.'

'None, Monsieur. For some months we are impassable. Now, here …
your bed. Table. Your chair. On here you see a letter from the Abbot to
you, a letter also from Dom Martin, the Librarian. This list is our timetable. Here is a small map. But I will fetch you at the times you will meet.
You are welcome to walk outside anywhere save the private cloister. You
are welcome, most welcome, to attend any service in the chapel and I will
take you in half an hour, to show you where this is, where you may sit, the
dining room. But for now I will bring you refreshment in this room, so
that you may get used to the place. You will meet the brothers also about
the monastery, the brothers at work. Of course, please greet them. They
are glad to welcome a guest. Now, I will leave you to become at home, and
I will return with some food and drink.'

The room was peaceful. The sun moved round to shine on the white
wall and the white cover of the iron-framed single bed. The window was
open slightly. I could hear the distant sound of the cowbells.

For a moment, I thought that I would weep.

Instead, the walls seemed to shimmer and fold in upon themselves like
a pack of cards and I fainted at Frère Jean-Marc's feet.

Eleven

I woke to find myself lying on the bed with the kindly and concerned face of the Guest Master looking down on me. There was another monk on my left side, holding my wrist to take the pulse, an older man with wrinkled, parchment-like skin and soft blue eyes.

'Now, Monsieur Snow, lie still, relax, You gave us a great shock. This is Dom Benoît, our Infirmarian. Il est médecin. His English is a little less than mine.'

I struggled to sit up but the old man restrained me gently. 'Un moment,' he said. 'You do not race away …'

I lay back. Through the window I could see the mountain peak and a translucent blue sky. I felt strangely calm and at peace.

In the end, Dom Benoît seemed to decide that I was none the worse for my fainting attack and allowed me to sit up. There was a tray of food on the table by the window, with a carafe of water, and I went to it after both men had left, feeling suddenly hungry. The Guest Master had said that I should rest for the afternoon, sleep if possible, and that he would come back later to check up on me and, if the Infirmarian agreed, take me to my appointment with the Librarian.

I ate a bowl of thick vegetable soup that tasted strongly of celery, some creamy Brie-like cheese and fresh bread, a small salad and a bowl of cherries and grapes. The water must have come from a spring in the mountains – it had the unmistakable coolness and fresh taste that only such water has.

I felt perfectly well now, but slightly light-headed. I supposed that I had fainted in the aftermath of the morning's awful drive, though I do not remember ever passing out in my life before. I noticed that there was a faint redness on my upper arm where Dom Benoît had probably taken my blood pressure. I was being looked after with care.

As I ate I looked at the letters that had been left for me. The first, from the Librarian, suggested a meeting that evening, when he would be glad to show me both the First Folio and any other books I might like to see. I would also be welcome to visit the book bindery. The letter from the Abbot was brief, formal and courteous, simply bidding me welcome and hoping that he would be able to see me at some point during my stay.

The timetable, which had been typed out to give me an idea of how the monastic day and night were organised, was a formidable one. There was a daily mass, all the usual offices, the angelus and much time for private prayer and meditation. The monks ate together only once a day, in the evening, otherwise meals were taken in the solitude of their cells, or at their work.

There was a map of both the inside and the outside of the monastery, with a dotted red line, or cross, indicating areas to which I did not have access. But I was free to walk almost anywhere outside. I could go into the chapel, the refectory, the library and the communal areas of the cloisters. It seemed that I was also free to visit the kitchens and the carpentry shops and the cellars, the dairy and the cowsheds if I wished.

When I began to eat I had thought I would take a walk in the grounds near to the buildings as soon as I had finished the last mouthful. But I had barely begun to eat the fruit when a tiredness came over me that made my head swim and my limbs feel as heavy as if they had been filled with sawdust.

I opened the window more, so that the sweet air blew in from the mountain, with a breath of pine. Then I lay down and, to the gentle sound of the cowbells, I fell into the deepest sleep I have ever known.

I woke into a soft mauve twilight. The stars had come out behind the mountain and there was a full moon. I lay still, enjoying the extraordinary silence. The morning's drive through the storm and the horror of almost running over the child seemed to belong to another time. I felt as if I had been in this small, whitewashed, peaceful room for weeks. After a few moments, I heard the bell sound somewhere in the monastery, calling the monks to more prayer, more solemn chant.

I got up cautiously but I was no longer in the least dizzy, though my limbs still felt heavy. I went to the window to breathe in the evening air. A fresh jug of water had been placed on the table and I drank a glass of it with as much relish as I had ever drunk a glass of fine wine.

I watched the sky darken and the stars grow brighter. I wondered if I could find my way outside. I felt like walking at least a little way, but as

I was thinking of it I heard quick footsteps and the Guest Master tapped and came in, smiling. He was a man whose face seemed to be set in a permanent beam of welcome and good spirits.

'Ah, Monsieur Snow, bonsoir, bonsoir. It is good. I came in and each time ...' He made a gesture of sleep, closing his eyes, with his hands to the side of his head.

'Thank you, yes. I slept like a newborn.'

'And so, you seem well again, but the Infirmarian will come again once more to be sure.'

'No, I'm fine. Please don't trouble the father again. Is it too late for my meeting with the Librarian?'

'Ah, I fear yes. But he will be pleased to meet with you tomorrow morning. I did not wake you. It was better.'

'I was wondering if I could take a short walk outside? I feel I need some fresh air.'

'Ah. Now, let me see. I have the office soon, but yes, come with me, come with me, take a little air – it is very mild. I will come to fetch you inside after the office and then it will be bringing your supper. We retire to bed early you see, and then tomorrow you will eat in the refectory with us, our guest. Please.' He held open the door for me and we went out of the room and down the corridor.

The stone staircase led into a long, cool cloister and as we walked down it I heard the sound of footsteps coming from all sides, soft, quick, pattering on the stone, and then the monks appeared, hoods up, heads bowed, arms folded within the wide sleeves of their habits.

But the Guest Master led me out of a door at the far end of the cloister and into a wide courtyard under the stars. He pointed to a door in the wall.

'There, please, walk out of there and into the cloister garden. You will find it so still and pleasant. I will return for you in twenty minutes. Tomorrow, you see, you will find it easy to make your own way about.'

He beamed and turned back, going quickly after the other monks towards the chapel, from where the bell continued to toll.

Twelve

I walked between the monastery buildings towards the cloister at the far end. No one was here save a scraggy little black and white cat which streaked away into the shadows on my approach. I looked with pleasure at the beauty of the pattern made by the line of arches and at the stones of the floor. There was no sound. The singing of the monks at their office was contained somewhere deep within the walls. At the end of the cloister, I stepped off the path and onto closely cut grass. I had found myself in the garden, though one without any flowerbeds or trees. I stopped. I was surrounded by cloisters on three sides, on the fourth by another building. There was moonlight enough to see by.

I wondered what kind of men came here to stay not for a few days' retreat or refreshment, but for life. Unusual men, it might seem. Yet the Guest Master was robust and energetic, a man you might meet anywhere.

I wondered how I would find the Librarian and the Abbot. And as I did so, I began to cross the grass. It was as I reached the centre of the large rectangular garden that I noticed the pool. It too was rectangular, with wide stone surrounds and set level with the ground. I wondered if there were fish living a cool mysterious life in its depths.

It was as I drew close to it and looked down that I felt the small hand holding mine. I thought my heart would stop. But this time the hand did not clutch mine and there was no sense that I was being pulled forward. It was, as on that first evening, merely a child's hand in mine.

I looked down into the still, dark water on which the moonlight rested and as I looked I saw. What I saw was so clear and so strange and so real that I could not doubt it then, as I have never doubted it since.

I saw the face of a child in the water. It was upturned to look directly at me. There was no distortion from the water, it was not the moonlight playing tricks with the shadows. Everything was so still that there was not the slightest ripple to disturb the surface. It was not easy to guess at his age but he was perhaps three or four. He had a solemn and very beautiful face and the curls of his hair framed it. His eyes were wide open. It was not a dead face, this was a living, breathing child, though I saw no limbs or body, only the face. I looked into his eyes and he looked back into mine, and as we looked the grip of the small hand tightened. I could hardly breathe. The child's eyes had a particular expression. They were beseeching me, urging me. I closed my eyes. When I opened them, he was still there.

Now the small hand was tightening in mine and I felt the dreadful pull I had experienced before to throw myself forward into the water. I could not look at the child's face, because I knew that I would be unable to refuse what he wanted. His expression was one of such longing and need that I could never hold out against him. I closed my eyes, but then the pull of the hand became so strong that I was terrified of losing my balance. I felt both afraid and unwell, my heart pounding and my limbs weak so that, as I turned away from the pool, using every last ounce of determination, I stumbled and fell forward. As I did so, I reached my left hand across and tried to prise the grasp of the small fingers away, but there was nothing to take hold of, though the sensation of being held by them did not lessen.

'Leave me alone,' I said. 'Please go. Please go.' I heard myself speak but my voice sounded odd, a harsh whispered cry as I struggled to control my breathing.

The hand still tugged mine, urging me to stand up, urging me to do what it wanted me to do, go where it wanted me to go.

'Let me go!' I shouted, and my shout echoed out into the silent cloisters.

I heard an exclamation and a hurried movement towards me across the grass and Frère Jean-Marc was kneeling beside me, taking me by the shoulders and lifting me easily into a sitting position, tutting in a gentle voice and telling me to be calm.

After a moment, my breathing slowed and I stopped shaking. A slight breeze came from the mountain, cool on my face, smelling of the pine trees.

'Tell me,' the monk said, his face full of concern, 'tell me what is troubling to you. Tell me – what is it that is making you afraid?'

Thirteen

There could have been no place more calming to the senses or enriching to the spirit than the great library at the monastery of Saint Mathieu.

Sitting there the next day in that quiet and beautiful space, I counted myself one of the most fortunate men on earth, and nothing that had happened to me seemed to be more than the brush of a gnat against my skin.

The library was housed in a three-storey building separate from the rest, with a spiral stone staircase leading from the cloisters firstly into a simple reading room set with pale wooden desks, then up to the one holding, so the Librarian told me, all the sacred books and manuscripts, many of them in multiple copies. But it was the topmost room, with its tall, narrow windows letting in lances of clear light and with a gallery all the way round, which took my breath away. If I could compare it to any other library I knew, it would be to the Bodleian's Duke Humfrey, that awe-inspiring space, but the monastery library was more spacious and without any claustrophobic feel.

At first, I had simply stood and gazed round me at the magnificence of the shelving, the solemnity of the huge collection, the order and symmetry of the great room. If the books had all been empty boxes it would still have been mightily impressive. There were slender stone pillars and recessed reading desks in the arched spaces between them.

The floor was of polished honey-coloured wood and there was a central row of tables. At the far end, behind a carved wooden screen, was the office of the Librarian. Along the opposite end were tall cupboards which contained, I was told, the most precious manuscripts in the collection.

The cupboards were not locked. When I noted this, the Librarian simply smiled. 'Mais pourquoi?'

Indeed. Where else in the world would so many rare and precious items be entirely safe from theft? The only reason they were kept out of sight was to protect them from damage.

The Librarian had brought me book after wonderful book, simply for my delight – illuminated manuscripts, rare psalters, Bibles with magnificent bindings. He was an old man, rather bent, and he moved, as I had noticed all the monks moved, at a slow and measured pace, as if rush and hurry were not only wasteful of energy but unspiritual. Everything was accomplished but no one hurried. His English was almost flawless – he told me that he had spent five years studying at St John's College, Cambridge – and his interest and learning were wide, his pleasure in the library clear to see. He had a special dispensation to speak to me, but he did not waste a word any more than he wasted a movement.

I had slept well and dreamlessly after a late visit from the Infirmarian, who had given me what he described as 'un peu de somnifère gentil' – a dark green liquid in a medicine glass. He had checked me over and seemed satisfied that I was not physically ill. Frère Jean-Marc had brought my breakfast and explained that the Abbot had been spoken to and would like to see me at two o'clock but that he felt a visit to the library would be the best medicine. He was right.

'And now,' the Librarian, Dom Martin, had said, coming towards the reading desk at which I was sitting in one of the alcoves.

From there, I could look into the body of the library, and the sunshine making a few lozenges of brightness on the wooden floor. The place smelled as all such places do, of paper and leather, polish and age and wisdom – a powerful intoxicant to anyone whose life is bound up, as mine had long been, with books.

'Here it is. Perhaps you have seen one of these before – there are over two hundred in the world, after all – but you will not have seen this particular one. I think you are about to have a wonderful surprise.' He smiled, his old face full of a sort of teasing delight as he held the book in his hands.

I had indeed seen a Shakespeare First Folio before. As he said, it is not particularly rare and I had looked closely at several both in England and abroad. I had also spent some time before coming to Saint Mathieu checking two existing Folios, so that I would be able to judge whether what I was to be shown was genuine. It was not impossible. The whereabouts of only a couple of hundred copies are known now, but the book would have had a printing of perhaps 750. Even if most of those did not survive, there was nothing to say several might not still remain, buried in some library – possibly, a library such as this one.

The book Dom Martin held in his outstretched hands was large. He laid it down with care on the desk before me but he did not wait for me to examine it. One of the innumerable bells was ringing, summoning him away to prayer. He walked out of the great room and I heard his footsteps going away down the stone staircase as the bell continued to toll. Two other monks, who had been at some quiet work, followed him and I was left alone to examine what I knew within a few moments to be, with precious little doubt, a very fine copy of the First Folio. That in itself was exciting enough, but in addition, on the title page, the book bore the signature of Ben Jonson. Of course I would need to check, but from memory I was sure the signature was right. So this, then, was his copy of Shakespeare that I held in my hands. It was a remarkable moment.

I spent some time turning the pages carefully, revelling in the book and hoping that I might manage to procure it for Sir Edgar Merriman. After a moment, I looked up and around that handsome room. I felt well. I felt quite calm. I also felt safe, as I no longer felt truly safe anywhere outside, for fear of what might happen and of feeling the small hand creeping into mine. I steered my attention quickly back to the book before me.

I spent the rest of the morning comfortably in the library before returning to my room at one o'clock, when the Guest Master brought my simple food. At two he returned to escort me to the Abbot. I had not left the building since the previous night, though I could see that it was a beautiful day and the bright sky and clear air ought to tempt me out. But whenever I so much as thought about venturing beyond the safety of the monastery walls, I felt a lurch of fear again.

The Abbot was unlike the figure I had imagined. I had expected a tall, imposing, solemn, older man. He was small, with a neat-featured face, deep-set eyes. He spoke good English, he listened carefully, he was rather expressionless but then his face would break into a warm, engaging smile. I warmed to him. I felt reassured by him and after ten minutes or so in his presence, I realised that he was a man with an unprepossessing exterior that concealed considerable human understanding and wisdom.

We talked business for a few moments in his tidy office, about the sale of the monastery's treasures and the Folio in particular, and I knew that things would probably be arranged smoothly. The deliberation about whether to sell anything at all had been long, careful and probably painful, but once the decision had been made, they would be quite pragmatic and arrange things efficiently. They had to ensure the upkeep and survival of the monastery for the future.

'Monsieur Snow, I would like you to feel you may stay with us here until you feel quite well again. We will look after you, of course. This is a very healing place.'

'I know. I feel that very much. And I am very grateful to you.'

He waited quietly, patiently, and as he waited I felt an urge to tell him, tell him everything that had happened, recount the strange events and my own terrors, ask him – for what? To believe me? To explain?

There was no sound in the room. I wondered what the monks were doing now and presumed they were in their own cells, praying, reading holy books, meditating. From far on the mountainside came the tinkle of the cowbells. I looked at the Abbot.

'I wonder,' I said, 'if I am going mad or being persecuted in some way. I only know that things keep happening to me which I do not understand. I have always been a healthy man and quite serene. Until – this began.'

His eyes were steady on my face, his hands still, resting on either side of his chair. His habit, with the hood back, lay in perfect folds, as if they had been painted by an old master. He did not urge me. I felt that he would accept whatever I chose to do – leave the room now, without saying more, or confide in him and ask for his counsel.

I began to talk. Perhaps I had not intended to tell him everything, even the details of my brother's own breakdown, but I found myself doing so. Once, he got up and poured me a glass of water from a carafe on the stone ledge. I drank it eagerly before continuing. The sunlight, which had been slanting across his desk, moved round and away. Twice the bell rang, but the Abbot took no notice of it, merely sat in his chair, his eyes on me, his expression full of concern, listening, listening.

I finished speaking and fell silent, suddenly drained of every gram of energy. I knew that when I returned to the guest room I would sleep another of the deep, exhausted sleeps I had grown used to having in this place.

The Abbot sat thoughtfully for some moments as I leaned back, slightly dizzy but in some way washed clean and clear, as if I had confessed a catalogue of terrible sins to the priest.

At last I said, 'You think I am mad.'

He waved his hand dismissively. 'Mais non. I think terrible things have happened to you and you are profoundly affected by them. But what things and why? Can you tell me – nothing like this has ever happened in your life until the first visit to this house entirely by chance?'

'Absolutely nothing. Of that I'm quite certain.'

'And this hand? This hand of the child at first did not seem in any way upsetting?'

'No. It seemed very strange.'

'Bien sûr.'

'But it was not until later that I felt any hostility, any desire to do me harm. Real harm. To lead me into harm.'

'Into these pools. Into the water. Over the precipice into the lake of the gorge.'

'But why?' I cried out loudly. 'Why does this thing want to do me harm?'

'I think that either you can choose never to know that and simply pray that in time it will be tired of failure and abandon this quest. Or you can choose to find out, if that shall be possible, and so ...'

'To lay the ghost.'

'Oui.'

'Do you believe this thing – child – whatever it is – do you believe it truly exists?'

'Spirits exist, bien sûr. Good exists. Evil exists. Perhaps the spirit of a child is disturbed and unhappy. Perhaps it has a need.' He shrugged. 'I do think you have suffered. I think you will do well to remain here and let us help you, refresh you.'

'But here of all places, surely, this should not have happened again? If I am not safe here ...'

'You are entirely safe here. Do not doubt it. You will be given all the strength, all the protection of our Blessed Lord and his saints, and of our prayers for you. You are surrounded by strong walls of prayer, Monsieur Snow. Do not forget.'

'Thank you. I will try.'

'This evening, if you feel well and able, join us in the chapel for our night prayers. These give great peace, great power to combat the perils of the darkness. And if you decide to confront le fantôme, and your terrors, then you will also be under protection, under the shield of our prayers.'

'What do you honestly think I should do, Father?'

'Ah. For me, everything is the better when faced. You draw the sting. But you only can make this choice.'

He stood in one graceful, flowing movement of body and robes together and held up his right hand to make the sign of the cross over me, then led me towards the door. As I left, he stood watching me walk down the cloister and I glanced back, to see that his expression was grave. He had believed me. He had listened attentively and dismissed nothing, nor tried to explain any of it away. For that I was deeply grateful.

I returned to my room and slept, but when I woke I longed for outside air and found my way, with only a couple of wrong turnings down stone corridors, to the courtyard. This time, I walked in the opposite direction from the one I had taken the previous night and went instead through the gate in the wall to the main entrance and, from there, headed towards the pine-covered slopes and a narrow path that climbed steeply and would, I was sure, eventually lead to the top of one of the peaks. I am no mountaineer. I walked for perhaps twenty minutes along the narrow path that wound between the great, dark trees. The ground was soft with a carpet of pine needles, my feet made no sound and when I looked up I could see violet-blue patches of sky far above the treetops. I came to a clearing where two or three trees had been felled and were lying on the ground. I sat down. There was no birdsong, no animal movement, but tiny spiders and other insects scurried about on the logs and at my feet. I realised that I was waiting. I even held out my hand.

One of the small spiders ran across it. Nothing more.

I made my way carefully back down the path. But when I went through the gate I heard voices coming not from inside the monastery but from somewhere beyond the outer courtyard. I found my way through the cloisters until I approached the inner garden. A group of about a dozen of the monks were standing around the pool. One held a thurible which he was swinging gently, sending soft clouds of incense drifting across the surface of the water. Another carried a cross. The rest were singing a plainchant, holding their books in front of them, heads slightly bowed. I stood still until the singing died away and then saw the Abbot lift his hand and give a final blessing while making the sign of the cross. I realised that the pool in which I had seen the upturned face of the child and towards which I had been so urgently drawn was being blessed, made holy. Made safe.

I was glad of it. But as I slipped back through the cloisters, I knew that the Abbot's precaution had not been necessary, for it was not the monks who were in danger, or indeed any other person who might visit this quiet and holy place. Whatever it was that had come here had come because of me. When I left, it would leave too. Leave with me.

Fourteen

Four Ragged Staff Lane
Oxford OX2 1ZZ

Adam,
Terrific news. Well done! I was sure you and the monks would see eye
to eye and am delighted you confirmed that it was indeed a First Folio
and managed to secure it. Lucky client.

Come to Oxford again soon.

Best,
Fergus

Ravenhead
Ditchforth
West Sussex

Dear Mr Snow

We are greatly looking forward to seeing you here on Wednesday next,
to dine and sleep and tell us about your visit to France. My husband is
on tenterhooks.

Meanwhile, having more time on my hands as I grow old than
perhaps I should, I have been delving a little into the story of the White
House and have turned up one or two snippets of information which
can perhaps be pieced together. But it may no longer be of the slightest
interest to you and of course you must tell me if that is the case.

We will expect you somewhere between five and six o'clock.

With every good wish
Alice Merriman

Hello. This is Adam Snow. I am sorry I am not available. Please leave me a message and I will return your call.

It's Hugo. Not sure if you're back. I've been thinking about what you told me when you came up here last time. I just wanted to say I'm sure it's nothing. Maybe you had a virus. You know, people get depression after flu, that sort of stuff. So, if you're worried about it, well, don't be. I'm sure it was nothing. OK, that's it. Give us a call some time.

Fifteen

Of course I had to return. As soon as I had arranged to go down and see Sir Edgar Merriman about the Folio, I became aware of the sensation. It was like a magnetic pull upon my whole being. It was there when I slept and when I woke, it was there at the back of my mind all day and it was there even within my dreams. I could not have resisted whatever force it was and I did not try. I was afraid of it and I think I knew now that the best, the only thing to do if I was to retain my sanity was to obey. I hoped that the monks were continuing to pray for my protection.

This time I did not get lost. This time I did not come upon it by chance. This time I had marked my journey out on a map a couple of days before and gone carefully over the last few miles, so that I knew exactly where I was going and how long it would take me from when I left the A road. This time I drove slowly down the lane, between the high banks, the elephantine tree trunks pressing in on me in the gloom, and I was aware of everything as if I had taken some mind-expanding drug, so clearly did I see it all, so vivid the detail of every last tree root and clump of earth and overhanging branch seem.

It was a tranquil day but with a cloudy sky. Earlier there had been a couple of showers and by the time I got out of the car in the clearing the air was humid and still.

I had come prepared. I had bought a pair of wire cutters and some secateurs. I was not going to let undergrowth or fences keep me out.

What would I find? I did not know and I tried not to give my imagination any rein. I would obey the insistent, silent voice that told me I must go back and once there I would see. I would see.

Everything seemed as before. I stood for a moment beside the car and then went to the gate and pushed it open, feeling it scrape along the ground just as on my previous visit, and walked towards the old ticket booth. The notice still hung there, the grille was still down. I stood and waited for a moment. In my left hand I carried the cutters, my right held nothing. But after several minutes nothing had happened. My hand remained empty. In a gesture that was half deliberate, half a reflex, I curled my fingers. There was no response.

The air was heavy, the bushes on either side lush, the leaves of some ancient laurel glistening with moisture from the earlier rain. I had put on wellington boots, so that I could push my way through the long grass without inconvenience.

I came out into the clearing. There was the house. The White House. Empty. Half derelict, the glass broken in one or two of the windows. The stones of the courtyard in front of it were thick with pads of velvety moss.

I turned away. To the side was another low wooden gate. It had an old padlock and rusty chain across it and both gleamed with moisture. But the padlock hung open and the gate was so rotten it gave at once to my hand and I went through. Ahead of me was a path leading between some ancient high yew hedges. I followed it. I could see quite well because although the sky was overcast it was barely half past five and there was plenty of light left. The path led straight. At the end, an archway was cut into the hedge and although ivy trailed down over it, the way was clear and I had no need of the cutters I had brought. I went through and down four steps made of brick and set in a semicircle, then found that I had come out into what had clearly once been a huge lawn with a high wall at the far end and the thickly overgrown remains of wide flower borders. There were fruit trees, gnarled and pitted old apples and pears, forming a sort of avenue – I know there are proper gardening terms for these things. On the far side of the lawn, whose grass was so high that it came over the tops of my boots and was mixed with nettles and huge vicious thistles, there ran yet another tall yew hedge in which was another arch. I turned round. To one side a path led diagonally towards woodland. I went in the opposite direction, to an open gate in a high wall. On the other side of it I found what seemed to have been an area of patterned beds set formally between old gravel paths. I remembered pictures of Elizabethan knot gardens. There were small trees planted in the centre of each bed, though most of them looked dead. I leaned over and picked a wiry stem from a bush beside me, breaking it between my fingers. It was lavender.

Every so often, I paused and waited. But there was nothing. Nothing stirred and no birds sang.

It was a sad place, but I did not feel uneasy or afraid in any way, there seemed to be nothing odd about this abandoned garden. I felt melancholy. It had once been a place of colour and beauty, full of growth and variety – full of people. I looked around me, trying to imagine them strolling about, bending over to look more closely at a flower, admiring, enjoying, in pairs or small groups.

Now there was no one and nature was taking everything back to itself. In a few more years would there be anything left to say there had been a garden here at all?

The silence was extraordinary, the same sort of silence I had experienced in the grounds of the monastery. But here there were no gentle cowbells reassuring me from the near distance. I wondered which way to go. I had come because I had had no choice. But what next?

As if in reply, the small hand crept into mine and held it fast and I felt myself pulled forward through the long grass towards the far hedge.

The soft swishing sound my boots made as I walked broke the oppressive stillness. Once I thought I heard something else, just behind me, and swung round. There was nothing. Perhaps a rabbit or a stray cat was following – I was going to say 'us', for that was unmistakably how I felt now. There were two of us.

I reached the far side and the arch in the high dark yew and stopped just inside it. Looking ahead, I could see that I was about to enter another garden, a sunken garden that was approached down the flight of a dozen steps at my feet, semicircular again and broken here and there, with weeds growing between the cracks. On the far side stood a vast cedar tree. A very overgrown gravel path ran all the way round. It was not a large enclosure and the surrounding yew hedge closed in like high, dark walls. Because of these and the trees on the other side, less light came in here than into the wide open space I had just left, and so the grass in the centre had not grown wild but was still short, something like a lawn, though spoiled by yellowish weed and with bald patches here and there, where the earth or stones showed through, like the skull through an old person's thinning hair.

I did not want to step down into it. I felt that if I did I would be suffocated between these dark hedges. But the small hand was holding mine tightly and trying with everything in its power to get me to move.

And then, as I looked down, I noticed something else. In the centre was a strange circle, like a fairy ring. I could only just make it out, for it seemed to be marked from nothing in particular – a darker line of grass perhaps, or small stones concealed below the surface. I stared at it and it seemed not to be there.

The grey clouds above me parted for a moment and a dilute and watery sun struggled through for a moment and in that moment the circle appeared quite clearly against a fleeting brightness.

The small hand was grasping mine in desperation now. It was as if someone was in danger of falling over the edge of a cliff and clutching at me for dear life, but at the same time it was trying to pull me over with it. If it fell it would make sure that I would fall too. It was exactly the same as it had been on the edge of the precipice in the Vercors, except that that had been real. Here there was no cliff, merely a few steps. I still did not want to go down, but I could no longer resist the strength of the hand.

'All right,' I said aloud, my voice sounding strange in that desolate place. 'All right. I'll do what you want.'

I went, being careful with my footing on the loose and cracked stones, until I was standing in the sunken garden, on the same level as the half-visible circle. But at that moment the sun went in and a sudden rush of wind blew, shifting the heavy branches of the great tree on the far side before it died away at once, leaving an eerie and total stillness.

'What are you doing here?'

The sound of the voice was like a shot in the back. I have never felt such a split second of absolute shock and terror.

'The garden is no longer open to the public.'

I turned.

She was standing at the top of the steps inside the archway, looking down, staring at me out of a face devoid of expression, and yet she gave off an air of hostility to me, of threat. She was old, though I could not guess, as one often can, exactly how old, but her face was a mesh of fine wrinkles and those do not come at sixty. Her hair was very thin and scraped back into some sort of comb and she seemed to be bundled into layers of old clothes, random skirts and cardigans and an ancient bone-coloured mackintosh, like a bag lady who preyed upon the rubbish sacks at the kerbside.

I stammered an apology, said I had not realised anyone would be there, thought the place was derelict ... I stumbled over my words because she had startled me and I felt somehow disorientated, which was perhaps because I was standing on a lower level, almost as if I were at her feet.

'Won't you come to the house?'

I stared at her.

'There is nothing here now. The garden has gone. But if you would like to see it as it was I would be glad to show you the pictures.'

'As it was?'

But she was turning away, a small, wild figure in her bundled clothing, the wisps of ancient grey hair escaping at the back of her neck like skeins of cloud.

'Come to the house …' Her voice faded away as she disappeared back into the tangled grass and clumps of weed that was the garden on the other side.

For a moment I did not move. I could not move. I looked down at my feet, to where I had seen the strange circle in the ground, but it was not there now. It had been some optical illusion, then, a trick of the light. In any case, I had no idea what I had thought it represented – perhaps the foundations of an old building, a summer house, a gazebo? I stepped forward and scraped about with my foot. There was nothing. I tried to remember the stories we had learned as children about fairy rings. Then I turned away. Somewhere beyond the arch, she would be waiting for me. 'Come to the house.'

Half of me was curious, wanting to know who she was and what I would find in a house I had thought was abandoned and semi-derelict. But I was afraid too. I thought I might dive back through the undergrowth until I reached the gate and the drive, the safety of my car, ignore the old woman. Run away.

It was my choice.

I waded my way through the undergrowth beneath the gathering sky. It was airless and very still. The silence seemed palpable, like the silence that draws in around one before a storm.

It was only as I reached the path that led out of the gardens between overgrown shrubs and trees towards the gate that I realised I was alone. The old woman had vanished and the small hand was no longer grasping mine.

Sixteen

The key was in my trouser pocket. I had only to open the car doors, throw in the tools and get away from that place, but as I went I glanced quickly back over my shoulder at the house. The door was standing wide open where I was certain that it had previously been shut fast. I hesitated. I wanted to turn and head for the car but I was transfixed by sight of the door, sure that the old woman must have opened it because she was expecting me to enter, was waiting for me now somewhere inside.

'Are you there?' she called.

So I had no choice after all. I dropped the secateurs and cutters on the ground and went slowly towards the house, looking up as I did so at the windows whose frames were rotten, at the paint that was faded and peeled almost away, at the windowpanes which were filthy and broken here and there, and in a couple of the rooms actually boarded over. Surely no one could possibly live here. Surely this place was, as I had seen it at first, ruined and deserted.

I walked up the steps and hesitated at the open door. I could see nothing inside the house, no light, no movement.

'Hello?' My voice echoed down the dark corridor ahead.

There was no reply. No one was here. The wind had blown the door open. Yet the old woman had been in the garden. I had seen her and she had spoken to me. Then I heard a sound, perhaps that of a voice. I took a step inside.

It was several moments before my eyes grew used to the darkness, but then I saw that I was standing in a hall and that a passageway led off to my right. I saw a glimmer of light at the far end. Then the voice again.

The house smelled of rot and mould and must. This could not possibly still be a home. It must not have been inhabited for decades. I put out my hand to touch the wall and then guide myself along the passage, though I was sure that I was being foolish and told myself to go back. I had only just regained my senses and a measure of calm since the awful things that had happened: in Oxford, in the mountains of the Vercors and the garden of the monastery. I was certain that those things were somehow connected with this house, and my first visit here, with the first time I had felt the small hand take hold of mine. Was I mad? I should not have come back and I certainly should not be going any further now.

But I was powerless to stop. I could not go back. I had to know.

Keeping my hand to the wall, which was cold and crumbled to the touch of my fingers here and there, I made my way with great caution down the passage in the direction of what, after a few yards, I thought was the light of candles.

'Please come in.'

It took me a few seconds to orientate myself within one of the weirdest rooms I had ever entered. The wavering tallow light came not from candles after all, but from a couple of ancient paraffin lamps which gave off a strong smell. There was even a little daylight in the room too, filtering in through French windows at the back, but the glass was filthy, the creeper and overhanging greenery outside obscured much of it and it was impossible to tell if the sky was thundery and dark or whether it was simply occluded by the dirt.

It was a large room but whole recesses of it were in shadow and seemed to be full of furniture swathed in sheeting. Otherwise, it was as if I had entered the room in which the boy Pip had encountered Miss Havisham.

In one corner was a couch which seemed to be made up as a bed with a pile of cushions and an ancient quilt thrown over it. There was a wicker chair facing the French windows and a dresser with what must once have been a fine set of candelabra and rows of rather beautiful china, but the silver was tarnished and stained, the china and the dresser surface covered in layers of dust.

She was sitting at a large round table in the centre of the room, on which one of the lamps stood, the old mackintosh hanging on her chairback but the rest of her still huddled in the mess of ragged old clothes. Her scalp looked yellow in the oily light, which shone through the frail little pile of hair on top of her head.

'I must apologise,' she said. 'There are so few visitors now. People still remember the garden, you know, and occasionally they come here, but not many. It is all a long time ago. Look out there.'

I followed her gaze, beyond the dirty windows to where I could make out a veranda, with swags of wisteria hanging down in uneven curtains, and another wicker chair.

'I can see the garden better from there. Won't you sit down?'

I hesitated. She leaned over and swept a pile of all manner of rubbish, including old newspapers, cardboard and bits of cloth, off a chair beside her.

'I will show you the pictures first,' she said. 'Then we can go round the garden.'

I had had no idea that anyone could possibly be living here and now I had found her I could not imagine how she did indeed 'live', how she ate and if she ever left the place. She was clearly half mad, an ancient woman living in some realm of the past. I wondered if she belonged here, if she had been a housekeeper, or had just come upon it and broken in, a squatter among the debris and decay.

She looked up at me. Her eyes were watery and pale, like the eyes of most very old people, but there was something about the look in them that unnerved me. Her skin was powdery and paper-thin, her nose a bony hook. It was impossible to guess her age. And yet there was a strange beauty about her, a decaying, desiccated beauty, but it held my gaze for all that. She seemed to belong with those dried and faded flowers people used to press between pages, or with a bowl of old potpourri that exudes a faint, sweet, ghostly scent when it is disturbed. Yet when she spoke again her voice was clear and sharp, with an elegant pronunciation. Nothing about her added up.

'I think you've visited the garden before Mr ...'

'No. I got lost down the lane leading to the house one evening a few months ago. I'd never heard of the garden. And my name is Snow.'

She was looking at me with an odd, quizzical half-smile.

'Do please sit down. I said I would show you the albums. People sometimes come for that, you know, as well as those who expect the garden still to be open and everything just as it was.' She looked up at me. 'But nothing is ever just as it was, is it, Mr Snow?'

'I don't think I caught your name.'

'I presumed you knew.' She went on looking at me for a second or two, before pulling a large leather-bound album towards her from several on the table. The light in the room was eerie, a strange mixture of the flickering oil lamp and the grey evening seeping in from outside, filtered through the overhanging creeper.

'You really cannot look at these standing up. But perhaps I can get you something? It is rather too late for tea. I could offer you sherry.'

'Thank you. No. I really have to leave, I'm afraid. I'm on my way to stay with friends – I still have some miles to drive. I should have left ...'

I heard myself babbling on. She sat quite still, her hand on the album, as if waiting patiently for my voice to splutter and die before continuing.

For a second the room was absolutely silent and we two frozen in it, neither of us speaking, neither moving, and as if something odd had happened to time.

I knew that I could not leave. Something was keeping me here, partly but not entirely against my will, and I was calmly sure that if I tried to go I would be detained, either by the old woman's voice or by the small hand, which for the moment at least was not resting in mine. But if I tried to escape, it would be there, gripping tightly, holding me back.

I pulled out a chair and sat down, a little apart from her, at the dark oak table, whose surface was smeared with layers of dirt and dust.

She glanced at me and I saw it again, the strange beauty shining through age and decay, yellowing teeth and desiccated skin and dry wisps of old hair.

'This was the house when I first found it. And the garden. Not very good photographs. Little box cameras.'

She shook her head and turned the page.

'The wilderness,' she said, looking down. 'That's what the children said when we first came here. I remember so well – Margaret rushing round the side of the house and looking at it – the huge trees, weeds taller than she was, rhododendrons ...' She lifted her hand above her head. 'She stopped there. Look, just there. Michael came racing after her and they stood together and she shouted, "It's our wilderness!"'

She rested her hand on the photograph and was silent for a moment. I could see the pictures, tanned with age and rather small. But it was all familiar, because it was all the same as today. The wilderness had grown back, the house was as dilapidated as it had been all those years ago. All those years? How many? How old was she?

'You!' I said suddenly. 'You are Denisa Parsons. It was your garden.'

'Of course,' she said dismissively. 'Who did you think I was?'

My head swam suddenly and the table seemed to pitch forward in front of me. I reached out my hand to grab hold of it.

She was smiling vaguely down at the album and now she began to turn the pages one after the other, making an occasional remark. 'The builders ... look ... digging out the ground ... trees coming down ... light ... so much light suddenly.'

The flicking of the pages confused me. I felt nauseated. The smell of the paraffin was sickening, the room fetid. There was another smell. I supposed it was accumulated dirt and decay.

'I'm trying to find it.' Flick. Flick. 'Margaret never forgave me. Nor Michael, but Michael was more stoical, I suppose. And then of course he went away. But Margaret. It was hate. Bitter hate. You see –' she rested her hand on the table and stared down, as if reading something there – 'I sent them away to boarding school. When we first came here, after Arthur died, it never occurred to me that I would want them out of the way. He had left me the money, enough to buy somewhere else, and I had never liked the suburbs. But when we came here something happened. I had to do it, you see, I had to pull it all down and make something magnificent of my own. And they were in the way.'

She turned a page, then another.

'Here it is, you see. Here it all is. The past is here. Look ... the Queen came. Here she is. There were pieces in all the newspapers. Look.'

But I could not look, for she was turning the pages too quickly, and when she had got to the end of the book, she reached for another.

'I have to go,' I said. 'I have to be somewhere else.'

She ignored me.

I stood up and pushed back my chair. The room seemed to be closing in on us, shrinking to the small area round the table, lit by the oily lamplight.

I almost pitched forward. I felt nauseous and dizzy.

And then she let out an odd laugh. 'Here,' she said. 'This one. Look here.'

She turned the album round so that I could see it. There were four photographs on the left and two on the right-hand side, all of them cut from newspapers and somewhat faded.

They seemed to be of various parts of the White House garden as it had been – the yew hedge was visible in one, a series of interlinked rose arches in another. There were groups of visitors strolling across a lawn. The one she pointed to seemed to be of a broad terrace on which benches were placed in front of a stone balustrade. Several large urns were spilling over with flowers. It was just possible to see steps leading down, presumably to a lower level and another part of the garden.

She was not pointing to the book. She was sitting back in her chair and seemed to be looking into some far distance, almost unaware of where she was or of my presence. She was so totally still that I wondered for a second if she was still breathing.

And then, because now it was what I had to do, I could not turn my eyes away, I looked down at the page of photographs, and then, bending my head to see it more closely, to the one on the right at which she had pointed. There was a caption – I do not remember what it read but it was of no consequence, perhaps 'A sunny afternoon' or 'Visitors enjoying the garden'. I saw that the cutting was from a magazine and that it seemed to be part of a longer feature, with several double columns and another smaller picture. But it was not the writing, it was not the headline at which I was staring.

The black-and-white photograph of the terrace showed a couple beside one of the benches and seated on the bench in a row were some children. Three boys. Neat, open-necked white shirts. Grey trousers. White socks. Sandals. One wore a sleeveless pullover knitted in what looked like Fair Isle. I looked at it more closely and, as I did so, I had a strange feeling of familiarity, as if I knew the pullover. And then I realised that it was not only the pullover which was familiar. I knew the boy. I knew him because he was myself, aged perhaps five years old. I remembered the pullover because it had been mine. I could see the colours: fawn, pale blue, brown.

I was the boy in the pullover and the one sitting next to me was my brother, Hugo.

But who the other boy was, the boy who sat at the end of our row and who was younger than either of us, I had no idea. I did not remember him.

'Come outside,' she was saying now. 'Let me show you.'

Yes. I needed to be outside, to be anywhere in the fresh air and away from the house and that room with its smell, and the yellowing light. I followed her, thinking that, whatever happened, I had the key to the car in my pocket, I could get in and go within a few moments. But she was not leaving the room by the open door into the dark corridor, she had gone across to the French windows and turned the key. Yet surely these glass doors could not have been opened for years. The creeper was twined thick as rope around the joints and hinges.

They opened easily, as such a door would in a dream, and she brushed aside the heavy curtain of greenery as if it were so many overhanging cobwebs and I stepped out after her on to the wide veranda. It was twilight but the sky had cleared of the earlier, heavy cloud.

I remember that she turned her head and that she looked at me as I stood behind her. I remember her expression. I remember her eyes. I remember the way the old clothes she wore bunched up under the ancient mac when we had been inside the house.

I remember those things and I have clung on to the memory because it is – was – real, I saw those things, I was there. I could feel the evening air on my face. This was not a dream.

Yet everything that happened next had a quite different quality. It was real, it was happening, I was there. Yet it was not. I was not.

I despair. I am confused. I do not know how to describe what I felt, though in part the simple word 'unwell' would suffice. My legs were unsteady, my heart raced and I had seconds of dizziness followed by a sudden small jolt, like an electric shock, as if I had somehow come back into myself.

As we left the shadow of the house and went down the stone steps, the evening seemed to retreat – the sun was still out after all and the air was less cold. I supposed heavy clouds had made it seem later and darker and now those were clearing, giving us a soft and slightly pearlescent end to the day.

Denisa Parsons stayed a few paces ahead of me and, as we walked, I saw that we must have come out on to a different side of the garden, one which I had not seen before and not even guessed about, a part that was still carefully tended – still a garden and not a jungle. The grass was mown, the paths were gravelled and without weeds and a wide border against a high stone wall still flowered with late roses among the green shrubs. I looked around, trying to get my bearings. I still felt unsteady. A squirrel sprang from branch to branch of a huge cedar tree to my right, making me start, but the old woman did not seem to notice, she simply walked on, and her walk was quite steady and purposeful, not faltering or cautious as I would have expected.

'I had no idea you kept up some of the garden like this,' I said. 'I thought it had all gone back to nature. You must have plenty of help.'

She did not reply, only went on, a few steps ahead of me, neither turning her head again nor giving any sign that she had registered my words. We went down a gravel path which was in heavy shade, towards a yew hedge I thought looked familiar – but all high, dark green hedges look alike to me and there was nothing to distinguish it. The grass was mown short but there were no more flowerbeds and, as we continued on the same, rather monotonous way, I thought that maintenance must probably be done by some outside contractor who came in once a week to mow and trim hedges. A couple of times a year he might spray the gravel to get rid of weeds. What else was there to do?

The shade was reaching across the grass like fingers grasping at the last of the sunlight. And then she turned.

We had reached the arch in the yew hedge and were at the top of the flight of stone steps, looking down to where I had seen the sunken garden, overgrown and wild, its stone paths broken and weed-infested. Below me had been the strange circle, like a shading in the grass, which had been there and then not there, an optical illusion, perhaps caused by a cloud moving in front of the sun.

But what I saw ahead was not a wilderness. It certainly seemed to be the same sunken garden, reminding me of somewhere Italian I must once have visited, but it was immaculately ordered, with low hedges outlining squares and rectangles that contained beds of what I recognised as herbs, very regularly arranged. There were raked gravel paths and, on the far side, another flight of steps leading up to some sort of small stone temple.

And then I glanced down. At my feet was not some shadowy outline, like a great fairy-ring, but a pool, a still, dark pool set flat into the grass and with a stone rim, and I saw that, as this was a very formal garden of careful symmetry, its exact counterpart was on the opposite side. In between them stood a stone circle on which was an elaborate sundial painted in enamelled gold and blue.

But it was the pool into which I stared now, the pool with its few thick, motionless, flowerless lily pads and its slow, silent fish moving about heavily under the surface of the water.

I turned to Denisa Parsons to ask for an explanation, but as I did so two things happened very quickly.

The small hand had crept into mine and begun to pull me forward with a tremendous, terrifying strength and, as it did so, a voice spoke my name. It was a real voice, and I seemed to know whose voice it was, yet it sounded different, distorted in some way.

It was whispering my name over and over again and the whisper grew louder and clearer and more urgent. On every previous occasion, whoever the owner of the small hand might be, that person had always been completely silent. I had never heard the faintest whisper on the air. But now I heard something quite clearly.

'Adam!' it said. 'Adam. Adam. Adam.' Then silence, and my name again, the cry growing a little louder and more urgent. 'Adam. Adam.' At the same time, the small hand was pulling me so hard I lost my balance and half fell down the steps, and went stumbling after it, or with it, as it dragged me towards the pool.

I closed my eyes, fearful of what was there, what I knew that I should see, as I had seen it in the pool at the monastery.

'Here. Here. Here.'

I flung my right arm up into the air to shake off the grip of the small hand and, as I did so, looked towards the archway in some sort of desperate plea to the old woman to help me.

She was not there. The arch in the hedge was hollow, with only darkness, like a blank window, behind.

I do not know if I cried out, I do not remember if the hand still clung to mine. I do not know anything, other than that the voice was still in my ears but wavering and becoming fainter and slightly distorted as the world tumbled in upon me and I felt myself fall, and not onto the hard ground but into a bottomless, swirling, dark vortex that had opened up at my feet.

Seventeen

I am sure that for a few minutes I must have been unconscious, before I felt myself surfacing, as if I had been diving in deep water and was slowly coming to the light and air. But the air felt close and damp and there was very little light. How long had I been at the house? I had gone there in daylight, now it was almost dark.

I was lying on the ground. I reached out my hand and felt cold stone and something rough. Gravel. Gradually, my head cleared and I found that I could sit up. It took me several minutes to remember where I was. The garden was dark, but when my eyes adjusted to it I could see a little.

I seemed to be unhurt, although I was dazed. Had I fainted? Had I tripped and fallen and perhaps knocked myself out? No, because I would surely have felt pain somewhere and there was none.

I was alone. The garden was still. The bushes and trees around me did not rustle or stir. No bird called.

I waited until fragments of recollection floated nearer to me and began to form clearer shapes in my mind. The old woman in the strange bundled clothing. The room in which she lived in squalor, deep in the near-derelict house. Their smell. The wavering sound of her voice. The garden.

That part of the garden she had led me into which was not overgrown and neglected, but mown and tidy, with lawn and trees, shrubs and flowerbeds, arches in the high hedge leading down neat flights of steps to …

I got carefully to my feet.

I saw the dark gleaming surface of the pool, the flat stone ledge that ran round it.

Golden fish gliding beneath the surface.

A bench.

Had there been a bench?

Bench. Bench.

My legs gave way beneath me again and I felt a wave of nausea. Bile rose into my mouth and I retched onto the cold ground.

And then I heard something, some ordinary and reassuringly familiar sound. The sound of a car. I wiped my mouth on the back of my hand.

I could not get up again and for a while everything was dark and silent, but after a moment I saw a light flash somewhere, dip away, flash again, and a few moments later heard something else, the sound of someone pushing through the undergrowth. And calling out.

'Mr Snow? Mr Snow?'

I tried to reply but made only an odd, strangled sound in my throat.

The light sliced across the grass behind me.

'Mr Snow?'

I did not recognise the voice.

'Are you there? Mr Snow?'

And then someone almost tripped over me and the beam of a large torch was shining into my face and the man was bending down to me, murmuring with surprise and concern.

I closed my eyes in overwhelming relief.

Eighteen

I lay awake for a long time that night. I had been given a stiff whisky on arriving at the Merrimans' and then encouraged to have a hot bath. Lady Merriman was anxious for me to stay in bed and be given supper on a tray, but I wanted to get back to normality by eating with them, talking, giving all my news about the First Folio, so that I would not have to spend time alone going over what had – or had not – happened. I was quickly restored by the good malt and deep hot water and felt no after-effects of my having – what? Tripped and fallen, knocking myself out? Fainted? I had no idea and preferred not to speculate, but certainly I was not injured in any way, apart from having a sore bruise on my elbow where it had hit the ground under my weight.

Lady Merriman said little but I knew that her sharp blue eyes missed nothing and that, in spite of her usual quiet reserve, she was the one who had raised the alarm and who had guessed where I might be found when I failed to arrive at the house.

She told me that the police had been called first, but that there were no reports of road accidents.

'Then I had a sixth sense, you know,' she said. 'And that has never let me down. I knew you were there. I hope you don't think that weird in any way, Mr Snow. I am not a witch. But people don't always like it if you mention things of this sort. I have learned to stay silent.'

'I am very grateful for your sixth sense,' I said. 'Nor do I find it in the least weird. A lot of people have a slightly telepathic side to them ... I am inclined to think it fairly normal. My mother often knew when a letter would arrive from someone, even if she was not expecting it and indeed hadn't heard from that person for years.'

'My husband is sceptical, but you know, after all this time even he has learned not to argue with my instincts. It doesn't often happen but when it does ...'

'Well, thank God it did today. I might have been lying there all night. I probably tripped on some of that wretched broken pathway and bumped my head.'

She said nothing.

The evening was enjoyable because of my host's obvious delight in hearing that he was very likely to be the owner of a First Folio within the next few weeks. How it was to be transported to him was a minor problem, though I warned that it would have to be done before Christmas or he would not get the volume until the spring – the monastery is usually snowed in between early January and March. He suggested the best and safest way was for me to travel to collect it – I knew the place, I would be trusted and naturally both the book and I would be heavily insured. But everything in me recoiled at the idea of returning to Saint Mathieu, not because of the responsibility of carrying the book but because I felt that anything might happen in that place, as it already had happened, and I did not trust that I could travel there and back without the return of something that would once again cause me to experience terror. Because I realised that, other than the slight mishap today, I had never actually come to any real harm. What I had experienced was the extremes of fear and they were dreadful enough for me to want to avoid them at all cost. I could not speak of any of this. I simply said that I felt a professional firm used to transporting items of great value would be better bringing the Folio to England. I knew one which was entirely reliable, if costly, and Sir Edgar agreed to let me suggest the arrangement to the monastery once the deal had been finally agreed and the money paid.

It was a close, thundery end to the day. The doors were open on to the garden and we could see the odd flash of lightning over the sea in the distance. Sir Edgar had brought up a bottle of fine old brandy to celebrate his latest acquisition and we talked on until late. Lady Alice glanced at me occasionally and I sensed that she was concerned, but she said nothing more until we were going upstairs just after midnight.

'Mr Snow, I have been rummaging about and finding some more things about the White House and its garden, if you are still interested. I have set them out in the small study for you – do look at them tomorrow if you would like to. But perhaps you've had enough of all that after your visit there today. I spoke to a friend who lives not far away and she said the place has been quite derelict and shut up for some years now. Everyone wonders why no one has bought it or had it restored. It seems terrible for it to be allowed to fall to bits like that. Anyway, I wish you a good rest and you know where the small study is if you do want to have a look through what I found.'

I had bidden her goodnight and closed my door, walked to the window and was standing looking out into the darkness and listening to the thunder, which was now rolling inland towards the house, before the meaning of what Lady Alice had said hit me.

It was hopeless then to try and sleep. I read for a while but the words slid off the surface of my mind. I opened the window. It was raining slightly and the air was heavy, but there was the chill of autumn on it.

I put on my dressing gown, but as I moved towards the door the bedside lamp went out. There was a small torch lantern beside it for just this eventuality and by the light of it I made my way quietly across the wide landing and down the passage that led to the small study. My torch threw its beam onto the wood panelling and the pictures on the walls beside me, mainly rather heavy oils of ancient castles and sporting men. Sir Edgar had a very fine collection of eighteenth-century watercolours in the house but up here nothing was of much beauty or interest. Once or twice my torch beam slipped over the eyes of a man or a dog, once over a set of huge teeth on a magnificently rearing stallion and the eyes and the teeth gleamed in the light. The thunder cracked almost overhead and lightning sizzled down the sky.

I found a number of magazines and newspapers laid out on the round table, opened at articles about the White House and its garden, but there were none of the photographs I had been given a glimpse of earlier, though I looked closely for the picture of myself, as a small boy, sitting on the bench with Hugo and the other child, presumably a friend. There was no reason why it would be here, of course – these were all photographs taken professionally, showing the splendour of the garden in its heyday, the royal visit. Two things made me shine the torch closely and bend over to peer at them. One was a photograph of Denisa Parsons. I had seen her before in the magazine Lady Alice had first shown me but here she was, I guessed, a decade older. She was a smart woman, her hair pulled back, wearing a flowered afternoon dress, earrings. Her head was thrown back and she was beaming as she pointed something out proudly to the King. I looked closely at her features. There seemed precious little resemblance between this handsome woman with the rather capacious, silk-covered bosom and the ragged, wispy-haired figure in the ancient mackintosh who had greeted me that afternoon. But faces change over the years, features decay, flesh shrivels, skin wrinkles and discolours, hair thins, teeth fall out. I could not be sure either way.

The second item was a long article from *The Times* about Denisa Parsons, the famous garden creator, internationally celebrated for what she had done at the White House. Pioneer. Plantswoman. Important Designer. Garden Visionary. The praise was effusive.

There was little about either her earlier life or her family, merely a mention of an ordinary background, marriage to Arthur Parsons, a Civil Servant in the Treasury, and two children, Margaret and Michael.

The paper was dated some thirty years ago.

I went back to my room, where the lamp had come on again. The storm was still prowling round and I could see lightning flickering across the sky occasionally as I lay in bed, sleepless.

Do I believe in ghosts? The question is common enough and, if asked, I usually hedge my bets by saying, 'Possibly.' If asked whether I have seen one, of course until now I have always said that I have not. I had not seen the ghost, for ghost it must surely be, to whom the small hand belonged, but I had felt it often enough, felt it definitely and unquestionably a number of times. I had even grown accustomed to it. Once or twice I realised that I was expecting to feel it holding my own hand. But in some strange way, the small hand was different, however ghostly it might be. Different? Different from the woman at the White House. Was she a ghost? Or had she been, as I had first assumed, a visitor, or even a squatter in the empty place, an old bag lady pretending to be Denisa Parsons? Someone who had once worked for her perhaps? The more I thought about it, the more likely that explanation seemed. It was sad to think that someone had gone back there, broken in and was living among the dirt and debris, like a rat, bundled into old clothes and spending the time looking through old scrapbooks and albums of the place in its heyday. But people do end their days in such a state, more often, I think, than we know.

It was only as I felt myself relax a little and begin to slip down into sleep that I remembered the part of the garden to which she had led me and which was tended and kept up, the grass mown, the hedges clipped, as if in preparation for opening to a party of visitors. I was confused about the place. I had walked across so many different stretches of lawn, gone through several arches cut in the yards and yards of high dark hedge, down steps, towards other enclosures, so that I had no sense of where the abandoned garden ended and the tended area began. And how many pools were there and where had the bench been on which I had apparently sat with my brother and our friend?

I drifted from remembering it all into dreaming about it, so that the real and the unreal slid together and I was walking in and out of the various parts of the garden, trying to find the right gap in the hedge, wanting to leave but endlessly sent back the way I had come, as happens to one in a maze.

I was alone, though. There was no old woman and even though at one point I seemed to have turned into myself as a boy, there were no other boys with me. Only at one point, as I tried to find my way out through yet another archway, I felt the small hand leading me on, though it felt different somehow, as befitted my dream state, an insubstantial hand which had no weight or density and which I could not grasp as I could the firm and very real flesh and bone of the hand that tucked itself into mine in my real and waking life.

Nineteen

I left for London the following morning feeling unrefreshed – I had slept, fitfully, for only a few hours and felt strung up but at least I left Sir Edgar a happy man and he had given me a new commission. He had become interested in late medieval psalters and wanted to know if I could obtain a fine example of an illuminated one. It was a tall order. Such things came on to the market very rarely, but putting out feelers, talking to people in the auction houses in both London and America, emailing colleagues, even contacting the Librarian at Saint Mathieu des Etoiles, would be very enjoyable and keep my mind away from the business at the White House. I also had some nineteenth-century salmon fishing diaries to sell for another client.

I even drove some twenty miles further, taking an indirect route back in order to avoid going anywhere near the lane leading to that place, though I knew I would not succeed in forgetting it. But I told myself sternly that speculation was fruitless.

As I neared London the traffic was heavy and I was stationary for some fifteen minutes. There was nothing remotely unusual about the place – an uninteresting stretch of suburban road. I was not thinking of the house or the garden or the hand, I was making a mental list of people I could contact with my various client requirements, remembering someone in Rome, and another in Scotland who might well be interested in the fishing books.

I glanced at the stationary traffic in the opposite lane, then in my rear-view mirror at a lorry. It did not matter that I was delayed. I had no appointment to rush to. I was simply bored.

I cannot say that anything happened. It is very difficult to explain what took place, or did not, as I waited in my car. Anyone would tell me that my imagination had been thoroughly wound up and become overexcited and likely to react to the slightest thing, because of the events of the past few weeks, and they would be right. And that is the point. My imagination did not play tricks, I heard, saw, sensed, smelled, felt nothing. Nothing. There was nothing. The strongest sensation was one of nothingness, as if I had been abandoned in some way. Nothing would come near me again, I would not be troubled or contacted. Nothing. I would never feel the sensation of the small hand in mine, or wonder if I was being watched, if something was trying to lure me into whatever lay ahead. Nothing. There was nothing. It had left me, like a fever which can suddenly, inexplicably lift, like the mist that clears within seconds.

Nothing.

I was entirely alone in my car, as the traffic began to nudge slowly forward, and I would be alone when I reached my flat. If I went back to the White House, or to the monastery, I would be alone and there would never again be a child dashing across the road through the storm in the path of my moving car.

Nothing.

I felt an extraordinary sense of release.

Half an hour later, as I walked into my flat, I knew that it had not been a fantasy, or even wishful thinking. I was free and alone, whatever it was had left me and would not return. How does one account for such strong convictions? Where had they come from and how?

Would I miss the small hand? I even wondered that for a fleeting second, because before it had begun to urge me into dangerous places, it had been strangely comforting, as if I had been singled out for a particular gentle gesture of affection from the unseen.

But the one thing I could not forget was the photograph the old woman had shown me of Hugo, his friend and me in the White House garden. I certainly had no recollection of the day or the place, but that was not surprising. I could only have been about five years old – though in the way details remain, I had remembered the Fair Isle jumper so clearly. I would ring Hugo when he was back from the States and ask him about it, though I really had no particular reason for my continuing interest except that coincidence sometimes forms a pleasing symmetry.

A couple of days later, I had a call from a dealer in New York who had a couple of items I had long been in search of and, as there were various other books I could ask about for clients while I was there, I left on a trip which then took me to San Francisco and North Carolina. I was away for three weeks, returned and flew straight off again to Munich, Berlin and then Rome and back to New York. By the time I was home, several missions having been successfully accomplished, it was late September. I was so involved with work in London for the following week or so that I completely forgot everything that had happened to me and the business of the photograph did not cross my mind.

And then I came in after dining with a potential client from Russia, to find a message from Hugo on my answerphone.

'Hi, Bro ... it's been ages ... wondered if you fancied coming up here next weekend. Benedicte's playing a concert in the church – you'd like it. Time we caught up anyway. Give us a call.'

I did so and we arranged that I would drive up to Suffolk the following Friday evening. Hugo always had an early start to his school day, so I didn't keep him long on the phone, but as we were about to ring off, I said, 'By the way ... I don't suppose you remember this any more than I do – but when we were kids, did we go with the folks to see a garden in Sussex? It was called the White House.'

I do not know what I expected Hugo to say – probably that he had no more idea than I did.

Instead, he said nothing. There was complete silence for so long that I asked if he was still there. When he did reply, his voice sounded odd.

'Yes,' he said, 'here.'

'You don't remember anything about it, do you?'

Another silence. Then, 'Why are you asking this?'

'Oh, I just happened upon a photograph of us there – sitting on a bench outside. You, me and a friend.'

'No. There was no friend.'

'So you do remember it?'

'There was no friend. I'll see you on Friday.'

'Yes, but hang on, you ...'

But Hugo had put the phone down.

Twenty

I arrived in time to change quickly and go along to the church where Benedicte was playing oboe in the concert, both as orchestral member for the Bach and as soloist in the Britten *Metamorphoses*. It was a fine and rather moving occasion and neither Hugo nor I felt inclined to chat as we walked back to the house. It was a chilly night with bright stars and the faint smell of bonfires lingering on the air. Autumn was upon us.

But it was not only our rather contemplative mood after the music that prevented conversation. I could feel the tension coming from Hugo like an unspoken warning, something I had not known since the days of his illness. It was almost tangible and its message was clear – don't talk to me, don't ask questions. Back off. I was puzzled but I knew better than to try and break down the barbed-wire defences he had put up against me and we reached the house in silence.

The orchestra and performers were being given refreshments elsewhere so we had supper to ourselves, an awkward supper during which I told Hugo half-heartedly about the First Folio and something about my foreign trips, he told me tersely about Katerina's university plans and that he was wondering whether to apply for headships. If he wanted to progress up the schools career ladder, now was the time. I don't think I had ever had such a strained hour with my brother and, as we cleared up the plates, I said that I thought I would go early to bed.

But as I turned, Hugo said, 'There's something you ought to know. Have a whisky.'

We went into his study. By day this cosy room which overlooks the garden and the path to the river is flooded with light from the East Anglian sky. Now the curtains were closely drawn. Hugo switched the gas fire on, poured us drinks. Sat down. He stared into his glass, swirling the topaz liquid round, and did not speak.

I knew I should wait, not try and hurry him but after several silent minutes I said, 'You remember all that stuff I told you … panic attacks and so forth?'

Hugo glanced at me and nodded. His expression was wary.

'You were right – they just stopped. Went. It all stopped. Whatever it was.'

'Good.'

Then I said, 'You'd better tell me.'

He swirled the whisky again, then drank it quickly.

'The other boy,' he said. 'I was there, you were there. On the bench. Then you say there was another boy? A friend, you called him. How old was he?'

I tried to bring the photograph to mind. I could see my boy-self, in the Fair Isle jumper. Hugo – I didn't remember Hugo clearly at that age, one never does, but it was Hugo.

'So far as I remember … younger than either of us, which made me wonder how he could have been a friend one of us had brought. Short hair, short grey trousers … oh, you know, like us. Just a younger boy like us.'

'What was his face like?'

I tried again but it was not clear. I had only seen the photograph once, although I had stared at it hard, in my surprise, for some moments.

I shook my head.

'There was no other boy,' Hugo said.

I opened my mouth to say that of course there was another boy, he had not seen the photograph and I had, but Hugo's face was pale and very serious.

He got up and poured us both a second whisky and, as he handed me mine, I noticed that his hand was shaking.

'The story,' he said at last, 'is this. We went twice. To that place.'

'The White House? That garden? What do you mean?'

'Mother took us. I was at prep school … at Millgate. I was out for the weekend. She brought you. It was an outing.'

I remembered little about Hugo being away at school then, though there was always a strange sense of loss, a loneliness, a hollowness at the centre of my everyday life, but by the time I was old enough to understand what it meant I had gone away to school myself, and Hugo was at Winchester.

'A boy drowned.'

I heard the words in the quiet room but it took me a moment to make sense of them.

'A boy …'

'He was the grandson – of the woman. That woman.'

'Denisa Parsons?'

'Her grandson. He was small – two? Something like that. Quite small. He drowned in the lily pond. In the garden.'

I looked at my brother. His eyes seemed to have sunken back into their sockets and his face was now deathly pale.

'How do you know this? Did someone tell you? Did mother …'

'I was there,' Hugo said. His voice was low and he seemed to be speaking half to himself. 'I was there.'

'What do you mean, "there"? At that place? Do you mean in the garden? Were we all there?'

'No. You and mother had gone to some other part – there were high hedges … arches … you'd gone through. You were somewhere else.'

He took a sip of whisky. 'I don't remember very much. I was by myself in the garden where there was – a big pool. With fish. Golden fish. Then there was – the boy. He was there. I don't remember. But he drowned. The rest is – is what we were told. Not what I remember. I remember nothing.' He looked directly across at me and his eyes seemed suddenly brilliant.

'*I remember nothing.*'

I heard Benedicte's car draw up outside and, after a moment, the front door. Hugo did not move.

'One thing,' I managed to say after a moment, 'one thing doesn't make sense. The child. The little boy fell into the pool and drowned, but what has that to do with the other boy with us in the photograph? The boy on the bench. We were both older. I don't know why she took us back – do you?'

He shrugged. 'I remember nothing.'

'Not the second visit? But you were older – what, eleven?'

'And how much do you remember of when you were eleven?'

There were footsteps across the hall and then the wireless being turned on low in the kitchen. My brother stood up.

'Hugo.'

'No,' I said. 'You started to say something, you can't leave it. You said there was no boy in the photograph. But I saw a boy. I saw him as clearly as I saw you. As I saw myself.'

He hesitated. Then waved a hand dismissively. 'Some tale,' he said. 'Always is some tale. About a boy who comes back to the garden – that boy.'

'What do … a boy who comes back?'

'Come on. I don't believe in ghosts, nor do you.'

'Oh, as to that … you know what happened to me. Hugo …' I went and put my hands on his shoulders, almost shaking him in my rising anger – for it was anger, anger with him for knowing something and trying to keep it from me. 'Tell me.'

He waited until I had let my hands drop. Then he said, 'A boy – that boy I suppose. He was said to go back to the garden – ghosts do that, don't they, so the tales go? Return to the place where whatever happened – happened. He was supposed to. That's all. Just a tale.'

'But the boy who was drowned was small – two years old. This one in the photograph was older … it can't be the same. This boy in the picture was a real boy, not a ghost.'

'How do you know? How do you know what a ghost looks like? White and wispy? Half there?' He laughed, an odd little dry laugh. 'The ghost went back there every year and every year he was one year older. He was growing up – like a real boy.'

'That's not …'

'What? Not possible?'

I fell silent. None of the things that happened were possible in any normal, rational person's world. But they had happened.

'How do you know all this? You lied to me.'

'Did I?'

'When I first told you about the small hand in mine, about …'

'Oh, for God's sake, that? I shouldn't think that's got anything to do with it, should you? That was just you having a bit of a turn. Coincidence. No, no, forget about it. But if you want to know, the whole story is on the Internet. One of those spook haunting sites. I happened to be looking one night – for the boys. We'd been reading *The Turn of the Screw* … you know how it is. You start browsing around …' He laughed the short laugh again. 'Can't remember what it was called but you'll find it there. The White House ghost … all good fun.'

He drained the last of his whisky, picked up both glasses and went towards the door without saying another word. I sat on for a moment. I heard his voice, then Benedicte's, low brief snatches of talk.

I felt suddenly exhausted and my head had begun to ache. I wanted to piece together what Hugo had told me, join it up with the things that I had witnessed in the garden to make a whole picture, but they were as disconnected as jigsaw bits in my mind. I was too tired. They would come together, though, I didn't doubt it.

I might look up the story on the Internet, but something about the way my brother had talked didn't ring true. I believed he had found the story on a website, but not by accident when looking up Henry James.

The next morning, Hugo had gone across to school by the time I came down for breakfast, and in the afternoon he was refereeing a football match, which he did for fun, not because he was on the sports teaching team. Benedicte and I went out into the Suffolk countryside looking at churches, and ended up at a bookshop which also served teas. Over a pot, and some excellent scones, I asked her if Hugo had mentioned my brief spell of panic attacks, and whether he ever had a recurrence of them himself.

'No and no,' she said, looking surprised. 'Adam, poor you. People often laugh at such things, but they are truly awful. No, his breakdown was over and done. But I wonder, now you say this, if there was anything connecting you?'

'Runs in the family, you mean?' I shook my head. 'I doubt it. A lot of people have what I had.'

'And have you an idea why you had? Is there not always a reason?'

I hesitated, then shrugged.

She smiled. 'Well, it is all over now I hope?'

'Oh yes.'

'That's good. Because for Hugo too ... nothing ever came back. He is now very strong and sane.'

We drove home through the darkening lanes, talking a little about music and books, more about Katerina and her prospects for getting into Cambridge to read medicine, and as we did so I felt a strange sense of lightness and well-being. The ghost story my brother had told me had explained a great deal. That the small child who had accidentally drowned should have returned to the place and wanted to be with other children seemed natural and I knew people had taken 'photographs' of ghosts. I had even seen one, a whole-school photograph with a ghostly master on the far end of the back row – though I confess I had always thought it some sort of fake. But those fakes, easy now with digital cameras, were once not so readily accomplished and as far as I could remember the boy had not looked in any way ghostly in the photograph the old woman had shown me. If he had, surely I would not just have accepted him as a third boy – our unknown 'friend'.

As I drove, I thought of the small hand, which I now believed to belong to the drowned boy. I had ventured into that place and he had caught hold of me. Had he found me every time I went near water and especially near pools? It seemed so. But why did he urge me forward? Why did I feel such fear of what might be about to happen? I shivered. It seemed beyond belief that he had such ghostly will and power that he could urge me to fall into water and drown and so join him. But what other explanation was there?

We turned into the town and drove down past the main school buildings towards the house.

Well, it was over. The ghostly power had faded. The only puzzle that remained was my visit to the White House when I had met the old woman. Had she been a ghost too? No, she had been real and substantial, though odd, but then, surviving alone in that near-derelict place would drive anyone mad. The drowned child had been her grandson and perhaps he haunted her too, perhaps she felt the small hand in hers, perhaps he took her down those gardens which led out of one another, to the place where the pool had been and that was now just a fairy ring in the ground. Poor woman. She needed help and care and company, but the world often throws up slightly deranged people like her, living on in a dream world, clinging to the past among ruins of its places. Presumably she would die there, alone, starving or ill, or in the aftermath of some accident. I wondered if I could return and talk to her again, persuade her to accept help, even to leave that dreadful, melancholy place in which her whole past life was bound up but which was not somewhere a once handsome, successful, celebrated woman should end her days. I determined to do that. And perhaps at the back of my mind was the thought that I would ask her, gently and tactfully, about her grandson, and whether the photograph was indeed of him as he might have been a few years after his death. And if she was visited by the small hand.

Even though it had left now, and I was quite free and quite unafraid, I could not yet forget the feel of it holding mine, or the effect its power had had on me.

As we went in I started to wonder if I could make the journey down to Sussex again. In any case, I expected to have news for Sir Edgar Merriman about his psalter, though I might have to take another trip to New York first. New York in the fall has a wonderful buzz, the start of the season in the auction houses, lots of new theatre, lots of good parties, the restaurants all full, but the weather still good for walking about. I felt a small dart of excitement.

Afterwards, I was to remember that delightful sense of anticipation at the thought of New York, my last carefree, guilt-free, blithe moment. Aren't there always those moments, just before the blow falls that changes things for ever?

I went into the house behind Benedicte, who was saying that it was strange the lights were not on, that Hugo must be having a drink with the footballers, though he did not usually linger after a match. It had been a pleasant autumn day but there was a chill on the air as we had come up the path, as if there might even be a frost that night, and now I sensed that the house itself was unusually cold.

'What is ...' I heard Benedicte's voice falter, as she went into the sitting room. 'Oh no ... has there been a burglar in here?'

I went quickly into the room. The French windows that led to the garden were wide open. Benedicte was switching on the lamps, but as we looked round it was clear that nothing had been disturbed or, so far as we could see, taken.

'You stay here,' I said. 'I'll check.'

I went round the entire house at a run but every room was as usual, doors closed, orderly, empty.

'Adam?' Her voice sounded odd.

'Nothing and nobody there. It's all OK. Maybe you forgot to close them when we went out.'

'I didn't open them. Nobody opened them.'

'Hugo?'

'Hugo had gone to school.'

'Well, maybe he came back. Forgot his kit or – something.'

'He took his kit and why would he open these doors even if he had not?'

'He'll tell us when he gets back. I can't think of any other explanation, can you?'

There was something in her face, some look of dread or anxiety. I led her into the kitchen and opened a bottle of red wine, poured us both a large glass.

'What can I do to help with supper? Potatoes to peel, something to get from the freezer?'

Benedicte was always well organised, she would have everything planned out, even if the time we would eat was uncertain.

'Yes,' she said. I could see from her face that she was anxious. 'Some potatoes to wash and put in the oven. Baked potatoes. Sausage casserole. I thought …'

I went over to her and put my hand on her shoulder. 'You haven't been burgled,' I said. 'No one has been in here. Don't worry. Hugo will be back any minute. He can look round as well if you like. But nobody's here.'

'No,' she said.

We made preparations for supper and then took our drinks into the sitting room. I had closed and bolted the windows and drawn the heavy curtains. Benedicte switched on the gas fire. We talked a little. I read some of the paper, she went back to check the oven. Everything was as usual.

The phone rang.

'Adam?'

She did not look worried then. Only puzzled.

'That was someone from school. They wanted Hugo.'

'Yes?'

'Gordon Newitt.'

I did not understand.

'The Head of Sports. He wanted Hugo. I said he was probably still having a drink with the team. But he said Hugo wasn't refereeing anything this afternoon. There was only one match and that was away. He wasn't there.'

She came further into the room and sat down suddenly. 'He wasn't refereeing any match.' She said it again in a dull voice, but her expression was still one of bewilderment, as if she were trying to make sense of what she had heard.

It may sound unbelievable to say that it was then that I knew, at that precise moment. That I knew everything, as if it had been given to me whole and entire and in every detail. I knew.

But then what I knew shattered into fragments again and I heard myself saying that the sports master had surely got it wrong, that perhaps Hugo had swapped places with someone without saying so, or that he might have gone elsewhere and confused his diary, hadn't had time to tell us, that …

I heard my own voice babbling uselessly on, saw Benedicte watching my face, as if she would read there what had really happened, where Hugo was.

And then there was a long and terrible moment of silence before I got up.

'I think I should ring the police,' I said.

Twenty-one

There is not much more of the story to tell. Hugo's body was found at first light the following morning, some way downriver. He had no injuries and the post-mortem revealed only that he had died by drowning, but not that there had been any natural reason why he should have fallen into the water – after a sudden stroke or heart attack while walking close to the edge. There was no note in the house left for his wife, no hint of any reason why he had lied about being out at the football match. We learned that he had been in school teaching on the Saturday morning, as usual and as he had said he would be. Around twelve-forty, several people had spotted him walking down the high street in the direction of home. After that, no one had seen him at all.

The towpath at that time of year is quiet but there is still the occasional dog-walker or runner. Not that afternoon.

Had he simply tripped or slipped, Benedicte asked again and again. The towpath was dry – they had had no rain for weeks, but he could have stumbled on a tree root.

It was a dreadful time. I stayed until Katerina arrived home from Cambridge and on the Monday morning I had to take Benedicte to identify Hugo's body formally.

We drove to the hospital in silence. She had been very brave and resolute, determined not to break down, and she was determined now, but she said she was afraid that she would collapse when she had to see him. That was why she wanted me with her.

I was as shocked as she was, but I had twice before had to identify bodies of the dead, including that of our father, so I did not feel any sort of fear that morning, merely a great sadness.

It was only when I looked at the still, cold body of my brother lying there that a great wave of realisation and horror broke over me. The expression on his face was blank, as it always becomes eventually, no matter what it may have been at the moment of death. It is the blank of eternal sleep.

And then I glanced at his hands. The left one was resting normally, in a relaxed position on the covering sheet. But the right one was not relaxed. Hugo's right hand was folded over, almost clenched. It looked as if it had been holding something tightly.

Of course I knew and then I understood it all, understood that the small hand which had relinquished mine for the last time had not given up, the boy had not gone away but, having failed with me, had moved to Hugo and begun to take his hand, and so draw him, clutching hard, towards the nearest water. I had not given in. I had saved myself, or been saved, though how I did not know then and I still do not know. I had not yielded to the small hand. My brother had, and died, like the boy, by drowning.

I told Benedicte none of this. We left the hospital in silence and by late that afternoon Katerina had arrived home. I left them together, partly because I felt that was what they wanted and needed but would never say, partly because I was desperate to get away. I would return for the funeral, of course, but that was not for ten days.

I drove fast away from the town and the river, desperate to put it far behind me.

I felt guilty that I had survived. I was appalled by what I knew had happened to Hugo, even though in the absence of any evidence to the contrary the coroner would record a verdict of accidental death. I would have to live with what I knew and I wondered if many others had been haunted in the same way, those who had once visited the White House garden and felt the touch of the small hand. I surely had not been the first, but I prayed that Hugo had been the last and that now the ghost of the wretched drowned boy could rest in peace.

Twenty-two

I thought that was an end to it. I thought there would be no more to tell. But there is more, another small piece of knowledge I was given and which I can never give back, can never un-know. Another, far worse thing which I must live with, for there is nothing, nothing at all, I can do with it.

When I got back home, I found a letter. It had been posted on the Saturday morning and it was addressed in my brother's hand and for a split second as I looked at the writing I forgot that he was dead but was fleetingly puzzled that he should be writing to me, on paper with pen and ink, not telephoning or sending a quick email.

But then, of course, I remembered. I realised. My hand shook as I opened the envelope, sitting at my desk beside the window on that late afternoon of a gathering sky.

Adam,
You need to know this. I have never been able to tell you, though there have been times in these past days and weeks when I have been close to it. But in the end, I could not. Perhaps you knew I had something to say to you. Perhaps not.

Now, having decided I can live with it no longer, I must tell you.

Please remember that we were children. I was a child. At eleven years old one is still a child. I tell myself so.

The boy drowned because I pushed him into that pool. No one else was there for a moment. No one saw what happened. You came to find me and I grabbed your hand and pulled you away, up the steps and through the archway in that high hedge that has loomed so darkly through my nightmares ever since.

No one knew. It was late in the afternoon, people were leaving the gardens. We were last. I pulled you across the grass until we found Mother and then we left too.

Nothing happened for some years. I pushed it down into my

unconscious, as people do with such terrible secrets. Nothing happened until my breakdown, which began suddenly and perhaps half by chance, after I read some story in the paper about a child who had drowned in a similar pool.

I had the same urges you suffered, to throw myself into water. The only difference seems to have been that I did not have to endure the grip of the small hand as you did. Not until it abandoned you – perhaps I should say 'gave up on you' – and came to me, not many weeks ago. I knew then that I should be unable to resist it, that I would have to do what it wanted, go with it. Of course I have to. It was my fault. I am guilty. You did nothing. You knew nothing.

I am sorry for this, for what I am telling you, for leaving everyone, for putting my family through what I know will be great pain. One thing, please. I beg you never to tell Benedicte or Katerina, however much you may want to unburden yourself. They will have enough to carry. Please keep this last secret between the two of us.

You are reading this in the knowledge that I have paid my debt and please God that is enough. That is an end to it all. The small ghost and I are at peace. The last hand that other small hand will take hold of will be mine.

With my love

Hugo